I0685599

"Paul Morphy's tragic story echoes Dostoevsky's *The Idiot* and Winston Groom's *Forrest Gump*—it is more than an overlooked chess story, it is a quintessential American tale, here told by Fullerty with Morphy's own combination of skill, insight, innovation, and passion."

J. C. Hallman, author of *The Chess Artist*

"Matt Fullerty spins a vivid and atmospheric tale around a key figure in chess history."

Tom Standage, author of *The Turk*

"Matt Fullerty has made an important contribution to the genre of 'historical chess fiction.' A must for anyone with a passion for history and chess."

Tom Robertson, author of *Napoleon Vs The Turk*

"From the facts of Morphy's life, novelist Matt Fullerty has imagined a rich and speculative tale. *The Knight of New Orleans* enters the psyche of a sensitive young artist developing his gift amidst judges and gin runners, generals and call girls. Even the pirate Jean Lafitte (himself a study in the tension between fame and honour) makes an appearance of sorts.

Morphy's ascent was meteoric; his downfall was appalling and total. Yet, he will be remembered for as long as chess is played. All of which makes it hard to place him with regard to another of Schopenhauer's pronouncements: "The longer a man's fame is likely to last, the longer it will be in coming." *The Knight of New Orleans* takes that fame in new and unexpected directions."

Macon Shibut, Three-Time Virginia State
Chess Champion (1993, 1999, 2002)

Winner

The Bookhabit Novel Award 2008

"What made Matt Fullerty's writing stand out, from the very first sentence, was an unusually strong and individual way with words. Taking us into the vanished world of old America and Europe he uses a highly textured language to give an almost physical experience of being in that place and time.

Drawing subtle lines between a society top-heavy with leisure and the profligate genius it produced in Morphy, he holds back the historical and personal reckoning while letting it gather and brood like the storm that finally washes away New Orleans.

In my view this makes *The Knight of New Orleans* a stand-out all rounder in the craft of literary fiction."

Geoff Cush, Bookhabit Award judge and author of *God Help the Queen* and *Son of France*

Second Round, Amazon Breakthrough Novel Award 2010

Novel Almost Finalist, William Faulkner – William Wisdom
Competition

Pirate's Alley
Faulkner Society

Novels by Matt Fullerty

www.mattfullerty.com

www.dionysusbooks.com
www.parkgateoriginals.com

THE MURDERESS AND THE HANGMAN

The story of female killer Kate Webster, the man who
hanged her and the missing head found 132 years later
in Sir David Attenborough's garden.

AMERICAN CON ARTIST

The infamous story of Elmyr de Hory,
art forger, criminal, painter, conman...
and innocent man?

To Jennifer and Peter, Mum and Dad—

For Katharine—

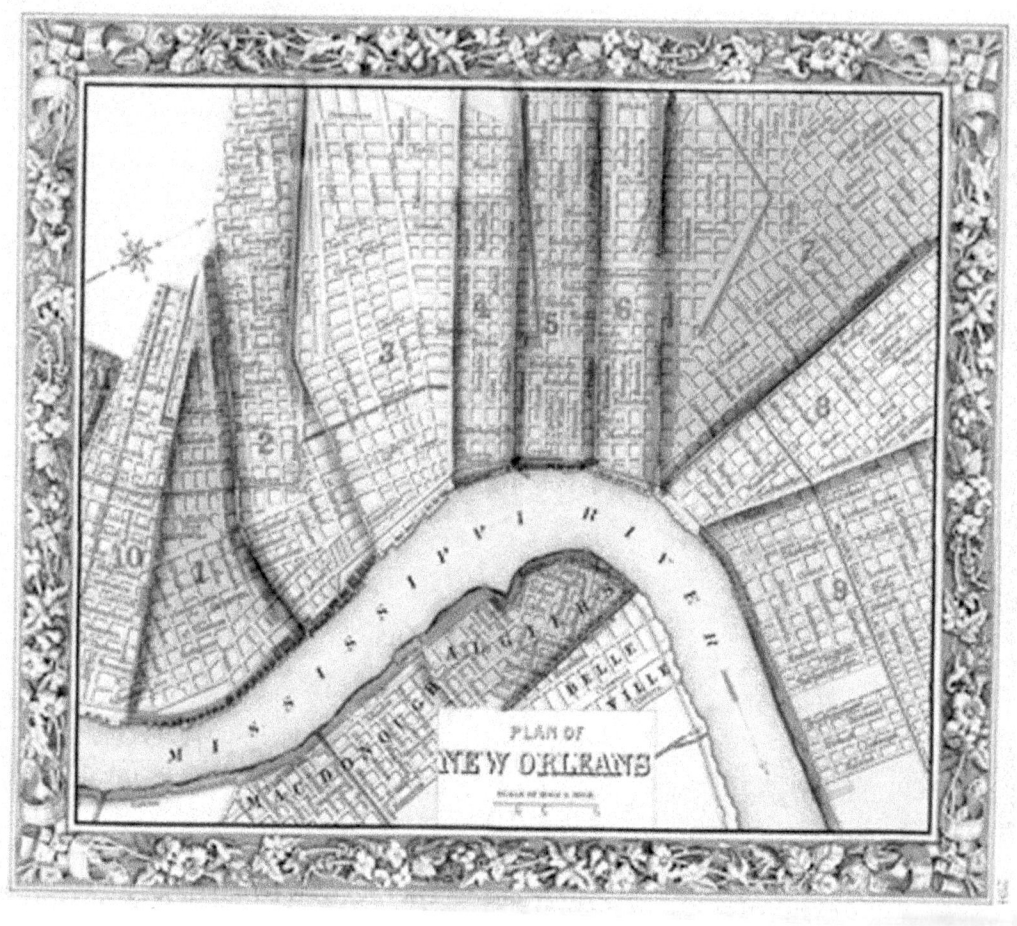

Credit: S. Augustus Mitchell Jr.

Plan of New Orleans, 1860, including Algiers, Macdonough and Belle Ville

www.theknightofneworleans.com

THE KNIGHT OF NEW ORLEANS

www.mattfullerty.com

Photograph by Ernest Bellocq

Raleigh Rye whisky and striped stockings

Basin Street, New Orleans

A pawn moves one square at a time, except on its first move. Pawns are often sacrificed for better position.

A king can only move one square at a time too, though his entire army will protect him.

A queen can move in any direction as far as she likes, for she is the queen.

The knight is the only piece that can leave and return to the board. He can leap over opponents, but often he pays the ultimate price for his loyalty.

Guide to How to Read This Book

Paul Morphy, "The Pride and Sorrow of Chess"

The game was his to lose

THE KNIGHT OF NEW ORLEANS

The Pride and the Sorrow of Paul Morphy

by

Matt Fullerty

Dionysus Books / Parkgate Press

Publishers Online!

For updates and more resources, visit
Dionysus Books and Parkgate Press online at

www.dionysusbooks.com
www.parkgatepress.com

Copyright © 2011 Matt Fullerty
All Rights Reserved. Permission is granted to copy or reprint
portions for any non-commercial use, except that they may not be
posted online without permission.

Page layout and cover design by Dionysus Books

ISBN-13: 978-1-937056-01-8

Library of Congress Control Number: 2011934697
Library of Congress Subject Headings:

Biographical fiction
Biography as a literary form--Fiction
Chess
Chess in literature
Chess players
Epistolary fiction
Fiction
Historical fiction
Psychological fiction

First Edition (UK) February 2012
[Parkgate Press: Dionysus Books reference number: 006]

"The woman that knows the most, thinks the most, feels the most, is the most. Intellectual affection is the only lasting love. Love that has a game of chess in it can checkmate any man and solve the problem of life."

Charles Dickens

"The game of the gods. Infinite possibilities."

Vladimir Nabokov
The Luzhin Defence (1930)

"Nothing in this book is true."

Kurt Vonnegut
Cat's Cradle (1963)

"On the chessboard lies and hypocrisy do not last long."

Emanuel Lasker
World Chess Champion for 27 years (1894-1918)

Cast of Characters

Morphy and Le Carpentier families

Paul Morphy, the pride and sorrow
Edward Morphy, brother
Alonzo Morphy, father
Telcide Morphy, mother
Ernest Morphy, uncle
Helena and Malvina Morphy, sisters
John Sybrandt, Malvina's husband
Joseph Le Carpentier, grandfather
Alex Le Carpentier, uncle

The Chess Players

Eugene Rousseau, French
General Winfield Scott, American
Johann Löwenthal, Hungarian-Jewish
Charles H. Stanley, English
Louis Paulsen, Swedish-American
Howard Staunton, English
Adolf Anderssen, German
Daniel Harrwitz, German-Jewish
William Steinitz, Austrian-American

New Orleans and Europe

Clara Young, a crib-girl
Charles Le Maurian, Paul's friend
Fred Edge, Paul's manager
LuLu White and Minnie Ha-Ha, New Orelans *madames*
Dan O'Neill, owner of *The Amserdam Dance House*
Léona Queyrouze, a suitor for Paul
Duke of Brunswick and Count Isouard, French aritocrats
Napoleon III and Queen Victoria

Characters in this book are composites of reality and fantasy. Names are maintained only to reveal shadows on the wall of Plato's Cave. All else is a gambit of steady play.

Contents

Part One
The Chess Players

Part Two
A Grand Tour

Part Three
The Floating City

Part One
The Chess Players

"Play the opening like a book, the middle game like a magician, and
the endgame like a machine."

Grandmaster Rudolph Spielmann
(*aka* The Last Knight of the King's Gambit)

1883-1942

THE KNIGHT OF NEW ORLEANS

Prologue
1842
A Chartres Street Playroom

It could easily have been a different toy or game. But on a balmy spring afternoon, four-year-old Paul is forgotten by the adults and left alone in the nursery of 1113 Chartres Street. The door is hooked to prevent escape; his nursemaid Titi is airing laundry in the courtyard below. Paul sits placidly watching the yellow walls. Dust dances in the fine light while high above, cloud-shadows rotate the ceiling. For hours he drinks in this world of light and shade.

Waking after a nap, the toddler stumbles onto the orange map of the East India Trading Company. Soon he discards it for a rubber ball, a glass wand from a magic box and a chessboard with diamond squares. He waves the wand over the chessboard, taps it, but nothing happens. The shiny board makes him dizzy. He notices a crack down the middle and traces his finger in the groove.

Immediately his nail jams and his face twitches. Something pulls at the skin. He watches his finger bleed gently from the baby slice. His face twitches, but despite the pain, he does not cry. He stares in awe at the wooden board.

Paul has discovered his future lying next to him. He counts the squares and lays the orange map directly over the board. Mountains and lakes fade to white, a transparent new world. He is distracted by the dark lines of trade routes, the borders of the European empires. The globe is carved like a flat apple bitten by foreign lands, all with strange names: Deutschland, Portugal, La France, Nederland....Here is an ordered world divided into regular squares, giants like the Midwestern states of North America. The boy smiles, a peculiar mix of innocence and intelligence. But there is something else behind his face, an uncertainty at those dark lines of trade routes, the moving borders of vast empires.

A minute ticks by, the boy frowns, and the light dims. Before pushing his new toy aside, Paul plays with its frayed edges. He holds up the transparent world to the skylight, so all children must feel unconsciously that this world, however small, is made for them. The boy peers for some clue, but sees only black-and-white diamonds.

The chessboard controls his imagination. The seed has been sown and the cut finger will not heal. Nothing else will do. Paul removes the map cover and frowns at the squares below, a chess terrain he invented. It could have been something else, another map or future, another game, another afternoon.

Chapter One
1844
The Funeral Parade of Jean Lafitte

In the courtyards of New Orleans the heart of the old French Quarter has stopped beating. The narrow cobbled streets are hushed. In a saloon doorway stands the old man Joseph Le Carpentier, auctioneer, slave-trader, respectable citizen of the city, and his small grandson Paul Charles Morphy. The old man is smoking a cheroot pipe and the young boy is sucking a toffee drop. The heat trembles in the air between them.

"Now wait Paul, the procession will be here," the taller figure says. "I know these things can be ex-as-perating. But the patience of the devil is wanted and you'll see something my boy. Quite a sight to behold!" Le Carpentier takes out his pipe and begins blowing in the glowing embers, cheeks swelling and reddening.

Paul stares at the burning tobacco, curious. "But *grandpapi…*"

"Ha!" escapes from the old man. "Humph! Oh! That's better." He grins down at his charge, careening smoke, and nudges the boy a mite hard in the ribs. "I split the cracks in m' own teeth!" A robust slave-trader, he rolls his head and laughs at the wantonness of the world. "Ah, my boy, one day you'll know the pleasure of a good pipe."

Paul is solemn and replies *"oui, grandpapi,"* and together they stare into the dusty street.

They don't have to wait long. From St. Philip and Bourbon a host of unwashed human forms emerge: drunken shadows merry with mourning drift into the heat of the day. Both black and streaming with colour, the funeral is here! A man stumbles and comically waving his hat disappears under the weight of the crowd. Another is squeezed along the iron grilles of the saloon, sucked back into the rolling bodies.

Already Le Carpentier has fallen inside *The House of Good Drinking* busy topping up his fortitude with a twist of rum in a dirty brown glass. For the time being Paul is alone. With the noise of thundering feet, singing snarls and trombones torturing a New Orleans melody from a balcony, the procession painfully sways and scrapes the corner without splitting its snakehead.

"Grandpapi...." Paul whispers. *"Je...."* but he cannot look away. There is attraction and repulsion, no fear but a strange steadiness in his eyes, awe unusual in a small boy. Paul is self-contained, his face blank. He steps back and finds a groove in the wall where the plaster has come away. Pressing his shoulder into dry masonry, he observes the funeral opera.

"The pirate is dead!" Le Carpentier declares, double fisting glasses of tequila, swaying in the doorway and feigning a whisper. "They killed him at last. The devil of the seas! Look my lad, an ad-mir-ab-le rascal!"

Over the crowd of defiance and dogs hauling along Bourbon Street rises the pirate Lafitte, floating on a wave of human fingers, lifelike and tomblike and strapped to a long wooden coffin. His head is raised on a glossy red cushion with jewels, flashing stones of emeralds and sapphires with a necklace of diamonds adorning his neck. "Fakes," says the old man, "or his own men would tear him down!" Paul shivers and stares, quiet and stony-faced at the hoisting up and down of the body. The mourners celebrate their leader; bursts of frenetic dancing begin. Women with painted hair are grinning and leaping, drumming fingers on washboards as instruments, ribbons in their skirts and stray chickens at their feet. At the fringes of the hullabaloo the spectators, American and French and Spanish, Creole and Cajun alike are pinned to the walls, by turns sympathetic and hostile to the passing parade.

Le Carpentier edges Paul back into the street and hoists him onto his shoulders. The funeral, a mix of dire colours and shiny black, glides in bewildered wakefulness at the death of long-rebellious and gloriously dead leader Jean Lafitte, scourge of the seas, captain of the islands, the swamps, the brushwood and the bayou. "Look! There is a man who dares, Paul! There is a man who will go one step further!" Le Carpentier's moustache bounces gleefully on his top lip. He readjusts Paul on his neck and gulps tequila *limón*.

For several minutes they watch the passing parade as raucous and dishevelled and happily uncouth, it thins to a trickle. The brass band *The Bold Boys of the Warehouse* brings up the rear with 'No Pirate Curse Ails My Heart' and 'Bury My Gold Deep In The Hole.' The music carries a two-fingered pomposity and swagger that even the mayor of New Orleans—currently regulating the city's red-light district with tax-boosting legitimization—would shadily appreciate.

After the noise fades down Royal Street, Le Carpentier deposits Paul on the banquette, poised and drained in his little suit of black. Proudly dressed by the old man in new mourning clothes, Paul is wearing a black tie, black gloves, and black shoes in the latest fashion. From his top pocket protrudes a delicate red handkerchief with black felt borders.

"Did you see?"

"Yes."

"In French my lad."

"*Oui grandpapi.* I saw him on top of the coffin. The pirate-man."

"Exactly. Now let me tell you of the past!" and he begins to toddle home along Bourbon. They are only five blocks from Le

Carpentier's and an extra block to Paul's home. Retired from his profession as slave-dealer for Louisiana plantations—auctioneer in the buying and selling of people—by inclination Le Carpentier prefers his memory of past adventures to his reputation as a card-carrying member of the Creole aristocracy. A mode other than shady scoundrel does not suit the colour of his cloak. "I knew Captain Lafitte. I'd know that swagger anywhere—he even swung it dead! But people, especially your parents, want me to keep that past a secret!"

The old pirate-lover finds nothing funnier than revealing the family secrets to the young boy. "They want me to slip into senility like an old man drooling in his dessert. A-hah-ha!" He taps his moustache and winks solicitously. "You want to know? My name was Double-Tongue with the Baratarians. Ha, how they hated me, Creoles and pirates alike! I would tell the laggards one tale and the Creoles a second. Call me the devil's merchant, the one and only Le Capentier!" On and on Le Capentier recounts his piratical days but Paul is no longer listening. Daydreaming, the boy walks placidly beside his grandfather, palm cupped trustingly in the fist of the old man.

Paul cannot get the image of the pirate out of his mind, Lafitte strung out on the coffin in the open heat of the day. Why did Louisiana come from all over to worship, mesmerized people gawping like thirsty flies, just for a glimpse of the body?

"The Baratarians were once brave and noble people, Paul. That is what you must remember. We would trade in the summer whenever I could get to the islands or Lafitte to the mainland." He wags his finger comically. "Don't judge them for living and lying outside New Orleans. The law is a flexible thing, my boy, a flex-ib-le thing, as you will come to see. Your own Barataria Bay is out there! You will go one day!" Exultant, he pulls the boy to his chest and looks steadily in his eyes. "No more than twenty-five leagues are those islands, Grande Terre, Cheniere Caminada and Grande Isle. Sandy beaches, marshes and lagoons. Pelicans, shrimp and delicious crabs! All you can eat! A choice paradise with…"

Paul is really no longer listening. All he can remember is the macabre grin on Lafitte's dead body. He knows that Lafitte was unwanted by the city, yet they came to worship him like a god at his death. A thousand followers and the Creoles of the Vieux Carré all paid their respects. He meant something in the world.

"Why was he bad?"

Le Carpentier is struck by Paul's peculiar earnestness. "Why? Because he was a genius and a rogue who met a tragic end. You'll be nothing like him, my boy. You'll prosper and drink with your *grandpapi* when you're grown. Maybe in five years when Alonzo lets you, then you'll see *me* off this earth! There will be a special circle of hell for old men like me. Brother Lafitte, lead the way!"

He scoops up Paul and swings him back and forth in the sunshine. "When I'm gone, will you remember today, Paul?" But a saloon catches his eye and the old entertainer—after tumbling over a bread basket—declares himself a 'modern pirate' and performs a little jig for his grandson. Then he disappears inside the establishment, promising "just a swift minute."

Paul is again alone. His mind slips back to Lafitte's grinning face and the mayhem of the funeral pyre. Cross-legged and head nodding, he feels a mixture of uncertainty and yearning. At eight years old, Paul is a boy with a gentleman's attraction to the wilder side of life. He has a curious look, pale and ephemeral, his eyes glazing under a reverie's spell. Half an hour passes. He imagines himself a king-pirate on the high seas, face one long scar, his brother Edward walking the plank. But smoke from a cheroot starts to tease his eyes. Balancing his tequila, Le Carpentier picks him up from the kerb. "You're a good lad for joining me, boy, especially when Alonzo don't know." Crouching again with a twinge of pain, the old man stares into Paul's pupils. "Let Lafitte's memory burn cold in the hearts of pirates—they never forget—and hot in the heart of New Orleans!" He matches a tipple with a little sway. "Pirates know man's desire, their ambition. Now it's your turn!"

"I will try."

"Time of your life, young devil. Roll up, roll up!"

Paul coughs from a pat to his back, resembling a push, and hops down Bourbon Street away from his enthusiastic relative. The church bells of the Crescent City ring out proud: the brass band of Lafitte's parade has entered St. Louis Cemetery No. 1 for the graveyard burial.

The mournful tolling is pleasantly audible over the crowd. In a spider's web the chimes touch the pretty iron grilles of the French Quarter. The death bells rise over boudoirs and shops, elevating the afternoon prayers of the Convent of St. Ursuline nuns, continuing long after a small boy's feet enter the Morphy home.

Chapter Two
1845
The Quiet Surprise of Alonzo Morphy

That night a dream keeps Paul asleep. He is walking through a mist looking down at his fingers appearing and disappearing. He is very cold. He is not afraid though, only slightly bewildered following his hand into the night. He is suddenly lost and outside the French Quarter, crossing over Rampart Street and among the shackled row houses, wooden-made and incestuously leaning. He shivers at the warmth of a red moon. From a window a cooing voice is heard, a woman's voice, more like a mermaid's than a human voice. He thinks of fishtails.

"Paul," whispers the voice. "Come inside. I need you!" He is puzzled but looks up at the window, diffused in a red glow, and sees a woman's face. She is grinning but her half crooked mouth is somehow appealing; her teeth are uneven yet the smile is warm and welcoming. He smiles back and the woman waves a lock of blonde hair. At that moment the mist rolls by and the dream is over. But Paul does not awaken. He turns in his cot-bed and finds his way back to the fringe of the French Quarter and suddenly he is down by the river. A boat has just landed and along the wharf a man appears, all dressed in black. He is a religious man and carries a twisted rosary entwined around his fingers. Paul feels drawn to the figure but in a different way, a colder attraction, uneasy and inverted. A moment later he is awake. In the half-light, the image of a black-robed bishop rolling his palms over and over flickers across the ceiling, then fades.

Downstairs his father Alonzo and his uncle Ernest are playing chess. It is early. Paul descends the spiral staircase to the ballroom and wipes away sleep, twisting small knuckles in his eye sockets. Before the dizziness settles his mother appears and sweeps him up in her arms. Over her shoulder he can see his father and uncle and a game of chess.

"My cherubim! Oh Paul, how delightful you look! We are so happy to see you." She is wearing a white bonnet and a flowing pink dress, yellow felt looped at the waist.

"Good morning *maman*," Paul says and Telcide clings on him intently before releasing him with equal gusto. His young *maman*, *nom complet* Louise Thérèse Thelcide Le Carpentier Morphy, is a talented musician and lady composer, a theatricalist and home-enricher. She draws away from her boy, tenderly but without eye contact, and disappears into the ballroom. Her white skirts trail in her wake, thinning in the light.

Paul wanders quietly into the *salle de compagnie*. The atmosphere changes and he senses the studied seriousness of the two players, Alonzo Morphy and the kind, suspicious and mysterious Ernest. The previous year Alonzo was appointed Consul for Georgia and both Carolinas, and more recently a judge at the Supreme Court of Louisiana. His brother, a former gambler and career drop-out, Ernest is now involved in the shipping deals or 'market shipments' that occur daily at the harbour. No one really knows what he trades. Both men are silent, focused on the glass chessboard in front of them. They are ready to spring into a duel if disturbed.

Paul doesn't want to be discovered so he stays near the door. A strong smell of French brandy and Havana cigars fetters the air. Paul watches a plume curl to the cream-coloured dome, displaying a carved deer hunt, where a silver-oval window permits the fine morning. The skylight opens a shaft of mellow light over the chessboard. For a small boy, confused between half-hearted affection from his mother and boisterousness from his grandfather, the atmosphere is tense.

Ernest looks up. "Ah Paul, come sit by me. I think I have your father."

Alonzo says nothing, hunched with head in hands, looking desperate. As Paul approaches the table the pieces come into focus. Alonzo's ivory-white and Ernest's purple, knights and rooks and bishops, settle on the squares. Paul feels his spine tingle. There is something magical in the contest, a strange quality of determination and flexibility. He cannot look away. A fairy-tale battle is taking place in hushed stillness. "If he escapes up the right flank," Ernest says, gesturing to Alonzo's king, "I trap him on that side. And if he breaks into the middle I fork his rook. See?" Ernest is so animated his bushy eyebrows crook into an 'M'-shape. Ignoring him, Alonzo taps his fingers.

Ernest fills his cheeks expansively, holds, and lets out a pleasurable sigh. "There's nothing he can *do*," he whispers to Paul and winks like a contented magician. Ernest's wicker chair creaks as he reclines his heavy frame. On this late Monday morning, the warm tobacco and nip of liquor are soothing him for the workday ahead. One hand is wrapped in his long brown breeches. He is about to head to the wharf when he plucks a piece to freedom: "I've got him!"

Paul senses what will happen but does not speak.

"Well, well," Alonzo says pointedly. "Good for you."

Ernest frowns and checks the board again. Eyes unfavourably pinning his own pieces, he senses Alonzo's words could be a trick.

"Well, well, well."

"Take your time," Ernest says.

Alonzo prefaces his move. "No, I think I must resign," and yet he does not move. His fingertips touch his wide forehead. Dark wisps of hair tumble to his ears, a gift from his Spanish heirs. His eyes are smaller and deeper than Ernest's. They flit over the chessmen, looking for an imaginary hole in which to tip his brother's pieces, to prize visible the invisible square. The delay is short. Alonzo puzzles in suspense of a new position, a new tactic, any opportunity. But nothing comes. Alonzo's sleeves dangle low to the chessboard: he is again the judge is in court gesturing a prosecution witness to the stand. Meaningfully he moves.

Paul stands at the table edge for better elevation, to see the move, the change, the decision. Alonzo sits up. The large clock in the room makes the initial chimes for nine o' clock, leaving fifteen minutes before both men must be gone, one to the office, the other to the river. Ernest thins his gaze; he takes a sip of brandy. Alonzo's palms close around the king and he looks up at his brother with a half-smile and a mock expression of pain—all too serious—on his face. "I hate to lose Ernest. But you won this one. This one! And winning the last of three! A good game my brother! Good game!" They shake hands over the table, like brothers should. Only now Alonzo notices the small boy.

"You didn't have to lose father," Paul says.

Alonzo regards his son, squints and takes a slow drag on his Havana. He replaces it on a silver clam-shell where it glows and crumbles some ash.

"Of course not," Alonzo says.

"You could have drawn the game."

"Impossible," interjects Ernest. "A clean victory!"

Alonzo smiles softly. "The boy doesn't know how to play. "But we will teach him."

"I know, *papa*," Paul adds quietly.

"How to play?" laughs Ernest.

"Your uncle is too good," laughs Alonzo. "He has been practicing by night, I swear." They sit in their chairs contemplating the table as chimes ring out on the clock. "He is growing so fast," and Alonzo points to pictures of Paul and his older brother Edward on the mantelpiece. In the austere photograph taken at the Chartres house, their birthplace of a few blocks away, the two brothers are kneeling on silk cushions, a sleeping dog at their feet. The photograph is damaged by smoke from the old chess room. Paul is five, Edward seven. In the Creole fashion for boys under six, Paul is dressed in the skirts and frocks of a girl's babyhood; Edward wears a sailor suit and is straining his neck in pursuit of greater height and looks proud of his man's short haircut granted the same day. Paul's hair hangs childishly long over a smile of innocence and charming vulnerability.

"He is older now," Ernest says. "Let the boy try."

They watch as Paul sets up the pieces. Neither comments but both see he is doing it wrong by intersecting the colours: he does not understand. Alonzo stands, but now something unexpected happens. Paul moves the pieces onto squares they recognize, a bishop here, a rook there, recreating the final position. It takes only a moment and the stage is set, down to three white pawns in a centre line before Alonzo abdicated.

"I can remember," says Paul.

The two men reach for their brandies and drink simultaneously.

"And what should I do?"

"Move the black bishop, *papa*," Paul answers. Instinctively he reaches onto the table, moving pieces minutes ago he was forbidden to touch. The black bishop takes up its new position as Alonzo tips back the rest of his drink. Cigars are no longer touched. Softly, ridiculously, Ernest makes his next move. Paul counters with a pawn and threatens the white knight. Ernest pushes the pawn. Paul moves his own knight and the board is locked.

"How do you know the moves?" Alonzo asks, draining his glass. "Your mother's been teaching you?"

"No *papa*. I learn from watching."

The moves continue, four on each side, polite exchanges. Pawns and pieces disappear. Suddenly Paul takes a single step backwards. "Stalemate," he says, fingers together. The two men stand and puzzle for honour over the chessboard. Ernest fills his cheeks but retains the laugh and swallows. He clears the cigars away, the water decanter, a vase of bougainvillea and carries everything to the mantelpiece. He looks down on Royal Street and the people shuffling through the hot morning air to work in shops and hotels and places away from this house, this room, this moment.

"The boy might have some talent," Ernest says. "He taught himself? Another chess player in the family…"

"Perhaps."

"To challenge us both!"

Alonzo is genuinely surprised and has not moved from the table. His hunched shoulders cast a shadow over the remaining position: a trio of black pawns all blocked by a single white pawn. The trap is successful and clearly foreseen by the small boy. More remarkably, both kings stand idly by, useless and mutually bound in non-defeat. Alonzo squints and struggles to understand.

"I missed it," he says. "And the boy saw it. The game is tied." He turns to his brother, clips his thumbs in his black waistcoat and smiles for the first time. "I believe cigars and brandy were too much for the hour. But the boy has convinced me. Bring the decanter, will you, Ernest! Let's have one more game."

But before the conspirators can fix Paul on the cushion Telcide appears, draped in the doorway. "No more chess," she says. "The time for a musical rehearsal is here. Paul, you must return to your room and kiss your uncle goodbye."

Alonzo says nothing. Paul gathers himself together and exits the *salle de compagnie*. Already he feels something bright and nervous, the promise of something stirring his stomach, a little fearfully.

"I wonder how talented he can become," Ernest says.

"More talented than you or me," replies the judge and walks to the window.

"*Quelle bonne chance!*" says Ernest and contemplates the women shimmering under their parasols on the street below.

That evening Paul returns to his room and discovers a present on the bed, courtesy of his grandfather Joseph Le Carpentier. A note is scrawled in loopy handwriting on yellowed parchment. *I heard about your talent from your father.* Paul regards the small wooden box and thinks of pirate treasure. Solemnly he removes the note and twists the metal clip revealing a miniature surprise in lemonwood and ebony, a regal beauty, polished and pristine, his own personal chess set.

But there are no pieces. The old man has forgotten the players, the chessmen, in this genteel war-game. Paul bites his nails. It does not matter. In his imagination he places translucent pieces on the back ranks and plays his first game against himself.

Chapter Three
1846
Telcide's Musical Soirée

Three days after Edwards's eleventh birthday the boys are alone in the evening. Alonzo is at his club, the Monsoon House, where the deals are struck with local business traders, putting right those offenders of Creole pride more in league with the 'fresh off the boat' Americans than the old aristocracy. Such blighted days and nights! Fine men by their own account, they inhabit the billiard library to decide who needs defending and how to redeem those attorneys who visit the bordellos of Rampart Street and must clean up their act. Alonzo will be gone late, Ernest is taking the balmy air and Joseph Le Carpentier—as ever—is no one knows where.

Tonight, *Chez Morphy* is reserved for music in the ballroom so Telcide's friends can noisily perform their harps, clarinets, French accordions and violins. As chief entertainer-at-home, Telcide is *chanteuse* and hostess. The Morphy ballroom is transformed into an experimental hub of poetry readings and small operettas, of piano sonatas and music written and performed by its untalented clientele. Miss Julie and Miss Monroe, the old Merchant sisters, Reverend Porteur from St. Philip, Mr Michaels the charmless banker and the overgrown infant Molly Stupor. The ballroom bisects the hall where the two boys are sitting.

"Let's use the courtyard," Edward says. "Amy or Matilde might whistle to us from the street." Paul, quiet by his side, is listening to the ballroom music. "Nothing ever happens round here," Edwards adds, twisting both arms behind his neck and joining the fingers. "Sigh, sigh, sigh! Why do you never want to do anything?"

"I'll play chess," Paul says hopefully.

Edward grins. "You're pale. But you can run if you want to, just not very well. What's the matter with you?"

"What's the matter with *you*?" Paul says and stuns his brother.

"You want to play chess. That's father's game."

"It's a good game."

"It's *only* a game. You're pathetic!" He peers in Paul's face; the answers are not there.

Paul looks at his feet, incommunicative. From the other room he hears the sounds of adult laughter, of instruments being tweaked and tightened, a ripple on the piano keys. Surrounded by music from his infancy, he has little inclination to sit outside the ballroom on the plume chair—the one shaped like a giant rose—as he once did. He feels neither at home among the strangers nor his family; he is more content in his room, behind a closed door.

"You go and get the board," says Edward, "and I'll see you in the kitchen. I can't stand this musical whatever-it-is." The eleven-year-old disappears into the kitchen to fix himself a glass of root beer. He pauses on the threshold, posing with fists on hips like a soldier, something he has seen other boys do. "Well, go on then. Get the board!"

Paul doesn't ask about Edward's change of heart. One moment his brother wants to dangle his feet in the fountain, the next pull creeper from the walls of the servant quarters. He doesn't like Edward's unpredictability. At least his father is consistent in his sternness or his enjoyment of Paul's newfound, if only, talent. Telcide is preoccupied with her dresses, her friends, and her musical compositions, although she too can confuse him with sudden bursts of emotion, self-indulgent hugs, and the desire to swing him under her arms as though he's still a swaddling baby. Now that Alonzo has taken to calling Paul 'the prodigy,' Telcide has even cut those bonds of closeness to concentrate on her acquaintances. She has grown bored with him like she did Edward. Soon she will turn cold and wish she'd had another baby, something Paul fitfully understands from his grandfather. "Telcide is always unhappy," Paul remembers from their Sunday walks, "and only children—like you Paul—can ease that pain."

Edward remains permanently unpredictable, Paul thinks, as he climbs the staircase, both hands on the banister. The hall upstairs is narrow and the candlelight dim. In his room Paul finds the lemonwood chessboard and runs his finger along the edge. There, too, is the box of pieces carved by his uncle Ernest to imitate the ones they used that morning—a year ago now—when Paul surprised his father. He tightens the box under both arms and pauses momentarily.

Across the room through the window he can see the convent wall, yellow and overgrown with Virginia creeper. A nun is in the garden bent over the vegetable patch, digging. She treads carefully in the soil moving row to row, her white cowl covering her head and neck. Paul smiles to himself. Outside in the hall he can hear voices from the ballroom. "Everyone, places now," Telcide is saying. "What a lovely gathering, I'm so blessed! I just want to play you a little sonata I've been practicing with good Mr Michaels." After a squeaking of chairs, the lopsided melody struggles into life and dances too fast through the notes. Paul imagines the piano keys touched awkwardly and tries to picture his mother's face.

"Paul," someone calls from the bowels of the house, "I'm waiting!" The voice echoes with impatience and Paul hurries down the stairs. He misses the last step and falls, catching dearly at both chessboard and pieces. Mouth open in horror he tumbles on the hard wooden floor. Rolling on his back, blinking, he finds the complete chess set protected, lying silently on his chest. His heart is beating. "Nothing is lost," he says.

The moment is short-lived and Telcide emerges upset from the ballroom. "What are you *doing?*" she screeches and stares wide-eyed in his face. He can see her lipstick and the hairpins behind her ears. The glitter from her pink ball gown flutters over his frame. He wheezes "I fell mama," and here is the moment to cry but he cannot do it. There is no flicker behind Telcide's eyes except her embarrassment for the hushed room of misfit musicians behind her. She unceremoniously picks up Paul and dusts him down. Then, almost an afterthought, she taps him on the shoulder. "Run along now," and louder for the listeners, "my darling young prodigy!"

"I'm still alive," Paul says, nursing his arm.

In the kitchen Edward has heard the commotion. Paul enters and sits on the cold floor. Already apprehensive of his young sibling, Edward has sectioned off the kitchen with a piece of chalk. Root beer and milk festoon his top lip. "That is your side," he says and they set up the pieces on a footstool. It's getting late and the chess armies are dimly lit by unseen candles tapering their long shadows. Paul is careful not to touch Edward's line of chalk. From the wall, faces of their extended family stare down. Telcide's mother, Lady Modeste Blanche, grins diamond-studded over the draining board. Mr Diego Morphy is next in stern maroon, a single gold tooth changing his personality from dour professional to secret daredevil. All prints are reproductions of the ballroom portraits and reminders of the Morphys' illustrious Spanish and French heritage. Between eggs and the cook's knives is a picture of Mr Joseph Esaü L. Carpentier, vagabond and smiling Creole cad. Paul gains a quiet comfort from the pictures. They are inanimate and impress him with their serious images. "Why are you looking at them?" Edward scowls. "They're all dead."

The first game goes Paul's way. A mistake by Edward forces his queen to be traded for a rook. Already the endgame is inevitable. Paul can do nothing to appease his brother who sulks through the second game and again loses. The pattern is set. Edward continues to play badly and halfway through the fourth game he scatters the pieces, stands in a huff and folds his arms.

Then he pretends nothing has happened, sits cross-legged and asks Paul to reset the pieces. Paul does so.

"King's pawn," Edward says, swivelling the board to control the white pieces. He sits bolt upright and radiates stern concentration, a caricature of his younger brother. "A gracious move in this game of kings," Edward says nonsensically and aligns his pawn with the authority of a bishop. Within six moves an imbalance is clear to Paul who begins to advance bishop and knight. He works the pieces in steady combination, a sacrificial pawn between them. Edward is preoccupied with his own attack and does not see what is happening.

"Check," Paul says, seeing there is nowhere for the white king to run. Edward lowers his body to the board and scrutinizes the position. Paul's black bishop is restraining his pieces. And there, on the opposite file, is a single black rook waiting to execute his leader, his lone king, already hemmed in by its own pieces.

"I'm lost," Edward declares. Paul waits, neither elated nor troubled, somehow soothed by the solitude of the final pieces: their dynamic fixity, a world of steady objects only he sees, imbued with power and dynamism.

"I'm lost!"

"Maybe you can…"

"Don't!" screams Edward. "Don't even say it. You know something? *S'blood*, I hate this game!" Something strange then occurs. Edward slumps back against the clothes-horse where his father's breeches are drying, and the soggy leggings dangle in his face. When he parts the legs, his eyes glow with a meanness Paul does not expect.

"Listen."

"What's the matter?"

"You cheated again," Edward says and pulls down the leggings which flop on the pieces, clumping wetly and hiding the alternate world. Edward stands, brandishes the pants in one hand and callously whips his brother over the head with the other leg. Water drops spin about the kitchen. Paul wheezes and pushes himself backwards. Then it happens. A slap clean in the face. The mark appears after a few seconds, right across Paul's cheek. Edward is taken aback from his exertion. Paul is white from surprise. Then the older boy is gone, out into the twilight of the balcony and down the steps to the courtyard. In his wake, Alonzo's leggings drag over the chessboard and tiny pools of water darken the lemonwood. Except for the black king, mournfully upright, the ivory pieces lie on their sides.

But something stops the victorious Paul from standing. The eight-year-old takes the king between finger and thumb, boxes the other pieces. He wipes the board and carries everything to the flower table below the stairs. Cautiously he opens the ballroom door hoping for some word or glance from Telcide, what exactly he does not know. He hovers on the threshold, drying the black king on his flowery sleeve, as welcome in the dark hallway as he is unwelcome in his mother's music room.

The guests hush as Paul enters, the bruise on his cheek hard to disguise. He cannot see his mother among her cultured Creole friends of the Vieux Carré, the *hoi polloi* of this clique of parlour music. The adults gawp from behind music stands, their violin bows suspended, sheet music and make-up surprised and tongues a-goggle. No one has seen the small boy before. "Oh, he's upset," someone coos. "Look at the poor child! He needs relief!" The word is out, and with Telcide nowhere in sight they encircle him. Yet all is too claustrophobic for a child brought up in a nursery with a brother and two sisters but only limited exposure to adults. "Give him a lollipop!" is cried. "Someone find his mother!" "No let him wait!" "Isn't he funny! Maybe he'll do a little jig!"

Paul stares in despondence at the guests imprisoning him with their fleshy bodies and warm breath. A prim girl of sixteen and tone-deaf, Miss Julie screams with inexplicable joy. The Reverend Porteur wags his finger with meaning while Mr Michaels removes a dainty comb and parts his toupee. Seeing no monetary opportunity the Merchant twins, penniless gold-diggers Maya and Ariana, curl up in a single frightened ball. Miss Molly the seamstress, who lives close to the bordellos of Rampart Street, sits down in a huff. But it's too late for Paul. He is prodded in his little gentleman's outfit and twirled as though changing the guard. After an unbearable minute he squeezes under flailing arms and makes for the exit. There his mother is waiting cast in the doorway as a risen Siren in her cape of canary yellow, bearing a glass of water on a tray. "Where is that Pierre when one needs refreshments?" she asks. "The children's wet-nurses are no doubt sleeping again!"

Paul rushes to his mother, who brushes him off, but he dangles on her skirt. Now in a woman's presence he feels the shame of his insult for the first time. The tray wobbles in Telcide's hand and, embarrassed, she smiles for the crowd. She lays a finger on Paul's head and turns his cheek for fleeting examination. Telcide knows a stage when she's on one. "Harmless!" she pronounces to muffled but appreciative laughter. "The boy will live!" She props him in the doorway. "Run along now child," as though speaking to a harmless lost boy or homeless orphan, "it's time for bed. *Mama* cannot concentrate on her singing."

"*Mama*," Paul pleads, half-heartedly. All he can do is unfurl his fingers and show the docile king wrapped in his palm. "I can do it," he says.

"Of course you can, Paul. I know! But we don't need to be disturbed. Run along now. Go play with your brother Edward. He is probably outside having lots of fun before nightfall. Go now!" And Telcide laughs as she strides into the room with Paul disappearing under her dress. Before she turns, with a twinge of regret to say 'goodnight,' he is gone.

Upstairs Paul drinks from his washbasin. He places the king on his window sill and climbs under the thin bed sheets. From downstairs he can hear the piercing tremolo of Telcide's soprano and the crashing blaze of the Reverend Porteur's alto, the muffled trilling of the twins and the booming of Mr Michaels's bass cough. The others join in randomly. A harp calls before the unpleasant cacophony falters and Paul can no longer tell the reality of the house from the world outside. All is noise. The memory of the violent chess game is gone and only sleep can bring succour. A church bell is muffled in the distance.

Sounds eventually soften until Paul hears Alonzo and Ernest come home, creeping heavily with the uncertainty of drink. Some paper crumples mysteriously in the house and the last candle from the hall is blown out. Paul knows Edward is still outside, which no one knows or cares much about tonight. Paul waits for the moon to rise. Then he sits in his window and peers at the cornflowers on the window sill, the Indian Blankets and Black-Eyed Susans. They seem to float there, waiting for something. Black night enters his lungs and he feels calmer. Under the starless sky, he sees Edward sitting alone by the fountain, crying.

Paul watches him not without feeling but knowing he cannot soothe Edward's woes: his desire to be popular, win his parents' affection and make his mark in the world heroically, instead of playing kids' games among the flowerbeds. But what Paul doesn't know is that chess now separates them, making one a talent worthy of investment and great attention from adults, but not the other. Edward does not see his younger brother's gaze at the window; nor does Paul see the true nature of his brother's burden. The moon clouds all.

Paul thinks of his sisters, Helena and Malvina, twice his age and away at convent school. He wonders about their lives, their lessons and if the nuns are strict. A blur of Helena's chestnut hair is all he can remember and a soft voice, Malvina's sad eyes and harsh laughter; no real moments only a few disembodied feelings that linger. Paul tries to imagine the men they will marry, businessmen, Europeans, sailors perhaps. Paul lies on his bed and imagines a chessboard projected on the ceiling. His mind paints the white squares and his isolation blackens the rest. Here are the sixty-four spaces of a different world, endless and immortal, the light and dark restorative. With remarkable clarity he predicts the future for both players.

But tonight Paul falls asleep after a few opening moves. A nightmare of a grotesque burlesque intervenes. All he can see is the frightening red teeth of the seamstress Miss Molly. He sees her leaving her apartment and wandering north of Rampart Street beyond the French Quarter. Then the grinning face of Jean Lafitte appears, trapped in his wooden coffin, martyred and wordless and feted in a swirling parade. Further down Bourbon Street Joseph Le Carpentier is there too, with twinkling eyes and curled moustache and a planter's hat. The old Double-Tongue is falling, falling and tipping back into Paul's dream with grandfatherly words in the spirit of New Orleans. "The patience of the devil is wanted and you'll see something my boy! Quite a something to behold!"

Chapter Four
1847
The Momentary Outrage of Winfield Scott

The coolness of winter bites at the edges of the Quarter along the riverbanks and the swamplands of the Big Easy. The cold is temporary and by February the warm weather descends as expected. The mists roll off the mighty Mississippi, circle the Place D'Armes, and are diffused along the fish markets from Levée to Chartres. Icicles hang in Exchange Alley.

Months pass. Parties come and go. But one event approaches rapidly on the horizon, the most famous of local celebrations. Paul is nine years old and ready for his first *Mardi Gras*. Le Carpentier takes special pride in dressing his grandson in the height of dualist fashion. A band of blue silk stretches from Paul's shoulder to his waist, a moustache thickens his lip and a straw hat sits on his brow with a red plume and turquoise feather vying for attention. At his side is a carved wooden sword sharpened to a blunt point. The weapon is secured in a leather pouch Ernest has acquired from one of his many dealings.

In this regalia Paul sits in the *salle de compagnie* before a packed room of onlookers. No one is there to admire his costume.

The morning is given over to chess and a very important guest. But first those who care for defeat can challenge the young master, the child whose name is known across the French Quarter and into the Warehouse and Garden Districts. Within one short year Tulane and Baton Rouge know of the chess boy wonder.

One man steps forward in a ruffled morning suit. The family steps back. It is Eugene Rousseau, a local amateur champion and one of the three best players in North America. He is wearing a white hat and a red shirt for *Mardi Gras*. He smiles jovially at Paul who is seated like a family jewel on one of Telcide's silk cushions. Rousseau begins with a casual air, affecting cockiness, while Paul happily places his pieces in the centre of squares.

"I wager one to five on the boy," someone whispers. "I'll take your money." The smell of gambling is given a disapproving "tut-tut" by Telcide at the door.

Rousseau is cautious. But Paul is a fast player by nature, releasing his pieces in flourishes. His chessmen move unseen to all parts of the board on a spider's thread, the thinnest silk in the world hanging intuitively between them. One move becomes five. The crowd drinks in the perverse intensity of staring at unmoving figures. Paul is not aggressive but he seems to know his next move within seconds; the flow and acceleration of his play alarms and delights the spectators. It always seems to be Rousseau's move.

"You are talented," Rousseau says, himself a young man. "La Bourdonnais should be worried!" His words hang in the air and he continues to make pointed remarks. "I wonder what the future holds for you. I think there is greatness ahead."

"Let the boy play," Ernest says.

"No need for silence," Rousseau counters.

They enter the middle game. Rousseau drinks a second glass of water. Nothing drastic in material or position has occurred for either player. The queens are exchanged and pieces drain the board. But something about the bout is odd, a pressure and symmetry that unnerves the audience. No one can work out the leader. Rousseau mourns the loss of his queen and sits sullenly.

At Paul's shoulder stands Alonzo, a father with a shadow to cast. He declines to play Paul himself now his son is to be groomed. "Talent is infinite," Alonzo jokes, "but I don't want to wear him out." His attitude is one of stern protection for Paul mixed with a kind of strange awe as though Paul were a changeling and not his own progeny. For Alonzo, his son *is* the Morphy name. He presents Paul's talents to the world as though showing a fine racehorse to a crowd of prospective buyers, expecting frenetic gamblers to swamp the display any moment and devalue the possession. Often Alonzo asks the boy how he decides but Paul cannot articulate his moves.

"I have a prophecy," Rousseau says cryptically, "that I am going to draw this game."

Between the chess players, specks of black smoke hover under the skylight. Paul nods politely with no malice and pushes a pawn. The die is set, the endgame commences and Rousseau, without knowing, is lost. The boy glances up, not in victory, but in public awareness of something. His rooks are free from the back rank. Pinned to one another, sturdy and powerful, they sweep the defeated pawns of Rousseau's army. A bishop is dispatched. The sword has fallen. "To the boy king," someone cries. *"Le petit roi!"* A toasting of drinks! The re-lighting of cigars!

The pieces are reset. Wearing his blue sash Paul is balanced on a folder of legal papers smuggled from Alonzo's study. He is shy of Rousseau, who makes an ostentatious show of shaking his hand, and not unkindly. "You will go far," Rousseau whispers, taps his own fallen king and gestures to Paul's king, solo but alive. "On the board *you* are the king. Trust that piece and the world is yours!" Paul nods from politeness but lays his hand on his king's crown, uncertain whether to trust his defeated opponent. Over the drifting smoke he sees Rousseau's retreating face and twinkling eyes, charm in his crooked grin and crumpled suit.

The atmosphere is now buoyant. Conversation in the boy's ears swings from how Andrew Jackson's pirate militia speeded the British exit from New Orleans in 1815 to the current price of lobster in the market. "Good old Chalmette fighters," Alonzo says.

"New Orleans will stand forever. Only the floods can bring her down!"

"Hear, hear."

The voice is unknown and the room goes quiet. The chatter of carpetbaggers, auctioneers, Mississippi merchants and boasters is over. Paul moves the king gently to his starting place. The General has arrived.

"Let the battles begin!" the voice booms and the men part before a typhoon. "Thank you. I greet you heartily, gentlemen, for old trials on the fields of glory"—with a spin of his hand— "and for the one about to be decided!" Ernest resists a smile. "Let neither God nor King tear us asunder. Today is a day for the cannons to fly! Bodies may strew the sidelines but ours will increase the glory of heroic *Nouvelle Orléans!*"

Seeing Paul's military sash and wooden sword, General Winfield Scott swaggers to the little glass chess table. His sword is clenched across his stomach, whiskers flying. "Well bonjour, *mon petit,*" he says, "surely you cannot be my adversary? I see you have a moustache like mine!" After a few smiles, Paul's tongue dries in his throat; he expects the portly soldier to draw his sword and slice his face like a pineapple. But he doesn't cry or twitch his costume moustache and is silent.

Recovering from his momentary surprise, the General mounts an attack on dignity itself. "I didn't expect such a rude *enemy*," glancing with suspicion at Paul already aligning the pieces, "until *after* I got to Mexico!" Laughter resumes. "Those Mexicans, heartless scoundrels, I tell you…" In his excitement, sweat beads line the General's brow.

"But battles must be fought!"

"Give that man a drink," General Scott replies.

In the first game, Paul mates the General in eleven moves. After much protest at the size, age and demeanour of his opponent, Scott is lured with port by Ernest into the biggest reclining seat in 1113 Chartres Street. There he sits twirling his grand moustache. He glares at Paul as though expressions reveal destinies and the game were poker.

"A humble error," Scott says inexplicably. "My cavalry attack the king's defensive line? Of course the queen would end up in a skewer!" He eyes the room suspiciously. "An amateur folly," and he leans over to worry his small opponent with his frame, "made only by amateurs."

The next game lasts fourteen moves until Paul announces "mate-in-four." Scott drains his port. He offers the empty glass to Alonzo who affects dismay. The next game sees Scott less impatient but the agony of concentration shows. He screws his lips to his teeth and stares at the open spaces. Someone in the back of the room executes a low whistle and another man touches the piano keys; Scott asks them to stop. "If I can only..." he begins, "it's just not clear." With patriotic fervour he plugs his fist on his knee. His foot springs under the table and surprises Paul, who smiles bashfully and wobbles on his book pile.

"I can't take this," Scott says forgetting himself, "it's like the enemy has more gunpowder in his cannon." His face plums up. Sure enough, Paul's prediction of the end transpires. Four moves later the big military man is cornered and suffocated by his own pieces. A firing squad awaits. He squirms in his chair, a reddening eel trapped in a basket. "I am the leader of the American Army," Scott announces, "fighting for all of us, you know. I'm fighting a war to keep us free. A real war!" No one speaks. Two games to zero. Ernest politely extends Paul's hand but the gesture is too much for the proud old warrior. "I've not played for a year or two. You've caught me off my mettle!" Alonzo looks to the skylight as though the Angel of Providence is about to descend. "They're not excuses, young man."

A break brings out coffee and cigars and Scott's *faux* English accent. "It really is unpardonable impertinence. How can you expect me to play a boy, a child? It's some ridiculous gaff or trick, I tell you, and I deserve to know what it is!"

For want of breath, the General loosens his purple necktie and the men nod meaningfully. He stands and affects a military retreat but not before arranging one final game for the evening. After a gumbo dinner, he desires a *gentleman's retaliation* without further *bons mots*. So a *soirée* is arranged at the chess club above the Sazerac Coffeehouse.

The re-match is equally swift. Chief Justice Eustis keeps score, the brothers Morphy watching carefully. Scott is bizarrely glum and chipper at alternate moments, his outer bluster failing to conceal his internal conflicts. Paul is newly dressed to emphasize the General's sense of infant mockery, in velvet knickerbockers and a lace shirt with a big spreading collar. He looks like an Elizabethan poodle. Underneath this daring outfit is his *Mardi Gras* costume of soldier's grey and fiery white pantaloons, invisible for decorum. In a corner of Sazerac's, his wooden sword rests under a portrait of devilish French chess artist Philidor, a flash of magic in his eye.

The adversaries choose a corner table. They shake hands and select pawns. The long room, only a few old men at the window, falls quiet. Alonzo takes a seat to relax and shares a carafe of *café au lait* with Ernest. Scott advances the English Opening, Paul the Sicilian Defence. Soon the contest speeds to the middlegame and an awkward position with four knights looking to control the space. But the young Creole can see the end. He looks up for confirmation from Philidor but the portrait is obscured in sunlight.

Scott moves, but Paul is dreaming of his first *Mardi Gras* night with Rex, the King of the Carnival, the Zulu King and the Comus Parade. Scott drums his fingers on the table, eyes imprisoned on the squares, not noticing the boy's reverie. Paul imagines a poster in The New Orleans Chess Club, red and gold, describing his defeat of experienced players during *Mardi Gras*: "This evening is Paul Charles Morphy's first night on the devil's town. See him there, if you dare!" He daydreams of the midnight commotion....

Tonight belongs to the street and the underbelly of the city. Twelve hours of fear to be embraced and exorcised and strange love to be found and lost. Ah, sweet wine of life! Slaves will be free between dusk and dawn, and the corrupt and downtrodden will embrace while misfits dance under the sordid moon. Come Comus! Come to New Orleans....

Paul moves the chess pieces fast, hurrying the moment when Alonzo tells him he can leave for *Mardi Gras*. Meanwhile Ernest tells Justice Eustice about his grandfather Michael Morphy, an officer in the Irish regiment. "He changed his name from Murphy to Morphy. Then he became American consul to Malaga and brokered a peace deal with the Dey."

"Who's the Dey? Lafitte and his men?"

"No, this is Algiers. The point is that Michael, my grandfather, paid sixty thousand dollars for American seamen imprisoned as slaves."

"Slavery is a terrible thing," Eustis says and comically winces. A fat man in a planter's white coat, he is bumbling in his bigotry.

"Times haven't changed much," a voice interrupts. The General wobbles overlooking the little wooden pieces, an exuberantly defeated look on his face. "Nor should they! And that, sir, is why I am going to Mexico. To defend our States and keep our assets. Slaves make for a healthy New Orleans!"

Clearly the General has lost again.

"Well, three in a row," Alonzo replies ignoring the conversation. He stirs his coffee and is proud of his son, albeit unknown to Paul.

Immediately Scott sets up a second bout and engages queen's pawn. The temptation is there to gambit but Paul resists. Within three moves the bishops spar openly in the field, leaving casualties. The knights open lines for the queens and at the tenth move Paul has the General in check. Paul marks the spot with his hand and announces "here is the place" for victory. He is right and the General is indignant.

Paul is taken home silent as usual. Chess, he now knows, is a serious game. He feels closer to his father but his mother will be annoyed at the late hour. Alonzo grips his hand and guides him through people already dancing in the streets.

Much later, after a colour-strewn night chaperoned through the Vieux Carré by his uncle Ernest, Paul returns to his room and sits alone. A strong smell of musk drifts in the window. Outside a solitary magnolia tree leans over Telcide's flowerbeds and trembles in the breeze. Its leaves curl upward instinctively yearning and silent in the warm night air. Feet on the floor Paul watches the rising moon's cleft palate and latent eye. Why is she grinning? He feels the burden of his family. Somewhere in the house a clock ticks and chimes the hour.

Paul listens, counts. Taking a pencil and dried grey parchment he creates a chess problem in loopy longhand. First he adds a black queen surrounded by darkness. But a memory troubles him. Who is this queen? He adds a white knight, a boy, himself. The crude black-and-white pencil marks glow like ghosts. Unlike chess itself, containing more possible moves than atoms in the universe or seconds since the beginning of time, every chess puzzle has a solitary solution. Paul's chess problem is finite.

Yet history would say chess moves are red herrings constructed by the chess goddess Caïssa. Without knowing it, Paul too is blessed and cursed by Caïssa the demon-angel. All chess players worship her because the challenge of chess promises fantastical release, escape, even love. For Caïssa chess players sacrifice themselves time and again for glory and immortality as sailors bewitched by mermaids.

But the day has been long. Sleep comes fast. Paul lays the pencil aside and the puzzle floats to the floor. It is the young prodigy's only surviving chess problem, a puzzle to fascinate generations, to be flung worldwide in newspapers after he is gone. Its charmed combination of black queen and white knight lingers still....

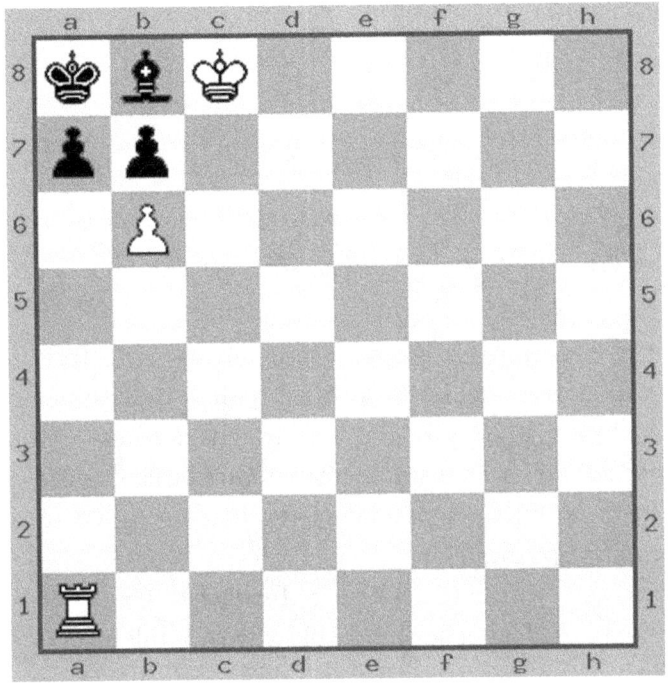

Morphy's Chess Problem

White to move and mates in two

Chapter Five
1847
Smoky Row on Burgundy

At the end of August Telcide grows sick from the hot weather and Alonzo is busy with a case appealing local shipping practices at the Louisiana Supreme Court. The house is quiet. Even Edward seems subdued, playing *pétanque* with himself in the garden or practicing his fencing moves in the full-length mirrors upstairs.

Without warning, Telcide's brother Alex Le Carpentier comes to stay. A dapper-looking fellow with a full closet of cream-coloured suits, Alex gives off a rakish air but a preoccupied expression suggestive of secrets and reasons to leave him alone. No one in the family really knows if Alex is comical or dangerous, effeminately dressed like an old-fashioned Creole dandy but insisting on a rapier under his jacket.

On a lazy Friday afternoon, the sky cautioning rain, Alex and Paul set out for a walk. "Let's explore," are Alex's words. "We have until five." Paul is happy—he's rarely taken beyond the vicinity of the house. The two drift through the arcades and slate-coloured roofs of the Vieux Carré. Paul surveys the lace-like iron balconies, the broken fruit stands and eternal cobbles. Sunlight divides the wagons into triangles of light. On Orleans Street a damaged-looking puke-coloured cat leaps off a drainpipe and watches them sourly. "Look at her licking her paws," Paul says, but Alex says nothing. He is watching three servant women with colourful striped *tignons* sliding by in the fat heat.

"That's Mary Thompson's, a cigar store." He releases Paul's hand. "Now you wait here and I'll be about thirty minutes." Without another word he disappears inside. Paul presses his hands on the glass. He inspects the unconvincing line of cigars in the window, without prices, over-straightened like dusty unread books. A red glow of lantern-light illuminates the back of the store. He peers and sees Alex in silhouette talking to a lady in a tight dress. They disappear.

After twenty minutes Alex returns sighing "she was busy," and the journey continues. They take Toulouse to Burgundy but not before passing the remnants of the Cheapside market. Alex buys two honey cakes and they sit on a basket of purple figs as the sun chips away at the awnings over the fishermen's wares. A disembowelled rabbit trickles blood upside down in Paul's eyeline. He regards it dubiously as he eats his pastry cake. Alex won't wait long. At the corner of the street they pass a retired sailor, his beard grizzled and hair in long shanks. He is baiting an animal cage with a wooden crutch. Inside are weary-looking crocodiles and giant crabs living unhappily side by side. "A penny for the dance!" says the sailor through his nose, prodding the animals with his crutch. Paul is wide-eyed and coughs. Alex takes his hand. The black fish and bloated shrimp of the market fade out of sight.

On Burgundy the sun is setting. They descend a dark passage to a sunlit courtyard and beyond. Here is Smoky Row, a single block dividing Bienville and Conti. Alex bends down to Paul. "Now listen young man, I brought you here because…you need to see other parts of the city. See that fountain," and he points to a depressed-looking corner gusher under a tall oak tree, its branches wheezing in the breeze. "No one will bother you, if you stay there, and don't come further."

"But uncle, *why* are we here?" Behind Alex's white suit and purple flower of his buttonhole, Paul can see the ramshackle houses piled on each other higgledy-piggledy like over-zealous bazarre stalls.

"The buildings are trying to breed," Alex whispers, clutching at straws, "but aren't we all…" He starts to feel dizzy as a few drops of rain touch his face. "Now you stay here near the fountain. No further! Just dangle your feet or something. You'll be fine!"

Alex crosses the street. Scampering towards a two-storey house, he parts a door held with ropes and is gone. Paul takes a step instinctively. He sees the peepholes in the walls covered by movable slabs then remembers Alex's words. Go no further. No one is around. But the feeling continues of eyes watching through obscure sliding panels. Paul hears a few whispers of Gumbo French, the patter of patois. He is afraid. But before he can retreat to the fountain a noise grabs his attention. A bright pink parrot dips its bill in a sewer puddle and looks up.

"Hello," says Paul and waves. The parrot cocks its head, gauging Paul's harmlessness, and resumes drinking. A low gust blows through and suddenly all the shack-houses tremble in the afternoon humidity. Near the bird a small collapsible doorway— itself containing another doorway—ejects a small girl. She is about Paul's height with golden curls and calm-looking accepting eyes. Curling her toes on the broken cobbles, it's clear she sees Paul and is making a show for him. She starts to skip around the doorway. Paul is bemused but cannot look away. The girl curiously twists on her heel. Whenever she seems about to skip forward, she skirts back as though caught by an invisible chain.

Nothing more happens. The girl sits in the dust and picks up an oak leaf. Paul remains under the fountain's marble tub, a manic-looking bronze shrimp for a gusher. He dips his finger in the water and wishes Alex would come back.

"Why don't you play? Are you scared of me?"

Blinking and standing, Paul moves away from the shrimp. The water gurgles and repeats the note of the little girl's voice. "Do you know Happy Charley? He's a barfly."

"I'm waiting for my uncle. He's Alex Le Carpentier."

"You shouldn't call people names," she says with a curious dirty giggle, "not real names. Not around here. You know why?"

"I'm sure I do," says Paul.

"Because. That's why. I know all about the new rules and regulations, the *licenses* and *ordinances*. You may well ask. I know more than you!"

It seems like the parrot she has decided Paul is innocuous. So affecting ease she approaches the fountain, only a mirage of coal-smeared skin, bruised legs, a black smock and frizz of overgrown hair. Paul is alarmed at her appearance. But reaching him, she extends her hand to reveal teeth more or less pale and friendly.

"I'm a shutter-girl," Clara says. "You can call me Clarabelle. Or Clara…your sweet belle and lover! Ha! *Mon coeur! Vous êtes mon vrai homme!*"

"I'm Paul Morphy," he says shyly.

"Ditto. Likewise! You want to play a game?" She sits in the dust cross-legged and squints up at him. From her green linen pouch Clara tips a handful of glass beads, each streaked with blue flowers on its oily surface. "Play marbles?"

They spread a circle in the dust. But the boy not comprehending the rules, and the girl not caring to delineate, the game is a chaotic collection of random throws. Clara grows impatient and knocking Paul's last marble from the circle she cackles with surprising hilarity brewed in her skimpy body. "You need some practice."

"I'm waiting for my uncle," Paul repeats and sitting on the fountain she takes his hand and pretends to read his palm. Paul holds his breath. She eyes him suspiciously.

"Do you know where you are?"

"I'm at home."

"Not here. This isn't the big happy Vieux Carré."

"How do you know?"

"I guessed right, din' I."

"What's a shutter-girl?" he asks.

"*It's* means I'm a *lady*. Look at my fine clothes."

Paul does. "I like them very much."

"I know so," she replies and pouts. "You can kiss me if you like."

Paul sits still. "I should…"

"Only joking. Ha! I wouldn't kiss you if your head was on fire! Boys are for mamas not for girls like me. I'm a fine jewelled lady." Just as quickly her mood changes to despondence. "You believe me, don't you?"

"I do," Paul says and nearly takes her hand.

"I'm a shutter-girl 'cos I'm shut in here. I'm to shut up all the time by shutt-er-uppers! That's what they tell me, so that's what I is." Strands of her hair accidentally flick Paul's nose. "So what's you?"

"I'm Paul. Paul Charles. Pleased to…"

"We had the introduction. You're a gentleman," she says. "And you're mine too."

"I'm a French and Spanish gentleman," Paul says. "*Mama* is French and *Papa* is Spanish. Titi is my nurse."

"Do you love your mother? I help mine all the time."

"I help my *grandpapi*. He's an old pirate."

Clara takes a moment to drop the marbles down her chest. Then she removes her hand with a tiny glass vial wrapped in leather. "These are knockout drops," she says. We use them in drinks to lull the men. For a *picayune* you get a drink of whisky to sleep the night *and* meet a lady. Do you like whisky?"

"I've never had…"

"You've never had whisky?"

"Never," Paul says solemnly.

She laughs tipping her head back and the sharpness bewitches Paul. The heat and fountain water blur and he thinks of an injured mermaid calling. "And for a *picayune*?" he whispers as though making an offer.

"I don't play for nothing," Clara says squeezing his hand and Paul is dizzy. Now a creature comes alive from the fountain, she begins dancing a two-step in the dust. "This is one of Happy Charley's songs, jus' like 'dis:

I am a man dat most of yer know
I'm known as a knocker wherever I go.
My fame it is fightin'; I kan't get enuff.
All over de town dey call me a tuff;
Yes, I'm a man dat de people all dread,
And when I gets rowdy I paints de town red.
I know all de cops; I stan' in wid de roughs,
—*she raises the note on high*—
Yer kin bet yer sweet life I'm er Nu'leens tuff!

Ha! *Encore!*" she eggs herself on, singing the melody in a comical voice. Paul is so lulled that without warning he slides into the fountain with a splash, cutting his head on the metal belly of the shrimp. Right then, Alex hauls him from the water with blood and the memory of a little girl's black silken dress in his eye.

"Sweet Jesus," Alex cries. "Sweet Lord. What happened?"

Paul coughs out water and whispers: "*I'm known as a knocker wherever I go!*"

"Alonzo is going to…" He wipes the cut. "Littl-lun, it's time we was gone."

"Where is she?"

"No one is here."

"*La belle de la bordello*," he whispers.

"What? Listen, Paul there are no *belles* here. The rooms are for men to smoke and talk. Like a club." He bends down and dabs Paul with fountain water. "But don't tell Alonzo you were here. It's our secret."

"She's gone."

"You're delirious, boy. But you have to see the real side of New Orleans, especially if you wish to be a Creole gentleman one day!"

"I don't want to be gentle-man," Paul says and Alex laughs.

"They play hell with your jackets in there. Ug! The chimneys of Smoky Row! Let's go to the river for *la glace*."

"Yes," says Paul. "What are ordinances and regulations?"

Alex eyes him with amusement. He notices how Paul's hands are like a woman's, undamaged by physical work. So what does it matter, he thinks, Paul will be a gentleman soon like the rest of us. "Those girls are banned from the Vieux Carré." Alex begins mumbling. "For crimes like play-thieving and money transactions…"

"Playing?"

"Sometimes they fight like animals. Like cats."

"Why?"

"You're too little, too young!"

"I won't tell," Paul says looking earnest.

"Well okay, but never tell your mother. Those girls are banned from city alleys for bad and mischievous behaviour. Paul, they're ladies who live outside the civilized world, you know. But they're happy. You can hear them singing all the time." He grins.

"I don't understand."

"Well, what should I do? I like to play cards and the Custom House and men tell me things. Anyway, all coffeehouses and places selling alcohol ban the harlots…I mean the bad girls…and their men too."

"Why?"

Alex sighs. "Look let's find the Spanish ice cream!"

"But…"

"Exactly!" and he breaks unconvincingly into a playful trot. *"Tu veux que la crème glacée fonde?"*

Paul says nothing.

Leaving Smoky Row the conversation fades, and from St. Peter they enter Jackson Square. Here they skirt the statue of former President Andrew Jackson riding high on his steed and vanquishing British redcoats. Alex doffs his hat and taps Paul solemnly on the head. "A great man of the city! Much loved." Paul squints up through the light, sees the devilish smirk of Jackson's horse and takes his uncle's hand again.

They arrive at the waterfront. "This is where my brother-in-law Ernest works," Alex gestures to a row of grimy buildings.

"Here's what I wanted to show you. Look! There, look harder!" He points. "The sea…"

"I can see the sea!" Paul echoes. "Can you see…?"

Alex holds his stomach, false-laughing. "A pun, young man. *Très bien!* You *will* go far with the ladies after all."

"I will?"

"I've no doubt of it!" They stop where Jackson Square meets Levée Street and there, on his uncle's shoulders, Paul can see the full bend of the Crescent City. The waters sweep north to Jefferson Parish and south to St. Bernard Parish. Nothing is as fine or beautiful as Big Muddy grinning in the sunshine.

All down the dock, bales of cotton, lumber stacks and barrels of molasses angle the muddy banks, threatening to slide into a watery grave. Piled with dry goods and liquid merchandise, tiny skiffs bob at a crowded jetty, while blue hats of the longshoremen grace the white tips of the choppy riverbank. The men joke and curse, all backs and arms. Within ten feet of the shore, mighty overloaded drays thunder up Tchoupitoulas along the banks of the old *levées*.

Alex guides Paul's fingers to the horizon and points to where the river becomes the sea—in imagination only. "All she does is feed the sea with work. Feed the sea."

Directly across the glittering expanse of the Mississippi lies Algiers, the bayou, and flooding wide over the wetlands, the womb-like Mother Delta herself, forever dying and reborn.

Paul squints and concentrates. In his mind's eye he sees Clara in a yellow sash skipping across a shimmering chessboard. "Go beyond the sea," she whispers. "Follow it." She dives off the board and is lost to deep waters trembling in the heat. Further out rolls the mysterious Gulf of Mexico and untold marine adventure.

There they stand, Paul with his cut eye and Alex with his shallow beard. They wave their handkerchiefs to outbound voyagers, human specks like birdseed on the decks. The departing vessels round the bend and float downriver to a future elsewhere.

Chapter Six
1848
The Gambling Game

The Morphys now return to the house for the wedding reception of Telcide's cousin Geraldine Le Carpentier, newly betrothed to her fiancé, the dry goods merchant Jacques Dupré. Left languishing in the hall is a long table of pork in apple sauce, poultry and *pomme de terre*. In the dining room, Telcide is singing her soprano solo for her impatient friends' daughters—Madeleine, bored and wilful, and Charlotte, bored and charmless. At pauses in Telcide's soprano, an undertow of laughter comes from far away. Aha! It is the boys chasing frogs along the wall of the St. Ursuline convent. The married couple Geraldine and Jacques sit politely in a corner full of food, waiting for their painted hansom to take to their new home near the Warehouse District. Meanwhile the men are in the parlour telling stories, smoking and drinking the brandy from Alonzo's glass cabinet and saluting the future sons of Jacques Dupré.

On a chequered tablecloth using salt cellars and napkin-rings for pieces, a merry game of confusing chess is taking place. Ernest has disappeared to locate a proper board. The games are non-stop and much to Alonzo's chagrin, gambling is being practiced openly. His face is a picture of disapproval but softened by the merits of the Spanish brandy. Men squint through their moustaches and monocles, hovering in their own smoke. Joseph Le Carpentier is relegated to a corner stool. Legs akimbo, rakishly leaning elbows on knees with chin cupped in his hands, the old devil's eyes shine. His creased brow reveals memories of youthful romance and honour, loves won and lost. But the irises remain sharp with the possibility of rolling a winning trick. "Like firebrand snake eyes!" the auctioneer calls from his old man corner. "Go on, move! Take the bull by the horns!" He curls a wisp of grey hair over his ear. "Make a move of deter-min-a-tion, young man! Let them bring the attack to *you!*"

Paul tugs his grandfather's sleeve as the old man lifts him before the gambling jury. Bets are whispered through beards on all sides and Alonzo starts to object. "Not with the boy," he says. "One game *sans façon.*"

Ernest returns with a proper chessboard with the edges trimmed. But nothing can stop the gambling. Paul makes the English opening, first defeats Ernest and then Alonzo and Ernest as a team. The crowd of burly men, dapper but sweating in double-breasted suits, call surreptitious suggestions the whole time. Paul is quietly seated on a brandy casing fetched from the wine cellar by Jacques—his first marriage duty—and rushes through the games. Amid the hullabaloo, the chessboard blurs piece after piece. Sometimes an opening appears beautifully crystalline. Sometimes Paul is intoxicated by the musty smell of brandy and the thick tobacco fumes. He wins and wins and wins.

All goes well for an hour. Then the singing stops in the next room and Telcide, horrified, appears in the doorway. Without looking at Alonzo she grasps Paul under his armpit; he half flies from his box. The gambling pawns scatter from the table.

"How could you?" she cries to the room of decadent innocent-looking gentleman. "He's only a boy. He's not even eleven!" she laments. "What were you doing at eleven? Don't answer that!" She prods a blanching, wiry man in the ribs. "Not selling yourself like this. Leave him be, just let him grow up before you pollute his mind! None of you see inside the cathedral. So don't prostitute the mind of my son with your vices!" Twirling on her heel, a white blouse swinging through the parlour, she is gone. Paul is dragged in her wake. Hair tousled by the men, he slides in the sawdust after her shiny white shoes.

The next morning Telcide is absent and naturally chess for money is continued. At eleven the game adjourns to Madame Begue's second floor at 207 New Levée. Brunch is served. Ernest had brought the chessmen but a board is not necessary. The positions are reaffirmed on a helpful Parisian tablecloth of gold and silver diamonds. Without delay, as one challenger falls another replaces him. Chess pieces and money fly over the food, and long after the men cannot put away one more mouthful, another course is sequestered on credit from the kitchen. Begue's pretty young owner Amendaïde, attired in *duchesse* satin of the latest fashion, declares *"Hostness excellente, non?"* with the arrival of every dish. The red wine, the *cap* bread, the *tub* butter, the veal cutlet, the tender liver and broiled tomatoes all arrive with a flourish. Paul eats and falls quiet with the aromas and a Bloody Mary befuddling his mind. He dreams up hearty fish chowder, hot baking powder biscuit, a huge roast beef with Yorkshire puddings, roasted Creole potatoes, mince pies and three kinds of frosted cake served with floating islands. But nothing is a dream now he is a boy among men.

Dusk arrives before the meal is over and the chess gambling adjourns. Exhausted, Paul is awarded nothing for his trials and victories except being carried home on Ernest's shoulders. "Can we go back again?" he pleads. "I didn't play very much."

"Of course," says Alonzo. "We can always go back."

Chapter Seven
1848
Rizzo the Amazing Man-at-Arms

In the winter Edward and Paul are taken to Dr Camille Rizzo, composer of chess problems and *maître d'armes extroadinaire*. Rizzo is a hunched-up Italian with bushy ginger whiskers, a top hat and a piercing gaze. He removes his hat to duel but retains the whiskers. A self-confessed deft hand over the chessboard, Rizzo also claims to be *sans pareil* in use of the rapier.

A knock at the door! Untwisting the bolt Rizzo sweeps aside the ridiculous iron grille, the portcullis to his chess and fencing school. With arms spread he welcomes the Morphys with a grandiloquent bow.

"At your service, my esteemed Count Murphy!"

"Morphy," corrects the Judge as he motions Edward and Paul inside. Alonzo looks dubiously around the barren room with its warehouse windows, excessive dimness and sawdust shavings. At one end a rack of broadswords lines the walls. At the other the clash of blades resonates from two old men busy practicing hitting a long green carpet, hung up for the purpose.

Nearby four chess tables are studiously displayed. A young boy sits at each fixed on a game. "My wife Telcide," continues Alonzo, "believes Edward should improve his chess to calm his mind." He indicates Edward, who imitates the Italian with a cavalier bow, to Rizzo's alarm and Alonzo's delight. "And Paul clearly needs instruction in the fashionable weaponry of duelling if he is to grow to be a Creole gentleman."

Paul looks up politely, careful to imitate no one. Rizzo stares pointedly at him.

"He is small for his age and thin."

"He is a dreamy-eyed boy with the hands of a woman," Alonzo says. "But no one will beat him at the royal game."

"Aha, but to which game do you refer?" Rizzo chuckles to himself. "Two games, both for life and glory, are practiced in my academy, sir."

"I see," Alonzo replies. "Well, I shall leave my boys in your good hands," and he nods approbation to Rizzo's so-called *initiation price*, the cost pointedly more than a Sazerac brunch but less than a box of Montecristos. "Send the bill to one Joseph Le Carpentier, 65 Royal Street," Alonzo calls from the stairwell. "And write this on it—*for all the Sunday dinners!*"

"Certainly, I will sir!" Rizzo laughs after him. "Thank you Mr Murphy. Pray for me sir! Pray for me!"

At last the boys are alone. The hunched-up Italian peers at them, suspicious of their fighting worth or intellectual merits. "So which is the dumb one and which one the weakling?" he charmingly enquires.

"I'm both," says Edward.

Rizzo draws back his hand to cuff, but relents and scratches his own ear. "You're less than the best, boy. The Judge says you need improvement. I say he's out of his gourd, but we'll soon smack you in shape. Ha!"

"My father says you're a loon," Edward responds, leaning on one foot. "We're only here so *papa* can go to his club."

Rizzo is taken aback but as *Esteemed Conductor of the Académie d'Échecs* only for the briefest second. Paul is quiet and hops from foot to foot, nervous.

"I *am* a loon, gentleman. But I can play! I can play! I'll dance you around a chessboard until it's off with your arms! That's more than you lily-livers can take. Now stand in line! Where do you think you are? This is Exchange Alley Number 149. I run both sides of this room gentleman. On every side! And I get free coffee in the downstairs *Café Regal*. And in case you're unsure, I'm not only a spectacular Italian specimen, but a master swordsman. I can *checkmate* you with the tip of my rapier in an instant!"

Alarmed, the old men Alfonse and Gregory slow-beat their carpet. Edward is quiet now.

"Are you ready?"

"I think I'm ready," Paul says loyally.

"*En guard!*" cries Rizzo and executes a little prance. He raises his hand. "Stand up straight! Here you will learn *scacchi sublime e meraviglioso*. Beautiful mates. *Il gioco naturale!* Delicate chess moves and even more delicate swordplay. Look! The noble arts shall lead us to the kingdom! Eternity!"

"Let's go," says Edward and takes his brother's hand.

"Wait!"

Rizzo dashes before the boys, kicking up sawdust, and plucks a rapier from the wall. "The board and the blade! Ho!" Tossing a chess piece—a white rook—from his belt, he kneels and swats it through the window crying out "Death and beauty, your mind shall be your rapier!"

The moment lingers. Edward claps and giggles. Paul turns white. Rizzo clambers to his standing hunch position breathing heavily and glares a final challenge. Jamming two fingers in his gums, he whistles shrilly. Immediately the old men in the corner cease their duelling with the carpet. They meander over, grumbling en route as though called for execution. Paul stands motionless, his whole chest heaving.

"You don't know these worthy gentlemen," says the jolly pretender, "though you should." He places a poniard under one grizzly old man's chin. "He is the saintly father of Marcel Dauphin!" He tugs at their knotty beards. "And here is Gilbert Rosière's pater!"

"*Bonjour*," the old men say in unison.

"Believe it or not, boys, both were outrageous swordsmen in their day. Unfortunately, the sons have inherited the sins of the fathers!"

The old men bow unconvincingly. "A lovely tale," says one.

"History worthy of a poet," says the other.

"Eternity to you both!" says Rizzo and releases them. He gestures through the window to the premises over the street where a full room of young bucks is swinging blades in severe practice. "Tremendous talents," says Rizzo. "Look at them! But here we have only the dregs of great swordsmen! Oh God, I can barely eat. Death and beauty! My meanest rivals, ha!" He scowls at the window. "There, see the *salles d'escrime* of my sworn business enemies. But peace have it! My fencing school shall overcome. Time will reverse my fortunes, boys!"

With a flourish Rizzo separates his pupils. Still speechifying, he pays the old men in cigarettes for beating his carpet and the room empties of elderly fighters.

"Now bring me a sword!" Rizzo cries. "Any sword will do." Edward unclips a sword from the wall. Rizzo unsheathes it and touches him under the neck. "Now go to the table, there's a good boy."

Edward sits before an empty chessboard and four boys appear, each behind his own board, ready to chess-duel: four individual games at the same time. Edward introduces himself all round with a hearty "*bonjour*." The boys look up, pale, sour-faced and look down. Edward grasps his knights and twists them forward yearning to be adventuring outside, anywhere rather than stuck *playing a children's game*. Glum and hapless he walks between the boards, playing both black and white. The boards grows complex and ultimately, resisting a triple loss for a single win, he stalls. The whole time he can hear Dr Camille Rizzo daredevilling Paul in the art of swordplay.

Peering over his shoulder Edward watches his paltry sapling of a brother. Paul is jumping with a wooden sword not unlike his comic *gladius* from last spring's *Mardi Gras*. He thrusts at the air without sound. Rizzo is dubious and says so, calling Paul a "prancing barely moving target." But despite his imbalance and lack of strength, Paul's gait is firm. He retains a surprising quality for one so small and harmless-looking: Paul is fast. Any thought is in the past so he is always quick to move. The sword flickers to his side.

"Good," says Rizzo. "You need to grow."

After an hour they swap over. Edward frees himself from chess by gesturing rudely to the other boys. The price of freedom, he is given permission to beat the carpet which he does enthusiastically. Meanwhile Paul sits before a set of sixty-four squares. As the newcomer, the boys challenge him one by one, his small height and frame wakening their blood. Losing one by one, flies broken on Caïssa's wheel, they quietly resume their own games or go home after a double loss. Few remain. Paul keeps winning until up steps Rizzo, local master of the sublime mate and so-called lightning game. Thumbing his ginger whiskers, he houses his dagger and sits.

"So you're the chess player? You can defeat your father, uncle, grandfather, brother," counting on his fingers. "Your mother doesn't play? Hmm…quite right too!"

"My mother plays music. She's composing an opera."

"Death!" cries the incomparable Italian. "I must see it! Tell me more!"

"She's writing it today and it's called *Louise de Lorraine*. I can hum the melody."

"Tell me, boy, it's a trio for piano, violin and cello."

"*Louise de Lorraine* is a five-act opera," Paul says and stares at Rizzo with a tilt of his head. "She's composing the score. *Maman* has *musicales* on Sunday afternoons. You can come along, sir."

Dust in his hair, a wheezing Edward calls out: "The parties are private. And *maman* has a *mezzo-soprano* voice. She is a pianist and a harpist. *Maman* is a genius. So is *papa!*"

"Yes," says Paul. "*A mezzo-soprano.*"

Rizzo watches Paul's eyes light up and the irises softly grow dim. Sensing his authority waning, Rizzo wraps the table with both knuckles. "You have just me to play. Then you can go home." Under the table, unseen, he nudges Paul's foot and a bead of saliva appears in the corner of his mouth. "Then you can go."

Paul plays a *fianchetto* opening in homage to the lurid old faker. Rizzo is somehow unnerved. "Only one move," he murmurs in his chin. But when Paul instinctively brings out his king's bishop's pawn, Rizzo bursts out: "Steady on, young pup. That's a technical opening!"

Paul sees his supposed teacher's mate in only four moves and becomes agitated. It is too soon to lose on purpose. Rizzo misses it, and ten moves later the young chess dualist can strike Rizzo's colours down. He forces a suffocated mate. Two more games go the same way, a mistaken rook sacrifice by Rizzo in the second, and a rook queen skewer to Paul in the third. All is lost for the Italian and the diminutive Creole begins to make his mark, unseen and unsung in a lost corner of the chess world. Far away the chess masters of Europe are murmuring in their sleep.

Edward is quick to take his brother's hand and sweep towards the door. But, before they can make it, from nowhere a dandy in a suit of green cloth and the widest of yellow neckerchiefs bursts into the room.

"Look at me!" Bastile Croquere trills. "I love to wear cameo rings in the afternoon, breast pins and even a bracelet in the evening! Can you imagine anything more daring? Come, embrace me Camille!"

The boys teeter in the doorway, surprised by the intruder.

"Bastile!" declares Rizzo, "you are interrupting my boys. How many times do I have to say I'm not finished until three!" Upsetting the chess table anyway, scattering pieces as though auditioning for a French farce, Rizzo springs to his feet. "I'll lament the loss of my *trustees*. But it's been a whole morning since we parted. Did you duel at midday?"

"Every day, my Captain!" and the two dandies beat sword blades in a delightfully sharp greeting.

"Cross swords with me in a private *assaut*, sir!" Croquere begins a joust with Rizzo.

"You've been sipping coffee and liqueurs all day long!"

"In a pig's ear, courtesan! And call me Croquere you dog!"

They mince and strike, pose and strike again.

"Where are your adoring young bloods, Rizzo? Chase them down the cellar, did you?"

"I cut off their heads with a grin, you impostor!"

"Face a challenge or leave the city, you ridiculous cad!"

"You know your problem, Rizzo," cries Bastile. "You never learn when to stop. You don't know it, but you need a broadsword diploma or a rapier mind to teach this grandiloquent sport. You, sir, lack both!"

"Chess or fencing?"

"Dancing of course!"

"Never!"

"Always!"

"Death and brandy!"

"Honour and eternity!

They drop on the floor still fighting so no one notices as Edward and Paul escape. They both carry a piece of paper stating "hereby the sons of the illustrious Judge Morphy are officially enrolled at Dr Rizzo's *School for Exquisite Swordsmanship and World Class Chess-Playing*. Let no man tear this paper from their hearts!"

Meanwhile Croquere raises a black glove from the floor.

"Should I tell you of the time I whipped Poulaga at the old French Opera House. He saw me crying at *The Marriage of Figaro* and proclaimed my cowardice. It's true! Pistols at dawn were insufficient for my thirst for vengeance, I was so young!"

"I remember it well. A tall tale if ever I heard one."

"No, sir. A smirk on my face at the interval! I slapped his face before his daughter and mistress with my diamond glove. That drew blood, but my speech cut him the most. *C'est vrai je pleure, mais je donne aussi des calottes.* They *still* speak of those words among the Paris opera Gods!"

"You survived, though, I see."

"We met at the duelling oaks. My man Rosière was my second, but I didn't need him. I put an end to comedian Poulaga and made a wife of his mistress!"

"You didn't?"

"And a mistress of his daughter."

"Eternity!"

The boys emerge into the heat and light of Exchange Alley and run all the way home.

Chapter Eight
1849
The Dancing Eyebrows of Herr Löwenthal

By May of 1849 before Paul turns twelve, Edward is attending Dr Rizzo's Academy weekly while Paul is permitted to drop out. No longer are the chess players of New Orleans, Alonzo and Eugene Rousseau, Justice Eustis and Joseph Le Carpentier any competition for Paul's precocious magic. In an inspired moment the New Orleans Chess Club sends a letter to the greatest player of Great Britain, one Howard Staunton. Although in European chess circles Charles H. Stanley is commonly regarded as the English champion, the invitation is moot. Mr Staunton writes back to decline the offer, being too busy in a grand editorial task illustrating the plays of William Shakespeare. Staunton is given a gentleman's benefit of the doubt.

The weather grows hot and humid and one evening, the outside air stifling, the Morphys decide to challenge their boy prodigy. So Alonzo, Alex, Joseph Le Carpentier and Edward all combine to make a winning quartet. But the family dream-team produces chaos and squabbles. Paul recognizes his own style of play in their moves and quietly capitalizes on this secret knowledge. On the thirtieth move they sacrifice a rook for a daring combination, and instantly the quartet is forced to resign. Paul is led by the nose to victory. The family scatters. Alex and Joseph set up the dominoes while Paul quietly resets the pieces for nobody. Sunday, according to the house rules, is the one day for chess. The game over, Ernest goes for a walk without saying where, while Alonzo goes for a drink at the Monsoon House since his card-playing friends are awaiting his whisky round.

A week later the silence is broken. *The New Orleans Times-Picayune* announces that *Hungarian chess master Johann J. Löwenthal is visiting the city. Mr. Löwenthal is one of the five best players in the world!* Paul will become a local celebrity if he defeats the famous European combatant. In the words of Justice Eustis, opening the New Orleans Chess Club in the new location of the Exchange Reading Rooms, "we are proud to welcome you, sir, to our beloved home. Gentleman, Herr Löwenthal has played *three* blindfold games simultaneously for a year. Blindfolded!" The applause shimmers through the room of fifteen men. There are no women. Drinks are brought by a butler wearing a tiepin in the shape of a knight, all double brandies and a glass of *sirop* for the child. "Herr Löwenthal has gone into exile," Eustis continues, "as a result of the struggle between the Magyars and the Austrians. A sad time for Europe, so we bow our heads in sympathy!"—which they do— "but if I may say so, calamitous events bring a joyous visit to the New World!"

The speech is misplaced but Löwenthal politely nods and takes a sip of sherry.

"You are most welcome to the Vieux Carré," booms old Joseph Le Carpentier.

"I simply desire a decisive match against Monsieur Morphy," says Löwenthal taking his seat. "It was decided on the fifth of May we were to play three games, two today and one on the twenty-fifth depending on time and other matters."

"Quite correct," replies Joseph Le Carpentier a touch uncertain.

"The victor shall retain the honour!" says Löwenthal.

Alonzo steps forward: "With the boy so young, there is no need for stakes."

"Have we met, sir?"

"Judge Morphy."

"I hope you won't be judging me today," Löwenthal laughs. "No stakes. That is fine. I earn my living by the sweat of my brow, sir. I have no need to pluck alms from a child."

Alonzo looks puzzled, but smiles broadly showing his fine white teeth. They shake hands and the preparations are complete.

Refraining for once from smoking, the men scatter about the room, sink into *fauteuils* under paintings and linger at the card tables. They take up small eye-telescopes, new to the city and designed for the opera, and centre them on the board. The effect is marvellous and ridiculous. In black coattails they strain for a new angle on the pieces, fold their arms and grunt through ruffled white shirts. Luminous drops form on their foreheads. In the corner, beneath the wide berth of the bay window the United States and the Louisiana flags crisscross in harmony. A channel of light breaks into colours between them. A dramatically oversized chessboard is waiting.

Mr Löwenthal, plucking his long coat from his hips to his ankles, takes his seat. He adjusts his white necktie and places his black bowler hat on the table then on the floor. He appears nervous but maintains a jovial air of disaffected concern.

"Won't you sit?" he says to Paul.

"It is very kind of you, Monsieur," Paul says. "But I often play standing up."

Löwenthal reaches and pats Paul on the head, a little too patronizingly for Joseph Le Carpentier who stoically sets his chin. "Make sure you're comfortable," the old man calls out.

They play. Löwenthal has a habit of comically raising his eyebrows at Paul's moves and his hairy cheeks and droopy moustache twitch when the eyebrows go up. Paul executes a speedy opening.

"All very interesting, Master Morphy," and the Hungarian peers down his long nose at Paul, affecting humour. The first game is a *bagatelle*, a rout for the youngster. "Not yet twelve years old, eh?" Löwenthal says resetting the pieces, "all very interesting! You have been practicing, not playing with the other boys?" Uncertain how to reply Paul nods pleasantly. He does not understand the implication of his victory now. This is no longer Winfield Scott, a pompous General on his way to war puffed up with Napoleonic vanity. Defeating Johann Löwenthal ranks Paul among a chess elite, a world of backroom gambling, rivalry and prejudice, not money, but prizes far more valuable, honour and fame. The brothers-in-law Alonzo and Ernest peer over the board, releasing their breath with Paul's win like fairy-tale Brothers Grimm directing the career of a Boy Snow White.

Game two produces a studied defence from Löwenthal ironically suited to Paul's attacking play. But the boy is distracted. The memory of that angel-devil girl from Smoky Row seeps into his imagination. The chessboard starts to recede from its position, blur but occasionally flicker into clarity. Something strange is happening, a feverish dream. The board is revolving, the pieces alive. On each one Clara's pale face starts to masquerade, cheeks chiselled and pouting. Her baby irises stare hollow and ghost-like from the queen's eye sockets. Paul's king carries her face, a frightening sight, a creepy male *doppelgänger* of Clara in a jaunty crown. His knight, too, grins from borrowed lips of the little shutter-girl. Even the mute and defenceless pawns twist their hourglass figures in copies of Clara's silken dress. *It's not real*, he tells himself, *none of it is real*. Terrified and terrifying all her eyes scrutinize Paul and all the pieces cry: "Pretty Clarabelle! She lives down by the river in the abandoned slums!"

Paul rocks in his seat, dazed by the obscene vision....Clara is not a chess queen, knight or pawn. She is trapped in a half-rotten house, alone in a crooked building and controlled by the brothel ordinances of the Vieux Carré. Nightly she hustles pennies from the fine gentlemen, twirls and dances. She is there and not here; still she frightens Paul. He closes his eyes and the pink tip of her tongue extends and mischievously blows him a red-mouthed kiss. Paul is in her room now, scared but oddly excited. Something is wrong. He cannot breathe or find the door. The walls are dirty. A *madame* with a crushed face is grinning through her single gold tooth and facelift hair. There are dark red stains on the sheets.

Clara hides her face and plays on the floor. A broken picture is on the wall, a handsome man in a white fedora and gold cufflinks; *Papa* is scrawled down his suit in a loopy hand. On a peg behind the door hangs a rag doll with no eyes….At that moment Paul shakes his head and Clara drains from the ivories and vanishes. The pieces abandon their fantasy and reality resumes.

When he delivers "checkmate" it is scarcely above a whisper. The game is long but decisive, and the victor, after pinning the king in the corner and using the rook and bishop to force mate, is the boy. Paul greets Löwenthal with a friendly glance as he executes the last move. For a moment the humiliation seems more than the master can bear. The room grows tense. A reaction is expected. Slumbering under a folded newspaper, Joseph Le Carpentier suddenly awakes with the words: "I wonder where General Scott is these days?"

Laughter is the tonic!

"Congratulations," says Löwenthal.

The opponents press hands and the older player's face breaks into a surprisingly wide smile. "You've just made history." On this note he rises, twists his moustache and bowler hat and remembers the men in the room. "Until the twenty-fifth," he says.

"By all means—we'll continue at my house," Alonzo replies. "89 Royal Street."

Löwenthal appears confused before smiling. "Something has fallen away from my soul," he says with a certain pathetic vulnerability and to Alonzo "of course, of course." Readjusting his necktie and inexplicably sad, he exits the room, adding "congratulations, young man." As a way of finding the door and avoiding the salute of the men, he fits his bowler to his head. "I look forward to seeing the city, yes, yes." The moment lingers in the air exposing the Morphy family's pride before the inevitable. Somewhere in the hall Löwenthal coughs to overcome a long repressed moan. "Terrible," he mutters, "I don't understand."

Back in the dim light of the Exchange Reading Rooms, the delightful victory boasts of the future. What is not possible? The double brandies, so soothing to the palate, sink down the gentlemen's throats. All is peaceful in the room, the final chess position suspended, and conversation absent. Only Paul trembles in his chair at the memory of Clara.

Then the room erupts. One by one the men heartily claim toasts to the young prodigy. The New World adventurers do not believe what has happened. Alex Le Carpentier and his father clap each other on the back. Alonzo stutters with joy at the achievement of his son. Sitting under a daguerreotype of Ruy López and Philidor, the Spanish and French chess masters, Joseph Le Carpentier cries: "What a buffoon! He couldn't outwit a *Kaintuck!*" In the picture, López is shaking Philidor's hand with united feeling. But that means very little to the old auctioneer. His manners are rusty as days spent trading with pirates and rag-tag sailors who came to New Orleans sixty years ago and lost their way in the city. For Le Carpentier the vein of xenophobia beats strong: any European is a foreigner who is not descended from the old Spanish and French ancestors, the rightful inheritors of Louisiana. The British are merrily departed and the Americans are another breed. No one can persuade him otherwise. Even a visitor from Hungary with his chess marbles intact receives only this dubious sympathy from Joseph's style of survival—very little to none at all. *"Bien sur, mes amis,"* he cries with Alex steadying him, "we will see him on the twenty-fifth of the month, if he dares!"

Paul Morphy moves a flicker of black hair from his forehead and is carried home a hero. Suspended between Alonzo and Alex Le Carpentier, bony wrists protruding from his jacket, he is heralded through the French Quarter a boy king. Strong and soft-hearted respectively, his father and uncle swing him sick and dizzy. Paul succumbs to the hilarity of two respectable men racing up and down Bourbon proclaiming a New Orleans chess champion and laughing out loud. The people sunning themselves on doorsteps murmur they know nothing of chess except that the Creoles like to play. "We are Creoles, we are Creoles!" is the reply from the singing gentlemen, with Joseph Le Carpentier at the helm three sheets to the wind. As they take Dumaine, Alex falls back on Bourbon and beard in hand, suddenly turns up St. Ann's towards Congo Square. In all the celebrations no one will notice his gambling and midday visit to the sleeping ladies of the night. The men are celebrating, so why shouldn't he?

On Royal the parade is joined by Creole wives taking their promenades in linen dresses, orange belt sashes and white parasols reflecting the heat. They join the men and cajole them politely. "Stay on the banquette, please," and "make it *all the way* home." Here and there, wooden doors of saloons mix with the fashionable shops of the day, filtering the musty smell of liquor into the street. Under barrelhouse arches suspicious men, sailors and footpads stare at the women but do nothing. The parasols twirl, the young girls skip and the heat beats down.

From his upstairs windows a reporter overhears the *melée* and falls into the street with pencil and notepad. An hour later, the morning edition of the *New Orleans Times-Democrat* carries the *Parlour Entertainment*—now chess column—trimmed to size by one Charles J. Woodbury:

> Boy takes on European chess player in the city. Paul Charles Morphy of 89 Royal Street defeats Johann J. Löwenthal of Hungary at the New Orleans Chess Club by two games to zero. In uncertain times, the *New Orleans Times-Democrat* congratulates the young chess player on his fine achievement and wishes him great nerve and aplomb on the twenty-fifth!

Three days later Mr Woodbury prints:

> ...in the final bout of their conspicuous trio, Herr Löwenthal, it seems, makes a near-fatal blunder. Paul chivalrously insists upon his retracting the move,

whereupon Löwenthal smiles at the naïveté of the child but declines the offer. A draw is deemed necessary and Paul Morphy will offer a draw because he is a gentleman, brought up chivalrously by the moneyed aristocracy of the city. But he is clearly a gentleman too in his devotion to Caïssa and the royal game.

Long live Paul Morphy chess champion of New Orleans! The Boy Morphy! Charged with electric fire! He throws away his strongest pieces with a reckless audacity never witnessed in this kingly sport! A Dionysian energy! His style of chess is passionate in positions and elegant in its direct attack, revealing his fast and calm temperament.

What goes on inside Master Paul after witnessing the private *Mardi Gras* of his family through the Carré yesterday is the question of growing public fascination. He feels love for the beauty of the board, its artful logic and abyss of chaos, without fear. He likes to build to a big sacrifice to win decisively. But does he show feelings over the table? Leave the questions to his Creole clan, in good faith, my readers! Young Paul is barely able to see the pieces, his tender frame propped by a pile of books, and none of them chess books. He hasn't read a single one!

The *New Orleans Daily Crescent*, twenty-seventh of May 1849, writes:

…to play Morphy is to be struck gently by a zephyr. His pieces glide about the board. You appear to gain an advantage then before you can tell, all is lost and won. He snatches victory from the jaws of death. In losing you learn! You realize all was artlessly planned and nothing could have been different. His moves are like the last steps of Fate. You are charmed all along so bewitchingly are you beheaded…

In Smoky Row the notorious glad-rag the *Red Book* carries a picture of the boy, opposite hair-grow products and the story of a young mother murdering her child by drowning him in a puddle. *Buy sweet*

Miracle Grow, drink Raleigh Rye whisky, use Octagon soap! Paul's photograph is uncharacteristic. He is caught in blurry mid-air dangling off the Bourbon banquette after the Löwenthal games. Alonzo and Alex's heads have been removed. On the *Red Book's* double page spread, Paul is encircled by an elegant gold border and the words "demure intellectual fighter." Adjacent are the prices and calling cards of the fine ladies of that street, Bessie Brown and "Dew-Drop" La-Fleur, Jane "Bonny" Webster, Isabel One and Isabel Two, Kathy "Duper" O'Malley and Clarabelle's own mother Violet Young.

The tabloid copy, printed in happy red, runs:

Paul's hair is dark as Alonzo and Don Diego's and shines like a knight starting an unknowable quest. He is asking good ladies for a friendly steed! Paul resembles his male lineage, but the aquiline severity of *Papa* Don's features, so typically Castilian, has softened in the son's case. The brainy scamp is short for his eleven years and skinny more than slim. But his face has grace and dignity, fragility, vulnerability and aristocratic blood that will *sans doute* make him a regular customer. A descendant of the great Ruy López, so I'm told! You see a Spanish gentleman in Paul, we see a chess wonder. Yet what was Paul doing with Alex Le Carpentier the other night in Smoky Row? Who is the devil-man's sweetheart? Who is the angel-boy's maid? Do they play chess in twos or fours? Meanwhile new faces are afoot in the so-called French Quarter. Who is Dolly McGrew? Why are her pantaloons in a hot twist? And where does she sleep at night?

The story of Paul is unconcluded.

At the base of the next page in tiny print:

The *Red Book* will circulate Burgundy Street to the Warehouse District but no further. Prices may change, as in life, but talent never dies.

Chapter Nine
1849
A Blinding Gift

On his twelfth birthday, June 22nd, Paul plays Alex after his uncle reads about blindfold chess in the *London Illustrated News*: *'Staunton Refuses Blindfold Challenge. England master Howard Staunton will not reproduce the magical displays taking place in France and Germany.'* The men gather in the subdued candle-lit drawing room of Judge James McConnell's house, on the beautiful wide avenue of Esplanade away from the heat and humidity. McConnell makes a speech claiming Paul "possesses a greater grasp of the board than all the players I know. And I am one of the best fifty combatants in the country!"

"You certainly are," says Judge Morphy.

Alonzo and Ernest knot a blue silk scarf on Paul as blindfold. The bows hang down his shoulders until he looks like a girl trying on a head-shawl. Newly coiffed by Telcide, Paul's hair tumbles wave-like from a centre parting. Placidly he calls out pieces and squares and Alonzo does the honours. After fourteen moves primed as a performer, Paul announces "I must now win."

"Take your time," Alex says, stroking his beard.

"Five moves."

After he wins Paul is channelled into a side-room where Dr A. P. Ford presents him with an expensive mother-of-pearl inlaid chessboard. Paul thanks him and runs his finger along the polished pearl, hard and cold to the touch. Only now, looking up, he notices the curious spectators. Alongside the Spaniards Alonzo and Ernest are Irish immigrant McConnell, the wiry Frenchman lower-court Judge Guy AuClair and their one time drinking friend Dr Ford. All applaud the prodigy, leaning together in a rakish semi-circle to herald the glory of the Morphys.

"A new chess age is born!" McConnell cries, topping his last pronouncement. Puffed with afternoon-alcoholic pride he encourages Paul to hold the chessboard aloft. With a little effort he does so triggering raucous cheers. AuClair refers to Paul's mental feat as "simply another language," while Ford, a new arrival to the city, says "as good as Staunton!" and proceeds to tell AuClair of his colonnaded house in the Garden District.

In a corner catching the breeze from the unlit fireplace the Morphy brothers toast each other enthusiastically.

"So the world waits," says Ernest.

"When the boy is old enough…let him choose. I'm happy either way, the law or the board. Both are chequered. Both have their problems and etiquette."

"True."

"So long as he learns how to fence, woo and dance!"

"That he will," says Ernest, "every man must have his vice."

"Indeed so, young brother."

"To Paul Charles, and the future!"

"Long may he reign!"

"And rule justly," says AuClair at their elbow.

As they drink, Paul feels the soft press of his feet on the rich maroon carpet. Curiously he notices the brilliant shine of the men's shoes, a magical moment of beauty he will fail to escape, the slender white of the Frenchman's pumps, McConnell's shiny moccasins and the black Italianesque trim of his father's pointy boots. With delight, he remembers his mother's shiny white shoes.

The candlelight wavers. With the curtains not yet drawn, and nothing but white sky outside, Paul dissolves his surroundings in his mind like pawns sliding forward into no-man's-land. The strange and familiar men disappear and human pieces sublimely vanish until only their shoes remain. With boyish good feeling Paul strains to remember the shoes little Clara was wearing long ago by the fountain. But he cannot, and is left wondering. Instead he remains in a side-room of the Esplanade drawing room, unwillingly gathering attention and praise but not succour or understanding. Set on a course by close family and friends he's already mounting a disturbing and deadly throne invisible to the eye. Trapped in a circle of ambitious men who blow bubbles of vanity and crusade for his dream, Paul teeters among them with fake joy and real fatigue, a crowned prince puzzled by the beauty of all these shoes.

The gathering is unusual, the Creole invitation extended to more recent European *émigrés*. At the higher echelons of society, the Crescent City and port of New Orleans are the last places for social distinctions to disappear. Divided along strict ethnic and class lines, the law of averages governs the Big Easy. Vieux Carré gentlemen run the courts, one eye regulating control of the Mississippi and the other funding *minutemen* on the bayou outskirts. Beyond the city's precious *levées* the whisky-soaked Judges rule, second only to the carpetbaggers, slave-trading pirates and the footpads of the no-go-areas. Young or old, rich or poor, everyone else is in the shadow of the brutal sun looking for a passage somewhere less crowded and cut-throat but equally elegant, musical and refined.

"Paul will live the life of luxury wherever he goes," Alonzo says.

AuClair continues the compliments: "Paul's *coup d'oeil*, his appreciation of all options, makes him a great chessist."

No guest takes up the mantle further until Paul himself says "I'm thirsty," and Judge McConnell without permission pours him a glass of Möet champagne. The boy gags but swallows and thrills his eyes for the amusement of the room. The blindfold slips from his forehead and Paul raises his arms as court jester and toy majesty. All cheer and take turns clapping him on the back. A strange ritual of making the boy a man, watching the champagne froth a moustache on his top lip, challenges his Catholic upbringing. But a typical Big Easy exception to the rule is made now he proves his worth at every gathering. Here at Judge McConnell's is the first time Paul has tasted alcohol, and he asks for the bottle. Alonzo denies him but the taste is sweet on the boy's lips.

Ernest is still looking at the board, grinning. "I'd bet on our little Ruy Lopez in any game," he says and removes his nephew's blindfold.

Paul blinks a few times.

"He's the Napoleon of chess," McConnell cries.

"Alexander!"

"An invincible young Philidor!"

"Look how he delivers *the coup juste*," AuClair adds, "so unexpected!"

There is a shallow knock on the door and a stern-looking African woman enters bearing a silver tray with cigars. But the cigars never make it to the men. Harried, she steps aside and reveals the visitor. A fluting voice says:

"He is my son, and he's going to the opera." A cross-looking Telcide Le Carpentier glares into the room, neck taut and raises her hand for silence. Either side of her are Paul's sisters Malvina and Helena, newly returned from school. They prance into bodyguard position and hold the tail of each other's dress.

"Good afternoon gentlemen," says Telcide. "One more Monsoon House? Yet another secret smoking-and-drinking society?"

The men stare. Faces flush with colour, and they glance about for allies but they're all in the same sinking ship. Caught Havana-handed, Ernest starts to apologize by speaking in circles. "Even the boy's finished with work."

Paul rushes over and disappears into his mother's skirts.

"Chess should be taken like all other vices," she says. "Too little is taken in small doses in this family." Her look conveys queenly victory over harmless knights and bishops. "And you've clearly got the other vices under wraps!"

The men, sufficiently chastised, retire and take their cue for Sunday brandies, cards and even a little chess at the Octopus. But they leave like sheep, so mother and daughters can take Paul to become an honourary society girl for the afternoon. They head straight for Canal Street boudoirs where Paul stands in the windows watching ball gowns being stretched and clipped. A turn in the park becomes coffee hour, hymns and poems are read aloud, while all manner of joyous and jealous female secrets are revealed. Paul's ears are mysteriously shielded, but burn nevertheless as he is exposed to a thousand whispers en route to the opera!

§

Until that moment Paul has never known opera's grace and excitement, silence and darkness, its contorted emotion and splendid releases. In one afternoon off Levée Street they see *Patience* at the Spanish Fort Opera and *Robert le Diable* at the old French Opera House. They return at midnight. Paul is wonderstruck. His head buzzes with the speeches, declarations and laments. The melodies with their pregnant *tremolos*, bursts of passion, declarations of hostility, murder, love and vengeance are sealed within his memory. Twelve years old, he drums his fingers during chess games periodically whistling Rossini or Meyerbeer. Whoever he now plays, amateurs, friends or national champions, blindfolded or seeing the pieces, he remembers the opera and its desperate feelings.

"Now you know life beyond the chessboard," Telcide says when they leave. "*Be* harmony! Life is song and passion like a duet. If one is missing, life is not even worth living."

"Life is more than sixty-four squares," echoes Malvina.

"Find your passion," says Helena with a smile. "You have three, Paul."

"You will be a lawyer," says Malvina, "because Papa wants the tradition."

"Papa wants what's best for Paul," says Helena.

"And Paul likes the law anyhow," says Telcide.

"You are a great chess player. And you love the opera," says Helena. "That makes three passions." She nods demurely. "As for the three of us, we have only one passion!"

"Music!" Telcide and Malvina laugh. "*Toujours la musique!*"

Having soothed her family, Telcide is content. Paul smiles at all three of his new accomplices swaying in the early morning chill rolling off the Mississippi through Jackson Square. The sisters pull their coats close, raise their parasols to the wind. Paul is beyond tired. He trips over his shoes, bounced along by a trio of impassioned Creole women caught between the summer heat and the devious pastimes of their men. They have to carry him, their last babe and hope, teenage Edward being already drawn to gambling and a fervid desire to "run someone through with a broadsword." Paul is different, they know. He is asleep before they reach 89 Royal and home. Telcide goes straight to bed while Malvina sees her fiancée John waiting up in the kitchen and disappears. Downstairs Helena carefully bolts the iron door. A caring sister, Helena gently lays Paul in his room, his mother-of-pearl chess pieces waiting on a small wooden table under the window. The moon is riding high.

That evening Paul dreams again. Wearing a cowl, a black bishop feverishly rises from the belly of Big Muddy herself, promising "a time and place." The phantom floats in the air over Paul's head. He has the body of a bishop and the combined, strangled face of his uncle Alex and John Sybrandt. Paul is too scared to move and struggles under the sheets. Meanwhile a storm sweeps the window half open. Night rain flecks Paul's cheeks. He rolls over and the dream shifts and the mysterious face becomes a heavy-lidded lady, smiling with crooked teeth and framed by a red glow somewhere down on Levée Street. Red lights and the riverbank are calling, calling. A hand down by the river beckons.

A coughing fit breaks the spell and Paul springs up in bed. He is convinced he has seen a devil and a whore, the opera's Robert the Devil with Mary Magdalene from his Sunday school lessons. Is it really them? Then he recognizes one face: John

Sybrandt, the intruder in the house, but the dream-woman remains elusive. Paul knows the voice belongs to neither Telcide nor his sisters and is afraid. He shivers in the dark. Closing the window, he sees his chessboard nearby and draws comfort from its stillness, patience, certainty. He breathes nothing to his family.

In the Exchange Reading Rooms on October 28th Paul again plays Eugene Rousseau, now considered far-and-away the best player on the continent alongside Louis Paulsen and James Thompson. Paul shows no agitation. He whistles air through his teeth for want of a tune and wonders for the first time what will happen if he wins again? Will he be rewarded with a gift? Will he be celebrated?

Rousseau is under the weather, it seems, but rallies to the game. Unfortunately he wrestles neither win nor draw from Paul and is the first to congratulate him. The curtain is fallen: the boy genius remains undefeated. How good can he get? Paul concludes their last game with a stylish rook and bishop checkmate thereafter known as *Morphy's mate*. The stirrings of history tell that story. Again Paul senses nothing more than his family's pride and the beautiful shapes on the board.

The same day Paul beats Judge McConnell and Judge Meek in concurrent blindfold games, held in the courtyard of 1113 Chartres Street where Malvina now lives with John Sybrandt. A board is set up on the flagstone patio and encircled by enough greenery to draw wasps and dragonflies away from the table. All is Eden-like splendour and innocence. Honeysuckle vines and wisteria ivy peel down the house. Peach and fig trees laden with golden fruit cover the lawn. Like many Creole courtyards, an open fountain dominates the centre, buzzing softly with a trickle of water. No ostentatious fish ornament the spout only a small naked boy with a book, presumably a Bible, balanced comically on his brow. He is reading lessons to the world. Meanwhile under the overhanging veranda diamond-shaped flowerbeds of mint and basil pursue their hidden lives. Reclining in the relative coolness of the autumn breeze, James McConnell and Alonzo Morphy wait with single breath while Judge Meek, four times slower than his opponent, commences a disastrous move.

"*Échec!*" replies Paul.

He is half in the sun and weary. While John and Malvina prefer the indoor shade and their own quiet game of pontoon, Paul is clearly being lionized by the family men as he is every Sunday. Taking a *dernier bout* from Judge Meek he speaks the winning words in French for the pleasure of his mother.

"*Et mat!*"

Telcide neither senses nor appreciates the compliment, though. Once again she and Helena rescue Paul from his devotees, adult admirers and general *passionnés*. Striding into the garden she wonders at the words "*et mat!*" She gathers Paul to her side and whispers: "A board game cannot replace music!"

"Unlike the opera," adds Malvina and marches Paul from the patio, the blindfold he has been wearing the whole afternoon trailing in his fingers.

The next day, feeling a surge of new importance at his growing position in the family and a swell of teenage pride, Paul visits Smoky Row. He searches all down Eclipse Alley but cannot find Clara. The day is hot. The girl from the fountain has gone and several of the shacks are missing. The cobblestones look more like uprooted stone weeds and seem to say "do not come here, do not forget yourself, young man. We hold the street together and we are dying."

The place seems dustier but less deserted than the time many months ago when Paul visited Bienville, Conti, and Burgundy Streets on Alex's "journey for the soul." Now Paul walks by wooden pit-blocks of traders in human flesh and looks for the right house, only the right girl. Sooner than he expects, he emerges from the edge of Smoky Row onto a half block he barely remembers called Eclipse Alley.

"There is no reason to wait," say the cobblestones, "there is old and new stock on the Turf. The people come, the people go. We watch you bump your way from one suicide shack to the next gin-mill. We are here perpetually, but the young girls never stay long."

"I don't understand. I can't hear you."

"Leave this place."

Paul stays nonetheless. Where has the water gone? Where did he sit with Clarabelle? Where did they play marbles in the heat? Paul decides to go home.

"She is buried inside, or long gone," the empty fountain murmurs.

The sun is much lower and the streets growing shadows. Paul stumbles onto Basin Street where the sewage drains and follows it down where African slaves are striking drums in Congo Square. The sound is harmonic and mesmerizing. Boys and women dance and fret in the heat while children with wild eyes clutter the flattened stones. Babies are screaming and colour is everywhere, carts, donkeys and strange noise. The Vieux Carré looms in the distance. Smoke and cooking smells replenish the sky. A Voodoo priestess dances naked, raucous arms painted with blood calling the dead and gone. The drums reverberate low. Paul hurries on, breathing hard. He is lost.

Running along Liberty somehow he is back on Franklin, pinned inside St. Louis Cemetery No. 1. His face pulses with his heart-blood. The unseen dead are restless. Tombs are mounted left and right in pre-made family vaults, and pinned to the earth above ground—this way the skeletons survive a flood rather than float to the surface and terrorize a fleeing people. Everywhere pure white caskets quiver in the heat. The pale coffins drip with humidity and green vines. The single family names Leblanc, Hogue and Trevelyan are all that speaks from the quandary of headstones. Paul finds a dead end and is cornered by the little stone houses of eternity. "Soon," they seem to say, "you too will come home."

Then he sees the family tomb for *Señor Michael and Señor Diego*. No dates, nothing more. Paul parts the tall weeds. There, on a shadowy marble block freshly chiselled, is the single word 'Morphy.' The letterbox where human ash is emptied is ready for future generations. The white stone waits. Seeing the future and the past, Paul is suddenly very frightened. In the blazing heat of the day he cries out, stumbles, and scrambles over the grass away from the tombs. The coffins blur and threaten to collapse. Death is in his mouth, until he is through the main gates and drinking in the windy boulevard and cypress trees of Rampart. As though he's never been away, nothing has changed in the narrow streets of the French Quarter. He thirsts for a cold bath or something to settle his nerves. Ice water is the tonic to soothe body and soul.

Weary from his adventures, Paul finds a seller of toffee drops and sits outside Mary Thompson's cigar store. Near the red glow from her outdoor lamp he feels a strange kinship. He doesn't know why. But a funny smell rises from the drains, so he moves on. The toffee drop dissolves in his mouth reminding of the time he saw the funeral of Jean Lafitte parading Bourbon. The panic over, Paul delays going home and ambles down Barracks Street. On the corner a blue parrot is drinking from a puddle and he stops to watch. The bird's foot is tied by string to the brickwork and looped around the corner. Paul follows it to the arm of a little girl sleeping in the alley. For a moment he feels it must be Clara and something sweet and painful stirs in his stomach. By coincidence she stirs and looks at him, a twisted dirty face. She could be Clara but she isn't. Clara would never sleep in the street. She lives with her mama and friends down on Basin Street.

Paul goes home and takes a long afternoon bath. His arms straddle the tin sides and he counts the tick of the hidden grandfather clock. Body still clothed, a habit lingering from childhood of bathing in his pantaloons and soft leather shoes, Paul sighs as his heartbeat finally slows.

Chapter Ten
1850
The Intervention of Education

Jefferson Academy is a white Spanish triple-storey between Bienville and Iberville. Paul walks to school most mornings with Ernest, leather bags strapped across shoulders, one for learning and one for the Custom House. Uncle and nephew are weary in the early hours.

As a teenager Paul is free to leave the school and join the coffee-drinking dreamers on Exchange Alley. He can grow a beard and embody the conformist career of Ernest the warehouse manger. But Jefferson Academy is too dear to the Morphys' family heart. Paul will follow in his esteemed papa's footsteps and become a lawyer. So chess will be abandoned, shelved with great reluctance but not without discernible relief for Paul, as much as for Telcide or Edward. The aspiring pupil will focus on his Latin and Greek verb declensions, Mathematics, Geometry, Physical Training and the good taste and deportment required of an aristocratic Creole gentleman. The big legal feat is to learn by heart the Civil Code of Louisiana—the Napoleonic Code. The Code is long and complicated. But by the time Paul leaves Spring Hill College,

Mobile, he will perform a memory trick for friends and family, reciting the entire Code blindfolded.

Before then, to graduate from Jefferson Academy, Paul must venture out alone, a solo pawn backed by the goodwill of his extended family. They release him on December 3rd 1850 and he leaves for Spring Hill College not yet fourteen. The Pontchartrain Lake Railroad heads from New Orleans on the slow train *Smoky Mary* and the journey is the longest of his life. Cornered in the last carriage and fingers latticed on the open window, he watches home thin to a spectre on the horizon and disappear. At Milneburg four miles outside the city he takes the steamboat to Pascagoula and the stagecoach to Mobile.

In a week Paul's schoolfriend Charles Maurian joins him on the Alabama coast. The Morphys and Maurians choose to enrol their boys in the winter term, since the 'infected months' of July and August see the decimation of inland towns in the grip of yellow fever. The cooler Gulf location of the college makes it immune to epidemics. Straddling the city limits, Spring Hill is a collection of what look like redbrick farm buildings. White colonnades imitating Greek temples welcome the students to each department, the library, gymnasium and dormitories. Long owned by Jesuits, for whom the Catholic strongholds of Louisiana express misgivings, by mid-century the college is monitored by cleric Napoléon Perché. From then on the Big Easy senses a benevolent leader long before he becomes Archbishop of New Orleans. The secular newspaper *l'Abeille* supports Perché and by the time Paul and Charles arrive Spring Hill is considered fashionable *and* a worthy place for a Creole to obtain an education. Every boarder has a bedstead, washbowl and private table, plus each departing boy donates a dozen shirts, six cravats, writing materials, a *surtout* and a fork and spoon. Several of the affluent Creole sons are shocked but Paul cares little for the relative material hardship. As someone surrounded by luxury from birth, he is desensitized to the glamour of good living and regards his primitive dormitories and shared washroom with stoicism rather than petulance. Nevertheless he quietly revels in his going-away present of a fantastic blue-cut jacket and pantaloons.

Far from the Vieux Carré reminders of home fall fast away. Paul can no longer hear the sound of Telcide's piano or harp, the gruff voice of Mr Michaels the banker or shrill trilling of Miss Molly. Clara is more often than not absent from his mind. So too is his worry for Helena's fragile health. No longer can Malvina with a pin from her sewing box prick his elbow or ankles. Or Alonzo make him sit on piles of books and perform for the New Orleans Chess Club. The reprieve is more welcome than a hiatus. The Morphys are, for once, at arm's length. Only Edward is here somewhere in the schoolyard, being cajoled by an older boy into swapping study work.

Still, Paul's beloved grandfather hovers on the edge of his consciousness, the sad old gentleman and his cheroot pipe too much of a fairy-tale memory to forget. Paul does miss the sound of Alonzo's voice waking him, the veranda overlooking the courtyard and the pale moon at night from his bedroom. He knows he must seek consolation in his studies, in self-improvement, and no longer in idle games.

The winter of 1850 is happily mild and suited to concentration. In mid-February he wins First Premiums in Latin, Music and Arithmetic, and Seconds in Greek, French and Christian Doctrine. He gets a note delivered on St. Valentine's Day signed anonymously—a cheap card that sends his heart soaring. He can tell from the handwriting it is from Telcide, but written by Helena:

Thinking of you, mon chère, with love.

He feels happy and embarrassed at the same time. Joseph Le Carpentier has etched a pirate's face in a corner, an immoral swindler's grin, unbearably scruffy.

Meanwhile Spring Hill College is dominated by hardwood desks, the practice of penmanship in the afternoon and swordsmanship in the evening. Timetables revolve endlessly. Lessons are learned by rote and the boys clash weapons in the gym as though preparing for war. On a mild Wednesday with a light frost tempering enthusiasm, a school trip is planned and the Jesuits lead an excursion ostensibly to gather cypress leaves for vague scientific experimentation. From the fields boys stare aimlessly at the sky, tap knuckles on trees and pluck ferns.

Another group has the same exploratory idea as six schoolgirls emerge from a woody incline led by their bony and oblivious mistress. Drifting sideways they parallel the boys with their unconvincing green buckets as a suspended moment brings the two bands of children together. They twist into a snakehead figure-of-eight, one girl showing interest in Paul, waving and nudging him. She clutches the hem of her skirt and sticks out her tongue revealing pointy white teeth flecked purple. Paul does not know how to respond. He feels he should think only of Clara. But this new experience—so rare at school—lingers.

"Wait for me!" she says, "like we've already met. We can make daisy chains and play games!" Paul stands and watches as she bites her arm and mouths, "I am yours!" She does not laugh. Her accent is Cajun Biloxi and music lies hidden in her sly glances. A bystander to himself, Paul calls out "what's your name?" only to hear 'Clara' echo back on the wind. He knows it's not her but he can make believe.

His bucket returns empty of ferns.

A week later Paul tries to forget this new reminder of Clara. He is elected President of the Thespian Society, and plays Portia in *The Merchant of Venice* with Edward conscripted as Shylock. At rehearsal breaks their conversation is limited. Paul values his role for its speaking part and its poetry, so different to his own life, while Edward is ashamed and jealous of Paul's lead. In the scene with the three suitors, Paul lifts Portia's caskets just as gently as he moves the pieces in chess. Edward delivers his "hath not a Jew eyes?" speech with flecks of spittle leaping on the orchestra. After two weeks the Italian soap-opera concludes, a success, and the boys find common ground in Edward teaching Paul to dance while holding a broadsword. No chess passes between them, nor does Paul play Charles Maurian, and he is careful to avoid the Chess Club.

For the Philomatic Society Paul delivers a speech before term-end on the wonderful discovery of the magical planet Le Verrier, later re-named Neptune. In his own words Le Verrier is "colder, but bluer and more beautiful than our own world." But while he makes the speech Paul is thinking of Clara and a world of shutter-girls, dark streets and abandoned fountains.

He must find a way to see her again.

Chapter Eleven
1851
The Spring Hill Infirmary

After the November holidays, Paul and Charles—plus Edward—travel back together to Spring Hill for their second year. Again Paul has neither a chessboard nor chess book since after a relapse Telcide persuades him not to play. Charles prefers his Latin oratory and conducting the school choir to learning how the pieces move.

Over time Paul is revealed as less capable in physical challenges, not generating that harmony between mind and body so essential for graceful development of both. Instead he garners repugnance for the contact sports of the school, football and lacrosse, a fear he dilutes with a refined attention to clothing detail rarely seen in a Creole. On occasion he is the focus of school ribbing and name-calling. But paradoxically by being less of a physical threat and determined in his neatness an uncertain respect broods around Paul. In the eyes of popular boys, those less mean and longer-armed in their brand of bullying, he is forging honour for the school by wearing a white carnation and always keeping his shoes blackened to shine.

But the spell cast by Paul's proud family name cannot last. The black and white game, neglected, will find a way and rediscover its primary player. But the time passes and no chess, not a single pawn or piece, disturbs the old walls and young minds of Spring Hill.

The burgeoning season dies quickly. The pregnant sky delivers a tortuous summer of storms and humidity. Warm rain flecks the barley and rapeseed while orchid pods implode mid-air and drift long into the autumn. An unseen hand brings relief to the land as the cypress trees cool in the breeze.

In December two gentlemen visit the school offering professional advice on matters of finance and business relations, one Raphael Carraquesde of Mexico City and Louis Landry of rural Mississippi. Attendance is compulsory. After their speeches, Edward is buoyed with newfound confidence for kick-starting his dream of owning a tobacco plantation. Fifty boys stand in the gym to hear the lecture.

Edward whispers to Paul: "Let's export Tobacco Road from Virginia back to Spain. We could link the Southern states through the Carolinas back to Old Dominion. Bring sugar from the plantations!" Paul nods politely, and Edward sulks and ignores the lecture, twisting his toe on the parquet floor. "It's a good idea," he says.

After the gym empties, Paul stays out of guilt and persuades Edward to join him for some swordplay. Edward absently chooses the long swords, comically gold and recently sharpened for a display by visiting *maître d'armes*. The cutlasses are off-limits to the boys but Edward pulls them from the cupboard anyway. Within moments Paul is cut by a lance to the cheek, and the blood trickles on his chin. He wipes his hand on his face and shirt. A single drop falls perfectly in the centre of his white carnation and fans darkly. Edward is uncertain how to react as Paul merely lets the blade fall to the floor. He must find Charles Maurian to help get clean. He cannot feel the sting but he trembles at the redness. The visible shock and mess of blood could get him expelled.

Later Edward apologizes by bringing a bowl of warm water to his brother's room. Paul is already asleep with a bandage on his cheek, his fingers curled protectively on his stomach. Edward leaves the bowl by the bed. He whispers "I'm sorry," and "I'll find you a chessboard. Father Beaudequin has one, I'm sure of it."

A week later measles invades Spring Hill and Edward is struck down ill for five days with a fever and vomiting. The illness touches Paul and Charles despite both having passed through their childhood diseases. Nausea and chills set in. The college physician admires the look of their tongues, red and swollen. Soon it is clear both boys are in the grip of scarlet fever and must move to the infirmary.

Soon the College is in pandemonium and many boys leave. Paul and Charles are housed in the same hospital room, a corner of the infirmary overlooking the garden. As they convalesce Edward brings them the chessboard of Carraquesde and Landry, and despite his promise to Telcide, Paul begins teaching Charles a few openings and simple tactics. Paul is a good teacher. Charles slowly learns. After the amusement of his first lesson, Charles flourishes at the game. "I can scarcely conceive," he says, "how a man who does not play chess could be happy."

Imprisoned sideways in bed, Paul laughs for once, the brotherly cut on his forehead long healed. Regarding the yellow lawn thirstily stretching from the window into nothing, he replies:

"Chess is no longer something to govern life. It's a hobby nothing more. A pastime for the gods! Or so I was brought up. But it is wooden pieces moving on a board, an illusory game for fools. How can it serve any true purpose?"

Charles is entirely serious, though, struck by the game's deadly partisanship as much as its honourable challenge. As a new devotee of Caïssa, he encourages the studious side of chess. Within three days of recovery, the bookstores of Mobile are overturned in the search for literature on the game's Asian and Persian heritage. Paul buys Horwitz and Kling's *Chess Studies*, Kieseritzky's *Le Régence* and Staunton's *Chess Tournament*. No book is free from error and, according to Maurian's sudden expertise, "especially Staunton's." Later Charles buys a French copy of Lewis' *Treatise* and they read and play, indulging the whims of each other's style. Paul offers his friend rook odds—the advantage of a powerful piece—and even though Charles wins only a third of their bouts, the chess pieces take over day and night until the scarlet fever recedes.

'Learned' in the grip of fever, Paul is again playing chess and Spring Hill permits his indulgence. He plays his Spanish teacher Carlos Pépé Sanchez, a tiny brown-haired man with a pointy beard, on a visit to Mobile. No odds are offered or accepted and Paul struggles not to patronize his teacher. Upon his return the words are spoken freely that, despite his family's disapproval, *the boy will play*. So after Charles is dispatched, Paul is challenged by Father Beaudequin to play blindfolded. Edward offers Carraquesde and Landry's chessboard for the contest.

The event is a blur for Paul. Pretending he is back at 89 Royal Street with the New Orleans establishment looking on, Paul wins both games quickly. As Father Beaudequin loses piece after piece in daring and hopeless sacrifices, he is advised by Carlos Pépé to restrain his play until his temper is ignited:

"Nonsense! I shall play *en lutte* in the style of the great competitors. *En lutte* I say." Paul quietly demurs, saying he believes an attacking and daring style with uncompromising sacrifices is noble indeed, and proceeds to win the game by the same method. Unlike Father Beaudequin, the young teenage master harnesses the power of his risks. Offering the illusion of attacks Paul converts apparent errors—feints, threats, material losses—into splendid victories. A magician half understanding his tricks, he controls all positions and predictions and senses his own power. But he cannot see the future. Paul and Charles Maurian are friends in chess, but relatively few games are played and Charles cannot improve beyond the odds of rook. The chess books are exhausted and work must again take centre stage.

Suddenly a drifting boredom descends over their lives caught in a round of study, swordplay and practiced social etiquette for which they have no outlet. Charles defers his attention to Greek myths and is always talking of the Minotaur, as less of a beast more of a man, and the tragedy of his imprisonment within the labyrinth. Meanwhile the Cyclops in Odysseus's adventures gives Paul more bad dreams of unseen enemies and Penelope waiting at home for his return.

Again the chess games wane to nothing. Paul retains a pocket set, a gift from Charles, but the miniature scale makes the games inscrutable and clumsy. But Paul is determined to play in spare moments using night-candles, despite his mother's disapproval. The weeks become months falling into predicable seasons, and nothing changes between the thumping acquisition of knowledge and brief holidays back in the Crescent City.

Paul graduates one year early in the spring of 1855. Despite trouble in the colonies, by now he is against secession of the southern states and delivers an address at graduation speech, 'The Political Creed of the Age'. Herein he sows the seeds of his Civil War predicament, namely his desire to stay loyal to Louisiana and the Union both. The address is largely ignored but with a scroll and elegant miniature sword, a pocket-book and prayer, Paul says his piece. Not without regret from Father Beaudequin, he is shown the door from Spring Hill College to the wider world.

Charles Maurian having left the week before, Paul returns alone. He takes the stagecoach to Mobile and the steamboat *James L. Day* north, paying five dollars for his berth. The ship sails from the bay of Mobile one evening in May entering Pontchartrain by a narrow passage and skirting its southern shore. Landing at Milneburg, Paul boards a little railroad car built on piles and overpasses the swamps. Jets of steam whistle from the wheels below his elbows as he leans out feeling hot steam through his fingers. Dangling from the open carriage, one eye on his pocket chess set, he challenges the other eye and plays himself. Neither opponent relenting Paul is determined to win at all costs. Both wonder what the future will hold and how his family will set him up in legal practice. In an hour he will be in New Orleans. Defeating himself victoriously, Paul exits the door of the train.

Walking the last mile, he stops at the Elysian Fields Coffeehouse and lingers over a glass of *sirop* and a brandy before meandering via Levée to Canal. In no rush, he dusts straw from his travelling suit and absent-minded and a little nervous, he wanders the banks of the Mississippi, wide and hazy and glorious in the afternoon light.

Christmas at the Morphys is always a raucous vigil. Long celebrations mix music, wines and fasting at midnight, before presents are exchanged after New Year revelry on Three Kings Day. This year Paul turns eighteen and publicly blindfolded, without chess playing, he talks of becoming a lawyer with dark hair flowing from the sides of his head. He can almost recite the *Code Napoleon*. Telcide observes that he retains a more confident gait but remains a slender child. Despite the fun of the homecoming, Paul feels a heavy pain for days gone by, and senses the end of his childhood with apprehension.

Chapter Twelve
1855
A Tenderloin Graduate

P aul enrols at the University of Louisiana, Baton Rouge in November 1855, and he same month witnesses the famous actor Patrick Le Mar play Falstaff in *Henry the Fourth Part One* at the St. Charles Theatre. Alex accompanies Paul who is distracted the whole time but relieved to be away from the house while Telcide basks in the glow of a *soirée* de gala. At the final curtain Alex persuades Paul to take a walk to kill the last hour of Telcide's music. They meander in the direction of Lake Pontchartrain on the gaudy boulevard of Canal.

"Fancy a drink?" Alex offers. He is smoking a thin cigar and looking sly.

Paul considers: "Not if we go down on Smoky Row." He realizes only he has mentioned the red-light district.

"Of course," Alex replies squinting in the sun. "The barrelhouses have moved anyway. They're all down by Girod now."

In silent agreement they head towards the Creole quarter called The Swamp. Run by barkeeps, the familiar barrelhouses intermingle with makeshift, cheap bordellos for flatboatmen and drifting *Kaintucks* who moor their skiffs nearby. Already these buildings, like Smoky Row before them, are sliding into the

Mississippi bounded by Liberty and Robertson on one side and Julia on the other.

"You are old enough," says Alex and nothing more.

"I've been old enough for two years."

"Just keep your wits about you."

Through dim smoke and rolling river fog they enter the district of red dust. *The House of Rest for Weary Boatmen* advertises itself on a crudely painted sign in the heat, can-can girls dancing in purple paint. Cackling is heard, a slammed door, held breath and then silence.

"Better known as the House of Shanghaied Sailors," Alex adds. "They stay too long."

Behind an open cart under a dim archway is *Mother Colby's Sure Enuf House*.

"Less than inviting," Paul says.

In moonlight the French Quarter lies peacefully on the hill, questioning their journey, and the cathedral's cracked bell chimes one. Taking Ursuline Street to Hospital, two blocks down Barracks Row and the Vieux Carré is gone. Together they enter the heart of The Swamp. A small boy, skipping one foot to the other, offers them a sweet. "I'm Charley, I'm a good boy," and he slips a card in Paul's hand.

"Don't take the sweets," Alex says.

"Come later, see, for relaxed hours," says the boy and hops back to his corner spot.

"So this is Gallatin," says Paul. "All these broken cobblestones...I wonder if that girl..." his voice trails.

"Who?"

"Only a girl I met a long time ago."

"Don't hold your breath," Alex says. "A lot's changed since you were schooling, including the girls." Paul glares at his uncle.

At last Alex chooses the barrelhouse *Tony's Lonely Keg*, offering 'five cents any spigot'. The two men enter wrapped in dreams, dip pewter mugs in the barrels, pay at the bar and sip slowly. Conspicuous in evening suits they try to stay out of the light, but Paul is nervous. Alex takes him by the elbow.

"Let's stay here. You'll feel better after a drink."

"Tony's is near empty," says Paul, an obvious amateur.

"It's early," Alex replies and takes the opportunity to explain a few things. "Remember the girls are banned from the Carré. They're no-go on our streets. That's what keeps them here. It's ten years since all coffeehouses and piano bars banned the working girls."

"Censored," Paul says, lingering on the word.

"So they're all back-o-town."

Suddenly Alex is distracted by a painting of the fields of Chalmette hanging over the bar. Corn drifts over a dying soldier in the Battle of New Orleans and in the foreground a maiden is tumbling to her knees. "This land is sinking." Alex grins at Paul. "It belongs to Big Muddy more than us. But Basin Street will always turn tricks. Why? Because she'll wash away first! You know building the Carré took a bit of help from *levée* loungers and members of General Jackson's forces. Go back to 1815! Bite on those profits! The sailors dug a drainage ditch erected shacks and hung out red lanterns."

Paul takes a sip of the watery gin. "But here?"

"Well Smoky Row *was* a merry place but the town grew unhappy and now it's reclaimed land for merchants and warehouses. Fish storage and freezing! As always in this city, lad, you drift downriver. You sink a little deeper in the mud to ply your trade, waiting to be swallowed by the dirt. We'll all drown in this city."

"Here, we're not even *in* the city," says Paul.

As they talk the barkeep takes their mugs designedly and dips them in the barrel.

"Drink fast pay and leave," he says, "unless you can't read." He jabs a crooked thumb at the wall and reads the sign: "*No suitors after midnight. Wear fine clothes, lose fine clothes. Rich Creoles go home broke.*"

His one eye stares as he lifts his hat revealing part of a matted frayed scalp. Paul is shocked but not Alex. A minute later they are out in the street and little has changed except their immediate neighbours. The touting corner-boy is gone. Next door, reclining on the banquette of *Elisse's Brew Cellar* are two old crones dipping snuff and chewing cigars. They twist their knotted skirts showing knees and laugh. One is interested in her smokes and the other flashes spiky teeth at passing clientele.

"I think I'm ready to go home," Paul says but Alex is ready for the plea.

"What was that girl's name?" he says.

Paul eyes him.

"She was only a girl."

"Clara you say?"

"I shouldn't have told you," whispers Paul.

"No, you should have. We can go there together!"

"What do you mean?"

"I mean," Alex pursues and takes Paul by the shoulders, mischief lurking behind his eyes, "I probably know where she lives. You can see her in a moment."

They lean on a crumbling wall. Alex takes Paul under a canopy and unfolds *The New Orleans Item*.

"I really should go home," Paul says. "*Papa* will…"

"Listen, they're cribs, just rooms inside decaying hovels. They pay the girl but she never leaves. Why would you want a girl like that? And how can she even spend what money isn't robbed? A bed, table and chair and forbidden to leave the premises!" Paul winces and says nothing. "They snatch men's souls who come too close."

"Like mermaids," says Paul. He senses Alex's mind game.

"Friendly mermaids! You know, we can't split up or stay longer, one nightcap or go now. Do you want to see this girl?"

"Clara. It's silly."

"Why?"

"She won't want to see me. She doesn't know me."

"That doesn't really matter."

They enter the next house, a one-storey building similar to Smoky Row, only danker and worse lit. A lazy-eyed woman accosts them at the door and leads them along bare walls, a decaying purple carpet and a staircase rising to unknown rooms. A few glasses of whisky on a crooked table feign welcome. They pay a nominal fee and keep quiet so they won't get turned away. Alex knows they need to abandon all their remaining money, and probably their jackets, to exit safely. The whisky is sweet and sour.

Small for their ages and miniatures of pinching poverty, the girls gather round and present their cards: Evelyn Shafer, Carol 'Snooks' Randella, Gertrude Dix and Coretha López. Each girl is wearing a one-colour calico dress imitating what Telcide will be wearing tonight, the evening gown of a respectable Creole lady. Together they resemble a demented rainbow, over-bright with no soft edges. Facing the wall the establishment's servant, a grey-haired old-timer, plays the piano forte 'In the Good Old Summertime' with a brisk melody. Glasses of *Mumm's Extra Dry* champagne, half drunk, rattle on the hood.

On cue Clarabelle appears, the same Clara of long ago, changed but recognizable. She pauses on the stairs for humble eyes to feed. The little girl has grown into her stripy red-and-white stockings, canary dress and three-quarter stilettos. Her neck and arms are bare, except for a genuine pearl necklace and a bracelet of fool's gold. Full to her hemline is a coquettish hoop skirt, translucent through her glowing frock and barely covering her thighs. Clara treads carefully, conscious this is her moment in the light, attempting the demeanour of a princess. But in flagrant disregard of her attempt at opera-display, her tight-fitting bodice less than veils the swell of her breasts. In one hand she carries a comb attached to an extravagant fan that she twirls boisterously through the air. In the other she grips the lurid newspaper *The Mascot* as though centrefold fashions were her life. Both men stare, as Clara's outline silhouettes the chandelier and she begins in a sing-song voice:

"Welcome gentlemen to Gallatin Street. Welcome to the true port of missing sailors. They deserve all they get!" She adds with a wink: "And don't forget the bartenders, bouncers, thieves and traders!"

"Here, here!" from Alex. "More footpads than citizens dirty the Vieux Carré!"

"Ain't that the truth gents! You are most readily welcome!"

The girls ignore Clara, but Paul stares earnestly at her. Immediately Alex leads him to her. "This is Mr Morphy," he says, waiting until Clara takes Paul's hand. "Tonight he wants to relax with you or Coretha López and drink some brandy." He squeezes Paul's shoulder and says: "It's going to happen sometime, Sinbad."

Clara looks at Paul.

"Well, aren't you the young puppy." Paul is struck dumb, but Clara is not short of words. "Been to the theatre have you? Ever read th' ol' dirty tabloid *On The Turf*? It's what I read every day. I can read anythin' you know."

"I know," says Paul. "I mean, do you remember me?"

"Remember you, ha. Come on, let's go upstairs."

"No. No."

"*Love* ain't no crime," she says and descends into a rote speech. She rolls her eyes bored and churns out words as if on stage. "There's this 1817 ordinance, says girls are punished if they 'occasion scandals disturbing the tranquillity of the neighbourhood.' We don't do that. And before you ask, the annual fee of the 'lewd and abandoned woman ordinance' is $100 for a girl and $250 for a bordello, half going to the informant. Are you an informant, Mr Morphy?"

"I'm a law student."

"We're also banned from drinking in coffeehouses, watching cabarets, living with black prostitutes, accosting men from windows and 'sitting on steps in indecent postures.' Oh, and we can only 'stroll the city if decently attired.' We've got a license upstairs you know. It's a fake. Gertrude Dix forged it with her boyfriend for nuthin'. He's not her boyfriend now."

"How old are you?" says Paul.

"Never mind," Clara says, "how old are you?"

"Nineteen, soon."

"I'm nineteen too. And the license is engraved very proper, with smiling Cupids. One of them looks like you." Paul blushes. "Do you want to come upstairs now?"

A purple girl brushes by Clara's arm: "She'll talk to you that way all night, if you let her."

"Get dead," Clara grins and snubs her thumbnail at Carol Randella. "You've pulled less than your weight this week, ha ha!" She sticks her tongue out, takes Paul's arm and he's instantly pinned between the two women. Clara tugs one way, and Randella lodges her foot in the door until Paul gasps for air. He is embarrassed by the bordello, but for the women the drama is a hoot. Fortunately Alex takes the initiative and they all ascend the stairs in a parody of courtly finesse, ladies promenading their men. As they climb Clara claps, Alex counts steps and Randella giggles. Paul looks dubiously over the high banisters.

At the top they meet a sad-looking clown, a *figaro fragile* in a bright red wig blue nose and teary eyes. Just discernible as an old man in drag, the *Auguste* bursts into juggling four silver tumblers he's carrying on a tray to nowhere. Carol pushes him aside and he takes to the banister and slides mournfully out of view, his green pants tearing. Unconvincingly, the music stops as he hits the floor, hands clinging to his ruined trousers.

Now towing Coretha López too, Alex leads his entourage through a low doorway. Paul is left standing on the balcony, overlooking the piano player and swirl of dresses below.

"I only want to sit and listen," he says.

Clara presses a finger on his chest:

"That's okay with me. But take no longer than your friend. When he's done, we're done, okay? You're a very pretty man and you won't cause *no* trouble. But I just got back from the ice house and could do with a rest." She wrestles her dress hoop sideways through the entrance and leaves the door ajar.

Paul considers his options. Disturb Alex, or sit while Clara makes fun of him, or go through with it. Feeling cornered he visualizes a chessboard but the pieces do nothing. He feels incredibly hot and hopes he'll pass out. Alex could rescue him and carry him home, where Telcide will dwell on his weak frame and revive him with cool blankets and soft sheets and Titi will apply drops of *sirop* to his tongue. But in reality dust is everywhere, he is awake and the swell of Clara, the grown-up girl, is pressing his chest. He cannot tell if she's the same little girl with innocent curls and that touch of sensitivity he recalls playing marbles that day by the fountain in the cluttered abandoned streets of Smoky Row. Or is she now a man-eater seeking out nightly unhappy victims? Paul shutters at his own lack of nerve. He takes a step backwards and actually cries out before she presses a warm hand over his mouth.

They enter. Clara's room glows darkly. Paul is expecting a basic bed, chair, table and washstand. Instead he gets a blanket box doubling as bed-and-table and a great deal of gaudy decor.

"You don't like my room?" says Clara.

She closes the door.

"I do," says Paul. "I didn't expect...scenery." A Persian tapestry, less than authentic, hangs on one wall adjacent to an oil painting of a sleeping cheetah by a Portuguese painter. On the other walls, chalk drawings display men and women in various poses dancing and cavorting with drinks. Here and there, potted palms are encased in large earthenware jars. Their stems climb the curtains, and ironically camouflage the more erotic pictures, their wide leaves splaying painfully over the ceiling. Glimmering trinkets, candles and curios are everywhere. The bed itself is loose-carved mahogany with plush brown bedding. The black satin top-sheet parades a common welcome.

Clara is proud but embarrassed by her possessions. She watches Paul as he pretends not to notice the room. Two bars of Octagon soap, ruffled with hair, rest on some laundry with Lysol used for washing customers. A trick girl now, Clara places her arms on his shoulders.

"We stopped using permanganate of potash a long time ago." They sit on the bed and Clara dangles her feet and sings a few notes.

"You really are her," Paul says. "Shouldn't we meet properly?" and he extends his hand.

"I remember you."

"I..."

"I'm teasing!"

Paul is quiet.

"But you do like me?" she wonders. "I've been here too long."

"Well…"

"But I'm moving to Basin Street, you know. I'm joining one of the palaces the politicians is buildin' with a proper manager. A *madame*. That's what they call 'em, *madames*, after the glossy French girls. Hattie Hamilton or Kate Townsend. They're both young but I've heard rumours. Maggie Mischief the Irish immigrant. One of them will get a place, and my bet is Minnie Ha-Ha, the one they call *La Sans-Regret*. Queen of the Underworld. She's a South Basin Street trickster, a dirty one too!" Clara licks her lips, tapping Paul on the knee.

"So you don't remember me?" he says, stuttering. "Clara, you know I can get you out of here. We could…"

"A flower of evil, Minnie, she knows the purple arts, that one."

"Basin Street is not the place to go. You have to stop moving. We could…I don't know. I play a tournament game and I'd gamble, and we could go somewhere, leave the city…"

Clara looks at him.

"A game?"

"Chess, it's a wonderful thing," Paul says. "A puzzle for grown-ups."

"Oh?" Clara replies and is distracted. "Minnie makes them all laugh, that Ha-Ha!" She wheezes at her own joke. "At Minnie's new bordello the *cribbers* are in stitches round the clock. *That's* where I want to work, you know. She's a Voodoo girl through and through. Ain't that the way! Not like those other poor wretches you Creoles keep in garden sheds. Minnie's only slave to her passions!"

Paul doesn't know what to say. After a while Clara says:

"So you love me. Do you love me?"

"Clara, I do."

"Hell on a string! It's like you just married me. Ha!"

"Clarabelle?" he whispers.

"No one calls me that. Not now. Anyway, come see me. Basin Street has beautiful avenues, you know. It's Esplanade's facing side in the Quarter. You know Esplanade?"

"Yes, I live…"

"Well, I don't need to know."

She kisses him and he recoils caught between desire and uncertainty, her make-up smearing his face.

"You look horrified."

"I…I don't mean to be."

She tries again and again he recoils.

"Can we just sit here and talk."

"Talk?" Clara goes red but her eyes glaze over quickly. "Sure, we can talk. But it's getting on." She draws her knees under her chin. Well, ask questions or something. I'm ready."

"You could just say things. I can listen. Tell me about your family."

"Tell me about yours. You still have to pay."

Paul considers. "I know. That's okay. Well, *maman* is Telcide but really Louise Thérèse. She likes music and right now she entertains guests. She's writing a five-act opera."

"Less about your mother…I've never seen an opera."

"Do you want to?"

"You're joking?"

"All you need is a dress, an evening gown. I can find you one."

"Are you kidding? I have a barge of 'em. We have more dresses than the Queen of France."

"Oh."

"Don't think we're poor!"

The moment hangs in the air. Paul can smell the Octagon soap and the palm trees and he looks up at the black and yellow marks on the sleeping cheetah's back. Gently he touches Clara's back. She lets him. For a fleeting moment she looks pained, strokes her own cheek and says:

"You won't tease me?"

"No…never."

"I'm only a crib-girl."

"You're the first I've met."

Clara smiles and takes a breath. "*My* mother didn't die of yellow fever. I tell everyone that. She just left me. Up and chasing that California gold rush. I had no friends and nothing. I came back to find you, you know that. You were long gone."

"Gone, but not long gone."

"I do remember you. We played together."

"I came back," Paul says.

"And you'll leave again."

"Maybe we can go to the opera?"

"I like the thought."

Clara takes his soft hands in her own, presses his fingers to her chest, uncurls them one at a time. Paul feels like crying, holds his breath and is more nervous than ever. His slender forearms noticeably tremble, as she touches her bracelet and presses his nails to her breast. She runs his fingertips slowly down and stops. With her free hand she places a *lagniappe*, a single cream oleander, in his buttonhole and a sticky blue feather behind his ear. "These will mark you," she says, "so the hustlers will leave you alone. The streetwalkers won't catch you 'cos you've 'ad your fill."

"Have I?"

"I think so. Listen, just ignore the 'Be Mine' women in the concert-saloons. Those *toughie* girls ask you to sit in a booth a buy them a drink. They'll drag you in."

"Don't they need sleep too?"

"They're just drunk and unhappy."

"I'm happy."

"Paul?"

"Yes?"

"I weren't satisfied, you know, when I was a kid. I didn't think the Smoky girls or the house robbed me, but I always had the feeling that *life* had cheated me."

"Clara, I'm melancholy by temperament."

"Big words." She grins: "Melancholy?"

"Yes and this may be hard to understand but I'm a lawyer or will be. I'm struggling too. After my family and my profession, only chess, well, inspires me. But it's a burden. I play easily, and fast, so I can't understand why people believe I'm special. But I have to play that role—to pretend—and it's difficult. Do you understand?"

"Of course! Sure."

"You do?"

"It's a game?"

"Yes, a trick. A talent for those little pieces found me, and I needed something."

"And I was a trick-baby," Clara says, "and I could always sing. My father was just another john. I don't blame my mother and I've no shame for her. Men can't help it, it ain't their fault. Just seems they don't have good sense."

"So your father is…?"

"Dead somewhere. So my work is a victimless crime. You have to murder your opponent in chess, I know that. Just like seven-up whist! You've got the cards and if you're not dumb, you win. Just like the killing that goes on chess-wise. I kill my men too, and no one gets hurt. We all get paid and everyone's happy-go-lucky. Chess and cards and living, they're all the same."

"Royal games…" murmurs Paul.

"Make sense?"

"I think so. But there's the money too?"

"What do you mean? Of course it's for cash."

"I wouldn't want any money between us."

"What's that? You'll pay me what you owe me, never mind tricks n' just talk."

"I will, Clara," Paul says and waits for her scowl to dissolve.

"Ha! Either way, it's a dollar in the pot. You have to pay up, that's how it works…"

Paul stirs and stands. "What's that smell?"

"Take your seat, minister. There's no fire."

"Something's…"

"I know what *yen pok* is and smells like cookin'."

"What?"

"They's in the back cooking up th'opium daze. When I was six, I knew then it put people to sleep. You want to know my life? Memories? Two ponies in the yard while some girl rides them naked, and the yen pok cookin' in the kitchen."

Paul stares. "I think I should leave now," he says. "But I want to get you out of here. And I do love you."

"Sit down. Listen the opium is new to you. Don't touch it or you'll sleep for two days. Irish whisky I know 'bout too. Take a barrel of spirits and a half-pint of creosote. We brew that one ourselves. I know what port is too. Prunes and cherries and burnt sugar, with olive oil for an old tawny taste."

"Clara, it's good to know what they put in the stock."

"Stock? Ha-ha! *We're* the stock."

He smiles. "But why tell me?"

"I read it in the newspaper that's all. Brandy in a barrel is grape juice and—get this—sulphuric acid."

"You're kidding."

"Nope, you just add chewing tobacco for the plug then fill it up with spirits!"

"All you could want in a drink!"

The seconds linger between them.

"You know, I've read that *Red Book*," he continues. "Well, my brother reads it…"

"You have a brother? You should bring him."

Paul frowns, and to change the atmosphere Clara twists herself off the bed. She hunts for the newspaper under the earthenware jar and pulls out a double copy: "*Thursday week. Mike Haden cut his brother's throat with a razor.* People, stay away from Mike Haden. Ha-ha!"

Paul says nothing.

"So be it," says Clara and flicking the pages she does a little trot. "Here's one. *Mary Schwartz blinded a customer in a row over a fifty-cent door fee.* Not true that one. It was a dollar! Anyway, here we go. *Who is Red-Light Liz, the one-eyed paramour of Joe the Whipper?* A whole two pages, that's good. *A daring and lusty man known as Mighty Joe is making a wholesome living on Gallatin giving beatings to masochistic harlots.*

But who is he? And why does fair maiden Liz allow his practices? Perhaps he is gentle like a caressing butterfly in his use of whips, switches, steel rods and canes. Be sure to visit 98 South Robertson from... I can't read the next line...oh!"

"Clara, stop for now."

She continues to read while Paul sits mournfully on the bed. The little girl has gone, it seems, but Paul feels far from disillusioned. Clara is animated and full of life her head cocked in amusement.

"I just need to show you the outer world," Paul says.

"I don't need rescuing."

"But I can help," he whispers. "You can leave the barbarity of living…"

"You don't judge me, mister! I'm happy. Now give me the money." She tosses the *Red Book* at him and holds out her hand. So Paul pulls his leather wallet from his pantaloons and counts out notes. She takes them all, kisses him on the cheek and straightens his *lagniappe*. "Now remember what I told you, and I'll see yo' again right?"

"*Sans doute*," he says and smiles.

Somewhere below, the tinny piano starts up and *Meet Me Tonight in Dreamland* climbs jauntily up the stairs. "Looks like dancing time is over," Clara says. "This is my favourite song. Will you dance with me?"

"I can't dance," Paul says simply. As she stands, he is entranced by her dark blonde curls and the delicate lace of her neck, and his eyes wander.

"Everyone can dance," she replies and pins him to the wall. "I didn't want to dance anyway. Go conquer the world at chess, or something. Weep like Alexander!" Voices interrupt Clara, and before Paul can ask her how she knows the boy king who cried for more worlds to conquer, Alex is in the doorway, brisk, satisfied and three sheets to the wind. A brandy bottle nestles under his arm. "Thirsty?"

Clara reaches out and takes a big swig looking Paul straight in the face. For a few seconds, he sees Clara's eyes through the eye of the bottle, wide and sad and desperate. The bottle is passed and empties. Time slips off their backs and the music plays and plays.

They're out in the street, Alex without his jacket, both swaying. Paul has lost his wallet and searches the ground for a memory of his *lagniappe*. He wants to weep.

"I'll never see her again."

"Another weed grows from her tomb," Alex replies and hiccups. "These girls are all the same."

"Only the same as women we know," says Paul. In the mud he finds a loose poppy and pins it to his collar.

They pass concert-saloons as rough-looking as their clientele. Together, they peer along horizontal slits of light exposing the belly of the dives where all is happening legal and less so. Burly men stomp and cavort with naked women on wooden dance floors. Raucous drumsticks swirl behind an upright piano and a trombone or two. The sweat is palpable. In the fat heat, a swearword flies here, a come-on there.

The next place is far different. An empty bar reveals an old man cutting his own hair under a candle swinging from the bar. All the barrels are rolled away for the night. In pale wax-light he squints hard, his false teeth shifting and a mysterious hole drip-dripping tar from his cheek. Paul starts back and bumps into Alex. In the doorway a scrawny tomcat looks askance at him, ready to hiss, then mews over some fresh bloodstain on the wood, another untold story. A solitary chair lies crestfallen on the banquette.

Paul encourages Alex to hurry to the next place where, alone and musing, sits songwriter-barfly Happy Charley. Paul hovers on the threshold and immediately Charley cranks out one of his ditties, sinking deeper in his chair. With rolling lips he delivers *Oh, Beautiful Doll!* with feeling and follows it with *When You Were Mine, You Were Mine, Now You Are Gone*. Paul drinks in the blur of melody and reminisces about his trip to the French Opera House.

Meanwhile Charley taps his bare toes in the dust and coughs for money but Paul misses the signal. Next Charley croons through his nose local favourite *My Wife She's Gone To The Country, Hooray Hooray!* Smiling Paul drops some change in his tin labelled *One For My Leg and Your Soul.*

"You'll have nothing left for the thieves," says Charley, "except yourself."

"Except my life, except my life," says Paul. "Words, words...." Feeling the intoxicated need to shed his poppy, Paul takes off the flower and lays it beside the tin. Then he makes a request. Charley plays *Meet Me Tonight in Dreamland* slowly but strangles the ending on a tiny wooden pipe. Then he offers his one-man audience a toffee drop.

"No thanks," Paul replies. "It's too late."

Meanwhile Alex is drunkenly reading a sign on the next block: *McClaren's cool stockings, three a penny pair.* He garbles a reply: "One good deed follows another." Then riverwards they weave, the warm night propping up their sloshed skins. The block ends suddenly vast and cool where the Mississippi crowns the evening with painful beauty shimmering and deep. Alex teeters on the ridge and calls: "Look, I could fall either way!"

Later in Jackson Square they pause beneath the statue of the old hero, the last *Monsieur President.* Alex touches his foot lightly and they bow to the pedestal. Shoulders touching they dream together. Light shines from the river. An hour drifts.

As dawn comes up they continue over St. Ann's where Paul sees Edward returning from either Rizzo's Academy or the bordellos of the tenderloin district. He sees Edward's feet caked in mud and calls out a jovial "*bon soir!*"

"*Bien sur.*"

"Hello."

In the mystifying morning air, Paul cannot even be sure the apparition is Edward.

"*Oui, oui, et tu as visité Clara?*" the wind carries and Paul knows he is imagining things.

"Is that you Edward?"

"Alex too! The Morphys and Le Carpentiers are not so different after all. It's all blood and music and self-destruction. A little chess on Sundays if the mood is right?"

"What do you mean?"

"Tread carefully, Paul, the way home is longer than you think."

The ghost is gone as though never there and Paul is left to take Ernest's arm. Like soldiers after a single night's leave, they stagger down the Mississippi by instinct back to 89 Royal Street.

Chapter Thirteen
1856
The Promise of Last Rites

From December Paul is away at university in Baton Rouge pursuing his law degree without Charles Maurian or anyone close by. The time is spent studiously and again he tries to avoid chess, surviving almost a year. Through 1856 he cannot stop writing illusory letters to Clara which he stores away in a private drawer. He develops evening migraines and one night sets up the little pieces. Within days chess is again a real comfort. No one can beat him locally so he travels to Louisiana giving odds of rook to most players. He writes to Charles who tells him not to worry. "Play if you like, since you're not gambling your education. Your family will not care."

Paul returns to the Vieux Carré on a Sunday in October so he's permitted a friendly chess bout without breaking family rules. Joseph Le Carpentier makes no bones of his former excitement. Paul offers odds of knight but the old adventurer insists on playing equal. But he can't see too well so the game mysteriously ends in a draw. Joseph is so elated he does not consider the possibility of Paul letting him win. Chess resumes a steady round in the household but still Edward refuses to play, leaving for Dr Rizzo's school the next Sunday and not returning before dusk. Dinner too is a strained affair. Paul spends the time walking the streets by day and avoiding Basin Street by night. He must focus on his future reading, appease Telcide as novelty-waiter at her musical *soirées* and prepare legal paperwork for his father, plus the payroll for Ernest at the Custom House. He is doing everything but feels nothing and retreats to his room behind the pieces of the purifying chessboard.

On April 7th, Paul receives his law degree having memorized the entire Civil Code of Louisiana. At home on graduation he presents a verbal display of the *Code Napoleon* to Alonzo's endless applause and Telcide's giddy clapping. Helena is charmed and Malvina sourly impressed. Edward endures the performance under great sufferance by inviting round his brothers-in-arms from Exchange Alley. Afterwards in the quiet afternoon, the house all sleepy with heat, Paul plays his father at chess. On the seventeenth move he castles the judge directly into checkmate. It's their last game.

"You're a genius," Alonzo tells his son. "The courts will be blessed by your legal brain." He points at the corner portrait of *his* father, a sternly confident man-of-action: "If Diego could see you now, he'd be happy I'm sure." He pats Paul's shoulder and jabs a Cuban cigar in his own smiling teeth.

"Thank you *Papa*."

"So when do you start work?"

"Soon, soon," Paul says, but more than a year is required because Louisiana requires all graduates reach their majority of twenty-one to practice the law. In youthful hours, idle thoughts begin. Alonzo's and Ernest's work slows for the summer and with no more school to focus his future, Paul sets out on the streets of New Orleans, alone.

With every step he is travelling back to a fateful day in his childhood, raking over a memory. A short walk becomes a loop and an excuse to head to Canal to meet Helena for a coffee. He tells himself he mustn't go back to Clara. But by the safety of daylight he returns to The Swamp, where he's immediately directed to Gallatin Street and the palatial brothels of new underworld queens, LuLu White and Hattie Hamilton.

Times are changing fast and the red-light district is coming alive. Girls are rising from gutters and growing into famous dames and real money is being made and trickling in all directions. The belle whores are patrolling Canal Street showing off their foreign dresses. Once, self-styled vigilantes the Royal Oak Boys weeded out the weak by keeping the women down: in league with the police they kept men at the top of the game. But the girls are powerfully organizing and looking to run their own places.

Clara is clearly somewhere in town. But Paul doesn't yet have the stomach to look inside the three-story brownstone mansions. "She'll be dead in a year if I don't do something," he whispers to the alley, "so there's no going back!" He stands on the corner as darkness falls, neither entering the palaces nor going home. There he waits, under the moon, playing and re-playing rendezvous with Clara like an imaginary chess game in his mind.

During his educational absence in Baton Rouge, news of Paul's chess prowess circulates in city newspapers from Atlanta to St. Louis, all the way to the chess capital of New York City. A rumour is spreading about a national tournament to decide the greatest American chess player. No such competition currently exists in the United States or anywhere else. Long after its infancy, the game is a private battle for gentlemen and yet to mature into international contest.

For two weeks Paul keeps to his room dwelling on Clara's uncertain whereabouts. He plays solo games on his miniature chess set. The house is a gloomy prison when one evening Paul is awakened by an unexpected and awful event, a bitterly unexplainable fluke. Alex breaks the news to Paul standing by the window of his room but Paul can already hear Telcide's sobs in the background. Helena enters as Alex turns to the bed and says "Your father is ill. We just brought him from the courthouse. It seems…" He cannot finish the sentence and Paul is left stranded. Alex bows his head and leaves.

Helena sits on the bed and takes Paul's hand.

"It's *Papa*," she says, struggling for words.

"I know," Paul replies, and when he looks up his face is grey.

"You know?"

"Alex told me."

"Tell me, Paul," Helena says, a desperate strain in her voice, "how could something like this happen?"

"Oh God, they just…" he searches for the right word. "It's like a cloud descends, the hand of God or a bolt of lightning…"

"Paul."

"I don't know, Helena. It's happening so fast."

"I think it's brutal and beastly and shouldn't be allowed!" and she begins to cry. Just as quickly Helena is angry with herself and dabs her nose with a tissue. She is a petite woman, uncertain of herself, reserved. The Morphys are not used to moments of crisis, always surrounded by servants and Creole neighbours. But now Helena feels a loss of courage and Paul knows that if the moment comes, no one will weep for their father like Helena.

"Since I was small, I was always his favourite," she says. "Malvina preferred the older boys outside the family!" She manages a smile and turns to look at him. "We were always matched Paul, *Papa* and me. Remember those quiet afternoons? Malvina and Edward would be abroad teasing the neighbourhood children or playing with sticks in the street."

"Striving to be popular," Paul says.

The recollection of long hot days, endless sunshine and a few floating clouds, comes back to Paul. The house would be creaking in the heat, the smell of roast pork climbing the stairs, beans and rice cooking in a gumbo in the back kitchen. Titi would be picking plums and tomatoes from the garden. He remembers the playroom on Chartres for a split second, and the map of the world newly in print spreading under his feet. Between Paul and Helena the air grows soft-hearted.

"I'd be dreaming by a window, or *Papa* would be reading to me," Helena says.

"Or playing a game of make-believe…"

"Charades…"

"Or the latest board game."

They sit and remember. Helena presses Paul's hand before he leaves to search for the room where his father is lying. Telcide has long since left the house unable to bear what is happening, retiring to Malvina and John Sybrandt's. She will be back in the morning. For now it's Helena and the older Morphy brothers, only Edward absent.

Paul enters the half-lit room and takes his seat near the line of men.

"Tell me one more time, *grandpapi*," he politely asks.

The old man coughs and gestures to his son Alex: "Do the honours, my boy! This one is too ele-men-tary for a devil like me. I'm the Double-Tongue. But one story is enough for every man. You know, I can only stand a few more hours in here!"

Alex frowns at his father and turns to Paul, now sitting at Alonzo's ear and given pride of place. "He was struck at the courthouse. As you know, not a noble blow but we'll it bear with patience." Despite his midnight excursions, his uncle Alex is a trainee preacher at St. Louis Cathedral, trying to escape the shadow of the Le Carpentier name. He touches Alonzo's forehead and makes the sign the cross. "He was conversing with a fellow lawyer, Edward McManus, when he turned and the brim of McManus's hat cut across his eye."

"His legal cases were over for the day," Ernest adds. "Another enforcement of streetwalkers, it seems, keeping them…let's just say, there are no secrets in this family and the job had to be done."

Alex continues: "Well, I believe the ordinance was to move them further away. To the lakeside of Basin Street. He was preparing the necessary ordinances, Paul, with Mr McManus when…"

"And my father," Paul says. "Tell me what happened."

"He means without em-bell-ishments," Le Carpentier adds.

"Be respectful, father," Alex says and stands to finish the tale. "By the time Alonzo was home late, the eye was a mess."

"Blood and dirt," Joseph says remembering the story from yesterday.

"The next day enflamed…"

Suddenly Alonzo says: "You took me to a dark room. Confined me. Imprisoned me."

The men all jump, leaning forward on the bench, Paul remaining on a small piano cushion. He is too intimidated to offer counsel to his father. Nobody speaks.

"On my death bed," Alonzo says, *"fortis et hospitalis."* Worn out by the trauma, his beard and moustache trimmed, Alonzo coughs a few seconds. He raises a hand, which Paul takes, and he presses the young man's fingertips to his lips. *"Fortis et hospitalis."* One eye is half open, looking murky but with a deep twinkle, a black dot of life.

"Brave and hospitable," Alex whispers. The men sharpen their ears, peering over the candles completely surrounding the bed. Nearby are good luck charms, fresh fruit and other offerings, pictures and dolls from Malvina, plus two coins from Telcide in her private joke with Alonzo to pay the River Styx boatman. A small sword from Edward lines the mantelpiece arranged by Titi as a military shrine among slaves. At the foot of the bed is a small table, bearing a single water jar and a single white rose, both from Paul.

"Paul," says Alonzo. "I can see you."

"Yes father. I know."

"Where are your brothers and sisters?"

"With Telcide in the next room."

"Close by," says Alex.

"They are definitely praying or something," says Joseph Le Carpentier. "Pray for gold, my son."

The men scowl at the old man, and Ernest tries to re-establish some decency in the room. "Go on, brother," he says, "Paul is listening."

Alonzo strains to sit up, not seemingly a good idea but they help. Bandages cover his head and one eye. "*Fortis*," he says. "You must learn the history of the colonies, Paul, for they are your blood and will carry you...I'm not about to make any great speech, though. As a lawyer you'll be making speeches for the both of us." He pauses and giggles but the men are sombre. "Learn the colony's history. Louis XV was told by the Duc de Choiseul—a dirty minister with no love for Louisiana—to gift the state to Charles III, his Spanish cousin. That means you *all* have Spanish cousins." He attempts a laugh and looks bleary-eyed."

"He'll be delirious by sun-down," Joseph thinks without speaking.

"After the Seven Years' War, France lost Canada and all of Louisiana east of the Mississippi. Choiseul decided to rid France of a place that was nothing but trouble, so Louisiana was ceded."

"Yes, father."

"Promise me you'll never gamble, Paul." He turns his firm and swarthy expression on his son, his favourite he realizes, because of Paul's desire to follow in his footsteps and because Telcide delikes Paul's sensitivity and prefers Edward.

"Helena," he says and starts to cry.

"Yes father?"

"Look after your mother."

It is too much for Paul and he has to remove his hand.

"But promise me you won't gamble at chess, Paul, no matter what happens. There is a lot of money in the family and you'll receive your share. Promise me about the chess. It's your mother's wish and mine too."

"I promise *Papa*."

Alonzo turns to the others gathered. "Bury me in the tomb next to Michael Morphy," he says. "Michael was an officer in the Irish regiment. As you know he changed his name from Murphy to Morphy and became an American. I want to die in the memory of my Spanish *and* my Irish forefathers. They all had the energy and the grit…" He starts coughing and his voice drops to a murmur. "I don't want to strain myself. But bury me there. With Michael and Diego. Write some lines on the tomb, Paul. You can do it. Make us proud, boy!"

Paul is softly crying and he thinks of Telcide alone in her room, no doubt praying. Joseph Le Carpentier takes up the reins, having seen too much death to let a family accident break his stride. His buffooning pirate attitude is gone and his face is pained for his son-in-law.

"I can tell a story," he says, "if you like?"

"I've finished mine," Alonzo says and sinks his head on the pillow. He strikes a listening air and gently closes his good eye. The blood on his forehead is fresh as he goes quiet, not alone, but with the men of the Morphy clan listening to Joseph Le Carpentier.

"Escaping a re-vol-ution on Malaga," the old man is saying, "is how this all began. Your heritage, Paul, past and present combined! Michael's son Diego was born and christened on that island. Isn't that right? The family escaped to America by Señor Diego placing *his* infant son—*your* father Alonzo—in a market basket."

"Like Moses," says Alex.

"He's smiling," says Paul and the men agree. Joseph continues: "Well, Diego's wife Vania was a produce seller and she knew how to cover the baby in a basket so he wouldn't be seen. She placed her child onboard an English vessel when the ship was at anchor, but destined for Philadelphia, City of Brotherly Love."

Nobody moves. After a few minutes Ernest takes out a single chess piece, the king. "The pieces are in your room," Ernest says and hands the king to Paul. "He wanted them. These chessmen are the oldest in the family. They're not ebony or ivory, but rosewood."

"*Merci*," says Paul.

"It's okay, don't say anything. They're for practice with your mother-of-pearl board. The choice is yours."

Paul takes the king and presses it to his chest. He knows Alonzo is slipping off this mortal board to no one knows where.

Paul squeezes the piece. "There's nothing I can do," he says. "Nothing!"

The men lean their shoulders on the wall. The night draws in and they continue to sit. Ernest and Charles play cards. Joseph Le Carpentier moans in a reverie, calling and re-living past adventures.

Morning light softly enters the room and Alex is the first to speak. "Look at Paul," he whispers, "*brave and hospitable.*" Head on his father's shoulder, Paul is curled on his velvet piano seat. The chess king is gripped trustingly in his fingers. "The boy not yet a man," Alex says, "is gone. One sleeps and the other wakes no more." Warm and cooling flesh, in the night air of New Orleans, father and son are suspended in grief. A minute or so passes before Ernest carries Paul to his bed, the king wrapped in his palm unbroken. Paul is laid down to dream, fully clothed, on the white sheets.

Mid-morning comes and naturally brings a moment of forgetfulness until Paul momentarily, heartbreakingly, remembers. He looks through his window and unwinds the ivy gently from the wall. A rattling breaks his concentration and he stops. There, behind the courtyard wall, he sees a solemn-looking man in a doorway playing a game of dice on a coffin. Pale flowers scatter the lid as the dice tumble, white roses sliding down in the mud.

"Good morning," the undertaker calls and out of sight Helena calls back: "Yes, this is the right place."

In a black-and-white dog collar, Ernest Le Carpentier is pallbearer and officiating priest at the burial. The house is weighed down, sunken under the loss.

Alonzo Morphy dies on 22nd November of apoplexy, old-world stress, too many legal cases plus brandy and cigars. He also dies of a Panama hat, left by accident overnight in a larder to grow sharp as a barber's razor. Morphy and Edward McManus talk one ordinary afternoon as friends, then one turns and unintentionally cuts the other one's eye. Nothing to be said only *"go home, I'm sorry, and convalesce. It's just a cut."*

Later that week, the circuit judge and the defendant agree: death by misadventure. The case is dismissed. The deceased leaves a sum of $154,590 and a smiling fortune for his children to fight over. Alonzo is buried in St. Louis Cemetery No. 1 and reunited at last with his father Diego and grandfather Michael.

A new age for the Morphys is set in motion. So begins a more daring time of greater heights and achievements, but a darker time too.

Edward is abject and malicious in his grief, blaming everyone but himself. He sees Rizzo and Gilbert Croquere all the time and stays away from the house. Malvina is strangely polite with her emotions, but uncompromising when looking for money. She schemes daily to acquire the biggest slice of the pie while her sister Helena locks herself away with her butterfly collection. Alex hovers every day over 89 Royal and drifts by night to unknown quarters. Only Joseph and Ernest, the dreamer and the new household head, seem relatively stable. Joseph is too old to care to even suffer, while Ernest is too busy protecting the estate. Realizing how much she painfully loves her husband, Telcide mopes. She drapes her bed in black and turns away her friends. After the shock recedes, she cuts the strings of her harp and descends into crepe-clad woe. Paul is somehow forgotten, falling between the cracks. The house looms large but he is no longer a boy, touched now by grief and guilt. As ever, though, he is caught between the sixty-four square madhouse and memories of Clara, a haunting, imaginary love for both.

From Basin Street down, from this proud Bourbon family to the mighty dreams of a Chartres Street playroom, the city sinks a little lower every day.

Chapter Fourteen
1857
The First National Chess Congress

Ten months after the funeral Paul receives a letter inviting him to the First National Chess Congress, the equivalent of an inaugural championship to be held in Manhattan. Still mourning, Paul daily wears a black suit and the jet-black cufflinks Alonzo gave him when he defeated General Winfield Scott. For private reasons Paul claims he cannot attend the Congress. But the organizer Judge Meek and Charles Maurian work to persuade him. The question of financing Paul's journey is covered by Crescent City benefactors, namely a handful of romantic-minded traders with pockets laced by sugar plantations. Seeking prestige these merry merchants step forward and in a small absentee ceremony, flattering to his pride, Paul is elected president of the New Orleans Chess Club.

The family money arguments begin before he leaves. The majority of the estate goes to Telcide as a widow desiring an expensive home orchestra to impress her friends. Ernest, Alex and Joseph Le Carpentier receive a handsome lump sum deposited in solid silver at the Baton Rouge Central Bank. Unfortunately Alonzo's *Last Will and Testament*, discovered in a moccasin shoebox in his bedroom closet, fails to confirm any sum should be split evenly. Thus along with the money Alonzo unwittingly bequeaths a period of persuasions, jealousies and outright lies. Malvina decides to employ a lawyer to address both Paul's and Helena's claims, arguing Helena's illnesses, a slight epilepsy, and Paul's unsociability make them unsuitable claimants. Each family member retreats to the point of his or her soul.

This time Paul seeks solace not in the royal game but in bodily escape. He wanders Basin Street and tipples in saloons on the local whisky *Raleigh Rye*. He avoids the brothels. On one occasion he witnesses an old man struggle with a teenage girl ripping her skirt in the street. The incident alarms him so much, for protection Paul takes a chicken knife from the kitchen. He conceals the blade in his coat, twice wrapped, and feels more worried for carrying it.

Still, his memory of his last encounter with Clara indefinably pains Paul. No other girl on Bourbon Street, or vicarious glimpse of one of Edward's play-girls, comes close to appeasing his memory. Clarabelle is all. Yet he won't enquire about her whereabouts. The one for whom he feels, he cannot directly pursue, lacking the daring impulse to penetrate the doors, drinking dens and hidden cribs. His repugnance at the idea feels insurmountable, a neurosis carefully kept under lock and key and dissipated over the chessboard.

Seeking the only other pleasure he knows, Paul longs for the nightly opera. His mother and sisters no longer interested, he returns over and over to sit by myself in the darkened gods. One night after a mute dinner at home, Paul trails the river streets, his eyes blinkered and focused. A touch of infamous Mr Hyde gripping his insides, he drifts to Girod and the less salubrious quarters of back-o-town. The whole time he ignores the whore-queens catcalling from glassless windows. Errand boys sit cross-legged in doorways ready for their next tip. On stoops, pennies are piled for the cops' collections. Eventually Paul tires of his own drifting. The lingering fear he collects while trying to walk off the death of his father dissolves. A decision has formed during his solitary jaunts and drinks. He will solicit a request from the Executioner of Alonzo's estate, a role adopted by John Sybrandt. Paul's inheritance will be transferred to the New Orleans Chess Club and remain in his own name.

With only living expenses for the days ahead, Paul murmurs farewell to his family, to tearful Helena and wondering Telcide. Somewhat deluded he laments the fact he will not see Clara until his return. Soon he will have the strength to seek her out. For the present he is rudderless, he tells himself, too upset to face her.

But one shameless last afternoon sipping *Raleigh's* in a dingy barrelhouse, Paul learns that she lives at Hattie Hamilton's place, *The Twenty-One*. Everyone knows *The Twenty-One*. Scenting it with lilac, Paul sends a message to 21 Basin Street, written on his old elegant 1113 Chartres Street notepaper, printed by Alonzo himself in the house where Paul was born. He receives no reply.

Paul leaves New Orleans the following week. He doesn't know now how long the journey will take. The distracted admirer of Clara Young is now twenty, a Creole gentleman and promising challenger for the first chess championship of the United States.

At this time no American champion let alone world chess champion exists. No single king—only great players. Before William Steinitz faces Johann Zukertort in 1886, their bout termed a 'world contest' by their own hand, and ushering in modern chess competition, no global champion exists. The question of deciding any national let alone world champion is as uncertain as a grandmaster feint. For mastery of the world, all that is needed is an opponent. But finding the right challenger long before the days of official champions reveals the troublingly narrow line between success and failure, patience and desire, pride and fall.

Blind to the future, Paul will challenge the best players in the Union in New York City, and from there the world. Nothing can stop him except lack of true players. Like the Macedonian boy-soldier Alexander he must gather between his fingers the dust of foreign deserts. Soon metropolitan men of the North with their extravagant monopolies of steel and railways will toast his honour with their burgeoning wine cellars. He must challenge the world before he laments its bitter taste.

§

On September 23rd, Paul takes the five o'clock steamer *Benjamin Franklin* upriver to Cincinnati. The journey is long and he suffers seasickness and spends most of the time in his cabin, listening to the sound of the engines. Under his porthole he watches the steamer cut mighty swaths of Big Muddy. Ridges of white water fly over her wide soft banks. The sustained plough of Ol' Man River is awesome and beautiful.

Though more expensive, Paul takes the train from Cincinnati, steam once again propelling him onward. He sleeps day and night over the clickity-clack of its pistons and eventually, on 4th October, New York's Grand Central Terminal encloses his carriage in darkness. Moments later Paul emerges into the light of a new world. Dragging his bags and weighed down by clothes and polished shoes he takes a Manhattan hansom cab to the St. Nicholas Hotel, alongside the Park, where his room already awaits.

The next morning, dressed in black for his father, Paul makes his way to the Manhattan Chess Club. The long lawns of Central Park dazzle his eyes. As he strolls by, ladies of leisure are trailing their dogs with wide parasols. Children lope in the sandy grass for an hour while city-men talk business on their half hour breaks. At the club, Paul plays a few games incognito, smiling and offering rook advantage. The players spurn his offers not knowing Morphy has arrived in town, and he is forced to leave mid-afternoon, following an openly physical threat by one of his opponents who is surprised when it materializes the New Orleans challenger is *not a member of the club.*

Paul re-enters Central Park on foot, escapes the rain under a canopy of trees and emerges on Central Park West. "The West Side is clearly less reproving of Southerners," he tells himself, meandering up Broadway to the rooms of the equally famous New York Chess Club. Unlike the East Side pretenders, here the club is focused on organizing the National Chess Congress. Paul is welcomed just in time to learn the so-called Grand Tournament needs larger quarters. He retires to the bar and sips a glass of ice water while the Committee of Management reserves 764 Broadway, the Descombes' Rooms. From the barman, a jovial-looking Yankee with a wide forehead and a cleft lip, Paul learns his friendly opponents for the afternoon will be Louie Paulson from Duluth, Minnesota and Charles H. Stanley from Brooklyn, plus the unofficial American champion, James Thomson from the Bronx.

"This way," says George Perrin, sprightly club secretary, "for a passage-at-arms." He guides Paul into a plush drawing room where Thompson and the other players materialize one by one reclining in leather armchairs. They stand to encircle Paul. Overhead, spectacular oil paintings of Yorkshire racehorses leap from the walls. Dust hangs in the air.

With goodwill to the amusement of all, George Perrin offers the first challenge to Paul. Meanwhile from the far corner, sequestered in a book-lined alcove and ruminating on Darwinian philosophy, a guffaw is heard. Here is lounging Louie Paulsen, the competitive young Swede from Minnesota. He snaps his fingers and blows air between them, affecting cool precision. Louie is heard to whisper, "the bout will play like a mosquito to an avalanche."

After the set-up and handshake, Perrin opens and Paul replies, but not before they are interrupted by shouts of "Stanley! Stanley!" A single knight and bishop are in play and instantly the game is abandoned, though not by Paul. All heads swivel. Perrin stands aside, resetting the board as a well-fed gentleman swaggers into the library. "Charles H. Stanley," he announces, pumping Paul's hand. Five spectators of a demented mobile fan-club cheer his entrance, "Stanley! Stanley!"

"I don't know these men, haw-haw! No, I do!"

Again, cheers.

"I'm sorry," says Paul. "We haven't met."

"Don't apologize for anything. We mean business here." With a flourish Stanley moves pawn to king four without offering Paul the white pieces. Paul tries to look like he'd anticipated this brash style of metropolitan chess, pulls back his seat, drapes his sombre suit-tails over his armchair and sits up as best he can. He replies with the Sicilian, queen's bishop pawn, two squares. The pawns face one another. Paul gathers his breath. One by one the pieces realign from his planned grandiloquent reply to Perrin, a now abandoned combination, and instead he must play a bluster game, facing the hour's most blessed player in America. The contest is a flourish of speed. The men lean in. Fingers dance over the board. Soon mate follows and Stanley rises from his chair in bewilderment, having lost. Within an hour the friendly introductions are concluded: four to Paul and nothing to Mr Charles H. Stanley.

Perrin immediately springs over and offers Paul his hand then his pen. Paul signs his name, his first autograph: *PCM* in loopy letters in the burnished leather album of the New York Chess Club. Unknowingly he makes himself an honourary member. Little does he know, Perrin will copy the signature and his nephew Arnold will sell it to all other members of the club. For the present Paul is following etiquette and correct procedure, the next stage of which seems to be defeating James Thompson in faster time and fewer moves, before his trip back to the St. Nicholas Hotel. Thompson is less pleasant in defeat, but manages a thin smile before disappearing into the belly of the bar. In the corner Louie Paulsen merely raises his glass.

"Mr Paul Morphy!" he announces to the room, nodding to Perrin.

Perrin echoes, "Mr Morphy has arrived!" and raises his glass. The chess players of the New York Chess Club all follow cue and drink a toast: "To Mr Morphy!" but no one can think of who he is or what to say.

No matter, glasses go up and the men peer over their drinks at the smartly dressed small Creole. In the communal eye he may be an American, but up north a Creole Southerner must clearly win their respect.

That night Paul dines late. After brushing his suit and climbing into bed, he takes pencil in hand:

Dear Clara,

I hope you are well. We shall surely see each other again. I am in New York now but I will return to New Orleans soon, I promise. In the meantime it is important for our future that you understand what I am doing with my life. My father died recently. It was a dreadful accident at work. That is why I am here, to keep a promise, and to excel in an ambition of mine before I reach my majority and can practice law like my father. You may have heard of him, Judge Alonzo Morphy? We never spoke about our families, except briefly you told me about your mother. Playing chess is how I can honorably live, away from my family, before making my own money. But I need to explain a little how the game works so you can prepare for future surprises. I don't mean how the pieces move, although that could add to our conversation! But more how the tournaments are managed.

Clara, I am here to challenge guardians of goddess Caïssa for the First National Chess Congress held at the New York Chess Club. I have already seen their wonderful clubrooms. The tournament will be a knockout but I hope to experience many other games during the official event, in friendly bouts and games-on-the-side, not for money you understand. Most games are informal meetings arranged by seconds like duelling and usually for 'stakes,' and the newspapers publicize them so the betting men know. I am refraining from all bets and stakes at my family's wishes. I must maintain their honor and protect the privilege of bearing their name while travelling and seeing fine new places. The Congress will continue to place bets. My games are organized separately so I shalln't raise a stake. This way I can keep my promise to my father.

I was thinking, Clara, I should have visited you. Maybe I can come and see you in a short while...

A knock interrupts Paul and he covers the letter with a pillow.

"Come in."

A waiter enters with a tray bearing a chicken dish and a glass of chardonnay. Paul tips the boy and the meal, the same dish, sparks a memory of the belligerent family words over Alonzo's will. Paul is reminded why he left New Orleans. The letter to Clara goes unfinished and he signs 'love' and draws his own face unconvincingly by pressing too hard. Paul Morphy, fortis et hospitalis, X. Declining to mail the letter from the St. Nicholas he leaves it on the table. Sleep comes quickly after the wine.

On Tuesday he returns to the Club for the Congress draw. Eight white tickets are chosen from a ballot box, declaring "Choice of Chessmen and first move." The tournament has begun. Paul finds he's playing a noticeably nervous James Thompson in the first round. The tables are prepared. The noise of the city's open carts, street-carriages and newspaper vendors is sucked away as the windows are sealed. The room falls silent as the First American Chess Congress edges into opening frays. There are no time controls. Eyeing each other, nodding and smiling, all thirty-two players take their seats for the long haul. The sense of competition is acute. Holding up his hand, George Perrin quietly says: "begin."

From the start Thompson retains an element of arrogance, physically swiping at pieces and toppling them when capturing. But he loses two games. At his request they adjourn for twenty-four hours. For the rest of the morning Thompson hugs the library, ridiculously advertising his mental exertion. Paul plays side games until—the next day—Thompson loses the last game making it three and advancing Paul to the second round. The same afternoon, Paul plays friendly bouts against Harold Montgomery and again against Thompson who's strangely keen to lose. No one pauses for breath or surprise as Paul takes all. Thompson is bullish in defeat: "A viceroy's luck! This tournament is chilling in its Southern manners!"

By contrast Montgomery is polite and charming and admires Paul's style and speed of play. At first, solemn expressions and general disapproving looks are discerned as Paul enters and leaves the room. But the more he extends his casual play, the more all faces are softened: they want to play him. The more he wins, the more his extraordinary gift becomes clear, and the more the disdain grows into an air of respect.

On 9th October an hour of warm-up occurs between Paul and Louie Paulsen, a draw. Then to undermine Paul with subtle friendly psychology, Louie plans a four-man blindfold display. Paul responds by volunteering to play as one of the opponents, also blindfolded. Louie will play three men and Paul will compete as the fourth. Actual blindfolds are unnecessary since they sit in separate hallways away from a room containing the boards. An amused old waiter ferries the moves, drinks and cigars. After three hours Paul declares "mate in five," and victory and fate are mutually sealed. Louie defeats the other three players but his blindfolded opponent is unstoppable.

At the weekend Paul draws Judge Meek in the second round, a less than challenging player whom Paul has defeated a dozen times in practice. Unsurprisingly Paul scores the first game in thirty minutes, an omen of everything to come.

For the benefit of the room, Judge Meek laughs boisterously: "I wish I could get a chance from Morphy sometimes." Seeing himself as a comedy challenger, Meek bemoans his own threats, knowing they fail to hover between menace and bluff, as good moves must. "I wish I could put him in my pocket and carry him off! But I can't, can I?"

Paul smiles under his delicate frown. He appreciates Judge Meek's humour, happy to play someone with Southern pride. That evening, face red and sides quaking, Meek stands to hail Morphy. He subpoenas the room's attention tapping his sherry glass full-on with a silver spoon; he feigns to save face by clamouring: "Gentleman! I exult to think that chess warriors of the Crescent City will catch a spark of enthusiasm from the New York amateurs. I veritably think those gallant southern spears, too long idle, will again be used! Morphy has jousts as brilliant as Stanley and Rousseau in '45!"

"Here, here!"

"Yes, to Morphy!"

"The Creole, the Creole!" they toast.

"Resurrect La Bourdonnais!" shouts Louie Paulsen without looking up from his match against Dr Raphael of Boston. But the toast is sober and the men applaud again. "Resurrect La Bourdonnais!" they chime like schoolboys with pale faces: "A new Philidor!"

On October 22nd Paul gains two wins over Theodore Lichenstein of Chicago. Meanwhile Louie Paulsen plays a tortoise-and-hare race against Dr Raphael taking the careful and cunning role in that parable. On October 26th both Paul and Louie win their third games. So they draw each other in a strangely parallel last round. The semi-finals are concluded with sherries all round. The pretender from Minnesota and the pride of New Orleans will now contend in the final.

"Hurrah for the North! Hurrah for the North!" is ominously chanted.

"Refill the brandy box," George Perrin tells the waiter, "a showdown is on the cards. But first a grand dinner interrupts play, and proves to be no ordinary meal, but a feat of inordinate celebration. Three dozen men retire to the Saint-Denis Hotel where The Bill of Fare presents a glittering cake in the shape of Greek goddess Caïssa. Each man will possess a slice of the chess queen. One half of the cake paints Egyptians playing chess 3000 years BC at the tomb of Nevtopf. The other half shows a mirror in Broadway icing, reflecting the players' faces. Other extravagant dishes appear, including an *Arc de Triomphe à la Morphy en pâté de gouyana, surmonté de la Déesse Caïssa Couronnant la Victoire.* The pastry course is a grand *Pyramide à la Philidor* and the fish *Bass à la Turgue and Morue à la Bourdonnais.* A Spanish castle, in the memory of Ruy López and draped with *paella* rice and seashells, is wheeled in by three waiters. After a drum roll, the lid is lifted to a communal sigh. *Vol-au-vent de cervelles à la Paulsen* garnish side-plates and for desert a magnificent *Pudding à la Franklin*, the kings and knights in jelly, the bishops and pawns in cream plus a huge *Baba Au Rhum* in the shape of a queen. After dinner, a speech by Vice-President J. A. Fuller satiates packed stomachs not too full to cushion brandy.

"He verifies the truth of the poet's line: *Westward the star of Empire takes its way.* He charms us, no less by his quiet unobtrusive deportment, modest and refined nature, gentlemanly courtesy, elegant manners and genial companionship than by his wondrous skills at our noble game...he reminds us of the mighty river on whose banks he lives, which gathering in its course the contributions of tributary streams, pours at last its current into the ocean, deep, clear and irresistible."

The Boy Wonder offers a few polite words and wishes "to thank Judge Alexander Meek, President of the First American Chess Congress, and to honour the New York Chess Club, its players and all his new friends." For a moment he stares at the room, uncertain of the expectant atmosphere. "I heartily wish you all prosperity on the unknown road of life," but he doesn't know how to go on. It occurs to Paul to say something about the richness of his surroundings. "We should all seek what each man in his true heart desires." The middle-aged men smile uniformly through their beards. As a body, they are pleased by the visitor's good manners and deportment. Paul calls: "Let the cigars circulate!" ensuring at least the temporary fulfilment of happiness.

After midnight Paul returns to the St. Nicholas tipsy and tired. He stumbles to the bathroom in the dark and digs in the closet for a candle, awash with feelings he can't explain. He has apparently come all the way to New York only to feel desperately alone. There he stands, gripping the porcelain sink and for bizarre comfort, he recites the Civil Code of Louisiana:

> ...Louisiana judges are obligated to consider written laws first. If no statute governs the dispute, a judge may decide according to hereditary custom. Article 3 defines custom as...practice repeated for a long time and so having acquired the force of law. A custom may not abrogate or conflict with legislation. Thus, Louisiana judges do not create the law. Rather the code charges them with upholding laws written by the legislature...

Pressing his face on the bathroom mirror, Paul slides to his knees and runs the taps. Managing to grip the sink and shut off the water flow, he broods darkly on his future.

Hours later he crawls from the refuge of the bath, not knowing how he got there, bruised and dazed. He must have blacked out. Retreating to the bedroom, he stands semi-naked in the soft morning air blowing through the window.

"I want to go home..."

Within twenty-four hours, on 29th October, Paul will vie for the first American chess championship. The rules are simple. The tournament uses Howard Staunton's Rules of Chess from his *Chess*

Player's Hand Book. The first player to reach five games wins and a draw mean no score.

Before modern time limits, manipulation of the clock is a tactical move and Louie plays for time. Paul responds by leaving pieces dangling, tempting fate. There they sit, hour upon hour, and it's always Louie's move. A pawn scampers one square only to leave endless drawn-out minutes. The atmosphere suggests Paul is foolhardy because he maintains his usual speed and must sit frustrated. Yet as ever he pursues a half-revealed mastery of the board, opening space and closing ranks simultaneously. It may always be Louie's move, but it seems that the Minnesotan can never steal the incentive, the beat, the nod. One two, three four, the knights and bishops are gone. Gaining space but losing pieces, the chessboard expands and shrinks.

At last queens are brutally exchanged. The spectators are hushed. The game accelerates, options narrow. Risk is only rewarded by a tempo, the tiny advantage gleaned by the proffered dubious move. In the heartbeat of a moment, the Greek wheel of fortune rotates. Paul places his army sacrificially at Louie's feet, all the important pieces except the secret to win the game. Like racehorses straining on the nod, Louie's pieces stumble and flail. One by one, they go lame reaching for the finish line, and the first game is broken open. Sublimating itself unseen, power is diffused to lesser pieces and victory is achieved gloriously on the wings of defeat. Working in combination the final knight and pawns gain the prize. Then from months ago Alonzo's words come back to Paul: "The king is the only piece that needs be taken."

Louie is politely advised by George Perrin to move out of check. He moves his king but nowhere is left to hide. The king is disallowed from moving into the death of check and starts his lonely run with an inevitable end. The randomness of the universe is beautifully curtailed—if only on a chessboard—until he is finally cornered, sliced and smothered. Double check!

Et mat.

In later games, the Swedish-American decides his moves after excruciating delays. With his foppish blonde hair and freckles, Louie emanates clairvoyant power. He distils all possible probabilities by draining and reconstituting the board's squares, literally taking hours. Nevertheless he draws the second game, a balletic slow-motion clash. The third game is an endless fifteen hours, with Paul's cumulative time less than forty minutes a move; Louie consumes eleven hours. He wears Paul down in a corner. The Creole is stubborn in his politeness, not permitting visible impatience, but enduring the wait. Nothing would pain him more than an accusation of ungentlemanly conduct. The game heads to a draw, but Paul is misguided for once. Louie secures a victory in one corner and checkmate is rapid. He gains a notch, but the fourth game is drawn and the fifth goes to the boy from the Vieux Carré.

That evening Paul takes to his bath, feet to the wall and a damp cloth over his face. He is always immaculate for dinner. Tonight he drinks only water. Past nine, he walks out to mail his letter to Clara, written a week ago and mulled over. Halfway across Broadway, he pauses to check the return address. A warning sounds on the wind and then a strange crunch. The bicycle skids, vanishes and Paul clambers to his feet. A hit and run. Paul's cry flies up the street but the envelope is gone, swirling in dust.

For a while everything is broken. Regretting delaying the letter, Paul wanders the storefronts of Central Park West. He spies a suit and matching tie, a set of bronze luggage and a deck of cards in a betting shop. He peers at the women's dresses in turquoise and gold then hurries on. At last he returns to his hotel, wondering what Clara is doing and whether she misses hearing from him, also unnerved by Louie's desire to prolong their encounter.

"Paulsen shall win no more games," he whispers and with finger and thumb he nips the candle. "Everything else must wait."

Trying not to breathe the dank hotel air, he lays the bathroom towel over his eyes. Darkness abounds. Close the mind, he thinks, and for once he has no dreams. Repair the mind...

The next day between games, Paul takes a glass of sherry and a biscuit with J. A. Fuller.

"Louie being slow?"

Paul taps his sherry glass and is surprisingly abrupt. "He'll never win another game from me while he lives."

"But it's two-to-one in your favour."

"I know. But unless I determine to win soon, forever will be now," he smiles, not convincing Fuller of much except his determination. The biscuit crumbles down Paul's shirt and he spends a whole minute removing the crumbs as Fuller watches.

Returning to the Descombes' Rooms and his small cushioned chair, the break has made Paul certain of something. He moves his queen into danger, *en prise*, offering her for the taking. Louie studies the position, deciding to decline the easy piece. Lips pursed, he announces "*Timeo danaos, et dona ferentes.*" But minutes later, with a reckless flourish Louie takes the queen anyway, reminding Paul that the Trojans "founded western civilization despite the fall of Troy."

Paul's strange offering of a queen sacrifice makes what now happens remarkable. By convincing Louie he's committed a blunder, Paul really did seek the loss of his powerful lady. Louie tries to expose a bluff, but accepts the gift, failing to see the deadly army of miniatures hidden inside, the blessed bishops and godless knights scurrying into position. Paul then waits, and seeing the game's final act, he looks up not in triumph but self-knowledge. Mutually protecting their ranks and files, the minor pieces employ a net and, without rooks for support, they swoop. The tipping point of the tournament has been reached. In future years Paul's co-editor of *Chess Monthly* magazine Daniel Fiske will describe Paul's play as "bold and rapid in move and swift in combination." In *Modern Chess Instructor*, future world champion William Steinitz will publish this famous queen sacrifice in gold lettering.

Paul graces a checkmate. The game ends and a man steps casually from the shadows, a long dark body in a long dark suit. As Paul leaves the building, Frederick Milnes Edge accosts him on the stone steps leading to the street.

"Mr Morphy?"

Paul turns, surprised. "Yes?"

"I wondered if I could have a word, dear chap. My name is Fred Edge, from over the pond. Yes, well, I'll get straight to the point. After you win this tournament, and clearly you are going to win Mr Morphy, Europe beckons. Chess is at home in the great cities from Prague to Berlin to Paris, and of course in my own capital's clubs, the London Chess Club and the St. George."

"I'm very sorry," Paul says and retrieves his hand from Mr Edge's silky grip, "but I'm going home after the Congress. I have business in New Orleans. I am a lawyer and I am going to practice, I mean start a practice and…"

"That is fine and so you should, so you should." The moment hangs in the air before Fred says, "I'm trying to take your meaning. I am complimenting you, Mr Morphy."

"But…"

"Yes, your play is fantastic. Your opportunity to play Howard Staunton is upon us and I know Mr Staunton personally. I can arrange the match. I am convinced he would accept your challenge most graciously. If you'll permit me, I can gather support for your berth across the Atlantic."

"The Atlantic?"

"Why of course, Mr Morphy. Did you think we were going to fly?"

Curiously, Fred Edge does not smile at his own joke and Paul is left momentarily bewildered, his coattails flapping in the wind. Edge's black eyes look enquiringly at Paul, not without friendly cajolement, but fixated so the smaller man cannot look away. "You would do well to let me manage your affairs, as your personal secretary." He leans in conspiratorially. "I know the continent well, the back alleys and finest seats in the opera houses. What do you think?"

"I'm flattered," offers Paul.

"I know it's a rush, but we can meet properly if you're interested?" He smiles keeping his lips together. Behind his slug-moustache and top hat, there is something of an obsequious Uriah Heep about Fred Edge. His ghostly appearance and the mischief in his sprightly limbs somehow hypnotize, and Paul is charmed and scared in equal measure. Yet the impression is an authentically thrilling one. Here is a man who would consider every detail, be transparently loyal in his emotions, and interpret the intentions of others. Despite usually travelling alone, Paul's gentlemanly psyche is curious about this *merrie* businessman leading the way. A well-heeled Englander could help navigate the labyrinthine etiquette of European society.

"I would have to think," Paul says.

"Well, naturally. I believe we can raise stakes for the game in Europe, just as…"

"No stakes," says Paul. For once he is terse and Edge gauges the reply. "There will be no gambling on my games. I have sufficient money for expenses, should I be interested in playing, or travelling." As Paul speaks, the pride of his family is tangible.

"Right now, you're the best player in the United States," Edge says. "Your country is less than a century young, its feeling of inferiority to Europe barely diminished, but toppling fast. What I'm saying, Mr Morphy, is that the champion of Europe *and* America would be the chess glory of the civilized world. It's that simple."

There, on the stone steps of the New York Chess Club, Paul's fate teeters. The sky overhead is grey with a condensed moment of pure contemplation. Paul ponders his future. A mirage hovers before him of reconciling his family through foreign achievements: Telcide and Edward truly happy, Helena overjoyed and Joseph Le Carpentier brimming with prestige. Surely that is Paul's aim? The image glitters, invisibly tangible, and impossibly real. No other motivation is as wholesome or duty-filled. Right there, Edge offers Paul his hand and within its darkness there swims a butterfly of fragile colours. All crystallizes before him.

Chess, fame, travel and the rescue of Clara from the brothel-mansions of Basin Street!

"Can we discuss tomorrow?"

"Your family will be so happy," says Edge, as though mind-reading. "Discuss tomorrow? Well, of course Mr Morphy. There are many days remaining for you to dispatch Mr Paulsen. Incidentally, may I call you Mr Paul?" With a swirl of his cape Edge is away, and Paul's demure affirmative, "yes, okay" is left hanging on Broadway, his small frame a little stunned and swaying under the green sign of *Broadway and Eighty-Ninth*. Looking forward to an evening at the St. Nicholas, bath-soaking away the sounds of the city, Paul walks to the corner and notices the Englishman again, the pale face and triangular eyebrows unmistakable. Fred dances from one foot to the other, performs an embarrassed bow on seeing Paul watching him, and is gone.

The next day Paul spends in Central Park reading the newspapers. He buys grapes in mid-town, poring over the small print concerning the future of the tobacco and sugar industries in the Southern states, frequently frowning. He walks off his concerns, popping grapes, and mingling with the busy crowds.

On the 10th November, a newly refreshed Paul wins seventh and eighth games against Louie, ending the match and consequently the tournament by five games to one. At last, he is the best player in America. No one is faster, younger or blessed with greater promise. Citing his amateur status Paul refuses the three hundred dollars prize money, so behind the scenes a special gift is prepared.

A week later he is presented with a silver service platter, a pitcher, salver and four goblets all engraved *P.M. Champion*. Louie Paulsen is presented with a marble chest-medal shaped as an American shield. In a backroom, less rouged and relieved, Paul and Louie pose for a brief pencil study by resident New York Chess

Club artist, Mr Henri Lester. Later they examine the etching, a bizarre portrait in which Mr Morphy is the jaguar to Mr Paulsen's puma, their tails disappearing into the Amazon rainforest. George Perrin accepts the image and further commissions the artist, congratulations are made all around, and at last the First American Chess Congress is adjourned.

That evening, a long formal dinner caps the proceedings. Full tuxedos abound with matching ties, belts and freshly pressed pantaloons. Mr Morphy remains the lion to be lionized, Paulsen the silverback ape to be endlessly preened by a close circle of male devotees. Everyone dines, drinks, smokes and cheers Paul, excusing their behaviour through revelry. The dinner goes into the night with toast after toast. After a little wine, Paul takes the dais and declares:

"Old Europe may be rich in devotees of Caïssa. She boasts Stauntons and Anderssens, Harwitzes and Löwenthals. Yes…and as Fred Edge would say, 'well, of course the Union has some catching up to do,'"—laughter reeling through the smoke rings— "it is the great boast of America that Mr Paulsen's blindfold chess has not been equalled."

Louie Paulsen, his voice uncharacteristically loud but his gestures slow and stand-offish, raises his glass. "We will face the Europeans head-on," he declares, "now we have Mr Morphy. We hereby challenge the much-vaunted chess Knights, and will master the magnates of the Old World!"

Thomas Frère stands on his chair and declares: "The game of chess, thank God, has no Mason-Dixon line!"

"Hurrah! Hurrah! Save the Union!"

"God save the South!"

"God save the King," Fred Edge calls from where he is lodged at a separate table. There being no room among the true players and devotees, he is bumped down among the journalists and secretaries. "And God save America!"

Paul sits and adjusts his bowtie.

"Quite so," Judge Meek retorts, and "God Save America" is taken up by both tables. Choruses sweep to the ceiling, while Paul is whistling piano tunes, long after celebrations have slid into sherry and cigars. Meanwhile, chess and Clara fog his mind with their decisions, moves, and unknowable impulses. Later, as the men disperse Paul offers 'Pawn and Move'—the advantage of a pawn and the white pieces—to the whole club.

There are no takers. James Thompson refuses to accept the advantage "as a point of principle," despite losing to Paul, while Edge deems Thompson to possess "no small amount of chess vanity." Paul is unconquered, but alone as first in club and nation. No one wishes to undergo defeat even for the common advantage of Pawn and Move. Any shame at handicapping a champion is usually dissolved by the honour of playing a great player, while in the chess publications of the day the loser's name is traditionally withheld. But here the players remain anonymous by simply not playing.

Eventually the former American champion Charles Stanley, without his usual fan-club retinue privately, offers a challenge to Paul, who then beats him in the Park before a modest crowd. They play five, the tally four to Paul and one drawn. The draw is not intentional, Paul never patronizing an opponent who proffers a consciously weak performance; rather he chooses to attack hastily to allow Stanley a careful defence. The endgame ties primarily because Stanley tries a 'forced mate in five moves.' He does so too quickly.

Afterwards Paul discovers the bout was a stakes game, which upsets him, the arrangements having been made in private between Edge and the club's gambling men. Paul chooses to dispose of the money. He has Edge—with whom he has signed to work for the duration of their European tour—send the money to Mrs Stanley to benefit their children because, on Edge's advice, Charles would have "drunk it up." Stanley, it turns out, was half-cut during the game and fully bladdered within an hour of defeat.

The First American Chess Congress: The Review is published by the New York Chess Club after Paul leaves December 17th for New Orleans. Eugene B. Cook from Hoboken, New York, composes a frontispiece chess problem: "Dedicated with the

Highest Esteem and Admiration to Paul Morphy, the Only." The name sticks and begins following Paul *the Only* Morphy around in the newspapers. He is *the Champion*; he is *the Only*; he is *the Pride of the South*.

By January 1858, D. W. Fiske is encouraging Paul, given his return to the isolated Louisiana delta and his lack of occupation in Telcide's words "owing to his being six months too young to practice law despite having passed the bar exam," to begin a co-editorship of a chess magazine called *Chess Monthly*. The enterprise is a success although Paul is less than anxious to spend his days annotating other player's chess games, let alone his own. He prefers his own memory of his matches compared to any physical record. In his brief editorial column, Paul again offers Pawn and Move to any American player. Again he receives no response, his readership no doubt viewing the New York Chess Congress as conclusive on the question of who might be the best player in America.

The first honourary clubs to appear are the *Morphy Chess Club* of Belton Bill Co, Texas and the *Morphy Lightning Rookers* of Portland, Maine. Meanwhile the New Orleans Chess Club, now Paul is back, secures new digs through the Mercantile Library Association at the corner of Exchange Alley and Canal Street. Home at last, the country will not forget him.

By April, for want of any challenging occupation or remedial pastime, Paul is busy giving eight-person blindfold exhibitions. One hot and humid afternoon a group of eager schoolboys from Jefferson Academy is invited to participate in such a feat. The boys' master is Paul's own former teacher, the demon mathematician Mr Gruber, who abandons his charges for a tobacco break and leaves them with Paul. In the schoolroom, barren apart from chairs and curtains flapping in the breeze, Paul seats himself in a brown leather armchair like an old-timer. One by one he calls out moves, a blindfold pinned over his eyes. Long loops of black hair sit theatrically on his shoulders.

"Queen takes pawn, table seven. Pawn to king's rook three, table eight. Table nine…"

Quietly mumbling, Paul drifts board to board determining the bluffs and strikes. The boys play the matches all fingers and thumbs, mesmerized by the black-and-white squares and group competition. The silence seems to say here is Paul Morphy, overgrown Jefferson Academy pupil. For the kids he is the American champion, clearly bored and a bit lonely. Sometimes their giggles reach him but Paul doesn't mind. He focuses his memory on the blue uniform of the school and the delicate green pumps; he can see the blackened chalk used for the lessons, each piece broken by the end of the day, and the image of his boyhood self quietly preparing his Latin verbs in the corridor, waiting to go home. Only five years older than his student entourage, Paul sits before them a young man, old in his youth.

There is a suspicious shuffling of paper, clearly indicative of schoolboy cheating. Concealed behind his blindfold, Paul tells the boys to put their copies of *The First American Chess Congress* in a pile behind the door, "to control their over-eager fingers."

"But why Mr Morphy?"

"Learn from the board itself, please, and from each other," he says, searching for the words that will guide and hopefully garner respect. He adds, without knowing why, "but mostly *beg* from the chessboard. Clamour for your pieces. Let them tell you secrets!" He feels strangely released from his usual taciturn self. "Lean over them," Paul says. "Listen, what do they say?"

"I can't hear, Mister," a kid snickers.

"*Moi non plus.*"

Without warning the curtain falls from the window and a blue, air-sharpened sky floods the room. Paul doesn't move and tells the boys to play on. The dust dances in the room, a thousand fairy specks, as heat troubles their necks and arms. The broken curtain yawns at the window. Time passes slowly. Paul begins to nod, drift. He calls out moves as though from a dream. Soon they notice he is asleep, hand in chin and elbow on armchair, his new-sprouting beard cupped in his hand. One podgy and ginger-faced boy tiptoes over and, grinning to his pals, tickles Paul behind his ear. The local hero appears to beg in his sleep, then falls to his feet and crashes to the floor. Paul wakes and abandons the session, apologizes, and returns their books individually at the door. The boys are more than amused.

"I must go home and lie down, I'm at a loose end in the Carré," Paul confesses. "And hot days can be wearying." Unimpressed, the boys stick out their tongues as they leave.

"You're the champion?" one says stepping on his foot. "We didn't finish a game!"

"Goodbye," says Paul, the blindfold on his neck like a school tie. The boys file away into a dark hall and run outside into the sunlight, away from chess and the strange brooding man. Paul watches them as he closes the curtains. That night, after the heat has died, he dreams of chess pieces falling through the air.

In late November an invitation from Fred Edge in New York is sent to England, requesting the pleasure of "the English champion hosted by New Orleans." Mr Howard Staunton, however, "kindly wishes to inform Mr Morphy, despite the pleasant offer, of his reluctance owing to the difficulty of reaching the city." The excuse is terse and frustrating: getting the Englishman to play will be half the battle.

That same month Samuel Morse patents the electric telegraph in the United States. Under Mr Morse's system, dashes and dots might signify chess pieces and moves. Soon it will be possible for Paul, seated on Exchange Alley amid Dr Rizzo's swords, to play a game of correspondence chess with Howard Staunton in London. Staunton would be seated in red plush velvet at the London Chess Club, St. James's Street, nestled under a bust of Admiral Horatio Nelson. But alas it's not possible—a problem of delay more than expense—and by the end of the summer Paul knows he must travel to meet his greatest adversaries over the ocean. Despite family squabbles and his continual worry about Clara on Basin Street, he must embark on a European tour to

London and Paris. Paul telegraphs Edge in New York declaring his intent.

Thereafter, Paul replaces chess with *Raleigh Rye* and Manhattan brandies as a new way of expressing devotion to Caïssa. Occasionally he takes soda water, edged with opium, to forget his family, his reputation and most of all Clara. He walks the balmy streets of the Vieux Carré during the week. He attends the French Opera House and St. Louis Cathedral by night. He sleeps all hours. At weekends his one respite is to leave 89 Royal Street and retire with Charles Maurian to the Elysian Fields Coffeehouse.

"I want to get away too," Charles tells him. "The Quarter is shrinking my soul."

In a backroom of the Fields, drinking and smoking opium through a ruffled tube, Paul plays the English Opening against Charles, ostensibly to prepare for his journey but really just to see what happens. Each game is a new birth, a step away from his Louisiana origins and ideally a step into the harmony and happiness of European enlightenment. He must prove that New Orleans can be left after all.

Chapter Fifteen
1858
Fat Tuesday's Scarlet Carnival

On the morning of *Mardi Gras*, a hushed brooding excitement descends over New Orleans. From dawn the markets of the Garden District, American Quarter and the Irish Channel are brimming with colour and excitement. Down by the river and Jackson Square, from Lee Circle to Basin Street, people are spilling onto the streets. The Vieux Carré is filled with gaudy string looped corner to corner. The costermongers and fish dealers are languidly sprawled, more by habit than affection, on their empty market stalls, children at their feet. The longshoremen and boatswains lie drying in the Mississippi mud. Even the dallying sword-parading bucks are sleepless from the night before, dotted here and there on stray patches of grass, while perched on stools with brightly coloured cushions the old men stare endlessly into the heat.

Above the slowly gathering *melée* Paul dresses alone in his room in a single white cravat, turquoise shirt, red pantaloons and yellow cufflinks. He regards himself in the mirror, the colours bleeding together, feeling dizzy but merry. Since childhood he likes

Mardi Gras, but wishes to strike a note of mixing with the crowd without *extravagance indécente,* or standing out. He takes a walking stick, a sleek blackened and strengthened bamboo pole for no other reason than amusement. He cocks his hat at what he hopes is a jaunty angle and leaves the house by the back door.

Beyond the fountain and the courtyard he can hear the singing and shrieks from the servant-quarters, but sees nothing. Today is everyone's day and more so for the indentured underclass than its Creole rulers. But any gloomy thoughts evaporate the moment he steps outside. For once again, Paul finds himself in a mood matched by the festivities. He begins his promenade on Chartres Street one move at a time. "By tomorrow," he says, "I will know Clarabelle loves me, as I love her. I can wait no longer."

A slow *Mardi Gras* parade guides Paul downtown. Young girls peer expectedly from shadows looking for cheap liquor salesmen and waiting for darkness to fall. A whistle blows and a sober bell replies, is cut short, then recurs with a playful jingle and note of correction. The churches are speaking of joy and woe. Up ahead a mangy black dog crosses Levée and looking for her owner the mutt begins rooting through the garbage distracted by hunger. Sensing something, the dog sees Paul and grins. The champion strolls Bourbon Street flicking his cane on the sidewalk unrecognized, accosted only by worry over his costume and whether Clara will look as she did before.

"Will she remember me?" he wonders and taps on the sidewalk. Glimpsing the lazy smile of the Mississippi, Paul leaves the crowd and drifts into a more open area off Magazine Street. Dreamily, he regards the brown beach and the rising tide washing back and forth. Down the sloping sand he buys a gin-fizz from a boy vendor and becomes a target for sales. A moment later, he is pestered and sold a piece of parchment from a hobbling old gent who guarantees his place among "the fifth seal of angels in heaven." Before the old fellow removes his skeletal hand, he compels Paul to sign a pointless piece of parchment. Paul curiously observes how his signature already reflects the *P.M. Champion* inscription on his silver plate from the New York tournament. "Just a coincidence!" the old man says mysteriously.

A second later, Paul is scrambling up the riverbank. He thinks he's gotten away but a girl is surprisingly quick at his heels. From her corsage she plucks a ghost orchid and pins the delicate drooping flower on his collar.

"For love and a charmed escape from death," she says and impersonates the flower. "Let me stay with you forever and a day, and a day and a day."

"I am mad but north-by-northwest," Paul says and takes a bow.

The girl is younger than her black cowl suggests. But she disappears through a *façade* of *The Chamomile Slipper* newspaper offices, doubling as a store concealing its red-light charms. So Paul doesn't get a close look at her. He needs to stop looking for Clara though. So he takes an Italian coffee at the junction of Common Street and Dryades where he tries an absinthe chaser diluted with orange water. The combination is sickly sweet and he can barely drink half. But the demon strength of the drink trickles into his brain and removes the mental trepidation he has been feeling over his career worries and the girl. Let the parade begin, he whispers, and downs the fizzing cocktail.

On cue, from the end of Carondelet the strange facemasks of elephants in *papier mâché* appear. The parade is pursued by martyred saints in various agonies of torture—Saint Lucy carrying her eyes on a plate, Saint Roch covered in sores, the Maid of Orleans herself, Jeanne d'Arc, dancing on paper flames in a full suit of armour. Constables and warehouse workers, dressed as skeletons and fiends, pass the *café* grotesquely intermingled. On carts, schoolchildren wave in the heat driven by teams of donkeys. Meanwhile all manner of wharfmen stand on corners and tease young girls with goblin faces. Everywhere little boys wander lost in white sheets. Meanwhile from beautiful iron trellises high over Common Street, all big drums and brass horns, an unseen band excites the crowd.

"*Mardi Gras!*" is the insatiable cry. "Tear it up, tear it down. Raise the crowd, raise the crown!"

The town dignitaries, businessmen dressed incredibly as babies, take centre stage. They stomp in steel boots and nappies with oversized safety pins, smoking cigars. Meanwhile the ex-pat Europeans parade in old and new styles, Spanish gentleman in threaded seersucker jackets and French ladies in silk spinning dainty handbags. Between them, Italian courtiers ride brown mares flashing ruby plumes in their hats pursued by heroes from Greek Mythology, from Achilles with his diamond shield to Adriane and her ball of string. King Midas is balancing a golden vase on his head, face agonizing, hand in hand with King Canute desperately trying to turn back the tide. On the last cart, Perseus wrestles the Minotaur on the back of an ox-cart with the beast's head decorated with gauze and tinsel.

"Everything dances," someone cries, "on a flamin' Fat Tuesday. Open your mouths and drink in the hot stardust!" One image dissolves and a hundred materialize. A face appears, vanishes, a foot, a shoe, a hand, a nose, a pipe. A black silk scarf waves over all and blows away. A cry of hilarious despair goes up, falls and goes up again. Perched under his café awning, Paul waits as the procession scatters colour in his hair, as in a dream. Twenty people wide, the *Mardi Gras* surges down Hospital Street, pursued by marvelling eyes, while astride a fine black stallion the King of the Carnival makes his entrance.

Brandishing a brass sceptre, the King ludicrously cracks people's heads crying: "Wait, wait, you are leaving your Rex behind!" At one point he spies Paul and lowers his regal frame. Paul, without thinking, stretches out his hand and touches the King's fingertips. The moment is magical. The King smiles and the stallion swishes its tail.

But only now, as the cart pulls away, does Paul notice the Queen seated behind the King. Lithe and barely dressed, she is sucking red-and-white striped candy, fawning at the crowd. As they depart she turns, this float maiden, and is clearly recognizable as

Clara Young. A pained expression is in her eye, not for the King but for Paul. Then she calls as loud as she can:

"Let the scarlet carnival begin!"

"Clara!" Paul cries. "Clara, come back. Where are you going?" He is on his feet knocking the table away. "You are the Queen of the Carnival! How did this happen? Clara!"

He stumbles down Common Street after the cart, followed by six white horses ridden by nymphs with purple hair. Heading the parade is the King's black stallion with a banner tied to the cart: "*Viola le premier car!* Worship and be saved! Paul watches as the mayhem rounds the corner. He cannot get close, so walks back to the quiet of Common Street and his half-drunk cup of tea. The sun keeps shining and burning the ground and he remains at the café until midday, somewhat chilled by Clara's cavalier performance.

"I don't understand. Couldn't she stop? I know I've seen her so little, but…" and he tries to gather composure in remembering his encounters with Clara. "Were they encounters?"

The long afternoon sets in. He takes in an Italian mask contest in the French market, drifting from stall to stall tasting the prize hams and bananas. Forcing himself, he waits for the King and Queen to return in case he sees Clara again. Since attending the funeral of Jean Lafitte, Paul knows the King and Queen will exchange lovers' glances and kisses. Suddenly they do return, high on the stallion and skidding to a halt beside a fountain. It now becomes clear that the King is the recently elected major of the city Thomas Gardiner, a former pirate-assassin and a bounty hunter, supposedly reformed. The crowds love him and sing his praises. At one point he climbs onto a balcony and dangles from the iron grilles while toasting his Queen. Paul is shocked to witness Clara climbing the vines. There, having ripped the cork with her teeth, she pours champagne into the King's goblet to the beat of his giggling. All around satyrs, fawns, mermaids, centaurs and a whole fairyland is dancing. A strange unreal quality descends over the market. Old men tease accordions, girls pound tambourines and someone is wailing boisterously into a megaphone.

The whole spectacle of *Mardi Gras* cuts deep into the blood of the people. From Rampart to Levée Street the annual purging of past and present, sin and heartache pours soul and life from St. Louis Cathedral over old stones and the long pier, down the banks of Big Muddy. A new rhythm rises from the north Quarter where the slaves are beginning their own celebrations for the night.

This same evening, Paul goes to find Clara at the bordello where she works. As it becomes dark he stumbles into *The Twenty-One* and is accosted in the hall by a fat silver-haired lady. Politely he declines her offer. If Clara is not there, he is not interested. The *madame* eyes him with vampiric concern, looking ugly and crazy in a white silk kimono. Gold bauble earrings dangle from her nose, a brooch inverted on her buffoon hair. He stumbles backwards off the stoop and clatters down the street.

Outside the noise is impenetrable. All down Canal the loose ladies of Basin Street are raised on carts catcalling the crowd and making gestures. Sometimes they expose themselves. Disgusted, Paul nevertheless looks for Clara on a float, wondering at what point her queenly duties end. None of these illusions is a happy one. Yet he feels now, more than ever, that Clara must be saved from the world she inhabits. She must be rescued from the bad tracks and welcomed to the easy side of town. Considering the predicament, Paul avoids an encounter with Alex and Edward after spying them drinking in a window of *Pavillon Bar*. He decides to head home. But he mistakenly takes Burgundy Street, the far end of which is bustling with the temptations of groggeries, guzzle-shops and gin-mills all peppering the street with tinny piano music and the promise of temporary rivers of Lethe and morning amnesia. Like a fly to a flame, Paul tells himself Clara lies behind those walls, and a moment later he is inside *Buffalo Bill's House*.

Aerated cider is selling advertised as champagne for two dollars a half-pint. Under the doorway's hanging axe, a life-size portrait of Don Quixote poses with affected heroism. Paul peers closer. The statue moves and scares Paul who rubs his eyes in disbelief. The Don is in fact whiskered proprietor Bison Williams, keeping order with a huge cudgel. Periodically he taps snoozing men on the head with the words: "I run my residence in the only locality in the city where decent people *don't* live!"

Soon Paul leaves "for the quieter bar across the street," away from giant windmill pint glasses and back to the Basin chaos. Opposite *Bill's* is *The Conclave* where the barmen dress as undertakers, serving drinks in miniature silver-handled coffins. Clara is not there.

The moon is up and Paul meanders upriver, tasting the street tequilas. A warm rain shower clears the alleys of sleeping bodies. Next he tries *Harry Rice's Green Tree Club*, where after a double he gets into conversation with a man called one-legged Duffy. They toast Ireland, Duffy for his "long-'go Ma," and Paul in honour of his great-grandfather, the daring Michael Murphy. Knocking back whiskies, Paul can't find his money and is thrown in the gutter old Duffy cackling in his ear:

"You gotta watch who you meet."

"And that includes you?" Paul replies.

Dragging his body on the ground, he sees something flash on the banquette and is tricked by its glinting air. On hands and knees, he digs in the earth and laughs when he finds a five-inch knife, a double-blade handsomely mounted in German silver. Having lost his kitchen knife, Paul secures this one tight inside his shoe, combining one of his greatest loves—delicate and charming footwear—with one of his greatest fears: any blade sharper than a Panama hat. He thinks of his father. Then he scorns the *Green Tree Club* and taps his shoe meaningfully, tricked by the knife's beauty.

"To Basin Street," he murmurs with hollow fervour, fully intoxicated. *"Pour finir ce roman* and little romance, *ce chemin ou un autre!"*

Despite the city's widespread carousing, the slaves of New Orleans often dress up to disguise their identity. The public lash is not worth the visibility. But the fear is too little to restrain them on

Mardi Gras night. After numerous *poses plastiques* before the looking glass, Benevolence Titi and her friends meet on the backstreets of Rampart and Esplanade around the cemetery and the cathedral. Stitched together last night, their costumes emerge twinkling in the moonlight. Men and women abound in white cotton gloves, spangles, tan shoes and red silk tights. Twirling parasols, they glance like fairground rogues as they march with barely concealed ecstasy in the same direction to the Square.

As the city's *Mardi Gras* slides into evening, the slaves' celebrations are just beginning. As their white masters sleep, the servants creep into the night for hours of wide-awake pleasures, teasing and taunting, swirling and drinking. The drums beat softly from Congo Square, slowly increasing pace and drawing revellers to the sound, the call, the welcome. Magic cloaks are funnelled from glassless windows. Cotton shirts slip doorway to doorway with diamonds and hearts sewed on pockets. Girls with false beards gather at street corners, while women in tall black hats and gowns of blue silk caress men in open doorways. In the St. Louis Cemetery No. 2, a boy with tarot cards crouches behind a headstone. Tiny children sell bright-coloured whips and tawny feathers. East of the Vieux Carré, clown pirates tumble in the street, bedevilling and arousing the snake charmers of Voodoo. Nearby banjos, mandolins and guitars dance along the white arcades. In faraway Creole courtyards, the black knights of Tremé reclaim the streets and the saloons smell of wet sawdust and beer in a burlesque of white *Mardi Gras*. For just one night, nothing can be stolen back that has not already been taken.

Down by the river near Burgundy Street, the savage chieftain Zulu King arrives on a water barge dressed in black knitted underwear, a hula skirt and a fuzzy black wig with a tin crown. He carries a sceptre, a broomstick bearing a black cat, and dangling from his fingers, a stuffed white rooster. The barge mounts the shore and immediately becomes a float surrounded by mules in a land parade. People slap the barge's watery haunches, and its catfish and mermaid graffiti is torn away. Waving his sceptre, broomstick and rooster all at once, the Zulu King cries long and passionate: "Welcome to *Mardi Gras,* my people!"

A cry goes up. The shore is filled with masks and billowing capes for one beautiful night. In the distance the Congo Square drums beat, listen and tremble with power.

Paul strays onto South Basin Street. Here the noise of Voodoo picks up the chants booming and buoyant in the blood. He approaches the concert saloons *Napoleon's Mistress, Bismarck* and the *New El Dorado.* A brass band meanders between the gutters and plays out a slinky ragtime march, the trumpets nodding to the gin-mills and low-slung taverns. One step at a time, the piping frivolity infects Paul's heart until, hands on knees and no lamppost in sight, all his feelings spill from his stomach onto St. Charles Street. He is sick on his shoes in a horrid fountain. *The Pavillon* on Baronne Street shields him under the National Theatre while he gropes on the street.

Then he sees her, his angel Clarabelle, cavorting with the so-called Mayor Gardiner. She is outside *The Pavillon* disappearing under blasé stars, winking and carefree, towards dancing and whoring dives *The Gem, Tivoli* and *Eden.* Was it her? Can he be certain? She stumbles closer but remains a few steps away. Desperately, Paul squints into the night and knows he's lost. For the first time he cannot go back; he doesn't know the moves. Where is he? How does he find his childhood self, the girl by the fountain or the boy watching his father playing chess on the veranda? Everything is moving too fast and the parts are loosening. He sits in the dirt in the street. What will happen to Telcide or Edward? He stares at an abandoned ghostly carriage of the St. Charles streetcar, long derailed and entwined by Virginia creeper.

Paul knows he must do something. He tries to envisage what his family or Alonzo might want. "I have to leave, I know that much," he says to the ground and closes his eyes.

Chapter Sixteen
1858
The Testimonial Watch

On June 21st, the day before his birthday, Paul wakes to the sound of *Louise de Lorraine*, Telcide's opera. Downstairs he finds the *soirée* ending and his mother alone. He crosses the room and sits with her at the piano. She is weeping. He plays a few notes.

"*C'est un désordre. C'est futile.*"

"*Maman*, you'll finish soon."

She smiles wanly and her fingers touch his cheek. "Such a good boy," she says and tucks a wisp of black hair behind his ear. Paul colours a little. "I wonder what will happen in the future. To the family. To you and me, Paul. Where are we going?"

"Well…" He reaches out to take her hand, feeling strange. But she is arranging the musical score and is already turning away. So he plays a tune, a light Belgian waltz he learned as a child, plays halfway, and waits for his mother to join in. She does not.

"This is a concert grand," she says and rests her hands on the lid. Gently she weeps.

"*Maman*, please don't."

"Your father was good. But he has left us. What can I do? I will never be a musician now." For a moment her eyes resist the anguish. "Maybe I can be a musician in the Quarter. Maybe even the composer!" The glimmer of destiny fades. "But now Alonzo…"

Once again, she is inconsolable.

"You will," Paul pursues.

"Why?"

"Persist."

"I don't know how!"

From his pocket Paul produces a watch awarded at the First American Chess Congress.

"Look," he says. "This is what they tell me I'm worth."

Telcide takes the watch in her fingers. Despite being his mother, instinctively something behind her eyes narrows, revealing if not envy then a kind of confusion, a miscomprehension of her own pain, an ignorance of its source. She sniffs and feels the salt drying in the corners of her mouth.

"It's only a watch."

"But it's beautiful, Paul."

She stares at the timepiece in wonder, and back at her son, uncomprehending. The watch slips through her fingers. In place of Roman numerals, the face shows chess pieces of red and black rubies and diamonds and so on. The pendant is edged with tiny king's crowns, while an exquisite emerald at the top acts as a push-piece to open the face.

"I've seen it before," Telcide says and turns the watch over sourly. But the back inscription changes her sense of admiration. *For Paul Charles Morphy, from the Testimonial Committee of the New York Chess Club, as Tribute to His Genius and Worth. A watch is more than a watch when a prize, a gift and a symbol of honor.* "More than a watch," Telcide whispers and strains a compliment. "You are the sum of your achievements, Paul, a man of the world and a Louisianan too. So I ask you Paul, as your mother. What am I worth?"

"Everything! The family really needs you. We need you, *maman*. I'll do nothing except bring a good reputation to Royal Street."

"To the Morphy and Le Carpentier names?"

"Exactly."

"You sound like your father." Telcide crosses the room and returns with Paul's chessmen and board, which she calls "the spoils of his victory in New York." Softly she adds: "But thank you. Now tell me about your prize."

"Well," Paul begins, "the pieces are Gaelic and Roman armies and represent the duel to the death between Christianity and Barbarism. You can play either side. Both are a matter of life and death."

"I can't change sides so easily," Telcide says. "If I couldn't compose music, I'd rather play chess…"

Paul laughs and his mother smiles. They look at the set.

"The board is gold and silver," he continues, "cut in rose-stone. Look, the Roman bishops have mitres and crosiers for battle-axes and swords." He takes the silver king with wings on his helmet and holds it up. "Gold pawns are Roman infantry bearing a double-edged sword."

"Real gold?"

"Oui, *maman*. The classic man-at-arms. He is defending the Western Empire on both fronts."

"The pawns are silver?"

"Solid sterling from the Manhattan Stock Exchange! You know a pawn is the soul of chess. Each one corresponds to the old Visigoth army, *maman*. The horns on his helmet are torn from the wild boar of Germanic forests. Plus he carries a knotty club to take on the might of the Romans conquerors!"

"Dramatic," she says.

"But look carefully," says Paul. "The king of the barbarian horde is falling over his armour and the knights are weighed down by their long hair. Those ridiculous rooks are in fact Indian elephants with *houdas*."

Telcide takes up the chase. "But note the eagle there, so elegant, like a musical *voce* spreading his pinions and ready to pounce upon his prey!"

"All the pedestals are polished in Cornelian, *maman*. The board itself is dovetailed in—look," and he opens it and folds it back—"rosewood."

"And here?" she points.

"*Proeliis ex sanguinatis facile princeps.* I am first among equals. And see, the engraved Sphinx and the illustrious names. I am there too!"

Telcide peers at the inlaid signatures and witnesses Paul's name, reminiscent of his childhood schoolbooks. The strangeness discomforts her as she reads off Petroff, Kieseritzky, López, Philidor, McDonnell, La Bourdonnais. Then the inscription *Climbing the pyramids of the past! Paul Charles Morphy, New Orleans.* She offers a sidelong smile. "Congratulations. That is you, Paul. Not me. My time is gone. I am just a part-time player, left in the sawdust after the actors have left the stage."

"No mother."

"Those eyes," she continues. "Look at them! They're all rubies, human, bird or beast. It's too much, Paul. I can't bear your prizes. All this for playing a game! Take them away, now, do. I can't see your testimonial watch, as you call it, your man-at-arms figures and all the rest!"

With a flourish, Telcide scatters a single pawn to the floor and rises to her feet. Her turquoise evening gown disturbs the candlelight from the piano top.

"Something is slipping away." She takes one step. Paul reaches out, galvanized, and his *maman* grips his wrist. "For the silver king I would be a wife, but for nothing less! I am a weak Southern woman, is that it? I can do nothing on my own. Nothing! Everything prevents me and no one helps. In time, friends are enemies. Now we're the embarrassed family with no head. Who will save us? Edward? Your brother! We know his unpredictable folly. Alex, if he weren't busy with his vices? And *papa* is too old and you're too young. *C'est un désordre.* Bring me a silver king! If only Paul Charles! I implore this city and all we've done for her. But no!"

"I don't understand."

"*C'est futile!*"

"Everything will...improve, *maman*."

"No. You'll have to grow up, Paul, sooner or later. Only then can we be a family or Creole again."

The note hangs. She waits, sighs and leaves him. At the door she doesn't look back. Any warmth in the room is gone. Slowly, Paul lays the chess pieces one by one on their backs, eyes to heaven. He says a prayer to the pieces, this comfortless little congregation mute and bedecked in jewels. He presses a key on the piano, then its minor companion, but the gesture seems more like comedy. Something Paul normally resists in a chess bout he now performs, sinking low and peering on the level with the pieces. A fleeting impression returns of what he once felt—magic, danger, meaning—for this strange battle, this mere table game. But the feeling drains into something closer to home, lethargy, a sadness and responsibility. He doesn't know how long his brother has been watching.

"So you were showing them to mother?" Edward stands in the doorway, his sword looped casually at the hip. Paul sees the blade is exposed. "She feigns being impressed."

Paul says nothing and packs away the chessmen. As he stoops to retrieve a fallen pawn, Edward is upon him. But the younger brother is adamant he will not make a sound, or cry out. No one will hear. Telcide must not know, nor any of the servants, nor his uncles, nor his grandfather. Edward stands over Paul in the moonlight and feels like strangling him with the watch, symbol of his brother's glorious talent and marker of their separate futures. He tries to break the glass face, but somehow the design is strong. So he takes the timepiece and is about to crack it on the piano when Charles Maurian pauses in the hallway to say goodnight. Edward says goodnight, waits a minute and turns to Paul.

"You cannot leave, Paul" he whispers. "You are selfish and foolish too. Keep the watch, but there'll be nothing for you when you come back here. You can't expect the family to wait for you...and..." He is breathless and wipes the sweat from his brow.

Then he hauls his brother by the neck onto the piano stool. "I am drunk, I'm know."

Trembling now, Paul squeezes the pawn in his hand. "You cannot...you have no right to."

"Stop it, Paul. I'm trying to keep things together. I'm warning you, don't leave now." He taps his sword. "I'll defend you with this sword, upon my life. But I will defend the Morphy name and family first..."

"What are you talking about?"

"I know what I'm doing. Don't upset mother anymore. She is working hard."

"On her music."

"While you play!"

"And you practice swords!"

"Swordsmanship brother! The word is swordsmanship, for men. You are the one playing games, and not even games girls admire."

"I don't like your girls," Paul says and the conversation comes to an impasse. Edward steps back into shadow and reappears in the red glow of the hall.

"All I'm saying is contribute. Work and make money, fight or something. Let 'em know we're not an easy target."

"Who?"

"Them. Don't you understand anything, Paul?"

Swaggering with his sword, Edward is gone. The room falls into silence and Paul is left at the piano. Telcide's *Louise de Lorraine* remains on the lid, incomplete.

Paul turns to a random page, rubs his neck and starts to play mournfully. But the music is a section of ribaldry, and Telcide's flair for crude pleasure underlines every note. Paul closes the book and plays freely. He adapts its mood to the spirit of a new kind of music, feeling the drums of Congo Square reverberate in his memory from his lost night on South Basin Street. His fingers move gently between the keys, pressing the edges, releasing them like breaths stolen under the magnolia trees down by the Mississippi under a full moon. But Paul has never spent the night down by the Mississippi. He can only imagine the river in the dead of night and the cypress trees and the swish of a lonely boat. Softly, he opens his hand to reveal the pawn pressed in his palm. It unpeels like a day-old plaster, and he sets it upright on the piano. Then he looks down at the mark it made, the silhouette of a temporary bloodline.

"Clarabelle," he whispers, playing the music and listening. "I am here *mon ami, ma belle*. Show me how to play, my Clara!"

Chapter Seventeen
1858
Welcome to The Twenty-One

Days become weeks. The weather broods hot and humid. The young chess prodigy stays cooped in his room, lying on his bed, arms folded on his chest. Titi brings him meals more and more frequently. A breeze troubles the pieces on his chessboard, but not enough to move them.

On July 29th Paul secures his chess pieces in a miniature wooden case. He collapses the case at the bottom of his *valise* forcing each piece to share the journey with its opposite colour. He closes the lid, locks it and runs his finger over the gold insignia *PCM* ingrained in the frame, a relic of his schooldays. Inside are his possessions for the trip: a few clothes, mostly cravats and the odd necktie, his father's Bible for dutiful comfort, pencils and a legal writing paper for Telcide to witness her home address on his letters, but not a single chess book. Paul puts his head in his hands. Soon he will leave again but not before securing the testimonial watch in his waistcoat pocket.

From the balcony, a clear moon illuminates the whole Vieux Carré. Downstairs his mother is absent, already retired after dinner. Ernest and Alex are talking about the old days. Eventually

Paul hears them leave with Edward too for the balmy night air and unspoken quarters. He waits a few minutes. The grandfather clock in the hall chimes. Below the balustrade he can see his sister Malvina standing by the front bay window, perusing the street. He hears her cigarette lighter strike, imagines smoke drifting under the window crevice into the night. Then he takes his hat, spotless gloves and walking stick, and leaves by the back courtyard.

The walk is calm and steady. Before long he reaches Basin Street and begins to count the numbers, seeking Hattie Hamilton's queen mansion *The Twenty-One*. At the corner of St. Louis some ragged-looking children are recreating *Mardi Gras*, pulling faces and clapping hands. They scatter red dust in each other's hair. Paul stares in wonder. At the centre of the group, wrapped in dirty linen, appears to be a tiny baby: the Comus of their worship. She is a girl no more than a year old, half asleep in the heat and rocking on a cardboard chair. The queen of the street, the baby is honoured on a childish throne of cardboard gold covered in drawings of fire. No adult seems to care. From nowhere, a child runs and throws a stone and Paul stares. Overhead fat men hang from the illicit red-lit windows with *flambeaux* spewing wreaths of black smoke. Shadows and torchbearers hover under the alley eaves. Someone is throwing *bagatelles*. As the light shimmers down Bright Alley, the overflow channel for the Mississippi and escaping city filth, Paul knows he has reached the end of Basin Street. Steam rises from the St. Louis Street bars. Down on Basin, Paul passes the *Amsterdam Dance House* and holding his breath, he counts a beat. He already knows from speaking to Alex Le Carpentier's workmen that Clara should be working.

A clock ticks.

"The caution of the tell-tale heart," Paul whispers into his coat. Poised in the entrance, he finds the place strangely quiet. Queen bee Hattie Hamilton is somewhere inside plying her music, drinking and trading on the smiles of her girls. Footsteps approach. From above a catcall surprises Paul and velvet curtains part as though an opera is imminent. Two bouncers step from the shadows, wide men with black hats and brass knuckles.

"A girl with a sash about her waist," one is saying.

"Or some ribbon in her hair."

"True."

"That one think she fancy, but the girls will pull her down."

Paul waits as they eye his presence. Presumably he looks sheepish, smaller by a hat, motionless despite his fingers rattling inside his waistcoat. There is no search, only tobacco juice spit suddenly at his feet to mark the threshold.

"Stay to the left," they trill, amused.

Inside, a crooked finger guides the way. Paul dips under a black veil like a spider's web, his hair becoming a troubled mess. A female finger beckons, its jewels winking. He follows obediently, nervous now.

They descend.

"We don't wear our Mother Hubbards every night," the girl says and touches the hem of her calico dress, whips it to her waist and lets it drop. Eyes steady, Paul smiles politely.

"Only on weekends?" he offers but receives no reply.

A string of red doors appears on the left famously totalling twenty-one: a door for every occasion. Paul begins to examine the door names, painted in nail-varnish and cut into the wood with a penknife. The light is dim and the names throb in the glow of the Orphean hall. They reach the final door and under Ellen Collins and America Williams, in loopy figures, is written Clara Young *à votre service*.

Paul stares.

"Clarabelle's upstairs. Ignore the doors. They're all fakes." She unhooks the latch. "But I'm not a fake." She extends her hand. "Mary Lamb. Or you can call me Rosalind. I go by both. Take your pick."

"Thank you," he says not knowing what to say.

"Welcome to Hattie's."

But Paul cannot speak. Mary swings open the door and vanishes inside the belly of the ballroom floundering on her own skirt. A cavernous room opens to ecstatic lights, giddy swirls of trombone music and a swollen dome for a ceiling. The strong nip of booze clouds the smell of sweat. From across the room, the single eye of Hattie Hamilton approaches, wide with amused detachment, leading the remainder of her fleshy bones. Paul waits, clueless how to react. A magnificent *madame*, Hattie 'The Hat' swings through the room, a monstrous vision of jewels and rolling limbs, her hips prompting her neck to stretch for air. But when she arrives by magic or mayhem she needs no breath. Her eye is prominent, rolling from the staircase to the piano to the chandelier to the new arrival. Wider than its patched counterpart, the eye performs an exquisite interrogation down Paul's tender frame. Her head supports an extravagant peacock feather, the daring bird poking at her forehead with its beak.

"Welcome to the house of horror!" The Hat says. "Be sure you want in before you come in!"

"Good evening," Paul says, feeling ridiculous.

"Stay a while! Few people see daylight again."

"I hope so…"

"Well, well," The Hat replies. "A freshman from the upper world? Always my favourite! I'd welcome you to hell but you found purgatory…" She leans in. "…which, if you ask me, is much better." She breathes out, looking conspiratorial. "I'm only pulling your leg. Never been in a Bastille bordello, young man? A flesh-pot paradise. We're the best around, all said and done. 21 South Basin Street," and she hands him a card. "You can call me Hattie, or Queen Bee if you prefer. I was joking about the horror!"

Hattie is a delightful monstrosity laden with diamonds, her white lace kimono pinned with sweat to the ebb and flow of her body. Under her peacock headdress, tawdry if it weren't for her other accoutrements, Paul discerns a bright red wig. Its tresses bleed on her cheeks. Amid a cloud of overpowering perfume, Hattie acts the *grande dame*, her masculine voice ringing with authority. A blue feather adds a touch of the macabre pirate to her ear. Girls lounge at her sides, their hair inelegantly imitating her peacock bumps, giggling in twos and threes in transparent evening clothes. Already for Paul, *The Swamp* of Girod Street is a forgotten memory, swallowed by a lusher and bolder whore-palace.

In the centre of the room Venus is kneeling rudely in a posture of inexplicable love. Attended by obscure divinities of light and nymphet-worshippers, the goddess of love brandishes two lighted *flambeaux*. Gold-plated portraits of sinning politicians and *Kaintucks* sailors melt down the walls. Grinning at them are sacrilegious cherubs amid a litany of fallen clergy. The Pope appears to be chatting with his neighbour the Duc d'Orleans, two powerfully devout peas in a pod.

An odour seeps through the wallpaper, the promise of wealth and intimacy, a sybarite's dream of luxury and repose. Each corner of the resplendent room winks at Paul. Splendour without comfort, the glitter suggests death and decay. Mirrors challenge mirrors, multiplying Paul's sleight frame with mock comedy. His own coattails approach and he steps back with surprise, prompting his alter ego's surprise, and he laughs as the incestuous mirrors fool his fragile ego. A tray of brandy glasses appears. A dozen hands reach out. For a lingering moment Paul's image nods at him and he feels an uncharacteristic twinge of envy. The doppelganger seems *debonair*, smarter dressed, more at ease. The impostor takes a sip of brandy and Paul copies his false half and gulps.

Meanwhile David Jackson, senator, paramour de Hattie and cigar-rolling pimp, quietly shakes Paul's hand.

"And you are?"

"Señor Morphy."

"Retain your real name, young man!" cries Jackson grinning. He lights up. "Of course Jackson *is* my real name or the courts would disapprove. Who are you looking for?"

"No one. Except…"

"I can tell," Jackson laughs. Chubby fingers gripping his cigar, he slicks back an egg-shaped head. "That's okay. Just follow, ah,"—he gestures to a small Mediterranean girl—"follow America. She'll show you way. So have you met my wife?"

"Enjoy," Hattie calls, snapping her fingers, and America whisks Paul away from the pimping couple.

Paul bows, almost curtsies a departure as Hattie walks by close enough to pick his pocket. She turns to Jackson with eye incandescent, eyebrow twitching into a rainbow of fury. Strange malice brews in Hattie's pudgy face, the peacock trembling on high, the red hair a shivering flame. The *demimonde* raises a crystal liqueur glass, ready to strike her husband for some unspoken offence.

Meanwhile America leads Paul up a wide staircase. Ball gowns flair on all sides. He already feels drunk with unreality. A triangular door reveals an ornate room overstuffed with paintings, sculpture and a boy with a broomstick. They turn a corner where pink rosettes carved in yellow wood decorate the ceiling. Stretching ahead, a frieze of winged figures splits the clouds with phallic golden trumpets; in the centre an imitation Renaissance tapestry depicts King Midas touching a chalice with one finger freezing to gold. Under this image a mantelpiece of white marble burns in a lick of Red Sea. They pass through the room into more halls.

"This way, Mr Morphy," America calls.

Every corner reveals lurid men and half dressed girls perched on fluted pilasters with jugs of water and whisky cocktails. Through closed doors laughter mingles with desperate pleasure. A ballroom door opens like a bitten apple and despite the grandeur, unshaved sailors and ruby-faced women skirt the room clapping and stomping to an unseen piano. False diamond chandeliers pinned to the rafters shake and extinguish their fake candles with macabre delight.

"All things good and true," says America. "Elegance and brutality, wouldn't you say Mr Morphy?"

"A wonderful mixture."

In a quiet corner, the mulatto butler Augustine whispers with a coachman named Lyon. *Bon mots* bounce back and forth. Augustine watches the room for his mistress, fingers tucked in his waistcoat with a proud air; one foot shorter and two wider, Lyon leans on the doorframe in his plum-coloured livery, high hat cocked at a rakish angle.

"We're lucky," says Augustine.

"Mebbe you," the coachman replies. "Not me."

"Mmm-mm."

"Raised up by the Lord, o'er tho' un-dig-i-fied floor-sweepin' beer-jerkers of Mahooogany Hall."

"I'll end up there one day," says Lyon. His eyes glint and they laugh.

"You know it coachman. For doin' nothing' *madame* will *bring* you to the whippin'-post *heer-self*. The Calaboose for you!"

"An' that's why *ah* drive the coach, boy. Gotta quik get-a-way."

"Mmm-mm."

"I'd take mee-self for tha' whip sometime, if ah ran this place," Lyon adds. "Don't make no difference to me." He picks at his teeth with a gold toothpick.

Augustine eyes him with amused suspicion and says: "Don't wait for the heavens tha' long! We jus' employed fur tha' ol' *vaudeville charisma*." They laugh.

"Just as long as they think I'm a jokin' comedian." Lyon replies, salutes, and gestures to Paul Morphy crossing the room. "Lookee 'im. New boy, boy."

Employed for their vicious loyalty, the old-timers chat and stare down their good fortune. Now they watch America Williams, the octoroon beauty in green satin. Their eyes dwell. Trailing America is a desperate-looking Paul in fine black threads.

"The overdressed *ingénue* is led to his fate," America whispers en route, knocks at a door and descends the catwalk past Augustine and Lyon.

"Come in."

Paul takes a tentative step inside and from the belly of the room a candle is lit. A glow reveals curtains of red lace, white dresses on the bed and the drowsiness of musk and incense in the air. On the *armoire*, surrounded by stains and strings of jewellery, is a miniature statue of the Goddess Venus copied from the ballroom. Paul eases the door back and stands breathless.

"Clara?" He takes a tentative step. "Are you there?"

A girl enters, smiling and carrying pictures of black madonnas. She pins them to the wall, unfolds the bed revealing a representation of Our Lady of Guadalupe inked into the sinful sheets, her praying eyes closed tight.

"I did that," the girl says. "I thought it was funny. I's very good, yes, no?"

"I…"

"You want see Clara? She in dat room. She wait a moment. She tired and get clean."

"I see."

"Is okay. She been not sleeping. She take bath and be good new. Very clean for you!"

The girl takes a step and shakes Paul's hand.

"Paul," he says. "Pleased to meet you."

"I's La Cubana," and she throws her head back to laugh, then flicks it tossing hair in her eyes.

"I came to talk."

"That funny! You want to be in bed now? I don't think so. Just sit. You funny too."

Oddly, Paul feels more at ease than he expected. The girl seems to not be troubled by him. She sits on the bed, takes his hand and playfully counts fingers. "Clara say you ten good fingers. And you do! I not expect nine. I know man three fingers."

"I'm sorry. She talks about me?"

"Alla time. All-la time."

"She does?"

"Yea she do." La Cubana smiles and winks. "She love pretty boy. You look lik' a girl."

"No, I mean…"

"You call me La Cubana. You like my room. Pretty huh? List-en me, see alla pret-ty dress? Well, always lotta dresses da Canal Street and we go buy. We got money, ya' know. Fancy dresses come from Bostonia n' Naw York place and cost lol' buy. They on Canal and us ladees know they don't come from Nu Orlean'. That way, da shop ladees dey know we *puta*. But we don't care. They married and dey all *puta* too!"

"They are pretty," says Paul. He stoops and picks up a woman's shoe, runs the laces through his fingers. "I like shoes too."

"See," says La Cubana, and offers the hem of her blue silk dress. He touches it curiously and feels strange.

"Clara, she not here yet. We have fun?"

"No. I mean, I came to see Clara."

"*La bella!* Ha! You no' like La Cubana? You know I not from Cuba? LuLu White, I use work for her in de *Rising Sun*, she has monocle. Big fat eye, she no see too good. She think I Mexican. Everyone think I Mexican whore, ha! So look,"— pointing at the mantelpiece—"all dose tings from store in Mexico City. Sombrero, mantilla n' serape. Everyone to tell you I da Mexican but I born in Dominican Republic. Dey not know! Where dat, you say? Where you born?"

"On Chartres."

"Dat an island?"

"A street," Paul says smiling, "in the city…"

"You born in Nu Orlean'. Why didn't you say so!" La Cubana takes his hand and lays it on her chest. "You feel dis heart. It beat for Santo Domingo, dat my home. *Take Me Back Perdito Street*, dat what I want sing."

"Is it beautiful?"

"*Take me back alla my home, Perdito, Perdito.*"

"Do you miss it?"

"You crazy! Everybody got a home somewhere jus' not here. You too. Or why else you here?"

"To see Clara."

"You see her now, I bored a' you. You like men downstairs. Dey who *don't* dance give more money a' piano player than those dance. Where sense? You got a coin fur me?"

Paul gives her a silver piece.

"So I take you now. She ready! Listen, La Cubana get up two in de afternoon, work, get up Soonday and look at store dresses. Last week, one *puta*—not your Clarabella—she marry salesman and leeve a Cheecago. All de women dey see us, Canal Stree' dey look our dress, an' know dey no' come from Nu Orlean'. I tell you dis story, all reddy? So dey know we all *puta*. But we don' care. Dey all *putas* too!"

"Yes," says Paul. "That's funny."

She opens the door and calls down the hall: "Where my po'-boy sanweech, no onion! Hey! Sandweech! So how come your family come Nu Orlean'?"

"Ah…"

"I serious. Tell."

"Well. You really want to know?"

"I waana know n-ow."

"Well, my great grandfather Michael was in a revolution in Malaga, and *his* son Diego escaped to America. Not him but his son, my father. Diego put the baby in a basket," Paul pauses, "like Moses, you know, so he got by the guards in a fruit basket and arrived on an English vessel."

"I like it." She frowns.

Paul feels foolish telling his family's proud story, their immigrant's liberty tale, far from the Sunday dining table.

"There's nothing wrong with telling is there?"

"No. Dat your history. Tell rest."

"That's it. Señor Diego never left Spain, but mother and child landed in Philadelphia's harbour. The baby grows up…and is my father. His name is Alonzo." Paul stops.

"You ask Clara, you know, about her grandfather. Her parents. She wil' like you den."

"Why?"

"Jus' ask."

La Cubana opens an interior door and without a word motions Paul into a boudoir where Clara is sitting on the bed.

"Come in." The door closes behind Paul. "You like to keep a lady waiting!"

"I was…" he begins distractedly. "She told me."

"I don't believe a word she says. Neither should you. But I love her like a sister, believe me."

Clara smiles openly. On both sides, the room is smaller with more candles dancing. Besides a chair is a washstand holding soap, a folding table with clothes laid out and nothing more. No window, no dresser, only a narrow bed in the corner and Clara amid the shadows. In the opposite corner a suspended brass cage holds a silent budgie faking sleep.

"That is Sammy," Clara says.

"He's alone."

She nods. Paul takes a step towards the bed where she's part sitting, part leaning on the wall, knees under her chin.

"I wanted to say goodbye," Paul begins.

"Did you prepare? Like a school test."

"I'm going away. We don't know each other but…"

"Please sit down," Clara says tapping the bed, but he stays standing. "You'll be more comfortable."

"I saw you in the parade."

"I saw you too."

"Don't you want to kiss me?"

"No. I mean, I don't know."

"Then I should kiss you."

Clara stands, raises her fingers and folds down the collar of his jacket. She touches his neck, and he stumbles back and makes a strange sound. Sammy in the corner squawks inappropriately but still pretends sleep.

Clara soothes him, whispering over and over it's okay, it's okay, but he collapses anyway and fumbles for the bed, embarrassed and confused.

"I don't…I don't know what's wrong with me."

Clara presses her lips on his, and coaxes him, but he pulls away, a hand over his mouth. "We are different…my family," he says.

"…is not here. We are all ladies, you know, but this ain't a debutante's ball," she replies. "No one can see us here. Your mother ain't here. And we're not going to get married."

"What?"

"I was joking. Hush." They kiss. "*My* mother is here though. You can meet her if you like! She's called Violet."

Paul pulls away, shocked, and is on his feet. "Clara, is your father here too?"

"Oh, I can't take this," she cries. "La Cubana! America!"

"No!" Paul says, moves over and takes hold of her.

There's a knock at the door but Clara calls: "Go away. *Todo va bien.* A false alarm!"

"Don't believe it," La Cubana says and a double door slams. Music from downstairs hums on the floorboards. One by one Clara undoes Paul's coat buttons, removes his blazer and opens his shirt. She runs her fingers on his chest and he shivers and somehow feels like crying.

"Can't we just sit and talk?"

Clara's hand remains in place. He asks her to remove it and she puts it back.

"Do you remember, Clara, when you were little and you played at the fountain on Girod with a little boy? You played marbles. Do you remember?"

"I do," she says and looks steadfastly in his eyes. "Tell me of the dances you have at home, I would rather talk of that."

"You don't remember."

"I was a child. How can I remember every boy who takes my hand? There were a few boys."

"I've grown up with a house of women," Paul says. "But I still remember one."

She smiles.

"What reason do I have to remember? You were a day like any other. For you, maybe it's different. For me it was children playing. And I wasn't a kid even then. We played marbles and you were gone."

"You came back to find me?"

"I…"

"So you do remember?"

"What if I do? It don't matter now."

"I like to think it matters, Clara. We knew each other as babies if only for one afternoon. You cried and you slept. Remember? We were together."

"Yes, as children, and now I'm banned from the city. You're going away anyway. I'd believe you, but how can I when I live in this place?" She sighs and Sammy feigns a sigh in her honour. "And I don't want to be rescued!"

"What does it matter Clara? You are the favourite of the town major. I saw you at *Mardi Gras* with him!"

"Another boy, so that makes two! Not true anyway. He was brutal. Why all these questions? Who are you Mr Morphy? You're just a client, a customer! You're house money, just a john right? You're nothing! This is my room and I'm the boss here. Don't make me call for the *madame*." She raises her voice and threatens a shout. "Jackson could hurt you."

"I'm already hurting, Clara," Paul cries. "You remember my name too!" He opens his hand revealing the pawn he took from the chess set on his birthday.

"I don't want a chess piece!"

"To remember me by," Paul says. "I might not make it back."

"Don't be so melodramatic. Now, did you come for a reason?"

"Can we not fight?"

"You came not to fight?"

"Clara?"

"What?"

"You don't really know me, and I don't know you."

"That's the first sensible thing you've said," Clara says.

He takes her hand. She moves it away. "Listen, I want you to know I'm not here for…" he searches for the word, "…just for the thrill of it. I want you to stop thinking that."

"I know, you're here to save me. And I don't want to be saved."

"No?"

"No, I don't. I'm perfectly happy."

"*The Twenty-One* is a prison."

"Yes but it looks like a palace, ha! You said you didn't want to fight. An' you don't want to make love so let's just sit here, sweet Creole," she says. "I've got all night."

"I would love you, Clara, if you'd let me. But not like this, not here."

"You sound like a woman. A baby girl."

"And you…you…" he gets to his feet, and without fear Clara relents and looks up at him.

"Okay, I'm sorry. Let's talk. Sit down."

"So…"

"So tell me something."

Paul sets the chess pawn down on the table. He picks up one of the candleholders. "I will tell you of the Marquis de Vaudreuil," he begins.

"The who?"

"It's a story. The Marquis de Vaudreuil, a French gentleman. A hundred years ago he brought his wife to Louisiana for the great balls at court. Officers and ladies were everywhere and they produced the first play called *The Indian's Father* in the governor's house, 1753…"

"Paul, I don't need to know about these people. I can listen to Cora DeWitt, Jessie or the girls at *The Phoenix*. They tell me all their good times…"

Paul groans but receives no reply. The budgie is finally asleep. "You could even read a novel," he says but stops himself. "Okay, here's a story of love. Does that interest you?"

She says nothing.

"I don't read thanks, but yes, tell that one. I'll give it a shot." Clara adjusts her skirt and makes a show of comfort on the bed.

"So you know the slave François Tiocou?"

"No, but I'm a slave of this city too."

"So you need to be free? I can help you with that."

"Tell the story please, Paul."

He smiles and tucks a blonde curl behind her ear. "You know, you look lovely."

"It's only a dress," she says. "A simple green dress, long in the knee, cut away at the neck." He watches Clara examine herself. A single pearl dangles from her left ear and straightening out her dress, she looks delightful. Paul begins again but suddenly the budgie is squawking, having clearly conned its human guests with acting. Its beak lifting the cage door, the bird takes off around the room crying freedom and death: "Hello Sammy! In the bed, in the bed, hello Sammy! In the bed!" Flying madly now, it crashes into the washstand before learning from exhaustion there's no window. It settles on the door handle. "Hello Sammy, hello Sammy!"

"In case you missed it, his name is Sammy," Clara says. They laugh and Paul gathers his composure and tries not to eye the clearly malevolent creature. "Carry on, Paul."

"Well, a long time ago François Tiocou marries Marie Alam. François is an emancipated slave but Marie belongs to the New Orleans Charity Hospital. She cannot be free and won't ever be free. They love each other dearly. What can they do? Maybe run away?" Paul raises his finger gently. "For historical detail, the year is 1737 and the chance of free slave is next to nothing. So François promises to *become a slave himself*. For seven years he works at the Charity Hospital too, on condition that after the seven years they'll both be freed."

"So you should move in with me?" Clara says wryly.

"No, I mean, theirs was a great love!" He counts the points on his hand: "Their freedom was signed over by Father Charles, Superior of the Capuchins, by Governor Vaudreuil of the Province of Louisiana, and by the Directors of the Hospital of the Poor, each with their individual coat of arms as seal and bond. François was declared a free man and Marie a free woman! He earned his freedom. He sacrificed his energy and life to be with the woman he loved and he was happy for it."

Clara is quiet.

"And? What happened?"

"Well, no one knows. They left and were free. That's the story. To go where they liked, free to work and never again answer to any master. To live! I don't know. Maybe they travelled."

Clara puzzles for a moment. "It's not true," she says.

"It's a true story," Paul says. "As true as this coat is black and your hair is yellow."

"My hair is blonde," Clara laughs. "It's real and the same colour as…"

"…as when you were a child," Paul adds.

"I have a story," Clara says, steps up and chases the budgie Sammy out of her way. "It's a horror story," and she winks. "Being scared is the way to feel safe, and the best kind of story after a soppy tale of love."

"François and Marie is a true story."

"They *were* and so is this tale. Quiet now!" and she leans jauntily on the table, and lays a bare foot on Paul's knee. "In the Seven Years' War your Creole friends ran this city with an iron whip."

"Iron *rod*."

Clara holds her hand up, imitating Paul. "Who's telling this story? So listen, Governor Ke-ler-ec ran the show with Swiss soldiers on a deserted horrible place called Ship Island. Just a dot of white sand in the Gulf. A pearl to see but a hellhole then n' now. Ever heard of it?"

"Not yet."

"Aha! Well young Paul, the fellow in charge was Captain Duroux, a brutal ugly thug if ever your ancestors free-licensed one. Ha-ha!"

"And where are *you* from Clara? La Cubana said…"

"Don't listen to La Cubana. Listen to me. I'm narrating here. So," and she takes a deep breath, "when his troops offended him, this Duroux staked them one by one to trees in the blazing sun, beat them naked and left them to rot and die, eaten by mosquitoes. So I'm told. And Duroux was offended a lot. So one day, some men decided to rebel against La Belle France an' join the traitorous English invaders. Duroux by now had sold their rations. They were forced to till his garden stuff like that. Cut timber, burn lime and trade water with Lafitte's pirates."

"Monsieur Lafitte."

"Listen! In desperation, some of the Swiss soldiers ran with complaints to Ke-ler-ec, the devil's own child. He gave them one piece of bread each and returned them to Ship Island. Guess what the Creoles then did to their own? They broke one man on the wheel, the one the English'd forced to guide them. And the others, here's my point about you Creoles, the others they nailed in coffins still alive and sawed them in two."

Unprepared for the conclusion Paul nods and swallows. "A good story," he says and despite himself, thinking about the punishment, he suddenly feels sick to his stomach. "I didn't expect it!" He waits for the queasy feeling to pass. "You know, this city was torn out of delta cane-breaks and dozens of men died in the mud."

"Oh, what do you know about it, Paul! I read *that* in the *Blue Book*. The local news has a history column. It's all true."

They sit together for another hour or so, telling stories. Despite the surroundings, no longer do they feel pressure to engage in profits, one way or another, for *The Twenty-One*. But Paul is careful to pay anyway when he leaves. Before then as it grows a little late they discover a shared admiration for the French opera, each one surprising the other.

"*The Barber of Seville* is coming to town next week," Paul says. But Clara says nothing. Instead she asks him how the pawn moves in chess, and he simply replies "one step at a time."

The last candle burns down to the wick. The light grows dim and the music dull. In the corner Sammy is no longer imitating life or sleep. From his desire to hang upside down, it appears the bird is trying to pay the boatman in the underworld. Yet his prison keeps him alive, and he will wake again, noisily and angrily, in the morning.

Clara kisses Paul, holds his cheek to hers then stands and closes the cage door on her tiny pet.

"You should go," she says.

"I'll come back. I want to!"

"Yea, I want to be a singer one day."

"You will." He dares to hold her in his arms, feeling his arms shudder. "You will Clara, I know you will. I'll come back. You'll write to me?"

"I will," she says. "I'll find a place." They kiss with some force. Then Paul takes his leave, trailing her hand and easing the door into darkness.

Chapter Eighteen
1858
Léona Queyrouze and the Pontalbas

T he Morphys are seated at a long open-air table in the Place
d'Armes. The bells of the St. Louis Cathedral are ringing
out, not for Paul who has reached his majority, but in
honour of renaming the old parade ground. No longer a military
arms depot, the Place d'Armes is becoming Jackson Square in
honour of Andrew Jackson, hero of the Battle of New Orleans 'the
war they did not need to fight' and the last battle of the War of
1812. The name quietly changes with the ringing of the St. Louis
Cathedral bells and a short procession of the New Orleans
defence force, the Louisiana Tigers. The Morphys listen as the
bells fade out. Silently, the sky casts a mistrustful eye over a brave
New World.

"The Place d'Armes will not change so easily," says Alex.

"Well, the Plaza de Armas is also Spanish," adds Ernest.

"French or Spanish doesn't matter," says Helena. "We are
Americans now. Paul is our first modern American!" and she
smiles sweetly.

"We've been American since 1803," says Ernest, but that doesn't mean we can't be both Spanish,"—he nods to Alex—"and a bit French."

"But we only speak French and English," says Telcide. "No one speaks Spanish at home. Alonzo wouldn't want Spang-lish any more than Frang-lish."

"No, we don't speak Spanish *chez vous* because of your *chèrè* Madame Le Carpentier," says Ernest, causing Edward to scowl at his affectionate presumption.

"Call me Morphy, dear cousin," Telcide replies, "that is the name I go by." She frowns at Ernest with mock disapproval. "But we can speak Spanish now perhaps. With dear Alonzo...."

"The funeral meats did furnish forth the marriage bed," whispers Alex, facing away from the table.

A voice now booms from the doorway of the St. Louis Cathedral: "I present the Louisiana Tigers, Seventh Regiment of New Orleans. Please stand and be faithful." A line of ragged troops emerges from a side alley in bright livery suits.

The Morphys raise their glasses and toast the defending army, somewhat self-consciously attuning to the new American order. But New Orleans, precarious floating city, was ever a city of change. Alex and Telcide raise their glasses higher than necessary. Helena sips her chardonnay, coughs has to sit down. Meanwhile at the corner of the table, Malvina and her husband John Sybrandt toast each other privately, whispering in mutual collusion.

"The last heartbeat of the old Vieux Carré can be heard," Ernest declares, "on this fine evening of June 21st. Paul has reached his majority and is also twenty-one!" They stand and toast again, congratulating the new adult.

"The boy's a genius," Alex calls, as though trying to raise the decibels over Ernest's new leadership. Edward turns away in disgust and continues to drink. The troops file past. Joseph Le Carpentier stays on his feet and even giddily marches a few steps before Telcide calls him back. The old auctioneer drains his glass and decides *his* troops are "just magnificent!" But the sun's glare seems to have piqued his thirst. He swings the port jug threateningly until the table is easily calmed. Then he takes his seat of honour and begins carving the roast duck, all eyes watching the knife. Sweat dripping from his hands, he says:

"The Place d'…"

"Jackson Square," says Alex.

"…d'Armes," he repeats "is *not only* where citizens used to meet for business, you know, or where the militia drilled. In wartime, public hangings and beheadings happened over that hill!" He swings the knife to the dismay of the table. "So beware!" Joseph passes a plate to Helena, one to Malvina and the third to Paul, the graduate gentleman caught between his sisters. "As I was saying…"

"I don't think we need to hear it now, father," Telcide says. "*Merci bien.* This is Paul's occasion."

"So I'll tell of our past chess games," he says. "Would that suit?"

No one speaks. The table is all too aware of Paul's exploits, the weight of the family name being what he takes to Europe. The changed family circumstances on the other hand remain the elephant at the table.

"Fame accrues to those close to the famous," John Sybrandt says, "and the Morphys are not immune. Somebody far from New Orleans cannot be expected to lift the family enterprises, more concerned as he is with entertainment than business…"

"…and more than our sinking plight," concludes Malvina.

"And what have *you* done lately, *chère* daughter," Telcide quietly retorts.

"Your first moment of Spanglish," says Ernest.

"You must triumph!" says Joseph. "Paul Charles Le Carpentier Morphy." He has the port jug and brandishes it like a trophy. "Make those European pretenders fear the name of the New World. Come back a hero, my boy, and everything will be yours! Families are all the same."

"Tolstoy," says Helena. "All *happy* families are the same."

"Happy in the same way," corrects Malvina.

"Do you want me to quote it?" adds Helena.

They eat.

"Joseph is right!" says Ernest. "We wish Paul all the luck we need to beat him at chess. *Santé.*"

Paul smiles and nods, hoping the pain of the family dinner will eventually slide into appeasement. The wind is audible over the table. Opposite, John Sybrandt crosses his legs and stares out into the square. Edward adjusts the caps on his boots and observes the fountain, the new statue of Jackson mounted on his war-steed.

Inside their chosen restaurant, *La Fin de Siècle*, the noise of the shrimp-and-crab dining crowd rattles the porch doors. Smells of gumbo and *cuisine française* vapours delight the family nostrils, tamed and quieted by years of pleasant indulgence. Outside, the Pontalba Apartments claim their majesty over the peaceful setting. The Morphys sit beneath a hand-wrought iron balcony, the window casements dripping with flowers, the stonework at their feet as red as the brickwork overhead.

A plaque on the wall nearby reads:

A decade has passed since Baroness Micaela Pontalba married her cousin Baron Celestin de Pontalba, and built the gracious and gorgeous Pontalba Apartments for the good of the Vieux Carré.

Underneath, some educated wag has etched in mauve ink:

causing a scandal when she left her husband and returned to New Orleans, building for herself magnificent living quarters on the banquette with splendid dining for the Creole crème à la Louisiana. Then she left everything for all of us to enjoy.

Below the comment and delicately hewn into the ironwork are 'A' and 'P,' the initials for the Baroness's two families, Almonester and Pontalba.

"One day, Telcide," says Alex, "that will be 'L' and 'M' for Le Carpentier and Morphy." Playing erring brother *à la Polonius*, Alex reaches over and squeezes Telcide's hand. She barely notices him.

"Let us toast young Paul again," Ernest says. "To Paul and his twenty-one!"

The family joins in and the glasses rise and fall. Paul thanks them.

"I will make you all proud," he quietly says.

"The pleasure of a chess combination," adds Alex, knowing no more of the game than his sisters, "lies in the feeling that a human mind is behind the game, dominating the pieces and giving everything the breath of life." The moment sits idly.

Edward somewhat unexpectedly takes up the challenge.

"The pleasure of chess, sir, if I may be so bold," he says, "lies in combat and individuality. All is energy. Examining the position, as Paul knows, does not motivate success only lines and diagonals and latent possibilities. War is all preparation and predicting the future."

"You talk as though he's already left," Helena says.

"Maybe he has," says Malvina and elicits a smirk from her husband.

"If Paul can face the Europeans," Edward says, "we will all be saved. The New Orleans Creole Society will take us back, and the council will recommend our business. People will come *to us*. There will be money."

"Enough!" says Ernest. He stands up and knocks the table with his fist, breathing heavily. "We are here to give Paul our blessing not to pick at his talent, and a God-given talent no less. We should be thankful. Most players have a style," he ruminates, "a chess fingerprint. But not *genius* in chess! We were a chess family not long ago, or have you forgotten? True revelation is akin to mystery. Chess is magic! The art of wonder!" The table is quiet at last. Ernest raises his hand as though preaching or seeking inspiration. "Fusing logic and art, recognizing pattern and an instinct for space, a talent for order and harmony, all mixed with creativity to fashion surprising new formations. This simply *does not happen* in drama, painting, poetry, ballet or *bel canto*, only music, math and *chess*. Chess may be slow but it creates something the world has never seen before. Does that not astonish us?" This time, his fist comes down on the table and he shakes with palpitations. "Let us not trivialize that!" No one looks him in the eye.

"You are right. Paul is the *creator*," says Telcide, impressed by Ernest's fervour. She raises her glass and again the captive audience toasts the boy wonder. Meanwhile Ernest wanders from the table recovering his cool. At the fountain he runs the waters through his fingers and dabs at his beard, wearied by the world.

"Will he come back with money?" asks Malvina, only to be stared at by her mother.

"Riches have led this family astray," Telcide says. "Paul will never play for money. He will play for honour and the family name. He is a gentleman."

"Then John and I respect Paul's trip as much as we can," Malvina replies. She turns her back on her brother, while at his elbow Helena starts to cry. Paul can stand it no longer and takes to his feet, but Telcide also stands to quell her son. In Alonzo's absence, all are apprehensive about the future and watched by their nearest and dearest.

Telcide folds her napkin and plucks a magnolia from the balcony. She takes it to Paul and pins his lapel. Her fingers trail across his cheek. "I've brought you here for a reason. She is here, Paul. We've brought her to you."

Paul trembles. "She can't be," he says.

With a turn to the next table Telcide raises a young woman by the hand and presents her. Unconsciously Helena and Malvina, somewhat stunned, move aside. The seat next to Paul is then occupied by a pale young woman, no more than seventeen, in a billowing white dress and wearing too much rouge. She looks nervous but smiles through her padded clothing and timid eyes. Paul's hair flops over his forehead in his surprise, but he acts the gentleman and hands the girl to her seat.

"Ah, daughter," chuckles Joseph Le Carpentier, "ever the matchmaker."

Alex jokes while Ernest admires the girl. Edward sulks. Malvina looks mean and pretends to pay no attention, but watches cagily while Helena quietly cries, no one understanding why.

"May I present the lady Léona Queyrouze," says Telcide. "Her father is Leon Queyrouze, son of the first officer of Napoleon's empire."

"Papa is a wine merchant," says Léona.

"No need for humility, my dear," Telcide softly adds and looks round the table, "not here."

"Here is nowhere," murmurs John Sybrandt.

Léona continues, "*Papa* was an importer of wines and liquors from the *Léona* plantation in St. Martin's parish. Before we moved to St. Louis Street."

"A plantation," says Malvina.

"Real money," whsipers Alex.

"Leon is president of the Democratic Club," Telcide says, "*L'Union Francais* and the *Casadoras Association*. He also helps the prestigious *Athénée Louisianais* to preserve French culture across New Orleans. Her mother is Anne-Marie Tertrou, daughter of Laurent and Louisa Beauvais."

"She is grand," Paul dares to say. "Pleased to meet you." Shaking hands, Léona presents her fingertips.

"Léona is wonderfully educated," says Telcide, embarrassing the table. "She knows Greek and Latin, Philosophy, European Literature, Science, Music and Art and is fluent in Italian, Spanish and German."

"Can you play chess?" asks Edward.

"Of course, *monsieur*. But only on Sundays."

"If I may ask," Helena says, "where did you meet *maman*?"

"At a Queyrouze salon *soirée* hosted by *papa*."

"At your home?"

"Oui, oui. I run the group myself. You are welcome there. Consider it an invitation and *papa*'s message from La Petite Mademoiselle de Staël à la Germaine Necker. It is my nickname! You can all call me Constance Beauvais. It's the name I am going to write under for poetic license."

The table is quiet.

"Maybe you can come for piano lessons?" says Telcide and Edward starts to giggle.

"I could, *madame*. I would like that very much. I already take fencing instruction from Monsieur C. S. Jones like my brother Maxim." She turns to Paul. "But my greater interest *c'est les échecs, le jeu noble*. I excel *en passant* and castling. I would like to learn the tactics and the artistry very much. I know *zugzwang* too!"

"Paul is going away," says Edward. Telcide offers him a blank stare. "But I can teach you fencing."

Léona lays her hands on the table. "I'm sorry, I cannot stay long. So Paul is twenty-one? Well in February 1837, the year Paul was born, my father saw the magical Chess Automaton *The Turk* paraded in New Orleans by Johann Maelzel. Even then no one knew its secret, how it played, how it worked."

"How it won," interjects Edward.

"Clearly there was a man inside," says Alex. "A contortionist. The crowd was blinded by mirrors and smoke. A cabinet here, a shuffle there and a false doorway."

"As I said, magic," Léona adds.

The table laughs uncomfortably, and Telcide begs the teenage Creole lady to stay.

"Well, do you know what Maelzel said? He said if he had a son, the boy would be a chess player of such rare grace and ability that people would think him a magician."

"Did he have a son?"

"No."

They laugh.

"That's how people feel about you Paul," Joseph says and no one corrects the old man for praising his grandson.

"I will be a lawyer," Paul says, "like father."

"Then when they come to you for legal advice, they'll see only a magician, an entertainer," says Alex.

"Not so," says Telcide staring while the men argue at the pale Léona.

"If you can't make the problem disappear," Alex says "they'll become suspicious, mistrust you. People will say, why not use your powers? Employ your intellect and foresight?"

"Paul would win every case as a chess logician," says Ernest.

"But they'll see the pieces in Paul's office," takes up Edward. "They'd rather risk all with an ordinary lawyer, a man with no claim to greatness, than with someone who makes their heart flutter one moment with excitement and fear the next."

"Ignore your brother, Paul. You'll be a champion but you'll never reassure the crowd," says Telcide. "They won't let you. But no matter, there is another world out there for our beautiful aristocracy."

"He is *already* a champion, *maman*," says Malvina.

Edward stands up, annoyed. "You know as well as I there is no trick to chess. The pieces are moved mechanically and the crowd sees the whole bout. There *is* no magic."

Telcide is stunned, leans back and smiles pathetically at Léona. "Excuse their impatience," she says. "You were saying about *The Turk*...."

"It is fine, *madame*. Perhaps I can call next week." She rises from the table before the traditional coffee and cream. Joseph tries to rescue the conversation, waves a dessertspoon for attention unnoticed.

"You know as well as I," Edward says, "people cannot play chess blind to what's important, women especially because they need to be inclusive. They cannot dismiss this move and that possibility. Chess is about *not* considering all the future positions. Victory lies in self-assured knowledge of the right move at the right time and always playing it."

"The rest is distraction," says Ernest. "Look, perhaps our guest would like to finish her story?"

"It's really okay," says Léona. "I'm very busy and must see some other tables." She turns quietly to Paul and says "but sometime we could play chess?"

"I would he honoured," Paul replies, feeling the glance of his mother's expression on his neck. He gives her his new lawyer's card. "Feel free to call in when I return from Europe. I will be gone a few months."

"*Charmée*," the lady replies. "I will."

Léona is gone and a moment later is greeting a table inside *La Fin de Siècle*. Telcide's anger is palpable but diffused by the family's sense of her staged manoeuvrings, their lack of consultation.

"No more chess talk, please," says Ernest in order to bring conversation back to the royal game.

"*Maman*, you cannot force someone onto Paul," says Alex, but regrets his mouth.

"She was not forcing," Helena says.

"He didn't like her anyway," adds Malvina.

Suddenly a different voice emerges. "Who knows what lies in the family interest?" says John Sybrandt, leaning over the table. "But the favour of an influential Creole like Léona wouldn't hurt any of you."

"Creative yes, influential no," says Alex. "She has no power."

"But connections, and job offers?" says Telcide

"She works at home," says Ernest, gauging the moment. "This is her first ever time in society and she'll be obsessed with nothing else for years. It's better to leave her alone. She won't marry. It's just…can't you all…" and he despairs a little and stops. "Léona's father has the real power."

Behind them, petite with jet hair, Léona drifts between the tables inside *La Fin de Siècle*.

"Strange ghostly translucent skin," says Joseph, eyes closing.

"As though she never leaves home," says Malvina, "like Helena."

"She looked preserved in a pickle jar," replies Alex. "She never breaks that glass smile."

They laugh.

"Mystical eyes," says Joseph. "I'm in love!"

Edward smirks despite himself.

"And a masculine mouth," Alex adds. "Like her friend *The Turk*. But I like a woman with a good mouth."

"I laid my hand on her arm," Edward says. "The flesh was hard as marble, probably from her constant fencing. But what did she say her brother was called?"

Telcide retires from the table to indulge her disappointment. She touches Paul's arm and, without warning, begins to walk home. No one follows. The young man, raised to his majority, watches his mother's shape shimmer in the heat of the square. The mist from the fountain seems to shower her. She emerges strangely untouched, enters the rose garden and does not look back.

Chatter continues between Morphys and Le Carpentiers, two families without a head. The new tensions between the north and south of the country, of more concern than the Spanish and French empires, are discussed for the first time. A conflict could be developing, but the speculation dies as the desserts arrive. Joseph is awake and grips his spoon like a knife.

Paul strains to keep his mother in view. She passes under the huge oak door of the St. Louis Cathedral, sits momentarily on the steps, then is gone inside. Accompanying her walk in his mind, Paul hears the piano solo of *Louise de Lorraine*, its jaunty sentimentality and suspended notes played over and over with draining sadness. Paul knows, at this moment, no longer will he follow his father or mother. No longer can he remain here.

"Joyeux anniversaire!" they proclaim as the desserts are tasted.

Paul makes a speech and blesses them all with happiness, feeling like a pompous priest, and receives patronage in return. He remains the boy chess player, the idler with a gift and the private brother, nephew, ally and enemy. He is the one they all feel at liberty to support and celebrate, but whom no one understands. Through coffee, cheese and biscuits and the remaining dregs of the meal, Paul says very little.

Gradually they disperse until only Helena, lost without her mother, and the sleeping Joseph remain. In the softer light of the late afternoon, the water of the fountain shimmers. Her eyes dry at last, a carriage takes Helena back through the square. Paul is alone with his grandfather. He takes the hands of Joseph Le Carpentier, feeling strangely close and in need of him. In the old man's hands, he can feel his own hands going cold. No one pays the bill. Paul remembers his walk, aged seven, with his grandfather to witness the funeral parade of Jean Lafitte. The eyes of the waiters stare as Paul struggles with the old-timer and slave-trader, and carries him gently to the fountain.

"Chess?"

"No, thank you, *grandpapi*," Paul says. "Not by the fountain. It reminds me of someplace else."

They sit there in the sun, staring into the heat of the day.

Part Two
A Grand Tour

"The reward of art is not fame or success but intoxication."

Cyril Connolly, *The Unquiet Grave*

1944

Chapter Nineteen
1858
Liverpool Docks and London Fields

Paul takes passage outside the United States on *The Philadelphia*, somewhat ironically reversing his own immigrant history. Beyond Big Muddy, water and land merge so harmoniously their partition becomes unimaginable. En route, Captain S. P. Griffin makes Cuba a port of call if only for an hour. Arcing eastwards from the Gulf of Mexico the ship is rewarded by the sight of Havana harbour at sunrise.

Dining at sea is more civilized than the passengers expect. Poultry is confined in coops on the upper deck while the ship's cow is quartered in a special deckhouse with padded sides. Fresh vegetables are protected from the weather by growing under overturned boats. Such foodstuffs are mere staples. The season is too late for oysters but lemons, kiwi fruit and pears are abundantly available. Champagne, the best remedy of all, becomes the captain's cure-all-ailments and sooner or later everyone partakes.

Paul suffers *mal de mer* soon after departure but eventually the calmer seas of the Atlantic beckon. *Old Glory* trails in the wake of the ship, dancing mischievously with its cargo of American emigrants, ladies and gentlemen on the European tour and the young prodigy who plays not a single game during the whole eight-week crossing.

Fred Edge meets the American at Liverpool's Mersey docks on June 20th. Sporting a welcoming suit of solemn black, Edge appears more unwell than the amateur sailor. He doffs his cap and helps Paul ashore before they shake hands warmly and head for a Merseyside hotel. "Welcome to the largest port in Europe!"

"Oh thank you."

"You know, Liverpool transports cotton from the factories of Manchester in the same privateers that return the silk, sugar and spices from the Orient."

"I didn't know that, sir."

"No need to call me *sir*, sir. Fred is fine."

"Right."

As a beardless youth with a broad-brimmed planter's hat, a canary yellow tie and Southern manner, Paul is immediately out of place in this rainy and restrained land. Mr Edge, resembling the populace at large in his death-black drapes, is fit to play the ambassador, though the margin is narrow. Leaving *The Philadelphia* behind, the Englishman points out empty tea chests floating under the loading docks. Paul imagines for a moment he has landed in Boston Harbor in a strange reversal of the colonial passage, although he has never been to New England before or taken a great interest in politics.

"Liverpool Chess Club extends its greeting," Edge says. "For a spot of tea before eight, that is."

"Tea?"

"Dinner, sir."

At the foot of the hill, the duo board a shaky cart driven by a cross-eyed mare. Without comment they head down the valley to Lime Street Station. Paul sleeps in the carriage and Fred shuffles him onto a southbound train. From that moment their close pact of servant and helper, if not friendship, is sealed. Edge becomes Paul's shadow, acting as his secretary and companion, a private Uriah Heep responsible for the books and the bouts.

"The best valet a man could ask for?" Edge says.

"You are a worthy manager already," Paul says. "Do not lower yourself."

The steam blares. Spending less time here than docked in Havana Bay, Liverpool is a memory only of chimneys, grey skies and streets with blackened faces. The overpowering smell of jasmine tea, pungent from spilled bags rotting on the docks, transforms into burning steam and the hardwood scent of their sleeping quarters. Paul takes to his bed while Fred sits up and reads the newspapers. London's *Euston Road* beckons eight hours from now. Afterwards it's plain sailing down the Tottenham Court Road to the West End, the heart of the Empire and *Lowe's Hotel*.

The next afternoon, a little under the weather, Paul embarks on a walking tour of the Royal Parks. Four miles through the capital entirely surmountable on foot—from Kensington Gardens and St. James's Park through Green Park to a loop of the Serpentine—he returns to *Lowe's* to find his first opponent Thomas W. Barnes waiting in the lobby. Edge tries to dissuade Paul by cautioning his health and reminding him of their schedule in a way that only secures the tie, essentially what they both want anyway. They can pretend the other is to blame if the match is a debacle.

"I can play."

"Good for you, Mr Morphy."

"Well, I walked for three hours on a morning coffee and an imported croissant. But we didn't cross the Atlantic to stroll amid the daisies of Buckingham Palace," Paul says, trying out a flutter of *poésie*. Thomas Barnes shakes his hand and laughs politely. They sit in the hotel foyer ignored by all, and begin a bout over an Italianesque coffee table. Thomas W. Barnes is a small man, smaller than Paul and possessed of his own lemon cake, presumably to assist his play, which he offers liberally but only Edge consumes with any appetite. Paul's chess manager, varying his black hat with royal blue handkerchief and splash of silver-pointed cane, sits in a corner and scowls at the unprofessional setting. A coat rack towers over the table flapping at both players' elbows. Edge pretends to read *The Essex Morning Herald*.

Paul starts to lose, one game at a time, but discovers the thread of his opponent's mind. He feels increasingly seasick, staring down at the table like he's still on the boat. But as the evening dwindles, he pulls back to salvage a five-to-five draw. They shake hands. Mr Barnes leaves the hotel without knowing his draw was more remarkable for not being a loss and in later circumstances would be counted quite a victory.

A curse in disguise, the match serves to usefully secure Paul in bed for the rest of the day. By the following evening, he is recovered enough to arrange bouts more confidently with Reverend John Owen and a re-match with his former adversary Johann Löwenthal.

"No more hotel lobby matches," says Edge and they shake hands with renewed meaning. For a while they part company to explore the local neighbourhood, buy gifts and accustom themselves to London.

On the evening of the third day, Edge invites Paul to stroll out after dinner just as the heavens open. At the corner they take a hansom, a low-hung two-wheeled cab drawn by a single horse, on a somewhat perilous trip down the South Bank. At the foot of Tower Bridge, Paul imagines the traitors' heads jammed on pikes infamously warding off challenges to the almighty Crown's power. Below, the Thames is no less a comfort and makes Paul mourn the Mississippi. The banks are low and he cannot run his fingers in the current, nor would he want to here where murk is no longer the warm mud of Old Man River but this city's Dickensian belch, a shimmering brown crawl.

"Spewing away the detritus of conquered lands?" offers Paul.

"And foreign fields forever England."

Paul casts his eye over Westminster. "I imagined it differently."

"Wait a while, look!" Edge points at the city lights over the Thames, winking with the promise of things undiscovered.

"It's cold even in June," says Paul.

"Don't worry," Edge replies, "you'll learn to love London. How could you not? Six million wasted lives."

They exchange a smile. Almost for a reason, the rain stops.

"The invisible clouds part," says Paul.

On the return journey, they trade the hansom for an open Victoria with its rubber tires and leather seats. They continue to plan.

"Are their any stakes for these games?"

"Of course not, sir, you were very clear on that point, I seem to remember. No wager will be made by yourself or the Morphy family."

"It's more than my mother's wish," Paul says. "My father didn't like gambling. We must find some other way of funding our contests."

"Daniel W. Fiske has taken care of it, Mr Morphy, through the New Orleans Chess Club."

"But where do they procure funds?"

"We already have, sir," Edge says, guiding the conversation. "Look, we can see the stars now."

Not undeterred, but willing to be led, Paul nevertheless admires the sky. "I think that is the boar and the ram."

"The nymphs in the forest. Look, the chase!"

"You know," Paul addresses his manager, "I am no fool. The journey must be paid and the chess players must be respected. I should know the source of the funds."

"Charles told me...."

"Charles Maurian," Paul says with surprising eagerness, "would want me to know."

"Well, if you must," Edge replies dubiously. "Our less-than-secret London backer is Lord Arthur Hay, an officer in the Queen's Guards and a member of the St. George Chess Club. The games cannot go ahead without stakes, sir."

"Yet, stakes imply gambling, Mr Edge, and lack of gentlemanly honour."

Edge is quiet. Nothing is seemingly more precious to Paul than his family name. They agree to defer to disagree and no further details are disclosed. Before practicing the law and making a living, Paul can do nothing but sanction the support. Self-consciously, he strains to see the stars and forget the stakes and the prizes. A strange fellow no doubt, Edge thinks, but nevertheless his concern remains securely, if a little insistently, with reputation.

"Let the victor take the heart-spoils!" Paul declares cryptically. "The only ones of any worth."

"The prizes can always be returned."

"The plough," Paul adds and points. "The humblest and most elegant of the constellations!"

Edge looks and acquiesces. "The stakes *can* always be returned. Whether your opponent wishes to accept returned stakes is another matter. Do you ever consider *their* honour?"

"You would be surprised, Mr Edge, who will accept their gamble returned, and on what premise."

Later that evening at The Grand Cigar Divan, 101 Fleet Street, they cautiously encounter the next opponent, bolshy Father John Owen *nom de guerre* 'The Reverend'. They sit adjacent the bar on a plush settee intended for card games. Nearby, an old woman is wrapped in furs drowsy with whisky. The terms are agreed. Edge and the Reverend's second, James R. Manlow, haggle over split stakes and ultimately decide life is short and the game should be decided for a set of Ivory Staunton Chessmen. One blunder follows another and the Reverend makes a cry each time as though surprised by the devil's helper. They play four games, and Paul wins twice with the Evans Gambit, securing two draws at Pawn and Move. They stand and the Reverend laughs and barks the excuse of being "a clergyman with responsibilities. My flock prevents me from upping stakes, Mr Morphy. You understand!"

"We can provide half your stake," says Edge, with a dour smile. "Perhaps next time we can duel for something a little warmer than a chess set? Say a hundred?"

"Outrageous!" says the Reverend and points at the board. "Those Stauntons are carved by hand. They're far more valuable."

"But not carved by the man himself," says Paul, eliciting a smile from both players, a delicate sense of bursting the egos of Fred Edge and John Owen that brings the proceedings to a delicate conclusion. They all shake hands.

The next morning Paul and Edge breakfast early at *Lowe's* overlooking Pavilion Square. Paul is not hungry and through the bay window he watches the shrubbery and two chaffinches at play in the fountain. 89 Royal Street, the courtyard, the fountain, the balmy heat, all return to him. Edge coughs into his *London Field* newspaper.

"Samuel 'Hacker' Boden believes you are a genius," he says, "and I quote: *Young Morphy possesses singular coolness and pursues an advantage once obtained with unerring truth and force. He is a veritable lion. His style of play is attacking and brilliant,*" Edge pauses for dramatic effect, "*but occasionally…overhazardous.*"

"*Le jeu est fait,*" says Paul.

"Bring on Staunton, I say! We shall see who is *the chess pariah.*" Edge lays the paper aside and opens their first letter, a challenge from Mr Johann Löwenthal that stirs Paul's memory.

"I'm surprised we don't hear from General Scott," he says. "Everyone wants a nip of my blood."

"No, it's not a challenge from Löwenthal," says Edge, "merely a comment on his defeat long ago. It seems the Hungarian likes publicity."

"Long, long ago," says Paul.

"He's often nice in defeat. *I was vanquished by superior strength. I saw all my combinations twisted and turned against me and I felt myself in a grip…against which it was impossible to struggle.*"

"We played two days ago," says Paul.

Edge tips the paper. "You played where? You never informed me. Where?"

"At the hotel."

"Here, at *Lowe's*?"

"The very same. You were walking off your lunch. Löwenthal was only here a week. It was a friendly. "

"We should set up another game."

Despite his chagrin, Edge takes the bait. He will set up another game. After breakfast Paul retreats to his room for a leisurely bath, claiming he needs to dust off his chess books.

"They must," says Edge. "You never open them."

Despite the distractions of London and lingering feelings of home, Paul plays his old adversary Löwenthal from 19th July through 11th August. A long bout, the match occurs at the St. George before relocating to the Gentleman's Club, the Hungarian moving for superstitious hope of improved play.

"Hacker Boden has printed another splendid appraisal," Edge is saying by the end of August. Paul declines to scrutinize the text. The chess columns fill daily with speculation over his next challenge, the next European-American tie. "*Nine-three-two Morphy, two drawn. Morphy awarded £100 for winning, presents Löwenthal with furniture worth £120 for a new apartment.*"

"A journalist's journalist, as my father would say. They need the blood money," Paul adds, "more than my family."

"Very gracious of you Mr Morphy," Edge says and comments no further.

Paul now makes a decision to avoid the Birmingham Tournament, the Grand Exhibition starting 24th August, to try and establish a match with Howard Staunton. The newspapers begin a story that the English chess champion is saying Morphy has already played him and there's no need to play again. No mention of the outcome of this match appears in print, a *telling omission* Boden calls it, since Paul is certain no such match has ever taken place.

"Unless I was sleeping."

"It's not possible, sir," says Edge taking everything seriously. "They should call it Staunton's fantasy! I fear that match." Speaking over breakfast, Edge butters his toast with an air of strict confusion, raising the slice to his eye-line. "But we'll find him Paul, don't you worry."

During the late summer evenings, they see an abridged *Hamlet* in Cambridge Circle. Paul also attempts to find out which operas are playing but cannot seem to discover the right district. Two strange men, Paul in a red necktie and blue pantaloons and Edge suspended in death-like black, they sit on park benches dotted around Leicester Square affecting grace but looking seedy. The chess columns of London and Paris breathe news of one surprising debacle after another in the Birmingham contest. One morning Edge confirms:

"It seems Mr Löwenthal knocked out the champion yesterday. Mr Staunton neither won nor drew a game."

"Mr Löwenthal is on for First Prize."

"And Mr Staunton for last?"

"Clearly."

"You pay such close attention, Edge. Let it go. Chess isn't everything."

Edge looks up as though Paul had wished his own death. "I'm only thinking Mr Morphy," he says, dropping the newspaper in a wastepaper bin next to their bench, smiling crookedly and folding his fingers, "that you would undoubtedly have taken that tournament."

"What do you mean?"

"You would be champion of England."

"Yes and Mr Staunton would never play me face to face. Now he's agreed, our bout will occur free of tournament complications. That's how it should be. All chess games should be contests of the soul played man-to-man for honour and…."

"I know, sir," Edge intervenes. "Let's just hope the match now occurs."

"What do you mean?"

Edge opens a later edition of the same paper. "Oh look," he says, "Sir William Jones's *Caïssa*:

Of armies on the chequer'd field array'd,
And guiltless war in pleasing form display'd."

"I know," says Paul. "A homage to our goddess. She will defeat all."

"You understand my point then, Paul. We should take our opportunities where we can."

"I want to beat him," replies Paul, "not on the London stage, but in private."

"My point—and William Jones seems to agree—is that Caïssa never refused a single bout and she became a god!"

"Goddess. This is not ancient Rome, Mr Edge. We're not chess gladiators."

"Sometimes you're too much the chess gentleman."

Paul is affronted and stands. "You sir…" His blood quickens. "I'm not to be spoken to in…" but just as soon he cools, recognizing Edge's thirst for victory, and regains his seat. "Just try and play the games," Paul says. "What games do *you* like?

"Marbles, sir. Look, all I'm saying is Staunton beat Pierre St. Amant at the *Café de La Régence*, November 14th 1843, and it's etched in my mind. Afterwards he was considered world champion, not European champion, but champion of the world. People still regard him that way. They discount the Americas and the South. Now is our opportunity, Mr Morphy. We must strike now!"

"All I know," says Paul, "is that Mr Staunton is a gentleman. I trust his saying he could not play because of the Birmingham tournament. You know a lot about Staunton. So if you want to swap statistics, sir, you'll know he organized the world's first chess tournament. It ran alongside the Great Exhibition, Crystal Palace, 1851 and was a glorious success."

"I know, Paul. Herr Adolf Anderssen won. So our friend Staunton wasn't the greatest then either."

"That's besides the point. He *is* the English champion."

"Aha! That's *my* point, again. We must play the champion, and he was in Birmingham last week."

"I will not chase Staunton like a schoolboy," says Paul. "There is a procedure."

"Yes, enter the same tournaments."

"Maybe, and yes, we staged the First American Chess Congress in New York because of that first London tournament. But there simply is no international tournament. There's no such thing as a world chess champion! We must beat him man-to-man. It's the only way. Don't you believe I want to win too?"

Edge breaks a smile for the first time.

"Okay, I see," he says, and puts his hand on Paul's shoulder. "You know something? Your face is turning red."

"You're too much," Paul replies. He walks towards Charing Cross waving his hand over his shoulder. "I'm going to look at the Palace. I'll see you for afternoon tea like the English do."

"Howard Staunton will be taking tea in Birmingham," Edge calls back. "We should take coffee in London."

"*Laissez-faire*, live and let live!" returns Paul. "The imperial capital is a long way from New Orleans."

Paul has fallen back into reading chess columns, if not chess books. He lies suspended in the bath.

One passionate Duke d'Orleans, in the middle ages, broke the chessboard on the skull of his conqueror. How then did Paulsen, with his superior magnetism and not too inferior skill, fail to affect Morphy? The moment that Morphy completed a move, he threw the whole board away from his attention. Surely, I thought, chess is a question of magnetism?

Paul skips on...

We saw Louis Paulsen with his vast head, sanguine temperament but coarse fibre indicating his rough almost pure-Bersekir blood; we gazed at Morphy with his fine open countenance, brunette hue and marvellous delicacy of features, bright clear eyes. It was the old combat between the Coeur de Lion and the Saladin. Strange that the Orient and the Occident should yet war! Paulsen huge, massive and ponderous; Morphy slight, elegant yet swift as lightning.

Picture the game half finished. Then Paulsen clasps long forefingers together. He lays them firmly on the edge of the board, counts a dozen moves of his opponent and evidently knows something. But what? You can hear him think. But not quite! At length, with a peculiar flourish of his arm, he seizes a pawn and moves.

With scarcely a moment's hesitation and eyes bent on the board, Morphy raises his arm as if to strike. He throws a piece right in the way of his antagonist. Another long pause, the Swede's hands close again. "Take the piece man!" is on everybody's unopened lips. Yet Paulsen pores for nearly half an hour over the board. He does not take the proffered piece but offers one of equal value. Then something like electricity flashes through young Morphy. The white forehead pleats up and he moves, fast. Caught with the same impulse, Paulsen responds click, click, click. Each move is a percussion of rifle, grape and canister followed by a clash of wooden swords. Then all is still. Flushed with the struggle, Paulsen looks up to see Paul Morphy sitting calm cold as an icicle. Looking down Paulsen sees his own mate only four moves away!

Paul feels dazzled, disgusted and tosses the newspaper aside, only to pick another off the floor. A glass of Cabernet Sauvignon in one hand, he scans the lines with an air of obsessive disdain, but feeling every blow….

> …embracing twelve to twenty moves and dozens of inter-combinations! This whirl of permutation with accurate results in thousands of combinations passes through Morphy's mind, as in Zerah Colburn and other arithmetical prodigies, through addition, subtraction and multiplication performed with the rapidity and accuracy of Mr Babbage's machine. Mental retardation might occur for anyone less gifted in this peculiar power than Paul Morphy, a man at the brake of a fire engine.
>
> This leads us to inquire, what is chess? Is it purely intellectual? What faculties does it call into exercise? The eye and fingers, the muscles of the arm and the peculiar power of viewing the chessmen in their places and of seeing beyond, elsewhere, always the imagination acting as one….

"Enough!" Paul says and folds the newspaper and dips it in the bathwater for purposes of penitence. Setting it aside he wonders about Mr Babbage's machine. "Last one," he promises himself, "then I must do something useful." But he can't resist opening the same newspaper to a column by Forest J. D. Woodbury and learning how

> Napoleon planned his battles on large maps with pinheads indicating each corps, division and brigade. He moved the pins about as thought required and so completed his Armageddon plan. But your chess player must go through this preliminary fight without touching map or pin. With strained reticence he must keep hands off until he makes a complete survey of the field. When he once touches a soldier he must be moved beyond recall. This requires very

> exhausting attention, nay, almost impossible; it is the faculty
> phrenologists term 'continuity'....

With a shudder Paul awakes in the bath to the sound of knocking.

"Monsieur Morphy!" The valet taps again. "I will leave the goods on the dresser table."

"Goods?"

"Letters, Monsieur Morphy."

Paul wraps himself in the silver silk dressing gown—provided by Lowe's for its favoured guests—and waits until the valet is gone. The bathwater is cold and he reaches for a robe and slips his feet pleasurably into the soft leather house slippers lent by Edge. He thinks of Titi and his lack of embarrassment as a child, happy to wander around semi-naked. But he is twenty-one and no longer a child. Plus he has developed a slightly paranoid sense, being away from tropical Louisiana, that to defy the English weather might induce pneumonia.

Letters strew the table, some bills, invitations to regional chess clubs and promises by ladies of society that dining would be discrete *so long as you first meet the husband.* Paul regards them in confusion and picks out the New Orleans postage stamps of Major Thomas Gardiner, flashing teeth and planter's hat. A note from Clara! He studies the letter in his room by the light of the *veilleuse.* The paper is coarse, but her writing is bold with lavender ink in a spidery hand, and smelling faintly of musk.

> *Dear lover,*
>
> *I would rather look at a beautiful loss than a dull win, boy. How are you chess-ing? Do you always win and what do the Europeans look like? Are they smaller or taller and are the ladies pretty? I remember your visit and wanted to write to show how I remember you! I am still practicing my 'victimless crime' just like the killings in a chess game.*
>
> *I work for LuLu White now, the one with the monocle. She threatens every day to open an octoroon house*

on North Basin Street and call it Mahogany Hall, but the joke is over. I thought it was funny the day before yesterday. Her place is the Calaboose but she can't be serious. Lots of mirrors and gilded chairs. The usual hokum! I quite like it actually. I am a lady now, ha ha! Walnut wood. Oriental rugs and carpets, silver grand pianos. You never met my mother, Violet, but she's here too. Foul-mouthed drunk all day and somewhere else all night. I'm joking. Until the next time she's sober. My joke of the day: It was her that got me into this mess. Well it's true ain't it?

We have a juggler too. But no evening gowns just Mother Hubbards. I can't work out if that's a step up or down. Maybe you'll have to rescue me after all? But LuLu is kinder than Hattie. We play seven-up most nights except when playing procuress on the doors. LuLu has a trick of finding a piece of old carpet on the sidewalk to announce 'a presence.' Then we load pots of hot water and drop 'em down the stairs. I've become quite the money-grubber too. A bordello, LuLu says, is 50 cents so I'm making better. On the sidewalk the rate was a dime. LuLu says I can run myself one day then I'll manage your chess games and we can be rich and live somewhere fancy like New York or Pennsylvania.

So will you write me? I have a few stories, mostly my upsetting LuLu's 'fleur de lys' for being late or not sleeping at the right hours. She calls it the flower of shame and makes us wear it and look sad. I don't have to pretend. Ha! There are mosquitoes here too. Anyways it's safe here and I wanted to tell you. We got some bodyguards though they mostly guard their own bodies. I'm saving mine for you, boy, as best I can. That's a joke! Those men, The Live Oak Boys, they protect us. They all sleep in a shipyard at Elysian Fields because their leader Red Bill Wilson says so. He's Red Bill because he's red where he keeps his knife. Believe me? I seen it! They all protect us with their oak cudgels, while you and your chess friends are away fighting! Write me back, will you?

Paul blushes and turns the page. Trembling to follow Clara's thoughts and decipher her mind, he drains his wine and lays the empty glass on his writing pad. The Victoria cabs of London trundle by beneath his window.

He draws the *veilleuse* close, shivers as dusk falls. The candlelight clings to the precocious letter....

> *You didn't think I could write letters, did ya? This is taking me four days. I now need a new feather to write with...*
>
> *I'm back! So you remember the Council ordinance no. 827 'Concerning Lewd and Abandoned Women.' I know it off by heart, like you and that Napoleon Code. Well the licenses don't work and we've abandoned them. The politicians love us here anyway, so it was only time. So unconstitutional, oooh! Or so it says in the Random Pamphlet. No more taxes or licenses. LuLu says it's very American and a victory. The case of Emma Pickett was even overturned and her bagnio city funded. Now that's progress! Let me copy it for you. She applied on May 22nd for Dirty Digs at 25 St. John Street and the case is now closed. Listen Paul this means I'm now free. I'm not chained to these streets! I can leave and do what I want, or in a few months we could live together. What do you think? I've been mulling it over!*

Paul leaps to his feet, but Clara doesn't continue discussing the future....

> *I can now eat on North Basin and even the edge of the Quarter. Yesterday a procession went right down Royal with hundreds of beautiful painted hussies...You should have been there. The locals called it obscene. You do really live there, don't you? Oh and one customer, Mike Haden, cut his brother's throat with a razor! Here is other good stuff from*

On The Turf: 'Mary Schwartz blinded a customer in a row over 20 cents. She left a trail of blood to her door, but when the customer returned with a live alligator he couldn't get the snapper through the door.'

This one's my favourite: 'Red-Light Liz the one-eyed paramour of Joe the Whipper has ended their long-running battle. That loving scoundrel, who made a living administering beatings to masochistic harlots using whips and steel rods, was sitting on the banquette rocking chair outside Kate Townsend's, dipping snuff. Liz walked over and lit him up in a gasoline bonfire. The Whipper's eyebrows are currently recovering along with his pride. Liz is looking for a new place to work but won't be leaving the neighbourhood.'

That's about it, Paul. I can't write forever. Do you love me? Shall we go somewhere? I want to know more. Write me back! Clara-bella-bella xxx

Paul lays aside the letter, a brutal mix of tenderness and promise and pours himself another glass of wine. He lights more candles on the desk, mainly for warmth. With an elegant paper knife he slits open a letter from D. W. Fiske and reads how certain news is making its ways back to the Morphy family.

Paul is told he must *"not challenge or accept a challenge to play a money match. Otherwise he will be brought home."* He can tell the line is Telcide's, rewritten by Fiske as temporary President of the New Orleans Chess Club. Clearly no dishonour must accrue to the Morphy dynasty, Paul thinks, currently dragging its belly to Jackson Square to impress the Pontablas. Why? So Paul can marry Léona? And now he is gambling. How much shame can one family bear!

"They play chess on Sundays," Paul addresses himself. "And they want to haul me home for playing an honest game?" He reads the lines again, denying him *to challenge or accept the challenge*...or someone will be sent to retrieve him. Who? "I don't play for money. And I never will! So there is no meaning here! Edge can keep the stakes if he wishes, it's no concern of mine!"

Tearing the newspaper in half he dangles the pieces in the candle flame. The words *we are only concerned because we are your family*...disappear into soot.

The last latter is from Joseph Le Carpentier, currently in ebullient mood at the prospect of a national Civil War.

Fever is gripping the nation, my lad, and I cannot get enough. If I were younger I'd fight. I got myself measured, privately of course, for the new gray uniforms though don't tell your mother. Soon you may be in the thick of it and prove your colour, Paul. Transfer all those Indian gaming skills onto the real theater! Chess does come from India doesn't it? Or is it Persia? Anyway, gather your sword!

    There is open warfare in Kansas Territory at least in the courtroom! The Dred Scott decision means fighting is inevitable. Never will they take New Orleans. Never! The 'militia,' as the Yankees like to say, is strong in our town. Remember the pirates, that's what. 1812 was not long ago. John Sybrandt has escaped the call-up and Alex has hot-footed away. Ernest is too old and I'm too young! And licking his wounds after a slapping from Rizzo-whatever-his-name-is, Edward is thinking of signing on. A wise move I told him. Let the Le Carpentier legends live even in the name of Morphy. Yes, young Paul! Write me a legend and I will sing you a tune!

    Oh and someone called John Brown, a farmer or something, is also stirring up the slaves and clearly a bad move. We must fight to keep them in their rightful place. It's like we're the whites on the board if I can be crude and the blacks are rising. Blacks were meant to be second. But we have the first move! The Democratic Party will come through, my boy. I hope you get this letter, by the way. They are censoring now. Abraham Lincoln is their man. Doesn't stand the chance in hell of a snowball. Not that I'm taking sides...

Paul turns the page and scrutinizes Joseph's bold-as-brash large writing. He almost has to hold the page at arm's length.

On that subject, my boy, you remember General 'Win-the-field' Scott? That Yankee you whipped royal as a gelding? Well old 'Old Fuss and Feathers' is just as old like me. I think he's stuck in Mexico City, the place he ruled with an iron glove. So looks like you beat him twice. He's retired!

Age comes to us all. But I intend to kill death when I see him and lop off his top with that scythe. Attack with my stick, ho ho!

One more thing. I went to see Maezel's chess-playing machine again last night. The so-called Turk! Turned out I had to go to Baton Rouge but I had to see it. I'll save you the trouble—there's a man inside pulling the levers. I definitely heard him cough. So much for pride! The only fool was the one he plucked from the audience to play…and he still got a draw. I was ashamed on your behalf, hahaha!

Must be a good player on the inside, Paul thinks. He lays down the letter and closes his eyes.

Chapter Twenty
1858
The Gambit Offered

P aul buys a baby daffodil, an odd choice in Edge's view, and hooks it to his lapel. Covent Garden smiles at the scene of their scheduled meeting with Howard Staunton, author, actor, Shakespearean scholar and chess prevaricator.

"London, sir, is all squabbles and shifting positions."

"Capital of the chess world, Mr Edge."

"For now," Edge replies, "for now."

Paul stops. "Look. What do you think of my flower?"

"The badge of the poor."

"A poor comment, Fred."

"Poor in purse not in spirit, surely."

They sit on a grass verge. Ragged people bustle through the covered market, exchanging wary glances or smoking under the marble parapets. On a balcony, the local aristocracy are lunching though it's not yet twelve. Snatches of conversation and scraps of bread from their plates fall through the wooden rafters. At Paul's feet, a small boy tosses a stone in a dirty puddle and fishes with his hand up to the wrist to recover it. He offers it to Paul, who smiles.

Edge misses the moment. "You sir, are a cross between the Spanish and French ancestry of chess, Ruy López and De La Bourdonnais. Agreed?"

"I'm American," replies Paul, amused. "Or did you forget the Louisiana Purchase?"

"Born American, but you remain a Creole."

"And you, Mr Edge, where are you from?"

"Ireland."

"Well, and so was my great-grandfather Michael."

"My great-grandfather was a Belfast stonemason. He left the Great Hunger potato famine to work in a Humberside cotton mill. From there he went to French Guiana, then to New Orleans." Fred contemplates the grass. "You know, in our American Chess Congress the champions were very young men. Mr Louis Paulsen was twenty-three. Staunton and Daniel Harrwitz won their laurels in their early thirties. At twenty-two, Charles Stanley won a match against Pierre Saint Amant, a first-rate player then aged forty. Now Stanley is the same age and past his prime…"

"And your point Mr Secretary?"

"The point is," says Edge, "there is no real excuse for Mr Staunton declining to play you. Listen to his pompous voice. *I take to my work, let the young gentleman take to his play.* I would defy his defiant air, sir. I would ask why Mr Morphy must suffer?"

Paul laughs. "As my representative?"

"Well, because Stanley is too old and the magic has gone. The English champion is just not up to the task. No victory is guaranteed, so he's scared. Look at Harrwitz. A most interesting study at the chessboard! Fine faculties, a splendid boxer quick with a combative temperament and a full physical imagination. More like you, sir, than Staunton. He makes the most beautiful combinations ever seen on a chessboard. Brilliant as fireworks!"

"So tell me, Fred."

"Well, sir, I've arranged a match against Mr Harrwitz in two weeks. But well, and this is the good bit. It's in Paris, City of Light." Paul says nothing. "I assume I did right?"

"You did. You did."

"If Staunton won't play, sir, we must take measures. A king should not throw away his crown before an unknown cavalier, however *preux*. This way we can hopefully play Staunton before we leave and dispatch two pretenders."

"One question," Paul jokes. "So when will I be king?"

"You will be, sir. The last time I looked you played the Evans Gambit well."

"Yes, kingly."

"You use it favourably, sir," Edge says, wringing his hands.

"Yes, the Scotch Gambit, the Muzio Gambit, but no Morphy Gambit!"

"I will extract it *extempore* from my mother wit!"

"Enough nonsense Fred, here comes Mr Staunton. Be calm please."

Edge peers. "He's actually here. You must be joking."

"If I was more serious, Mr Edge, I'd be laughing."

"Well, that would be a rarity."

The Covent Garden crowds part and Howard Staunton strides into present company at a clipped pace. In the manner of a public *soirée*, Howard 'Defender of the Faith' Staunton, Lord Lyttleton, Mr Avery and Mr Wills skip to a silent beat, lining up before the diminutive Creole and his Uriah Heep counterpart. Staunton's entourage hovers at his heels like brutalized dogs. They size up the foreigners, Edge looking like death-warmed-up and Paul like life-delayed, one in solemn black and the other in debonair green.

"He dresses like Charles Dickens in drag," says Mr Edge, trying to break the ice. Paul twists his yellow daffodil into place.

Staunton, hair frazzled like burnet barbed wire, stretches his neck as though scaring flies from his head. One by one he grips his adversaries' hands firmly and steps back.

"We came to make terms," says Lord Lyttleton, a fat man with jowls like a bulldog and a dainty Scotch waistcoat. "Unfavourable terms."

"Delayed terms," says Staunton, trying to appear equable despite his associate. The other two flunkies, half witnesses and half bodyguards, stand well back for intimidating effect. "I am in bonds to my publisher," Staunton continues. "*The Collected Works of*

William Shakespeare, Illustrated Edition comes out at the end of September. I simply cannot spare the time," he smiles, "despite your long journey. I would like to apologize. It's simply not possible." He extends his hand to Paul Morphy.

"Mr Staunton, will you play in October, November or December?" Edge leans forward. "Mr Morphy would very much appreciate a game with an English gentleman."

"Then why don't *you* play him?" replies Lord Lyttleton, upbraided in height by the lanky Edge. The bulldogs Avery and Wills hover nearby.

"Be careful gentleman," Staunton adds and reaches for a pinch of snuff. He makes no bones about using a small vanity mirror without offering round the goods. "We are armed with mischief."

"According to honourable law, if you refuse," says Edge, "we must declare a rejection and in lieu of a game, the press usually takes a view."

Staunton tucks away his mirror. "Now, I did not say I would not play. But practice is a delicate matter when one has committed work *and* the need to defend one's reputation."

"Mr Morphy," Edge says brimming for the opportunity, "has a reputation to defend too, especially at sensitive times like these."

"Humph! Great Britain will never help fight an American War if that is what you are referring to," interjects Lord Lyttleton bursting with fervour. "Slaves or no slaves. We got rid of ours. I don't see why you shouldn't get rid of yours!"

"We are getting a little off subject," Paul says and looks up at the decision-makers. Staunton is looking right back at him, determined to stare him down. Paul looks away feeling foolish and listens to the rest of the conversation.

"I am engaged on a great work, sir," Staunton says. He is puffed up by his entourage and sees nothing to fear from Paul. "This month I am in bonds to my publisher. But I don't see why a match shouldn't be forthcoming, say, in November."

"Let's fix a date," says Edge. "How is the beginning of the month?"

"Beginning of November," Staunton ruminates, his companions momentarily quiet. "Hmmm not good, no. I will see my publishers and let you know the exact date in a few days."

"You will confirm."

"I will, sir."

Edge pauses. "Well splendid! We very much look forward to your certainty." He extends his hand but Staunton is ruffling in his valise, and with a grandiose flourish he produces a book packed with papers. Paul sees the name Lady Macbeth on the flyleaf in her own words *unsexing herself*, literally a distracting illustration of her naked. Realizing his error, Staunton stuffs the lewd lady into the depths of his case. Without a word he produces his own published book, familiar to Paul from his days at Spring Hill College.

"In 1853," Staunton says, "a sixteen-year-old boy called Morphy scribbled in this copy of my book…"

"That's my book," says Paul.

"I know," Staunton says, "that's my point."

"How did you get it?"

The reversal unbalances him. "I bought it, Mr Morphy, I paid money for it. How dare you? Now if you will permit me I'll finish. Is this your writing, sir?" Staunton holds the book under Edge's nose, no longer wishing to address Paul.

"No, it's Mr Morphy's," Edge says.

"No, not you. This is no laughing matter either of you."

"Of course not."

"I wrote this book about the 1851 London tournament as you know, sirs. I did not expect to acquire Mr Morphy's copy. It was sent to me by a Father Beaudequin. A former teacher of yours, I assume? Anyway, I want you to know we *will* play Mr Morphy! You wrote on the flyleaf

Property of Paul Morphy. By H. Staunton, Esq. author of The Handbook of Chess, Chess-players Companion &c. &c. and some devilish bad games.

And some devilish bad games? And some devilish bad games, sir?"

"It was a private book," Edge says. "This is nonsense."

"I just wanted you to know," Staunton scowls and turns on his heel. "You'll see some devilish bad games!" He starts to shake uncontrollably.

"I hope so," says Paul.

"Why you…how dare you laugh at me, you scoundrel! We *will* play," and Staunton raises double fingers and clicks them. "Let's go." He snuffs up once more and Edge gives the bulldogs a devilish bad look as they leave. Lord Lyttleton is already gone, whipping along Avery and Wills. They mutter together then ascend to the overhanging restaurant for a spot of lunch, Edge and Paul watching as they reappear on the deck.

"Let's not have them look down on us," Paul says.

They exchange a smile. Edge straightens Morphy's daffodil and pats it flat.

"What an odd man," the manager says. "Howard Staunton, the British Coeur de Lion of the noble game. He looks like a maniac."

Three days later on August 28th, the *London Illustrated News* covers the encounter. In parsimonious language, and acting as editor of his own chess column, Staunton upbraids Paul's rudeness and *his effrontery in bringing along a business whipping boy and no honourable associate.*

"Apparently," Edge says, "you have neither stakes nor *seconds* fit to play. I believe, Paul, this man Staunton struggles with elements of journalistic impartiality."

"I do not have stakes."

"Of course not. Ah, but you do have a second."

"Who?"

"Me, I think."

"So he's right."

"Well, but we didn't discuss either stakes or *seconds*. And you could have both quite easily."

"I play…"

"I know, Paul, for honour. Sometimes isn't it a lot less painful to present monetary terms? Staunton is known to be mercurial."

"When a man resorts to such means as these," Paul tells his only confidante, "he will stop at nothing until he has committed himself. Let him go on!"

Later that morning, Paul gives his first blindfold exhibition in the King's College chess rooms. The whole time, a dark portrait of Howard Staunton is framed directly in his eye-line. Short of asking to change seats, as per the ancient tactic of placing the sun in an opponent's eyes, Paul finds it necessary to avoid the painterly Staunton gaze. Soon he is sitting under the lozenge window with a delicate etching of Caïssa above him. The chess goddess is graffitied with the happy words 'she came, she saw, she conquered but I had my time!' under her golden crown.

Paul ties on his blindfold. He faces the room and astounds the English students with five games blindfolded and no defeats. As the bouts begin, somewhere he hears: "We are all defeated in some fundamental way. I'm just accelerating the inevitable." He muses during the games that we're *all* defeated in some fundamental way…we're all defeated in *some* fundamental way…

It is a long time before Paul is relaxed, one arm thrown carelessly over his cushioned chair. When a piece on one opponent's board is accidentally shifted, he calls "impossible move" and alerts the room to the accidental deception. No one is harmed and Paul relishes the quiet darkness of the chess realm he constructs behind his eyes. He imagines himself lying in bed, the warm air licking the buildings south of the Vieux Carré. There, unseen and unheard, ghostly patterns shimmer softly on his childhood ceiling in the moonlight. He thinks of the world map in the playroom on Chartres Street, and his first discovery of a chessboard with its amazing patterns of bright and black squares. The porthole window of his room opens magically onto the courtyard below. Reaching out, he can feel the waters of the Mississippi with its endless rolling promises, deep in the mud of home.

"The emerald isle," whispers Paul. "I thought this was England!"

The room applauds his wit and offers him whisky at the bar. For once Paul partakes and he talks of John Bunyan and the mysteries of Rembrandt, the art of self-deception, getting a little tipsy. No one tries to seduce his mind of its secrets, though he is not entirely certain. Later he returns to his hotel to bathe, sleep and wander in dreams.

Chapter Twenty-One
1858
Le Café de La Régence

After crossing the English Channel, Paul and Edge take the slow train from Dunkirk and trickle through French fields to the metropolis. Paul stares at the flat-baked countryside with its Norman towers and drainage canals, the surprise of old men fishing in roadside ponds. On a whim, Paul remembers Clara's card game seven-up and asks Edge to teach him.

"Do you want to play with stakes?" Edge jokes and enjoys the idea of beating the chess player. "You know everything in France is better? From *lycées* to French furniture and couture, everything is a cut above Louisiana." He lays down a card and sweeps the game.

"So they say, Mr Edge, so they say."

"An unpredictable victory! Don't feel too bad, save your energy. I promise not to tell anyone! Can you tell if I'm joking?"

Paul eyes his companion. "I really don't know. Are you my manager, businessman or friend?"

"All three, of course."

Over the clickity-clack of pistons the cards scatter the table. Paul plays with affected concern, one fixed on the streaming scenery as though expecting change. Edge literally holds his cards close to his chest and plays a cagey game. He emerges as victor over the fast-dealing Paul, who finds his chess style does not transfer well to cards.

"I thought you'd be better, Paul," Edge comments with barely concealed pleasure. "Save your best cards. You should be more cunning!"

"I play the only way I know how," Paul says and lays down the queen of spades. He watches a farmhouse trail beside the train, a dirt track and a church steeple. "I am not used to concealment. In chess, every piece is visible."

"Quite so, but not everything is chess is it? Whist is a far more cunning game!" Edge lays the king of hearts on the table and claims a third game. "Nor are you used to losing."

Paul fixes his fingers to his temples and laughs. "As long as you're on my side, you can play the cardsharping. Then we'll stay in a fine hotel!"

"I see, and despite there being no money in the royal game, you're still all for the sport of kings?"

"You mean polo?" says Paul.

They laugh.

The game is concluded and Edge offers some advice: "You must consider what I'm thinking. You can ignore my thoughts in a game like seven-up and still expect to win. But not so in chess! Play the board, not the man."

"Is that what you think, Mr Edge? Then you really must play a little more chess!"

"I leave that to the experts. Smoking break," Edge adds and leaves the carriage.

Paul is suddenly alone. The comforting monotony of the train lulls him for a while, and he is almost asleep when the carriage door is peeled back with steady force. The inspector checks Paul's ticket and passport and looks for the other passenger, frowns and leaves.

Moments later two men enter, sit beside Paul and engage in conversation about the South going to war. They sport dark blue suits, red handkerchiefs in the top pockets. For civility they produce cards and hand them to Paul.

"We specialize in accident lawsuits, young man."

"Very discreet."

The new arrivals appear to be father and son, hair slicked back in the same direction as their pinstripe suits. Their eyes are deep in their foreheads, suggesting great scrutiny and application of the law.

"If you fall over," one says, "we are there."

"To pick you up."

"We work out of Boston. If you're in the area, feel free to request the Johnson twins. We operate on a client-by-client basis."

"I surely will," says Paul, and elicits a long friendly stare from the brothers who fold their arms and smooth down their moustaches. Slowly the larger man opens out the *Boston Evening Herald*. The smaller produces *Le Parisien* from his breast pocket and fixes half-moon glasses to his nose. This French farce entertains Paul and although he does his best to stare out of the window, he cannot help looking back to see what the two men are doing next. Before long, the larger one tires of the news and takes out *Les Fleurs Du Mal* by Rimbaurd.

"I shall soar on the wings of poesy," he says and settles in his seat.

"When in France," his companion replies.

Paul sees the opportunity for conversation and proffers being American as point of interest. But the twins frown and lean on their reading material as though to cross-examine the rude Creole gentleman. The carriage falls once again into silence.

Alarmed he is seeing double, Paul now watches the men without their knowledge. The double image of the Northern lawyer ferments in his mind. He would never turn his back on Louisiana roots. But something in the cut of those pantaloons, the black felt of those fine gold-lined briefcases stirs Paul's sense of decorum. He feels attracted and at once repelled by the confident gentlemen, their legal and rational minds personifying the honourable and moral life. What he desires for himself, they are the splendour of the city attorney and the career-minded gent combined.

Despite reservations, Paul simply stares in unmediated admiration. These are men at peace with their place in the world, he thinks, and who seek to improve it for others. Here is the right kind of person, he muses, the clean-hearted moralist.

"I am a mere chess player," Paul says out loud and draws his hand to his mouth. The lawyers lower their reading material slowly.

"We know who you are," the smaller man says, laying his hand inside his jacket and producing a long cane with a metal shaft and a silver tip.

"We read about you in the paper this morning."

"You are mistaken," Paul says.

"It would be better if you turned back now."

"You should probably leave the train," the bigger man says. He raises his hat to reveal a single chess piece balanced on his head, the white queen, which he lays on the table.

"High time you turned back!" the smaller man shouts and the unholy cane flies up. "You abandoned your family. Now you're gambling away money they don't have, blaspheming with a board game, bringing your good name into disrepute!"

"No," Paul screams, "that's not true. I don't understand." He makes himself into a ball while the white queen is glowering. The man raises a black finger, which grows in size and admonishes the chess player. Now on his feet, Paul raises the window of the carriage and strains back the cover. "Somebody help me!" He desperately fends off the men with his hands.

Suddenly Edge rushes into the room and finds Paul alone, his head trapped half under the glass partition and hair pulled back by the fast-moving train. His guardian wrestles him to a seat and discovers blood on his cheeks. Then Paul slips away into unconsciousness, while Edge rushes for water and throws it in his face.

Paul bolts upright. "What happened? Where have they gone?"

"Who?"

"Those men! The lawyers! The..."

"I caught you with your head out of the window," Edge whispers. "You were suffocating."

"Where?"

"No one is here, Paul. There are no belongings. You were asleep." He gestures about the carriage. "Asleep. A smothered chess piece. You know, *zugzwang*, that's all. Sometimes we invent feelings, right? You just dropped off and had a bad dream."

"That's all! I was dreaming of a white queen. She was torturing me..."

"That's all Paul. A daydream."

They change carriages and Edge watches Paul for the rest of the journey. They no longer play cards, or any other game.

On the outskirts of the Paris, the *lycées* and convents pile up on the horizon. Edge explains how, at the edge of Louisiana's former mother city, these homes "would provide sanctuary for the offspring of liaisons no one mentions in polite society."

"Creole rejects," Paul says, staring at the long dry lawns. They see children skipping over logs tied to the train tracks. A few turn to look at the locomotive rolling by. Most faces ignore them.

"Take your pick," Edge says, "octoroons or mulattos. You're a Creole, the existence of these children is no secret."

"London has them too," says Paul.

"For sure, we're no saints. The suburbs of Paris are where they end up. The receding tide of empire. We have the same schools in London, only better hidden." He waves at the children. "Nothing ever changes."

"Søren Kierkegaard," says Paul. "*Life is lived forward, but understood backwards.* What chance do these children have in France?

They'll be better treated in New Orleans, I can tell you that much, Mr Edge."

"Better to die on your feet than life on your knees. No slave is happy enslaved."

"Do you know any slaves?" says Paul. "And they are voluntary servants? Most don't even apply for emancipation."

"Because they know they'd be swiftly released of their services."

Paul is quiet.

"I speak for myself," continues Edge, "but it's better to be a lion for a day than a sheep for a thousand years. The problem isn't that these children are not white. The horror is that their parents try to erase their transgression by exiling the kids."

"The problem is that the children are not white but not black enough either. No one wants them."

"Except Paris," Edge concludes, as though the French capital were a black hole. "It's always Paris dragging back the unholy fringes of empire."

Inherited opinions given, they sit and wait for the train to arrive. Eventually, dusk falling, they continue by carriage to Meurice's Hotel and retire. The lights of *La Cathédrale de Notre Dame* wink through the nearby bathroom blinds. When Edge is asleep, Paul creeps to the bay window and stands under the shimmer of steeples. He takes a drop of absinthe to soothe his mind. Then he lies on the couch, no longer troubled by renegade chess bishops or flamboyant Yankee lawyers.

Mid-morning they repair to the Rue St. Honoré and the *Café de La Régence*, the famous centre of Parisian chess. Past and present *lumières d'échecs* would gather here in times gone by for public display and private admonition. Named for the Regent Duke of Orleans, the Café shares its elegant history with the founder of Nouvelle Orléans, before Spanish rule and the Louisiana sale of the century. Before Paul's arrival on 31st August, the *Café de La Régence* has boasted clientele from Jean-Jacques Rousseau, Benjamin Franklin and Robespierre, to

Napoleon Bonaparte himself who moved pawns over the balmy fields of Europe.

"Before the frozen terrain of Russia and hellfire of burning Moscow stopped him," says Edge. "And, of course, the English at Waterloo."

"Touché Mr Morphy. History was ever written by the victors."

"Yes, and what is history if not a series of victories?"

"A series of defeats?"

"You can beat Harrwitz, Paul, you can."

They stand beneath the white, colonnaded pillars at the Café entrance. A canary-coloured canopy flaps overhead. The wooden chairs are loosely piled on the banquette and for a moment, the cab traffic dies away. They peer inside and see the chess tables, the waiters pouring liquor in delicate black-and-white fluted glasses. A large blue parrot squats calmly in its cage.

"See, just like at home, but with more style."

"Right down to the parrot," says Paul.

Chapter Twenty-Two
1858
A French Duel

The match is confirmed with Daniel Harrwitz's secretary for September 5th. Telegraphic dispatches are sent to the Méry and the Duke of Brunswick, holidaying on the Rhine. Striding from his bath, the Duke declares his intention to defeat the young pretender immediately after his siesta for *l'honneur de la vieille France!* He calls for his robe and his diamond-encrusted chess set, and plays his lady friends that same evening. He lets them win, and learns nothing, but the Duke drinks from crystal brandy glasses and is entertained in a marvellous manner.

On the other side of France, the *Café de La Régence* is crowded. The *maître d'* partitions a triangular corner to resemble a stage. A table is elevated and draped with Tricolour velvet a foot above the spectators, in an attempt to encourage discipline. Meanwhile the whole room is cunningly constructed with mirrors so all drinking angles retain a view of the chess game. The blue parrot is moved to the cellar. Some mirrors are dirty and some hooked with magnifiers, thereby creating rumours about which player retains the advantageous position.

The French spectators are crammed into the Café, causing gentleman to rub shoulders with their own servants as drinking partners. The working lads about town drink themselves silly at the bar, while a lady or two slips by the doormen, seen but not heard. Among the crowd a wily Artful Dodger relieves the occasional pocket of its tired purse and giggles with hangman's courage. No motivation is otherwise needed for merrily illegal gambling focused on Morphy and Harrwitz. French francs skip down the bar like lost souls in search of salvation. Bottles of wine share tables with cuts of cheese, while greasy lapdogs hunt the floor near their owners' knees. Oil paintings of the past glories of French military heroes wobble and glint from the sweating walls.

A hush descends, as Harrwitz and his challenger enter the room to shouts of "Vivre La France!" Stoically they seat themselves at the Tricolour-covered table. Neither player wishes to joust on the French flag, Harrwitz ostensibly for his German fatherland and Morphy for his strain of Spanish-American blood. But France is the host and the men politely play along. Harrwitz strokes the tip of his beard meaningfully and nods to the crowd with mock appreciation. He is the favourite. For the gamblers suspicion falls on the unlikely American, the young pretender. Paul feels a sober chill and for the first time realizes he is daring to challenge the chess prowess of Europe. The crowd offers one long crooked smile in hope of his defeat and the fulfilment of their bets.

Meanwhile the players shake hands, pausing for the artists to make a quick sketch and sit down. Harrwitz is thirty-five and a chess professional permanently installed at the Café. Some days he is host and ruler of his realm; other days he feels tied to a rock like Prometheus for stealing fiery new insights from above. The Café is his home and his prison, the boundary of his fame. Playing the role of interloper, Paul is twenty-one, a child of no fixed race, nationality or religion if not New Orleans.

The chess is prepared on a small marble table engraved 'Napoleon Bonaparte, 1795.' Paul rubs his fingernail along the signature and shivers. A point came, he knows, when even Napoleon was defeated as Edge was only too happy to indicate. But for Paul the genius of Napoleon was vying for the world, not like Winfield Scott, *Grand Old Man of the Army*, taking a piece of Mexico City. Paul knows that no individual battle has a pre-ordained outcome. Who decides each bout is a mystery between the greatest players of the age. The popular vote is the decider of glorious victory so at this moment, the contest is here under his fingertips. The entire Rue St. Honoré shakes with the expectation of glory and the equal spectacle of defeat.

Herr Harrwitz wastes no time in laying his elbows on the table in authoritarian rule. Paul pushes back his coattails and studies the proportional cut of the chessmen. Nothing is unusual. They are wooden and elegantly tailored in the French style, light, witty and malleable. Harrwitz moves his King's pawn forward two squares and lets his hand linger, before releasing it in a flourish. The game has begun.

"Santé," the barman calls, and the room cheers and descends into the pretence of whispers and occasional shoves. Someone is singing in the street, and everyone laughs. From the first move Harrwitz employs psychological tactics, stretching his legs when Paul is about to move, blowing his nose, winking at the crowd. Playing a losing game he offsets pieces from the centre of their squares, hoping to pervert the board's only natural shape. Paul is keen to see how his opponent tries to seduce chaos into order and so redeem his position. But neither player knows who possesses the true line and who will escape the pressure to lose. Frequently Harrwitz swoops on a piece with a theatrical arc, before committing, simply to strike the spectators with wonder.

Meanwhile Paul stares intently at the board. The first hour slides away in barely fifteen moves. Still, Paul is distracted by Napoleon's actual signature under his thumb. Feeling self-conscious he tries to channel any feelings of awe into his own game to overcome the rulers of the past. The longer the game lasts, the more the Creole is distracted by the playful intimidation of the German, who now begins drumming his fingers on the table with incessant gaiety. Not a word is a spoken between them. But Paul maintains a sobriety of demeanour despite Harrwitz's tactics; he will look up only when he knows he has a winning game.

Standing nearby, Paul's *seconds* Jules Arnous de Rivière and Nelson Journoud set up an imitation table. Here they grin and play out the future possibilities of the game, not without a little gambling of their own. Their green board of maple men and oversized four-inch kings merits the comedy of their roles as stake-guardians and speculators. Journoud resembles the hangman waiting to be called for duty, Rivière his victim hunched over the board in fear of the chop. Lounging quite merrily in the shadows, they clink their goblets of aniseed wine with absinthe spoons and grow steadily blotto. Their counterparts in the Harrwitz's camp are burly-looking men of uncertain nationality, lurking even deeper in the Café and opening casks of wine, dripping blood-coloured drops in the sawdust.

Like a master theatrical host, Fred Edge stands nearby frowning at all the chaotic posturing of the Café and wondering why Paul is sometimes uncertain at the chess table. Tapping his walking cane on the bar, he eyes the game warily noting how Harrwitz is a sturdy-looking man and knotty of limb. There is something of the hunched goat about Harrwitz, he thinks, with his clipped beard and pale skin.

The first game meanders from its opening stalemate to Paul rescuing defeat from the jaws of victory. In the second the American blunders under the fanfare of the *Café de La Régence* crowd. Harrwitz remains quite still, a little surprised to find a good position. While covering his mouth with his hand as though playing a children's game, Paul mumblingly vows not to crumble before the German's reputation. But the moment does not last. As he moves his hand from the white queen, Paul feels an alien self-consciousness. The move is wrong. He has created a poisoned pawn suffocating the king's escape. For a while he plays *à la cavalier* but the die is cast. Harrwitz puzzles for seconds only, then without his usual merry antics, he captures Paul's sacrificial rook; the risk of capture is worth the potential bluff. A tortuous descent due to Harrwitz's sheer advantage of pieces is set in motion. Paul will be worn down.

At the close, Harrwitz makes a point of knocking down Paul's king.

"Da-da!" he declares and bounds into the air with unexpected gusto. The crowd senses his frenzy and all hands go up, while a piano man in an unseen room leads a spontaneous and rambunctious burst of the Marseillaise. *Daaa-da-daaa-da-daaaa-da-adaaaaaa-da-da!*

"Congratulations," says Paul and looks bewildered.

"Well, it is astonishing!" Harrwitz says regaining his seat but not his composure. He offers a limp claw, blood vessels exposed like poisoned tributaries, and grips Paul's wrist. Playing to the crowd, Harrwitz declares: "You know, his pulse beats no faster than if he'd *won* the game!" The crowd roars and Paul blushes. The pieces are set up for the second game. Meanwhile the challenger retreats to his *seconds* and is warmly honoured while they offer advice.

"I know what happened," Paul says. "I saw the position and the move that would cause the error. But the more I thought, the more it slipped away."

"Don't worry," says Journoud, chewing on a piece of liquorice.

"It's *bien fait* for the Allemand!" says Rivière in broken English. "He will lose *à toute a l'heure!*"

"I appreciate your words gentlemen," Paul says and sits for an aperitif.

Stepping out of the shadows Edge offers one word.

"Fate!" he says. "Mr Morphy loses because he is not yet ready to win. Is that not so Paul? New Orleans is a long way from here. But you carry it with you, sir. Now's the time to let it out!"

Rivière and Journoud nod with meaning and return to their private gamble on the next game, hoping to rake in a pretty franc or two.

"We bet every game for you, Paul," says Rivière.

"It is just a question of how much."

The two men seem sincere. Paul smiles wanly and returns to the chess stage, already strewn with roses for Harrwitz. As he sits, pieces of the Tricolour tablecloth are torn away with ironic zest by the crowd like religious relics. Flags are no longer sacred, he muses, and sets out his pawn army one at a time.

The third game is tight and in no sense a certain victory for Harrwitz. He plays a tactical game creating glass weapons of Paul's bishops. But Paul neutralizes his foot soldiers by maintaining the *tempi* of the white pieces. The sheer energy of Harrwitz's enthusiasm carries him forward and the knight, with its grinning jowls making it look alive, clefts the head from Paul's queen in a final fork. Victory is secured by a pawn storm in the corner. Game four is Harrwitz's too. But in losing again, Paul has learned the way to win. The rise of Harrwitz and the overbearing militarism of his manoeuvres shall become his downfall.

Every chess player walks a thin line between harmony and disaster and the German's game is no exception. Despite his speed, Paul too needs calculation within calculation to restrain delay from defeat. No player can counter the rapid mastery of chess pieces in play. During game five, Paul delegates more pieces to lines of harm than support. Unfortunately the plan doesn't work, and like so many aspects of the game, it breeds a singular loss. Meanwhile Mr Harrwitz is rollicking in his seat like a delirious baby. A beat, check and mate!

He is on his feet.

"I am Tamburlaine, conqueror of men! *Je suis le vainqueur du vainqueur de la terre!*"

"You're Napoleon," replies Paul. "The last game was the best." He admires Harrwitz's antics and almost savours the jubilation; to know such manic delight is so foreign to Paul. The mournful gap between their responses encourages the journalists in the room to create the *weird zealot Harrwitz* and the *sour-faced foreigner Morphy*. At the next break, Paul simply declares that Harrwitz will not win another game. Reminiscent of his match against the equally moody and ungentlemanly Louis Paulsen, Paul takes Edge aside and outlines his intent. Edge agrees victory would be a step forward and nods sagely at Paul's plan for Philidor's defence as though well versed in the school of classical French tactics. The table is again prepared.

Outside the Rue St. Honoré is quiet. Dusk has fallen. Several hours have passed within the stuffy Café and the last game of the session is announced with a plan to reconvene on September 18th. Over the next hour the Café falls into mute surprise, and step by step into brawlish discontent, as Paul wins the next three bouts. Harrwitz gets a respite. Then he feels unwell and must take a break for at least a few days. Before the last game, the score stands at three-three. The crowd prepares to listen to the American's words.

Paul announces a week from now he will perform eight simultaneous blindfold games, a feat never yet witnessed in Europe or the United States. The barman and the scribblers immediately take note of time and place. Eight games and eight opponents while seeing no boards. Impossible! Within a few hours, Paul's future opponent the Duke of Brunswick receives a telegram at his watering-hole on the Rhine and quietly coughs up his champagne.

"Now there is a reason to return to Paris!" he declares and orders his carriage prepared. "I will depart after dining!"

Meanwhile the combatants agree one more game, a friendly. Harrwitz makes snorting noises at Paul's moves and refuses to place pieces in the centre of the squares.

"There is no rule!" Harrwitz cries. "There is no rule!"

Checkmate is given by Paul on the thirty-third move using Philidor's Legacy, sacrificing the queen to give mate on the next move. It is a spectacular conclusion to a tawdry affair. The mirrors around the room seem to shimmer and threaten to break in mourning, so many eyes are pinned to the build-up and the sacrifice. Harrwitz, the game already lost but refusing to decline, worms in his seat and twists his pieces round the board while trying to escape the danger. In the corner, Rivière whispers something to Edge and receives a scowl from Harrwitz's *seconds*.

Edge nods and whispers back to the admiring Frenchman. "If Morphy sees no danger to his exposed king, he will allow it to stand brazenly."

The game finally generates a beat in Paul's favour. Like a horse winning a race on the nod, the benefit of the first move is returned, the wheel of life rising as it rolls. Paul dislikes administering the *coup de grâce* but there is no kind way. The game is won solely on stamina and Paul risking a sacrifice. He rises from the table and looks down at Napoleon's ostentatious signature carved in the wood, which retains the air of a fake penned by Harrwitz but is in fact genuine.

"*Au revoir*," Paul whispers and shakes the brooding German's hand.

"You are left with the Emperor," Harrwitz says. "I mean, you are the king *today*. But we will see…"

"The king and the knight," Paul corrects. "To be concluded," and he smiles sympathetically. "Don't you think?"

"The knight of New Orleans?" Harrwitz suggests and looks at the board in puzzlement.

"*Zugzwang*," says Paul by way of apology. He walks to the back of the Café and sits on a wine casket dazed by the hours of concentration.

"*Bien fait!*" cries Journoud. "Mr Morphy, you've just made me a lot of money!" Meanwhile Rivière stands unsteadily and shakes the hand of his new friend.

"I thought you were telling a lie for a while," he says.

"I am a gentleman," replies Paul. "I always play with the truth."

They laugh.

"Come on, gents," says Edge. "Let's get out of here before the fun starts. Taking their coats, they quickly exist by the Café rear, as planned.

On the way out Journoud says: "You don't have to push it, Paul, because it's the truth. If it's a lie, you have to push it."

"Nothing can be pushed except a lie," Rivière replies. "The bigger the lie, the better!"

"But that's no way to play chess," Journoud laughs. "And Mr Harrwitz is not finished yet. He is too much at home in the Café to stop now…"

"I have a chess fever!" Paul declares and the general merriment climbs to a new height.

Paris is waiting. The night is young, and they are all young. The cafés nearby are famously open. All night, they will serve phials of absinthe with a semblance of welcome to strangers from faraway lands.

Chapter Twenty-Three
1858
The Magician's Trick

Paul remembers a séance with everyone sitting round a table joining hands, and a small boy with a tray of blue drinks. But that is all. In his dream he extends the odds of a champion—Pawn and Move—to the whole world but there are no takers. Around five he wakes and examines his face in the mirror pressing his fingers into his soft fleshy cheeks. He wonders about the toll travel takes on the human heart and goes back to bed. He plans to escape Edge's company and wander Paris alone.

The following afternoon, he boards a ferryboat and drifts down the dark Seine, watching the cane-birds land in the reeds beyond the city fringe. He imagines himself fishing on the Mississippi. Slowly the city recedes until only the sound of the water remains, a soft happy-dumb gushing. The boat circles the sandy waters and meanders back upstream. All at once, the domes and riverside quays of the French capital beckon to Paul. They whisper for him to extend his stay and never leave saying: "You are home, you are home. No need to go back to New Orleans." The search for home clouds his mind, an enveloping fog promising embalmment, couching him in stupor and forgetfulness. The river Lethe is close at hand, he muses, not the Mississippi or the Seine but the great river of hell into which all rivers flow.

"Where rivers go to die," he says and feels a chill through his fingers. He drifts back into a troubled sleep in the early morning cold.

The next day, Paul rises early and adjourns without Edge to the second floor of the *Café de La Régence*. From the ground floor coffee-house and delicatessen, the upstairs library resembles a gentleman's club fitted with marble banisters and red lacquer walls. The trappings of male seclusion are all present: false bookshelves, cigar trays and half-full brandy bottles. Between two billiard tables and a cord is a single, large armchair. As Paul enters a gentleman leaps from the chair as though stung and becomes the *maître d'*, a portly man with red cheeks, thin scalp and a long squint.

"Welcome, Mr Morphy, I was just warming your seat. "*Suivez-moi* if you'd be so kind." There is a twinkle in his eye. "We're all ready for you."

"I hope I'm not late."

"*Non, pas de tout.*"

They pass behind the billiard tables until the armchair and chess table announce themselves. The ceiling hosts a mural depicting Caïssa, immortal defender of the royal game, suspended on a white cloud. She is naked to the waist, her eyes covered for shame. Her long golden hair spurns gravity in loops propelling fiery bursts of light and inspiration. Kings and castles, grinning footmen and chivalrous knights spin in her hair, captured and captivated by her beauty. In her hand Caïssa delicately displays a single pawn, tempting the mortals to borrow chess for a day but at the price of their minds. A smirk adorns her face in lurid rouge.

"Do not stare too long," says the *maître d'*, "or her mood may change."

In the background a Greek warlord, Ares, perches on a grassy boulder. At his feet lies an open casket: he has recently presented his beloved Caïssa with the invention of chess and tremblingly awaits her verdict. Meanwhile Caïssa ignores Ares, grins towards the heavens and revels in her new-found toy. He loves her but she loves the game more. Everywhere tree spirits peek from oaken hovels, singing out the immortal republic with exquisite diamond trumpets: *liberté, égalité, fraternité!*

"The story is incomplete," says the *maître d'*. "You must regard the magnificence of the carving." Paul strains to look, his mouth open in wonder as he drinks in the terror of the human chess pieces caught in the goddess's malevolent grandeur. "We too are caught in Caïssa's web and await a verdict," the *maître d'* continues. "We too must struggle for salvation without understanding the game."

"Monstrous," Paul says. Dropping his gaze, he is surprised to find he is not alone. In the middle of the library eight men are waiting on a crudely hewn carpet of chequered black and white. Rivière is there, separate from the group, and he steps forward to make introduction of the strongest chess players in Paris. The men raise glasses of port with affected humility.

"Hello," says Paul. "I'm Paul Morphy."

"No earthly title is required," Rivière says, "as far as Caïssa is concerned. The challenge, acceptance and the stake are the only rules."

"A player's reputation must be built on his confirmed wins. Based on supportive evidence," adds Monsieur Seguin. "Witnesses and the like."

"Plus the chess columns," adds the sculptor Louis Lequesne.

"Of course," says Rivière.

Paul stands a few feet away in awkward shadow from the ceiling.

"A few tricksters slip through the gap," continues Lequesne. "But why impersonate a chess player? For the fame? Certainly not for the money." The men laugh.

"Indeed," says Rivière. "What would be the motivation?"

"Embarrassed exposure must follow," Bierwith offers, a large man with heavy spectacles. "Victory and defeat follow every chess game. Like a double-edged axe. The sword that separates the worthy from the fallen!"

The room goes quiet.

"But today is different," says the *maître d'*. "The match is friendly. You know of Paul Morphy's blindfold feats in New York. Well, now meet the man himself."

One by one, they step forward and greet Paul, who barely moves. Their congratulations for the First American Chess Congress are delivered out of welcome, but clearly in awe of the youth from New Orleans. Each Frenchman shakes his hand, looks him in the eye searching for the secret of his soul, and step aside. All find him graceful, if not faintly debonair in his mannered gentlemanly conduct. No one is shorter than Paul, and conscious of this fact he bows like a colonial servant, a little dazzled by their general sense of *largesse*. He admires the extravagant fabric in the cut of their suits, their flamboyant purple-and-white shoes— attractively irreligious for the end of summer—and their breast pockets dipped with yellow handkerchiefs. Feeling underdressed and troubled by their flattery, Paul is almost quivering.

Fortunately the delay is short-lived. The gentlemen adjourn to eight tables dotted haphazardly in alcoves and under window sills. With a nudge from Rivière the *maître d'* calls out numbers and after a little confusion the players swap tables, cigar trays, and settle down: "Baucher 6, Bierwith 2, Guibert 7, Lequesne 5, Morneman 1, Potier 3, Pret 4, and Seguin 8."

Paul is led to his separate miniature room by the Café's host. The blue baize billiard table momentarily in his way, Paul allows his fingertips to linger on the cloth, sensing its luxury and poise, and a shiver like pins-and-needles goes through his frame. He rolls a ball down the cloth, watches it ricochet in a jaw and disappear. He smiles, surprised. Gingerly he steps over the rope and is caught for a split second before achieving his apartheid from the community of players. No one has prepared a stiff drink for him on the other side. A single glass of water and a blindfold lie ominously beside his solo chessboard, strangely empty of its army of courtiers. Paul senses a practical joke, as though his opponents will leave the room when he announces the first move blindfolded. How long would he remain? Would anyone tell him?

Fortunately Edge appears, uncharacteristically late for which he offers no apology, but immediately works to settle Paul's nerves.

"Only a magician's trick," he says and claps covetously on Paul's shoulders.

"Mr Edge, I have only water for Dutch courage!" Paul whispers.

"'Tis better than French liquor," Fred says and instructs Paul that he needn't wear the blindfold so long as his back faces the library.

"I would rather be playing billiards," Paul says and pulls the blindfold over his face.

"Many a truth whispered in jest."

"Well, I cannot play chess forever. It's only a game after all."

A tad puzzled at such blasé comments, Edge retreats under the rope to a small writing table and *Encyclopaedia Britannica* open at the chess page. "Take your time Paul," he tells himself and pours a glass of brandy. "The stakes are all clean."

"No mention of the money please," Paul calls from his dimmed room. "I may be blind but I can hear you." Alone again on a raised dais, he resembles the boy of long ago. Telcide and Ernest seem more like memories. But he clearly remembers playing his beloved grandfather seated on a pile of papers.

Without more delay, Paul calls out "pawn to king four on all boards." He imagines the hands of eight players, each with his superstitious manner, making that first move so familiar and innocent, and consequently so loaded with opportunity for mannerism and theatrical display. One hand darts, another slides the pawn sluggishly and another raises it high and hurls it down like a bomb. Meanwhile time runs away without the sound of a single clock. Paul grows uncertain of his solitude until he gleans the next murmur, or sigh or slurp of brandy from the adjoining room. The French and American empires are far from this little room. And yet the sense of destiny is narrowed all the more into these few players, and this single arena, due to the private nature of the enterprise. Paul wonders if his match with Daniel Harrwitz, for all its public spectacle and brazen competitiveness, could ever be as memorable as sitting in this room blindfolded with only a glass of water and memories of Basin Street to occupy his mind.

Time passes as it would and does. Far from losing track of the moves, the pieces, the tables and the players, the library gains an increasing clarity for Paul. He has no idea of the origin of his illusory power. Neither the clairvoyance of Louis Paulsen nor the inspired dalliance of Charles H. Stanley can explain his crystalline visualization of the ever shifting sixty-four squares. Each one is a mirage and counterbalance to its neighbour, ever diffusing their power elsewhere. Deceiving pieces and players, ever reeling back upon their own possibilities, Paul harnesses something special in the silence of a purely imaginary chessboard. And one by one he calls unique moves as though delivering party tricks to a group of mesmerized children.

"All I can say for certain," he tells himself, "is that I can see the ceiling in my bedroom and the open window. The moon is shining over the French Quarter. Edward is outside sitting by the fountain. I close my eyes and a board spreads out above me, quite still, and the pieces are steady too. Only then do they completely disappear and I'm alone. *Maman* is playing the piano downstairs and *Papa* is there too, both watching…"

As he calls the moves, Paul develops a musical distraction. From memory he thumps a tune on the soft arms of the *fauteuil*, his fingers dancing rhythmically. The chess patterns multiply. Gradually the orchestra of the games, each musical duel, seeks the endgame, the final movement, the *denouement*. The last days of imaginary kings must arrive. One by one the boards reach a dangerous equilibrium, hovering with anxious energy, before descending the other side of a solitary and fateful journey. All is chamber music chess, subtle and intricate. Then suddenly *le jeu est fait*. Paul plays unconsciously, instinctively, and with his trademark style, releasing pieces from their confinement and as soon as possible willing them, under threat, until a winning pattern emerges.

He remembers the portrait of Philidor from the Sazerac Coffeehouse and draws inspiration from that daunting moment. He needs a patron who is more of a teacher than a manager, and François Philidor the chess playing musician is ideal. The French master cast a spell over the *Café de La Régence* a hundred years earlier, with astonishing blindfold exhibitions in Paris and London. Six opponents, though, was enough competition during the first age of chess. Like travelling in carriages at high speed, any greater mental velocity was considered harmful to the soul and brain.

"All he ever wanted was to write music," Paul says, realizing he is speaking. He can hear Edge's voice and a murmur from the *maître d'*. Moments later, all is calm. Paul does not raise his hand to indicate a break or any sign of trouble and the voices recede. "The tragedy of wasted talent," he whispers. "Except Philidor was a great musician. He was exceptional in every way."

Over in the library, after several hours without a break, the games are concluding. An opponent calls out "bravo, Monsieur Morphy," or leaves the room *incognito*, ruminating.

"The game with the four-knights-variation proves a rapid victory," Edge is saying.

"And the English opening," someone replies.

The games go on. And on! Without hope of ending, seven hours go by without Paul moving in his chair. Edge checks on him regularly—all is good. The excitement of stylish chess play, from endless skewers and forks to the Levenfish and the Najdorf variations, fly from the mind of the young Creole. One by one his opponents defer and the victories are claimed, all of them noted by the players themselves. Every move is a statistic to be corroborated with the chess journalists tomorrow, printed and lost and recovered from the cavernous newspaper vaults under old cities.

Drifting into the final hour, Paul seems to gain some advisors, some puzzlers over his health, and even a waiter who tops up his water jug. Not once in hours does he take a break, go to the bathroom, eat or stand up. Water is his only comfort and the illusion of chess somewhere on the ceiling of his childhood playroom.

The games begin to take their toll. One adviser, an octogenarian chess player, is first to congratulate Paul—as the music of the last game fades—and seemingly after a long supernatural spell, Paul returns to a room of silence. Literally at the eleventh hour, he collapses from his table, spilling water and ripping his precious coattails. The magnolia falls from his lapel, her home since Paul's last night in New Orleans. On his knees he moans some words, deemed incomprehensible, and is taken from the room supported by Edge and Rivière.

"I have been too long from home!" he cries, and rising from his *fauteuil*, staggers under the rope.

"The games are over, Paul. Everything is all right. You won six and drew two. You've made history!"

"Life will never be the same. Please, Clara."

"Clara?"

He waits for his father's hand but Alonzo does not appear.

"Where is Titi? Helena?"

"It's okay, Paul."

"*Papa* take me home."

The octognarian strokes Paul's hair and says: "He conquers without seeing."

"Stay back!" cries Rivière. "Can't you see he's not well!"

The chess players Thomas J. Bryan and Louis Lequesne are already celebrating the young man's daring feat, and plan to head out to the Palais Royal and drain the dregs of the night at the *Restaurant Foy*. One by one they clap him on the back. Setting up the billiard table, they smoke cigars and open a magnum of champagne which few have the strength to hold, let alone drink, until Edge raises the bottle and pours froth all over his waistcoat. They all jump back with delight. Paul lies slumped on the sofa, forgotten. The old man soothes him and whispers in his ear. Suddenly Paul retains consciousness and drifts to the window. He realizes he was thinking of Clara. What would it all mean to her? How could any of this make sense?

The men watch Paul, but do not disturb him for genuine fear of his collapse. They presume he'll be okay but none of them is a doctor. The following week, news of the incredible chess bout is released. Paul Morphy is famous as a chess player can be. In a gentleman's world of club dinners and gambling duels, his name is burnished with the force of a politician or a stage illusionist. A human no more, he is free to wield belief over a sea of disbelief! The game is his to lose.

Paul Charles Morphy, of New Orleans, Louisiana—a prescient moniker—appears in red letters in international newspapers. His name can be heard in the omnibuses on Broadway and in the lobbies of the theatres. His face is displayed on placards and posters in the hotels and barrooms of Europe all the way back to the city that care forgot!

For three days Paul has not left his room at Meurice's Hotel.

Edge enters on the fourth afternoon and immediately marches to the bed. "Lots of people know you, Paul," he says. "They could help because you're famous."

"Thank you, Fred."

"Good doctors are everywhere in Paris."

"Thank you," Paul says. "But I don't need their noses in here."

"A doctor's conscience," Edge pursues, "is all a matter of taste, as the philosopher wrote."

"I know, but I don't need someone poking around inside my head."

Having spoken, Paul collapses again and is feverish for four more days. When he wakes, like Byron to find himself famous, he is heralded as a master of social ceremonies and genius of the age. Society thirsts for him as a public speaker *extraordinaire*, a role to which Paul is less than suited. Instead, Edge declines Paul's messages on all occasions but quietly accepts a few himself.

"I hope my speaking is okay?" he checks with Paul.

"New Orleans is far away," the unsteady genius whispers like a child learning his first nursery rhyme, "far, far away."

Chapter Twenty-Four
1858
A Letter from America

Paul is sprawled in bed recuperating with the recently delivered mail. He has a letter from Clara. He cuts it open with the absinthe spoon and unfolds the yellow scented pages:

My champion!

LuLu White is the most accursed scoundrel. She's the one with the monocle I told you about. She put me in a crib! A single room with no light only a candle. Told me I was looking funny at her David. I swear I wasn't, Paul. Believe me! And now I want out. I want to come to Europe and be your magical assistant like at the circus. Can I? I have to get out of here. You were right! It's no place for a lady. Ha ha!

I'm trying to get in at a new place. It's a shame but I have to go somewhere. I know you'd always help me. Anyway here's the bit from The Mascot on the new place:

Gorgeous tapestries and *real* oil paintings, leopard skins, potted palms and curios, heavily-carved plush-coloured furniture and an all-round red-blooded Old World rocco atmosphere is what you find at the *Amsterdam Dance House* with Dan O'Neill. Come join us, temporary at first and permanent if you like it. Gold-embossed cards for your friends. Möet & Chandon 'White Seal' champagne for your first client, stripy stockings $6 a pair and free when you hit the house hundred.

We are back-o-town off famous 101 Gallatin Street, a nice quiet spot and an easy walk to Canal and all your Boston dress stores. We have deals on ball gowns at the finest official bordello and groggery shop in the upper Quarter.

Glass door *armoires*, damask sofa and French mirrors (with gilt frames) in every room. Plus after three months you'll have earned a sideboard with armchairs and tête-à-têtes to match. Bed hangings at even the mosquito bar are lace with a blooming basket of flowers by the bed every day. Sunset carpet of the finest velvet! Good money to go around!

We pay $100 a year for saloon bands with instruments, $200 for singing and $300 for a platform show. Come enjoy a night at the *Amsterdam Dance House*. Ask for Trudy Martin or Little Bobby or Jeffrey Tarango. I am your host Dan O'Neill. We now have Craig T. Miller as doorman, a celebrated hefty Big Boy Brawler who lost his arm last month and now wields an iron ball the size of a baseball. We'll be safe and you will too!

Paul, I tell myself 'listen to the voice of reason!' At least until you get back. I don't deserve what LuLu is putting me through and Violet can't leave and start again. She's happy anyway. But I must do something and this Amsterdam Dance House sounds like the place. What do you think?

Right now the city is also caught in a spell of yellow fever so it's better you're away. People have spots in the street and everyone looks yellow to me, 'jaundice-ed' as LuLu says and they're calling it Bronze John. Violet says it's like the big epidemics of the thirties that pushed the California gold rush!

I'm sorry this letter is so one-sided. What's happening in the chess? Did you write me? But how would I know? They keep the letters at the desk, unless it's from a client. Keep writing, though, I get them when I leave and then I'll rail at them. LuLu and David are away anyway 'cos a new place is being built, Kate Townsend's at No. 40. A shot of Raleigh Rye for everyone who walks through the door! Should I move there instead? Oh, I don't know what to do!

I miss you, Paul, and I remember your last visit well. I still want to know how the chess pieces move! Ha! No one here knows or plays or seems to care. If it ain't a card game it's a duel and horrid fighting all night. Backroom dancing, drinking and humping to hell, Paul, it's more than a girl can take sometimes. A cathouse one minute and the girls all smiles and sleepy eyes the next.

I wish you'd come back. I don't want to be a good-time girl no more. Ha! The other option is The Irish Channel, Corduroy Alley, that dirty hole behind Rousseau's cook shop but they say it's bad! Too many Murphys and they're hard. It's somewhere near the Soraparu Market but I don't want to risk even a visit. Do you know where it is?

The day you come back, Paul, is the day I leave and get some legitimate business. Maybe I could run a hat shop and be a what-they-call-em, a millina? Your friend Charles could do the accounts. Oh, everything's such a dumb dream. I might as well be dead. I want to be an opera singer. Not even the lead girl! If I can run my own singing business and give lessons I think I could be happy. My mother says it's never too late, but that's our Violet and look at her. But I love her and you Paul. Come back soon. Your mate-to-be, Clara

Paul lays the writing aside and closes his eyes. He somehow cannot connect her letter with the gentle Clara, the one he knows from Basin Street. How can she be the outcast from polite society? And the girl he met at a fountain all those years ago? Yet he knows she's the same girl. He knows he must save her from sliding into obscurity, abandonment and ill-health or she'll fall under the street and no one will pick her up.

"I will find you," he whispers in collusion with the mystery of his desire. Clara's weakness, he reasons, must be the source of his strength. "Go to sleep, now, my love, sleep." He is sure he cannot love the girl of his imagination without the other Clara, the one he doesn't want to imagine.

Chapter Twenty-Five
1858
Last Orders at the Café

The next morning two letters arrive at the *Hotel de Breteuil*, a further delay from Howard Staunton and a provocation from Daniel Harrwitz to finish the match. Edge brings them to Paul in the hotel garden with news he has also arranged a match with Herr Adolf Anderssen of Breslau, Germany.

"I am a little tired of chess," Paul says. He is dressed in a long blue coat against the wind and twirls a yellow flower through his fingers. "Paris is not for sitting inside playing stuffy games." Edge waits as Paul reads the letters. "Why can't it wait until Sunday?"

"*We* can wait," Edge says, "but Mr Harrwitz desires the satisfaction of the remaining games, in a private room."

"You mean alone?"

"Not quite, with *seconds*." Edge sits on a bench facing Paul across the gravel path. "But it will cause resentment among the backers. It changes the gambling." He hands Paul a glass of orange juice. "But that's no concern of yours."

"Harrwitz requested the private room?"

"Apparently," says Edge. "Plus Staunton says he'll play you at the end of the month. I assume he means this month?"

Paul sips his orange juice. "All is well then," he says and waits.

Edge is flustered for a second, folds the letters and stands. "How do you feel, sir?"

"Please don't call me sir…." Paul turns to look along the high wall beyond the Tulieres Gardens to Versailles. "You know where our hotel is located, Mr Edge? That is the palace. Right…there." He points.

"Like a prison," Edge says, a little lost. "So perhaps I'll see you later for dinner?" He begins to walk away. "I hope you'll remain indoors. At least until your chill has gone."

Paul offers a friendly expression. "I'm sorry, Fred. I was in another world. I didn't sleep at all last night." They shake hands. "Shall we choose a restaurant for the *soirée*?"

"*La Lumière Blue?*"

"Certainly. We are in Paris after all, Mr Edge."

"Indeed we are, Mr Morphy."

A day later the match at the *Café de La Régence* is reconvened on Daniel Harrwitz's terms. He sends a note in English: "Three o'clock. No more spectators and no more gambling. Come straight upstairs."

Paul and Edge arrive to find the room bare. They sit at the chess table, already prepared, and face each other.

"This room…"

"…is barely a room," Edge replies.

Nothing is there except the chess pieces and a huge velvet curtain concealing part of the wall. Light filters at the window. Some mothballs roll around the skirting boards. There are no paintings or furniture besides a few scattered chairs and some mysterious old boxes with bruised faces and crippled locks. Paul pushes them away from the table with a smile.

"This room reminds me of where I'd practice swordplay as a boy," Paul says. "Dr Rizzo's Academy."

"You mean a warehouse?"

"It had a long window and nothing but sawdust. This is in New Orleans, of course. At least the velvet curtain is new!"

They sit in silence and after ten minutes the opponents arrive. Edge and Harrwitz's second Julius Coquère face each other in mock imitation of a duel then disappear in the shadows. They engage each other in unfriendly murmurs and comments, paying more attention to the body language of their respective gentleman chess players.

Paul sits a measured distance from the table, low down, calm. Meanwhile Harrwitz rocks his chair left and right, an opening gambit, and drills his elbows deep in the table. Answering these stage antics Paul twists loose hair from his forehead. Just as quickly, Harrwitz responds by staring blackly at the pieces in deep concentration. Their eyes remain on the board.

Two hours later, the match is over. Music pulses from the *Café* under their feet, and the expectant voices of Harrwitz's backers cause the floorboards to shake. Every gambler along the Rue St. Honoré is singing and begging the *garçon* for an update on play. When the waiter arrives, Coquère sends him downstairs carrying new scores to the cheers and cries of the merry drinking mob below. By dusk Harrwitz knows the bout is lost. The conclusion is five wins to Paul, two to Harrwitz and one draw. The intent is to play to seven wins but Harrwitz resigns.

Paul and Edge remain upstairs while the German descends the stairs to face the music of his unhappy supporters. On the way out Harrwitz turns his puzzled face: "I am a lord, for so my deeds shall prove."

"Tamburlaine the Great, Part One," Edge replies. "I have been educated too, Mr Harrwitz." Paul says nothing.

"And shall I die and this unconquered?" Harrwitz adds ruefully and closes the door. Downstairs, his stakeholders are furious. The noise increases and Paul begins to doubt their safety.

"I think Harrwitz is in trouble."

"It is not your concern, Paul. We have to eat too, you know."

"Man does not live on bread alone, Mr Edge."

"No, nor fresh air."

Paul has to be persuaded to be victor and claim the two hundred and ninety francs. He intends to deposit the money with Monsieur Delannoy, the proprietor of the *Café de La Régence*, for the good of the community. As a response Edge moves pieces on the chessboard in quiet puzzlement. "I do not understand, Paul. You've won. You *can* be happy."

"What did I win? Harrwitz's shame?"

"I'm content. Take the money so we can go."

Paul waits on Delannoy who eventually ascends and lays the heavy bag of coins on the table. Paul requests the balance of his stakes be sent to Adolf Anderssen.

"It will subsidize his journey to Paris."

"Of course," Delannoy replies and disappears with the bag.

"Indeed," says Edge. "So much for getting rich."

An hour passes before they leave with sufficient coins to honour their appetites at *La Lumière Blue*. "I will see Lord Hay in the morning," Edge adds.

"He's happy so long as I'm winning," says Paul.

"You are winning," and Edge claps him on the back. "You should hold up well against Mr Anderssen. I was reading of his games with Kieseritzky in the London Tournament. An immortal game. He shows no concern for pawn formation or the delicacy of strategic defence. Similar to you, wouldn't you say?"

"I really don't know how I play."

"You have a touch of false modesty," Edge laughs. "They're calling Anderssen the inspired barbarian. He's a gentle man with an extremely aggressive style but spellbound by the beauty of combination. Since 1851 he's been pretty much the world champion. Staunton is just pretender to his crown."

"As am I."

"You are challenger, Paul, challenger."

"Spellbound by beautiful combinations?"

"Just as I said."

They leave the Café for the last time and stroll down the Rue St. Honoré. When they arrive at the *Hotel de Breteuil*, Paul discovers he has a package. They stand in the lobby while Edge uses a chess rook to tear it open. George H. Lovett has engraved a bronze medal for Paul, to Edge's delight.

"Spoils of war," Edge says and hangs the medal around the champion's neck. You are the king of Paris."

"Don't let the Emperor hear you."

"Oh, he's the pretender. Not exactly Napoleon Bonaparte is he? You are the real emperor!"

"King is fine," Paul replies, touching the bronze face and turning over the medal. "It has an inscription:

For Paul Charles Morphy. Who beats Harrwitz in chess playing and Staunton in courtesy. New Orleans must be proud."

"Lovett wants to marry you," says Edge. "It's his engagement ring."

"Oh."

Paul stares at his manager, puzzled, and argues George Lovett must keep the medal. "I cannot accept such an expensive gift outside a chess club. Lovett is free to donate it to the Divan. I believe that's his club."

"The one on the Strand? He must be staying somewhere in Paris."

"Take it," says Paul and hands over the medal, the relief noticeable on his face. "It's yours."

Upstairs at the *Breteuil* something strange happens. First Paul settles himself by the fire while Edge begins reading column extracts in the *Paris Gazette*.

"The chess hacks of the *Café* consider you *solide*." Edge lifts his feet on the table. "They admire your play in the French style, and if I can dare to translate, you *perceive chess like music, the melodies stretching along various lines*. Yours is *une science exacte*." He plucks a letter-writing feather from the table and twirls it through his fingers.

"You know," says Paul. "I no longer wish to play without giving odds."

"After you play Anderssen and Staunton of course."

"Of course," Paul says, warming his feet by the fire.

"It says here that Mr Harrwitz, *whatever the outcome of his match with Monsieur Morphy*—clearly they smell defeat—*will undertake eight blindfold sessions*."

The chambermaid knocks at the door and delivers a card. There's a pregnant pause, then a gallant man walks into the room.

"I am Prince Galitzin, I wish to see Paul Morphy!"

Edge teeters at the table and Paul stands near the fire. The open door projects hot fluttering ash in the air.

"I am he," is all Paul manages.

"It's not possible? You are too young," the intruder grins with a quiver of his moustache. "Allow me," and he whips off one glove and shakes Paul vigorously by the hand, still flapping dust particles. "I first heard your deeds on the frontiers of Siberia." He turns to Fred Edge as though realizing his presence for the first time. "I hope I'm not interrupting."

"Well..." Edge begins, "we were..."

"Good. I am here to offer, how can I say, a mighty invitation to Paul to visit my homeland. Not Siberia so much as the great City of The Arts founded by Peter the Great..."

"Petersburg?" offers Edge.

"The very one!" Galitzin cries. "I would like make invitation you visit the chess emporium in his majesty's Imperial Palace. Emperor Alexander II and his beautiful wife Marie welcome you." The Prince raises his hands, stretching the silver buckles of his red shirt, and grips his shiny brass belt. "They await you with enthusiasm!"

Paul is uncertain how to reply. He proffers thanks, looking between the strange arrival and Edge and back to the strange arrival. "This is an unexpected honour. St. Petersburg? Well..."

"Mr Morphy is tired after playing," Edge cuts in. "He usually takes a bath at this time."

Paul blushes.

"A bath?" says Galitzin.

"Yes," says Edge. "A bath. Chess is physically tiring."

Galitzin takes a step back and bows with a flourish, his sword trailing the carpet. "Paul, I've heard of your extraordinary deeds on the chessboard. I've read your chess essay published in Berlin's *Schachzeitung*. Ever since I've been wanting to meet you."

"I'm honoured," says Paul, puzzled but guessing D. W. Fiske must have written the essay.

"Perhaps you would like to leave your card," says Edge, a little embarrassed. "We usually leave cards." Suddenly he realizes he is talking to a nobleman of the Russian empire albeit from a disaffected corner of Nicholas's reign.

"A card is helpful," Galitzin says. "We leave messages the same way!" He snaps his fingers and the teenage girl who appeared to be a chambermaid is transformed into his personal *aide-de-camp*. After whispers in which the names Nicolai and Livia are exchanged, the girl scrawls on a piece of parchment, pressing on Galitzin's shoulder. The Prince unfurls the paper magnaminously into Paul's palm.

"This is our address in Paris. If you choose not to call before Sunday, his majesty must visit *you*!" Galitzin unexpectedly laughs and his audience feels compelled to respond, Edge smirking and Paul offering hiccups.

"I'm flattered," Paul says, feeling silly.

"I must depart," Galitzin replies. "The charms of decadent Paris await!" He clicks the golden spurs on his heels, twirls a semi-circle and marches his female consort from the room. The door closes and the prince is gone.

"He came all the way from Siberia," Edge says

"I'd be scared at the court of Nicholas and Marie," Paul replies.

"If only Russia had good chess players. Then it might be worth the journey."

The interlude is over: Edge writes a polite rejection letter and safeguards it in his top pocket, where it resembles a handkerchief. He notices other letters and sifts through them. Meanwhile Paul has gone to bed. Before his head sinks in the pillow, he is dreaming of the *Café de La Régence*. Suddenly he is making a snow-laden voyage into the foothills of Siberian permafrost. Memories of New Orleans, white queens and fountain girls trouble his mind until he wakes with a start.

"What is it now, Fred?"

Edge is quiet for a moment before he leans closer and Paul noticeably draws his knees up in the bed. Edge sighs and invisibly Paul curls his toes back. But he is mistaken. Edge merely brandishes a letter from Johann Löwenthal, concerning one of Paul's blindfold games from the *Café* billiard room.

"Should I bring a board and a light?"

"Now, Mr Edge?"

"Well, Mr Löwenthal feels a mistake was made in one of your blindfold games published in the *London Illustrated News*. We could set up the board."

"Tomorrow," says Paul. "We'll dine in the saloons of the *Pestel* restaurant. What do you say?"

Edge peers at him, uncertain to push his desire to foil Löwenthal's article, or let the young Creole go to sleep.

"Of course," he says and lets the matter drop, before adding, "but if I don't look out for your reputation, who will?"

"Definitely the *Pestel*," Paul says and sinks his head in the pillow. "French cuisine will give me the illusion of home."

"A good choice, Paul. Yes tomorrow."

"Where there's gumbo crab or fresh fish, Fred, we'll go there."

"You know what they say about the crab, Mr Morphy? Though it walks sideways the crab believes it goes forwards. Why?"

"Because it goes its *own* way."

"Very good, Mr Morphy," Edge says surprised.

"The crab is lost," Paul replies, closing his eyes. "Just tell it to go backwards."

They laugh and Edge puts his hand on Paul's forehead. The chess player is uncomfortable and Edge leaves soon after.

Chapter Twenty-Six
1858
An Audience with The Barber of Seville

Paul arrives at the Paris Opera House alone. He stands before the grand building after walking the Champs-Elysées in the fading afternoon light. He looks at the card he received from the Duke of Brunswick, black and gold with the words, "Come join us again soon for evening's entertainment and conversation."

As it starts to rain, Paul finds himself drawn to the Place de l'Opéra where he sits momentarily under the fountain of Napoleon I. It reminds him of the statue of Andrew Jackson in New Orleans. He looks to the sky through the drawn sword of the former French Emperor, through the flaring of his horse's nostrils, his austere trilby hat, to his one hand holding down silver hair flying in the cold hard air. Only one eye is visible against the dark storm clouds. Paul can hear the faint rise and fall of music from the Opera House, the long mournful tremolo of the strings, the occasional hopeful bravado of a brass instrument. Meanwhile the wail of the operetta's soprano defies the weather, the city and everything the audience can throw at her.

No one is around as Paul enters the opera's side-entrance. The doorman takes his coat and deeper inside, his heart swells as he approaches the opulent staircase, neo-baroque and lined with multicoloured marble. From the hall he heads to the first gallery, asking directions to the upstairs bar. En route he discovers a treasure trove of classical and modern busts, all paying homage to Greek and Roman philosophers and European musical geniuses of the day. The staircase is so steep he rests half way, laying his hand on boyish Mozart's miniature head. The composer's hair is pulled from his forehead and his gentle beguiling smile is seemingly reserved for Paul alone.

Next in line are the dynasties of the current rulers of France, ending in current Emperor Napoleon III as a life-sized statue in full military regalia. Paul touches Napoleon's beard. Gold tassels dance on his shoulders, while his sword makes a parallel with his moustache so thin and sharp he could rest a glass of wine there. Paul trails his fingers over Napoleon's breast-buttoned suit. All is solid stone. He shivers at the cold touch and is looking in the Emperor's eyes when a voice whispers in his ear. He turns to witness a red carpet and a line of gilded mirrors stretching to the opera arena.

"*Bonsoir* Monsieur Morphy, I hope you don't mind my speaking French."

"Surely not, madam," he replies trembling.

The Duchess of Trémoille extends her fingers. "Did you come alone?"

"Yes, I was hoping the Duke of Brunswick was attending the opera and I was walking nearby…"

"Karl is here somewhere, I'm sure. In his box no doubt. Do you want to see him?"

"Yes, we attended *Norma* a week ago…"

"Ah, the Druid-opera! Just like me," she smiles. The Duchess of Trémoille, a regal noblewoman defying age with overwrought white dresses and yellow maquillage, takes a step closer to Paul. Her eyes flicker under the candle chandelier, framing her triple neck in the mirror. She reaches up to Paul and brushes his cheek and he half laughs, nervous, as her fingernail curls a loop of hair from his mouth.

"You should not hide your face," she says. "You're a young man." Her hand rests over his lips. "I'm no longer a married woman."

Paul's feet grow hot and cold in small flushes. The Duchess throws her head back and laughs. "I am teasing you. You know, I can see the melancholy of my own face in your eyes. That's all."

"I'm sorry."

"No, don't be sorry. You are beautiful. Come with me. Let's play a quick bout of your favourite game."

Before he can politely excuse himself, Paul finds himself in a small stuffy room adjoining the bar. Across one wall is a fresco of a giant capturing a salmon from a river. He feels queasy on entering the room. The idea of another chessboard is something he cannot bear without a drink. Fortunately absinthe is on hand. Together they drink from special thimbles produced from the Duchess's boson. They settle down, the waiter bringing two chasers—olive margaritas strong enough to suck their teeth back— while the Duchess pushes the pieces around in a fruitless impersonation of play.

"You're not trying," she gleefully declares after her first victory. "Don't drink too much. I want your best game."

"My best game?"

"I'm no amateur," she grins and sucks the olive from the glass, tipping her tongue back like a fruit fly.

Paul winces. "No amateur?" he repeats under his breath. "Wouldn't that be a bad moniker to live by?" His hand hovers over the white queen and he looks up at the frowning duchess, emeralds and pearls twisting together at her neck.

"Of course," she says. "An amateur is a poor excuse for a professional, no? A man who can't love his profession is wasting his time, don't you think?"

"That's undoubtedly true," says Paul. "The nation is built on the backs of soldiers, after all, and the French Emperor is a great leader!"

The Duchess smirks and folds her arms in delight. "There! I think I have you!"

"You really do," says Paul and feigns the escape of his rook in order to encourage her planned entrapment. As soon as he moves she veritably squeals with delight, her bosom a glittering parade of flashing jewels vying for the honour of her chest. Meanwhile her fingers nimbly exterminate Paul's king. The victory of course induces another game and the Duchess plays far better in the second. Paul now has to convince her that the black pieces can turn genuinely in her favour. Even though she wins, she is not completely fooled by his performance.

"Thank you Paul, you may go now." She touches his wrist. "I am a little suspicious of your concentration in that game. No matter. You respect a woman's touch and that's what we're playing for, isn't it?"

At this point, Paul feels a rush of blood to the head but manages to excuse himself as politely as possible. He pauses at the oak door long enough to see a reflection of the leaping salmon fresco, the fish suspended in its freedom. Paul hurries from the room spilling his drink and tripping over his own shoes.

In the hall he encounters famous baritone Grazianio, who "will play chess with Paul if he will sing a duet with him?" The big man grips his shoulder with passion.

"I'm flattered but I would like to see the opera now."

"After the performance, Mr Morphy," Grazianio replies. "I am singing first."

"I didn't realize you were performing."

"Shall we say at nine?"

"Oh," says Paul and now the Duchess is at his shoulder. A secretive smile is exchanged between the older couple: clearly Paul is out of his league. Together they witness the chess player squeeze a gap in their obsequious double act and slip away down the hall, scurrying somewhat.

"He walks like a girl."

"I like him," the Duchess replies, "but he is here for Karl, not us. "I love his innocence. Look at him. He is another lazy Creole like myself."

"You are *more* than lazy," Grazianio replies and is ignored.

"Paul Morphy is one of the *immortelles*. A gentleman with a talent. Just don't suggest he's a professional. He takes offence at that."

"It's not his company but his gamesmanship I'm after. How good can he really be?"

"Well, I just beat him," the Duchess replies and crosses to the bar in search of an olive margarita. She tells the barman "I want something to match my emeralds." But when she returns Grazianio is gone.

The sound of the opening overture is audible from the chamber room.

Inside the Duke Karl of Brunswick introduces Paul to Count Isouard. They shake hands, the Frenchman holding on a little long.

"Delighted," says the Count. "I've heard a lot about you, Mr Morphy. Karl tells me of your love for the opera." He pauses. "Do you know my friend is heir to the Duchy of Brunswick?"

"Prince regent and heir," the Duke says. "It's just a joke."

Paul smiles at the Count and nods in appreciation. "I knew he was close to the ruling princes. And yes, the opera means a lot to me. *The Barber of Seville* is a wonderful…"

Amused by his enthusiasm, the two Frenchmen stare at Paul. The Duke is small and amiable, his gold-brocaded uniform and frazzled hair suggesting a fake connoisseur of the arts. The Count is tall and wiry in the Fred Edge mould, though wholly unlike his counterpart. His suit is canary yellow and he wears a peacock feather behind his ear. "I am bohemian in the extreme," the Count explains, running his fingers over his bald head.

"Please follow me," the Duke offers, "to my private booth. It appears the show is starting." At this point he remembers the little girl clinging to his knee and twirls her into Paul's vision. "Oh and before I forget this is my niece, Chalmette."

"A place near your home city, I believe?" says Isouard.

"Quite so," replies Paul and bends on one knee and smiles. Instantly Chalmette disappears behind her uncle's leg where she grins, curtsies and vanishes again. Her swish of golden curls stirs a long-ago memory and he thinks naturally of Clara. He senses Chalmette's quiet bewilderment, gracing the opera with this group of flamboyant men. "A pleasure to meet you, young lady."

Standing up, Paul discovers Isouard looking at him strangely. But no more words are exchanged and they move deeper into the house. A circular walkway reveals a vast dome overhead and a drop to the orchestra pit far below. Permitting fifty private viewing alcoves, the stage is offset by extraordinary blue marble obelisks. Paul is taken aback. All around, a golden firmament is bound by a giant damask curtain, interwoven with giant butterflies of the French Tricolour. Before they arrive at the Duke's booth, Paul glances to the ceiling's turreted white dome. Zeus is firing his thunderbolts down from the heavens, nymphs and wild animals fleeing in alarm at his majesty and might.

"A strange mural for a musical setting," Isouard says and nudges Paul on the shoulder. "Says a lot about the French empire, wouldn't you say?" Paul regards the Count, trying to gauge his self-amusement for a face as smooth as his head. "I see the same power in music," Isouard continues, "as the power of Zeus. He was god of gods, after all."

"Quite so," the Duke replies, climbing into the show-box. He takes Chalmette under the arms and sweeps her over the lace balcony of their *loge grilée*. He throws his arms up in celebration. "You know this opera house has seventeen levels—but the magic is seven of them are underground."

"The beauty and the mystique," says Isouard.

"Just look around," the Duke says. "This is an emperor's playground with grand staircases, mirrors and balconies..."

"Proscenium boxes in a horseshoe!" Isouard takes up. "The gallery is so high, you can't even see the *groundlings*. A river of seats!"

"The whole place is a labyrinth," says the Duke. "But under the opera house there's an actual river with cellars and fountains and watery chandeliers. There's even a ghost of the architect Charles Garnier."

"I know nothing of a ghost," Isouard says. "And there's no river. Only a lake! You can see her on the seventh underground floor. She ebbs like the Seine. A natural city lake!"

Finally Paul says: "You know, to the passer-by, the building looks like an old railway station."

"And inside," Isouard adds, "it resembles the lounge of a Turkish bath! But what is its style? It's not Greek or Louis XVI."

"No, those styles have had their day," the Duke says. "This style is the great Napoleon III!"

"And no one's complaining," says Paul.

They stare at him slightly offended. Meanwhile the wide-eyed Chalmette, dizzy with rumours of ghosts and underground lakes, starts to giggle. Instinctively she takes Paul's hand. He squeezes and returns Chalmette to her uncle where she perches suggestively on his legs. The Duke bumps her up and down then tells her to play in the corner with her doll.

Tight for room, all four patrons now wait for the opera, looking down at the delightful amphitheatre. Already half the seats are filled with ladies in ball gowns, delicate fans stroking their cheeks, and serious-looking gentleman with their hair pinned back. A procession of Paris's fine aristocrats and court pretenders rolls ceaselessly below their box as the Duke and the Count squeeze around a chess table Paul feared but somehow expected. Both his opponents already seated, Paul is left stooped under the handrail, his back to the stage. Meanwhile Isouard pours champagne as though all is perfect comfort. As per the New Orleans French Opera House, the orchestra bows at the shimmer of a symbol and the Duke is on his feet clapping. He takes the opportunity to call to the full auditorium: "the presence of Paul Morphy is here, chess genius from America and new resident of the *Café de La Régence*."

Before Paul can correct the Duke, hundreds of curious faces turn, mixing envy with light applause, mostly frowning. Neither group can discern Paul's head amid the rows of bodies since he's facing backwards.

"I was unaware of the invitation to make me resident of the *Café*."

"It's just a point of reference they recognize," the Duke replies. "No harm done." Two young women in the row below persist in staring at the celebrity, until with a wave of his glove, the Duke dismisses them. Paul sits, quietly wondering.

Il barbiere di Siviglia now begins with the gentle *mezzo-soprano* voice of Rosina, the pretty young ward of Dr Bartolo. From the moment she sings Paul recognizes the same tone of his mother's voice, though far more polished than wavering. Nevertheless he listens and hears the soft yearning of Telcide's breath through Rosina. He no longer hears Rosina on the stage, but disappears inside his memories of long mornings when music would fill the house on Chartres Street. Afternoons, walking home on Royal Street after school he would hear her sing, even and sweet, before her voice would strain in disappointment. She would watch him come home from the window, her singing over with his arrival.

"I'm sorry you can't see," the Count says, straining to see over Paul's head. "If you set up the pieces, though, I'll describe the scene on stage."

Paul obliges and lays out the chess game.

"This is my new private box," the Duke says, "but it's not satisfactory. The next one I request will be so close to the stage, you can kiss the *prima donna*." He laughs and Count Isoaurd joins him in revelry; they calm each other with a mutual slap on the back. Paul blushes at the high jinks, feeling even more uncomfortable. He is preoccupied with the chess pieces and blind to the crowd. Meanwhile his dreamy vision of Rosina becomes a memory of Clara in her room, half dressed, waiting on LuLu White. He remembers her desire to sing opera, but she was a child the last time he heard her voice. When the chessboard is ready Paul waits, closes his eyes and hears Rosina singing from Clara's body. The broken notes especially remind him of her. Even checking and mustering concentration, he creates her face over and over. Silently, sweetly he follows Clara's body and voice, her trembling words, her gestures as she moves across the imaginary stage.

A moment later Chalmette is troubling Paul's shoe. She is trying to undo the fashionable blue buckles he's adopted with a trace of the self-conscious *de la mode* of the French capital. While she struggles, Paul feels an overwhelming sense of the women in his life fusing together. Suddenly the voice of Telcide, the face of Clara and the spirit of Rosina rise in his chest. At the same time he visualizes the painting of Caïssa high on the ceiling of the *Café de La Régence*. The goddess is there alone. Judging by her golden chessboard, she only bestows her love on the silent black and white chess pieces, those adorning her throne. All is a game of mental wit and energy with women, Paul thinks, exactly those skills it would take to woo a Caïssa.

"I always keep a chess set in my private booth," the Duke is saying, "and you've already seen *Il barbiere di Siviglia*. So I hope you don't mind?"

"I'm honoured to be here," Paul says and delivers a foolish smile, unsure how much aristocratic patronage he can handle. Feeling trapped he suggests they begin the game and is surprised when he learns the draw.

"Count Isouard and I will play as a team," the Duke says. "We feel it's better for our honour to combine our skills. You understand? It makes an all-round challenging game."

"We could play Pawn advantage or Pawn and Move?" Paul suggests. "That's the usual…"

"We *are* playing the advantage," Isouard laughs, "of player and move."

The triangular game, one of the fastest and most skilful games ever played, begins.

"You know, Paul, you will have to come visit my duchy at Wolfenbüttel," the Duke says. "We can play the same way. I'm enjoying myself so much I can barely consider *not* combining opera and chess in such fine circumstances in the future. I'll voice the notion at court! Everyone should watch the opera with a chessboard at hand!"

"Come on Karl, let's play," Isouard says, "or the barber himself will be singing. You don't want to miss the gentle knives at his throat!"

"No, my dear Isouard, I do not."

They laugh and the chess progresses. The two allies engineer their moves conferring loudly, while in the booth below a Madame Penco, who once played the Druid priestess in the opera *Norma*, is staring at Karl. No doubt inspired by the opera's Druids 'chanting fire and bloodshed against the Roman host,' she taps on their box with her cane.

"Can you be quiet? We cannot hear ourselves think!" The hidden chess pieces rattle and the Count politely remonstrates with her. A couple of pieces, knight and queen, drop on the bewildered audience below.

"A ridiculous game!" Madame Penco says.

"Well you should take up a silent game," Isouard replies, flicking the top of his head contemptuously. "Like chess. We don't need a sword, *madame*, swung over our chessboard!"

"I care not," Madame Penco replies. "We suffer the opera for *écarté* only. We're not about to suffer *l'échec* for you!"

Spying the fact that Madame Penco has only female friends—so his chances of a duel are limited—Count Isouard stands. "Do you know who this is?" he opens with, waving his arms at the general disturbance. "This is Count Morphy of Baton Rouge. He is a Creole king. I dare all of you to disagree! He is an angel called to the highest circle of this theater, do you hear? Higher than the very roof. I will not have him spoken to in that way!" The moment lingers. Then Isouard and Madame Penco calm down with exaggerated sighs and mutual disgust. Madame Penco is shaking a little. The game of *écarté* presumably recommences. Simultaneously the chess pieces are repositioned. Buttons improvise for the two missing pieces and the Duke restarts the bout with the same opening move.

As they confer, Paul listens to the opera from his crouched spot—from the music alone he can picture the action on stage. Doctor Bartolo, Rosina's guardian, is being shaved by Figaro as a ruse, so he'll be out when Rosina's lover comes to court her. Figaro now sings of the joys of being a barber in a great city. The scene remains Paul's favourite from childhood and he begins to mouth the words and drum the happy vocal on the edge of the chessboard. Yet in current circumstances the words don't fall merrily from his lips. All he feels is Figaro's razorblade, flicking and cutting deep into the frothing lather of Doctor Bartolo's beard. Paul shudders horrendously at the fountain of blood projecting in his mind. At the same moment, the aristocratic duo make their move. The game passes to Paul who stares confused at the board.

Filling the chamber, Figaro sings with holy joy about the work of clipping his clients, the old and young of Seville. He is the happiest man alive! But for Paul, Figaro may as well be Sweeney Todd. In his cramped spot, the music now chills the American, stirring memories of the swordplay of his youth and the fights with his brother Edward. With each cut of the music, he re-imagines the freak slash of a Panama hat to Alonzo's eye. *Fortis et hospitalis!* Hands shaking, Paul envisions a thousand cuts, death-in-chess, while the blood from Bartolo's throat overpowers his brain and he can no longer move or speak. Figaro becomes a soul balanced on a circle of Dante's hell.

"I cannot die," he whispers. "I cannot die or fall down a level…"

Presto il biglietto….
Tutti mi chiedono, tutti mi vogliono;
Qua la parruca, presto la barba,
Presto il biglietto, ehi!
Figaro! Figaro! Figaro!, ecc.

Ahime, che furia!

Ahime, che folla!
Uno alla volta, per carità!
Figaro! Son qua.
Ehi, Figaro! Son qua.
Figaro qua, Figaro là,
Figaro su, Figaro giù,
Pronto prontissimo son come il fulmine:
sono il factotum della citta.

Ah, bravo Figaro! Bravo, bravissimo;
fortunatissimo, fortunatissimo,
fortunatissimo per verità!
a te fortuna non mancherà.

Paul wakes from his reverie. The stage remains empty while the music conveys a thunder storm. He makes his chess moves rapidly and waits for his opponents who deliberate and continue to argue. The storm on stage rages in the young Creole's mind. The music carries him to a new pitch of concentration. Traceable only through his fingers, he moves his toy-like army along the magical lines and flanks of his mind. Then he makes a stunning move. *The lover and Figaro climb up a ladder to the balcony and enter through a window.* Isouard and the Duke reply with a pawn, challenging Paul's knight, and together they discover a skewer. Paul brings out his rook to counter and risks losing it. Naturally the twins take. *Figaro and the lover climb into the house through Rosina's balcony. She confronts them both with their perfidy.* A pawn is gone! The bishop is taken! Paul draws his chessmen into a net and advances through the open file. *Wind and lightning fly! The lover reveals he and Lindoro are the same person and Rosina joyously agrees to marry them both.* Paul covers his ears and drowns out the stage, the promise of love reunited. He digs deep into his brain for the right move, the tease, the glimmer of hope feigned to his opponents that will seal their fate. *The music teacher, Basilio, arrives with the notary but his objections to the marriage are quickly silenced with a bribe.* The audience sighs! Paul offers his queen and risks everything. *Dr Bartolo returns with the police but it is too late. Rosina and Count Almaviva have signed the eternal marriage contract!* The Duke is appeased by Paul's move and standing with applause for the delightful couple, Count Isouard takes the queen! All is over!

"Checkmate," says Chalmette and smiles from her corner and takes Paul's hand.

Isouard is stunned and falls back in his seat. "No, it can't be!"

The Duke laughs out with dark glee. He picks up his king and hurls him in the audience. "A pawn, a pawn," he cries, "my dukedom for a pawn!"

"You've lost!" Isouard says, disbelieving.

"Checkmate," Chalmette repeats giggling.

"Tell me about your genius," the Duke says crouching before Paul. "What is it? Can you describe it? Is it the ability to have imagination?"

"Keep asking questions. You might scrape a little stardust off his shoulders," Isouard says. "Just conceive positions and bring them about."

"Be quiet, Monsieur," the Duke says. "I'm being serious."

"I really don't know," says Paul, "how to explain the patterns."

"Aha, the Napoleon of chess," Isouard dares. "A master strategist with not a single word to say."

"I go for the direct victory," says Paul. "There's no other method."

The Duke narrows his eyes, uncertain of Paul. "The most direct victory? That's it?"

"I just play pieces in combination and never fix one attack. The game shapes itself."

"So you don't have a plan?"

"I wouldn't say that, exactly."

"You are an enigma, Mr Morphy," the Duke laughs. "I despair."

"Oh, don't say that," the Count smiles. "Only a genius despairs of his talent. Wouldn't you say?"

Paul is quiet. "I don't know. I don't plan on despairing."

Curiously, the other men laugh. They clap Paul on the shoulders and help him to his feet.

"Come on," says the Duke. "Let's go for a whisky. I believe there are a couple of people looking for you, Paul. A Duchess of Trémoille and Baritone Grazianio. Plus a man who works in my stables who's dying to play you at chess."

"Delightful," says Count Isouard and leads the way. The French teammates forget Chalmette, so Paul lifts her out of the opera box.

"I knew a little girl like you once," Paul tells her. "A long time ago in a fairyland called New Orleans."

"Tell me, Monsieur."

"I will, but forgive me my memory, it was a long time ago."

Chapter Twenty-Seven
1858
The Perfect Woman

The valet brings Paul a letter to accompany his breakfast and morning headache, and cuts the envelope with a knife, making him shiver. Paul recognizes the scent of Telcide's flowers on the envelope and the careful looping of her handwriting.

> My dear Paul,
>
> I trust you are doing well in the fine cities of Europe, seeing wonderful sights in London and our thankful motherland. London is a place I dream about often. And how are you finding Paris? I hope you are keeping to your promises about pursuing chess *sans fortune*. By which I mean play for honor not the loss of our name. Consider that gambling often leads to the tarnishing of a worthy Creole family.
>
> So it seems the whole world has gone mad! Your grandfather is convinced a war is on it way and sharpens the point of his bayonet daily and twice at weekends, if I can bear

to joke. The men here are already practicing duels. We cannot allow war to overtake New Orleans. So I hope the news in more favourable overseas? Have you heard anything about how the British might support the South?

Anyway, I'm writing with news of Léona Queyrouze. You remember the delightful young lady we met in Jackson Square? Well, last week two of her musical expositions *Victory March* and the *Fantaise Indienne*, were performed for the World Cotton Centennial by the 8th Calvary of the Mexican Army and directed by Captain Encarnación Payen. I thought you'd be interested. I don't see Léona able to write a full opera or operetta. But the performances were impressive, especially for someone as musically-minded as me. If I can be so bold, I believe she would make a good match. Her brother recently became the Southern Fencing Champion. He beat Edward in the semi-finals down on the shores of Lake Pontchartrain. It was quite an event with outdoor seating-and-eating. But I think Edward was pleased to see Daniel win the whole tournament. Funny how you respect your rival so long as he goes on to defeat everyone else. Are you finding the same thing in Europe?

So yes, I'm writing to caution you and to say 'hurry home.' Léona returned from studying in the Netherlands where it's rumoured she met a Times Democrat reporter named Lafcadio Hearn. But their romance is not certain, Paul, if you would make some commitment in her direction soon, everything could be different for us all. She has published some French poems you may want to read in *L'Abeille de la Nouvelle Orléans* under pen-name Constant Beauvais. I'm told she is accomplished academically too with an Étude sur Racine published in *Les Comptes-Rendus de l'Athénée Louisianais* more than once! And last night I heard her give a public reading of some poems for the Athénée Louisianais at the Grunewald

Hall on Baronne Street. She really is a lovely girl, so gentle and quiet-looking, and so dedicated to the world of print! She is quite the goddess of literature—who is that?—in human form! It seems Léona also publishes poems under the names Salamandra (Greek for Fire-Lizard, I looked it up) and Adamas (Greek for Unconquerable) in English for the *Times-Democrat* and in Spanish for *El Moro de Paz!* How could you fail? She knows all three languages! I think she's learning Italian too and clearly has a classical education. Oh I forgot *El Buscapie* in Puerto Rico which is now sold in New Orleans. Ernest told me about that one. Apparently he went to the islands with your grandfather and saw the article but that's another story as they say.

Anyway, my dear, I just had to write. She is the perfect woman! I've no doubt she'd love you and stop all this silly chess obsession!

Your maman,
Telcide Le Carpentier Morphy

P.S. Among her better received poems at the club were *Atlas, Magdalena, Samson* and *Ce qu'ont dit les montagnes*.
P.P.S. Something strange occurred on Monday. A girl came looking for you in rags, a dark-skinned girl but not one of the servants. She was terribly poor-looking. I can only think she had the wrong address. Do you know a Clara Young?

A small additional note on Helena's private notepaper falls from the envelope.

Dearest brother,
How are you? Please come home soon, Paul. The family is falling apart. No one talks now. We all miss you so much. Please.
All my love, Helena.

There is a second note:

Dearest brother,
I am writing this at the post office. I'm sending you
some money. Don't tell maman or Ernest. It will be
concealed in the next envelope I send. Grandpapi
showed me how. Just warm the edges a little and peel.
The money will help with your journeys. Will you be
home for Christmas?
Always, Helena.
P.S. Good luck with the chess games.

Paul wakes sweating. Dark light and bright shadows juggle images from his childhood across the ceiling. But mostly deformed creatures of the chessboard torment him, old kings and black-hooded bishops. Suddenly he is swimming in a drowning street. Water, water everywhere, nor any drop to drink. Is he awake or asleep?

A sneering pawn rides a horse past his face and Paul screams. Then a scurrying rook, legs backwards and shaped like a grasshopper, walks towards his bed. Clip, clop goes the castle with manic energy, eyes flashing and chequered like the squares of a chessboard gone mad.

Paul curls into his bed whispering "I have a chess fever. A temperature, that's all, just a fever...." He passes out before the sweat breaks.

Chapter Twenty-Eight
1858
The Professor and the Boy Wonder

O ver the next three days Paul is feverish after napping near a window and taking a cold bath. The hotel doctor diagnosess intestinal flu and no one discredits him, so Paul is leeched for two pints of blood; no one knows where the blood goes. He takes three days to regain a modicum of strength, sipping soup until he can sit up. Fred Edge continues to bring him newspapers, letters and his slippers for the occasional shuffle about the room. Day and night become perpetual twilight as Paul drifts in and out of delirium and nausea, exchanging sleep for dreams and his waking hours for fitful sleep. On the sixth day, Professor Adolf Anderssen arrives at the *Breteuil* for the arranged chess bout, due to begin at midday. Paul is heaped under the bed sheets, glassy-eyed and faint. Nevertheless he rises, seizes a pawn grimly and offers a choice of hands to Anderssen. He reveals the white pawn: the German's choice is correct.

Spectators line the walls plus Paul's *second* Jules Arnous de Rivière, Anderssen's *second* Hubert Longfellow, and a waiter to operate the telegraph machine to replay the moves to Anderssen's home town of Breslau, Germany. The four men blend together in dark suits and starched white shirts, a dab of colour on the waiter's folded napkin and a silver watch chain glistening on Longfellow's waistcoat. Holding a single breath, they appear poised to receive chess inspiration like injections for inducing a strange dream. Meanwhile the contest is reaffirmed as the first to seven games. Edge and Arnous pass the cigars while Paul retreats to the bathroom to mop his brow. Longfellow waves his hand at the cigar smoke with half serious contempt, whether to benefit Paul's condition or for Anderssen's own sake, it is hard to say. Longfellow stares from No. 1 Rue de Dauphin, over the Tulieres Gardens of the Louvre, and back into the street. Then he draws the curtains to block out the dusty haze of Paris's sunshine.

The match is the greatest to date. Anderssen is introduced as winner of the first *world* chess contest, the International Tournament of 1851 in London. As Longfellow concludes magnanimously, Edge feels inclined to present Paul as "the champion of the Americas currently vying for Europe" and the next world champion. The players merely shake hands and smile. Paul apologizes for his health and Anderssen offers condolences. Thus they take their seats in the small room, bringing old challenges and New Worlds together.

Unlike the glory of the matches against Paulsen, Stanley, Löwenthal or Harrwitz, there is something decidedly comic about this occasion. Most of all, Anderssen resembles the placid and humorous university teacher he actually is, with a bald head, slight stoop and inclination towards friendly solicitude. He jokes that Paul will position him looking into the sun, as Ruy López advised, if it "weren't for Longfellow handling the drapes." Anderssen's expression is so warm that Paul says it was only "accidental intent;" they laugh and for once Paul feels his gentlemanly pride is safe. The waiter constantly appears and disappears, as though attached to an invisible pulley, and murmuring apologies he returns with sherry and crackers. The men consume all except for Paul who makes do with a *chai* tea and *petit fours*. Seemingly ill-prepared for a day of chess, Anderssen eats with barely concealed delight, persuaded by Longfellow not to accept the sherry despite fear of incivility. The German nods sagely at this wise counsel while concluding the first game. He wins handsomely, albeit in seventy-two moves, against Paul's losing Evan's Gambit.

"If you win," Anderssen says enigmatically, his egg-head leaning to the table, "nothing will stand between you and Caïssa's sun."

"If I win," Paul replies.

Longfellow and Rivière set up the pieces. The first player to seven victories already seems a long road. And increasingly the games become farcical as the day wares on. Given Paul's illness and Anderssen's famous disdain for practice, both begin game two casually. Soon the intoxicating slow rhythms of the game induce new levels of puzzle and concentration. The experience of so many bouts of competitive play kicks in. But as the positions on the board intensify, the conversations grow calmer. Diffusing the tension in play, each man senses a kindred spirit in this strange world of toy battles.

"If it weren't for grown men at our elbows," Anderssen says, "we could play as children."

"Chess *is* for children," Paul adds, "despite what people say. It is a game of wit and alarm but seeking the praise of adults."

Anderssen looks up smiling. "You were a child prodigy?"

"They made me do it," Paul says.

"You're joking."

"Well, my father would play every Sunday. I learned in a playroom. But chess was like a hobby. My family would play and sometimes my mother would stop us…"

"Yes…and…"

"Then we would play outside…" While Paul speaks, clearly still under the weather, his appearance borders on the ridiculous. He hunches over the board, red-faced and trembling, but not unwell to the point of groaning or requiring his bed. Periodically he says "my head is relatively clear," to the dismay of his advisors who prefer limited comments on his fit state of play. Due to the lack of crowds and lack of gambling, Paul again demands no money stakes. Thus they play for honour and their managers and *seconds*, protectors of their morals and tactics, become merely spectators and admirers of majestic patterns forming and dissolving on the chessboard.

"You played Herr Harrwitz recently," Anderssen inquires, "and you were victorious?"

"Yes," says Paul, "though it was a struggle."

"Well, I thought you'd be interested in Harrwitz's challenge for your blindfold record, here in Paris. He attempted it last week."

"Oh."

"Indeed. He aimed for ten simultaneous tables and completed the feat, and in less time. But the journalists don't believe him and that's all that counts."

"But the display took place?"

"Yes, it took place. But many of the players left pieces *en prise*," Anderssen says conspiratorially, "as though designedly." Foldig his hands behind his head, he looks over at the other men. "I don't say Mr Harrwitz cheats. But let's say, he writes a chess column in *Le Monde Illustré* and doesn't permit a single one of his blindfold games to be made public."

"Well, that's his business," Paul says. "I don't play blindfold games for any sort of glory. They're entertainments. They're a trick to encourage interest in the kingly game for people who find chess tiresome."

"And long may you perform them," Anderssen says. "I hope you'll publish the games too. But you're in a minority if you only see the moves as conjuring tricks. They're quite real."

"I have no desire for publication," Paul says politely. "I leave the publishing rights to Mr Harrwitz and Mr Staunton and my friends in America with newspaper connections. Playing is more rewarding than reading about games, wouldn't you say?"

Anderssen smiles. "So you can't learn from a chess book? Well, perhaps. But clearly chess is changing, and you are helping Paul. We need to know openings or gambits or chess will remain in the dark ages."

"I am only a player," Paul replies and moves a piece to demonstrate.

An hour passes before Anderssen plays the Ruy López and secures a draw. The third game is rapid and Paul wins with the English Opening again. Disheartened at being two behind, Anderssen somewhat crumbles. Another draw settles play at six games to Paul, one to Anderssen and two draws. They break for lunch and Anderssen walks around the block. Meanwhile Paul resists the temptation to take to his bed and with encouragement from Edge, they sit at the window awaiting the return of the German professor.

By twilight Anderssen has pulled one game back, a proud victory. Yet Paul's adoption of the French defence in the eleventh game secures the match before the sun goes down. Everyone shakes hands. Anderssen, more than any previous opponent, affects ebullience in defeat but genuine pleasure at the talents of the younger man. He strokes his scalp mournfully and claps Paul on the shoulder.

"Welcome to Europe," he says without a hint of patronage. "I think you'll do just fine."

Three days later Edge reads an article by touring American journalist Forest J. D. Woodbury out loud from the *Paris Herald*. Paul is carefully administering himself a bowl of soup, napkin covering his lap and cautiously pushing the spoon away from his body according to French etiquette.

"Listen to this. Woodbury wonders why Anderssen didn't play as well against you, Paul, as against Jean Dufresne and Anderssen replies *"No, Mr. Morphy won't let me."* How about that? *Mr. Morphy won't let me.*"

"He has a fine sense of humour."

"Here's another Anderssen one. The Paris correspondent of the *New York Express*: '*In all Morphy's games he not only plays in every instance an exact move but the most exact.* Charming! You are perfect!

And another: *I win my games in seventy moves and Mr. Morphy wins his in twenty. But that is only natural. He is truly the American boy wonder."*

"I wonder what he means?"

Edge ruffles the paper. "Clearly he's quite the professor."

"I read one this morning," Paul replies. "Sometimes I think he *actually* knows me."

Edge looks over and frowns. "What do you mean?"

"Well, I quote Anderssen's words, *Paul is a wonderful talent. It is, however, impossible to keep one's excellence in a little glass casket, like a jewel, to take out whenever one wants. On the contrary, a gift can only be conserved by good practice."*

Edge frowns. "Who's talking about conservation? And what does he mean by good practice?"

"I agree," Paul says, "the game is there to be played. Our bout was one of the few games of chess I actually enjoyed!"

Later at dinner, Paul is well enough to sit at the window and eat almost a full meal. Edge is still buried in the newspaper, lulled by the chess descriptions and all the puzzling compliments talented men set for each other in print.

"Don't believe everything you read," Paul says, buttering his toast.

"I'll believe anything, just not everything," Edge replies looking down the page with a smile. "But I could get used to these testimonials. It's ironic Anderssen has such wit given his lack of chess practice. I wouldn't say he was the hardest opponent you've faced."

"Wouldn't you, Fred?"

"Okay, here we go. In a letter to a colleague in Breslau the professor says: *"If Morphy yields you a chance, examine it carefully. You will find accepting the advantage will lead to disaster!* You know, I prefer the comment about the jewel in the little glass case."

Paul presses his hands on the tablecloth and Edge senses the subtle gesture and reluctantly curtails his amusement. He lays the paper aside. "What would you say," Paul says, "if I were to challenge for twenty blindfold games?"

Edge swallows. "I would say you were balmy."

"Mad?"

"Quite mad! You could challenge Harrwitz again, Pawn and Move, for 500 francs."

"Fred, I already said no stakes."

"We need the cash."

"I'm having money sent from New Orleans. It will be here soon."

Edge leans forward, gleaning Paul's ambition could fall either way. Persuasion is not impossible. "Here's what we should do. Forget the twenty blindfold games. You said so yourself, it's a display, a performance." He raises his arms. "Here you are, the world champion, quietly eating your toast."

"Except for Howard Staunton."

"Exactly. So we offer Pawn and Move to Staunton who may commit, but may not. If he refuses we offer Pawn and Move to any player in England, France and the whole of Europe. Soon you can weep like Alexander for no more worlds to conquer. They'll be no one left!"

"Touché!"

"Mr Staunton's match is all that will remain."

"Like Alexander the Great," says Paul and lays down his knife. "Did we receive any letters from home today?"

That same afternoon Edge returns with a new batch of newspapers, the morning edition. He already has the chess challenge printed and shows it to the American champion, busy watching his feet in front of the fire. Paul reads the declaration in Porter's *Spirit of the Times* to be distributed in France and picked up by the foreign nationals across Europe: *To silence all cavil in regard to the English Champion, Howard Staunton, Paul Morphy offers him Pawn and Move to play for any stake.*

"There," says Edge, "it couldn't be simpler. You will challenge the world and the world will refuse. That will make you world champion."

Paul looks up over his shoulder and says: "You know, Edge, when I was in school I studied law, not chess. I didn't play a single game the whole year. I can still recite the Civil Code of Louisiana by rote. I have a sound memory of facts and cases and I passed all my exams. I am a lawyer at heart and I want to practice the law. There I've said it."

"You want to go home and be an attorney and make your family proud? Just throw away your talent?"

Paul says nothing.

For a moment Edge weighs his reply. "You know, Paul, the law is well and good. But that is the rest of your life. You won't get a second chance with chess. Don't stop now. We're almost at the endgame so to speak! You can help fight legal battles and pursue that proud family career for the rest of your life!"

"You don't understand," Paul replies calmly. "I came to play Howard Staunton. He is the best player in the view of the newspapers *and* my chess friends. That may be wrong but that is why I came. And we cannot play him. I despair of the fact that..." Suddenly without warning he cries out, having rocked a little close to the fire and burned his feet. To Edge's alarm and surprise, Paul begins dancing round the room calling out chess moves for the streets of New Orleans. "Oh the knight of Bourbon! For the queen of Levée Street!" Trapped in pain, his torments are released as though he imagines chess pieces lost in the alleys of the French Quarter.

"Paul, what's happening?"

"Clara!" he replies. "I mean, my feet! Oh Fred, help me please!"

Bearing a basin Edge rushes from the bathroom and throws cold water over Paul's feet, causing a comic sizzling. Over a few minutes this solution proves correct as Paul feels only a throbbing in his toes. The debacle becomes the bizarre sight of Paul limping about the room. But the atmosphere calms. Only recently recovered from flu, Paul retreats from his manager to his bed.

Questions await him as he slides under the fresh sheets. Can he forge Alonzo's past into the future? Will he return home triumphant on the wings of Caïssa or be stranded in Europe forever? If he does get home, will Clara be okay or drowning under the splendid squalor of New Orleans? Overall, isn't he better off playing chess as a magical retreat from the chaos and ambitions of those surrounding him? The choices are spectacular and foreboding and Paul does not want to face them. But he cannot relax for fear of chess moves, old and unmade, running constantly in his brain like unquiet clockwork mice.

Edge meanwhile leaves the *Breteuil* for a few days. He returns weary after seeking distraction in the streets of Paris. Paul thinks of Alex slinking away to the red-light district but cannot imagine Edge pursuing this kind of indulgence. One evening after sleeping all day, Paul feels recovered from his illness and the accident with the fire. He takes to Paris himself. He leaves by the back door, sensing all that makes this evening amid the lights and music from the cafés, and the bleak romance of the night-watchman lighting the street-lights, all the sweeter for being alone.

"I am sick of chess tricks," he writes in his mind, "both on and off the board." He decides to write an open-air letter to Charles Maurian, his only true friend. "There are no more chess kings, Charles," he whispers. "Not because Staunton won't play me, but because *I will refuse to play*." He repeats the speech echoing "I refuse" all down the Boulevard St. Michèle. Weaving under the evening lights, he ducks and strides along the northern Parisian quarter.

Paul walks hours without getting weary, until his head is completely clear. Eventually he emerges into his favourite part of Paris, the Rue de Rivoli and the moonlit Louvre. He lingers in the Place Napoleon and the Place du Carrousel. Some of the time, he sits on the kerb watching a rat scurry between doorways. Down the street a man begins unloading pumpkins. Paul is reminded of the festivities of *Mardi Gras* and the fruit market where he saw Clara as queen of the parade. He waits until the market is opening and walks to a street jeweller. He buys a necklace, a locket of fool's gold for Clara, and drops it into his coat pocket. She will find it later, he thinks, when all is over.

At a newspaper stand he blames his temptation to read the chess columns on Fred Edge. Then he buys the day's edition anyway. George Walker in *Bell's Life in London* quotes from D. W. Fiske, Paul's family friend. Walker says *We have Paul Charles Morphy, aged twenty-two, who offers Pawn and Move to every other player in the world. And large as the world is this—we at The New Orleans Chess Club—honestly believe the boy can do!*

Paul smiles and feels a surprising tremor of hope and recognition for the feelings of people at home. Walking past a street bin, he resists discarding Walker's words or sentiments and tucks the newspaper protectively under his arm. At the corner he stops. There, high above the turreted grey buildings, the sun and moon no bigger than each other share the same sky. Consciousness awakens from the long night and Paul becomes aware of carriages rattling by and sad-looking horses. The moon sinks and the sun struggles through the gaudy haze. Beginning the last walk to the *Breteuil*, he intends to take a bath and climb into bed wearing a fine pair of silken socks. To sleep perchance to dream, he muses, and makes his way through the waking streets.

Chapter Twenty-Nine
1858
The Emperor's Gardens

That weekend Paul is subpoenaed to the royal lawn hidden inside the Tulieres Gardens, a less than secret haunt of Napoleon III. He feigns awe as the Emperor greets him personally at the gate with a sly smile.

"My letter arrived?" the Emperor inquires.

"Yes, your majesty," Paul says. "Your seal was unmistakable."

"I know."

Paul is led along the gravel path through a labyrinth of hedges. At each corner the yellow sash on the Emperor's shoulder pompously twists, his sword rattles, and he appears to be talking to himself. Striding ostentatiously into a croquet garden, he declares himself Louisiana's spiritual ruler.

"I am nephew of the beautiful mastermind of French liberty, Emperor Bonaparte!"

Paul walks to maintain a close but measured distance. If Telcide could witness the proceedings she would tremble with delight. But her son feels only trepidation as the hedges move to reveal the splendour of lords and ladies of the French court, all reclining on their bellies eating a picnic. Instantly Napoleon marches up and down. He casts his eyes about mischievously and claps gleefully at his ruse. The courtiers scramble to their feet, the ladies giggling and the men bowing, all sixes and sevens and dusting grass from their clothes. Meanwhile the Emperor waves his sword to and fro while coughing and skipping and generally disturbing the calm. He strikes a mighty figure in his open shirt, military espadrilles and trimmed leather boots with golden tassels.

"This is Paul Morphy, a great Frenchman of New Orleans and chess genius! Who would like to challenge him at croquet?" The Emperor cocks his ear and listens to the wind. "Come now, aren't you the finest men of the land? Or have I been led astray? Who cares for a *partie* with a known champion? I will only ask once!"

A man in a blue coat steps forward, his voice suggesting confidence. "Certainly your majesty, it will be a pleasure." Napoleon regards the Duke of Normandy and dismisses him. "No, I will do it myself. I was just testing you. Prepare the pitch."

Paul is handed a croquet stick and the men clear the lawn. Before he can realize what is happening, the Emperor of France is swinging a wooden mallet behind him in deep concentration. A clear thud sounds the first strike of the game. Applause! The white ball bumps along the croquet hoop and stops half way. Confused, the audience cheers and the Emperor scolds them and demands they applaud "merit where merit is due" and "adversity overcome," or else they can "perfect the art of silence!"

Paul feels his hands shaking. The reality of the event is all too real. Along the grass twelve metal hoops stare haphazardly at him, each a multitude of options. Focusing, he determines three possible routes from hoop to hoop. But with no experience, no solution is clear. How is this new game played? He cannot even watch by learning since Napoleon—leaning rakishly on his mallet and less than amused—is watching him. So without quite knowing why and having only read about croquet at school, Paul approaches the only possible play on the turf, a black ball near Napoleon's foot.

"I was marking it for you," the Emperor says. "*Bon chance.*"

"*Merci bien,*" Paul says and the Emperor daintily steps out of the way. Paul lines up the ball and begins swinging the mallet between his legs, slightly too high. The crowd titters and falls quiet. Somehow Paul cannot determine when to release the shot. Panic starts to set in as he feels the weight of the swing, leans into the stroke, and fires off the ball at a tremendous pace. The light breeze in the garden holds its breath. His heart stops. The ball flies ten feet before touching the grass, skims the head off Napoleon's ball, and by an inexplicable stroke of good fortune ricochets through the first hoop and rests under the second. The crowd is dumb. Paul lifts his hand to block the sun from his eyes. Napoleon applauds, throws back his head and laughs uproariously. Nothing could be wittier in the Empire, it seems, than a severe croquet beating.

"You are clearly a genius at all games!" The smile vanishs *tout de suite* from the Emperor's face. "Nevertheless, this is *my* game." Confusing Paul even more, he grins broadly.

Shot by shot they move up the garden. The crowd hops over the little grass border of flowers and gravel, following the competitors. Here Paul's beginner's luck, to the Emperor's contempt and happiness, falls away. He is exposed as a croquet charlatan before the French lords and ladies, the men in frilly collars and crimson stockings, the ladies in giant evening ball gowns. All take their cue and applaud Napoleon as required. Finally the Emperor clears the last shot clean through the hoop and draws his sword for the mock sighs of the crowd. He bows with majestic subservience.

"*Merci, mes amis.* Twelve shots for eight, I believe. But I owe my competitiveness to my devilish accomplice. Here he comes! Let's help our friends the Americans to *liberté*, no matter how strained the civil rebellion of their country. To Mr Paul Morphy!" Everyone claps dubiously. They eye the small drab-looking Paul in his long-sleeved suit as he trails the black ball with his mallet.

Meanwhile Napoleon rolls his ball underfoot, symbolically suggesting his divine right to rule. Paul refrains from copying his host. Instead he executes a long bow to all assembled. Unexpected by his audience, the theatricality and excess of his performance seems to do the trick.

"It's a pleasure to be in the Tulieres gardens with his majesty," he manages. "I enjoyed the game."

The show would be over if it were not for the sequel Napoleon prepares. He dismisses the revellers, who instantly return to their banquet of breaded cheeses and bottles of exquisite wine.

"What else do you do beside chess?" the Emperor asks.

"I go to the opera."

Napoleon swings his arm. "Music is the cushion of the soul. That's why I sing. And you?"

"I feel safe there."

"You feel safe at the opera? Let me tell you. Three years ago I arrived for the *première* of *débutante* Grace Fontainbleu. My wife was there, *Eugénie de Montijo* the blessed Countess of Teba. A happy evening lay ahead, young man. But someone tried to kill us. Not to assassinate, to kill. Divine royalty was bombed by so-called dissenters. Vile creatures! Over eighty were killed."

"I never heard…"

Napoleon twirls his moustache into a coiled spring. "And at the Paris Opera of all places! Can you believe it? Music and death! So I built a side exit for a mid-show escape! That, *mon ami*, is a secret. That is why I ordered the splendid new building!"

"I've been there," Paul says. "It's quite a marvel. I played a game against the Duke of Brunswick."

"A pointless fellow." The Emperor parades Paul beyond the hedgerow into the next private garden. They meander along a gentle brook and under the weeping willows until the grass becomes bare ground. Momentarily Paul fears for his life since he hears Napoleon draw his sword and ask him to turn around. But it appears the Emperor wishes to spoof the English court by knighting the American beside the Seine, in the heart of Paris, to send him back to the United States with a clearer sense of his French soul.

"Sir Paul, arise!"

"My manager will be more than happy," Paul says. "He is an Englishman."

The inevitable now occurs. A crystal chess table with see-though pieces materializes behind the trunk of a willow, its headdress reaching out over the brook.

"Those trees lean as though to drown themselves," the Emperor says. "They're all like Ophelia, waiting for flowers to bear them up in the water.

"And dignify their death," says Paul.

The Emperor begins a game. The chess pieces are confusing, however, because of mingled light and shade from the overhanging willow.

"Kalmyk tea," the Emperor says. "One part Russian, one part cream and a dose of salt."

Paul accepts the cup and glances into the strange coloured liquid. He makes sure he smiles.

"Thank you."

The die is cast. They commence play and Paul realizes he has to try and lose gracefully while still seeming to try. Having eluded embarrassment during croquet, he must serve Napoleon's ego without being discovered. He plays a mysterious rook move. The Emperor is delighted but Paul is nervous deep in his stomach. Clearly he is expected to win but why should he prod a sleeping lion? Does Napoleon believe he can outwit the American chess champion by inviting him to court and electing to play under a tree? Paul tries to engage the game even-handedly but he develops hypocritical tendencies, a double pawn, a twisted rook, a deceiving bishop. A draw is soon declared as both players experience mutual losses. Napoleon appears drained but satisfied, and leaps from the table realizing a stalemate could predict a victory. Instead he slips on a loose log near the riverbank and—still living in the long shadow of his uncle—the Emperor unsheathes his sword and swings it in a boisterous frenzy over the stream.

"Take note, young Morphy," he cries. "The combat is only just beginning!"

Paul deceives his opponent into winning the next game before silence is broken over the board.

"How is the tea?"

"Delightful."

"It is a recipe," the Emperor says, "to calm ambition and desire! Would you like the ingredients?"

The Emperor now showing signs of boredom, Paul conjures a strategy where Napoleon can win. But the position looks false and only draws out the kill longer. Paul begins sweating. Due to a lack of pieces, the pawn line he left immobile demands movement. Carefully he advances several candidates for promotion and transformation into a new ruler: the all-powerful queen who will sweep Napoleon to dust. However, despite Paul's fear of being cast in the river, the Emperor brings about his own destruction with a grandiloquent leap to his feet:

"Young sir! You fly your true colours! I witness the true Monsieur Morphy!"

"Well…"

Napoleon hitches one hand into his yellow belt buckle and whips the other through his beard. "I admire your honesty and openness."

"I had the advantage…"

"Clearly, and you took it. And so you should sir. One tiny pawn and the game is yours! What François Philidor says is true! A pawn *is* the soul of chess. Paul, you're the pawn to my mighty king, see? So you win!"

He laughs and encourages the Creole to copy him. The table still begs checkmate. Paul has to make the final move. But after years of war-like chess, he delicately resists moving his queen to the correct square. Paul certainly does not say *et mat*, but chooses his words and actions carefully.

"Pawns are souls," he says, "but playing the pieces wins the game."

"Very true," the Emperor smiles. "*Touché.*"

"Merci, *votre altesse.*"

Napoleon frowns. "But no need to flatter. Yes, you win. Take a seat please. Very good." He looks comically over his shoulder, and whispers as though revealing an espionage plot or national secret. "The American Ambassador in Paris has elected you to the *Cercle Impérial,* to which only the Princes Imperials, highest *noblesse* and foreign ambassadors belong."

"It's an honour…" Paul begins.

"Do you understand?" Napoleon asks.

"I'm not sure I do."

"It means as a former citizen of France, dear Paul, you will now play on my behalf. For the honour of the Empire!"

Paul looks at the stream. A single bulrush is caught in the water and he waits for a butterfly to alight on the reed. She stretches her fragile wings in the dying sunlight then flies away. There is only water down by the Seine and reflection of the empty sky.

"I appreciate the offer," he replies. "But I am an American."

"You are French, Paul. Do not disregard your heritage. I have given you a great honour and I can take it away."

"I don't know what to say."

"Then say yes."

Paul wonders how he got here all the way from New Orleans. How can he find a way out, a loophole or exit from the maze?

"Morphy, listen to me. I am under pressure. I am recently returned from Branitz and ready to visit the Chalons camp. The fortress at Vincennes is to be enlarged. Eighty million francs are needed to complete Cherbourg." He leans forward conspiratorially. "You would not believe those nobles you saw on the lawn, how vain and jealous they can be! They squeeze me in all directions until I have nothing but blood. My breath will expire, see?" He breathes in and out, in and out. "You know something, Paul. You have no idea what men of power can do. Do you know the depths of misery we endure for our prizes?"

"I don't, *votre altesse*."

"No, I'm wrong. You are one of few who understand, Paul. Listen to me! We have a draw at chess and you remain the croquet winner. We are equals! Accept the honour and declare France your benefactor."

"My family will not..."

"You will never have to gamble or fight a duel. And your family will never know. I know how they feel. Gambling remains illegal so they're a little concerned. Monsieur Edge can be replaced. Do you know he is writing a book about you as we speak? Cast him aside, he's no friend. Take what I am offering you and power and glory will flood your nights! I can make you immortal in my wake."

"I'd have to tread in your footsteps," Paul whispers.

Napoleon is momentarily stunned.

"Pardon monsieur?"

"I mean, my family does not permit sponsorship or the earning of money through the game. Chess is a gentlemanly tradition in our family and I must retain that value and prestige or we Creoles..."

"We Creoles? No...what did you say before that?" the Emperor asks, cocking his head.

Paul notices the sweat trembling on the end of Napoleon's nose. "Let's play one more game," the younger man offers, "to decide the issue. That's a fair wager between gentlemen, isn't it?"

After a coughing pause, the Emperor says "okay Paul. That sounds fair to me." A curious smile crosses his face. Napoleon twirls his whiskers and taps his sword handle with newfound gusto, seemingly forgetting Paul's comment. They reset the pieces and play. But soon a single thundercloud, a malign spectator, opens a competing gambit. Ignoring the raindrops, they play on. Paul starts to shiver. Meanwhile the chess pieces cloud as though by magic and the gloom increases with every move. Royal heads bob along the nearby hedge as court ladies and gentlemen race for shelter, laughing and scattering the picnic party. Paul stays focused. But as pools of water collect on the squares, Napoleon grows more suspicious of his play and begins to tut-tut.

"Play as you would normally."

"Normally?"

"I know what you're doing," the Emperor scowls then clips Paul on the arm. "You don't know how to handle the Emperor, it is understandable, but I value our meeting, Monsieur Morphy. You bring out the best player in me, don't you think?"

"Undoubtedly."

"A common saying in chess is that a threat is more powerful than an execution, Monsieur. Don't you agree?"

"I do."

"Do you believe in the awful triangle of chess, math and insanity?"

"I'm...I'm sure I don't."

"I'm teasing," the Emperor says. "I consider my opponents, you know, abstractions. I hear *you* play the person, never the board. You are the greater man. I cannot play the person or I would be my uncle, you see. Sometimes people cannot forgive me for not being him. Do you understand? I am not Napoleon *the First*."

"No, I mean yes," Paul says. "I sometimes wish I had been born in my grandfather Joseph Le Carpentier's time."

"How can you?" Napoleon replies. "No one can understand the loneliness of greatness. You see? Only the Napoleons share this great power and understand the burden. Ha! But you can listen, right?" Paul finds himself nodding.

Within minutes a carriage arrives, led by two graceful white horses, and twisting his sword Napoleon retreats inside. The coachmen whip the beasts back over the grass through the rain.

Paul is left alone with the chess table, the last sensation of the Emperor's fingers from their handshake beneath his skin. He takes his seat and moves the pieces to completion. Without a word, the game in the Tulieres gardens is forever abandoned. He walks to the garden gate. Not for the first time he swears off chess, but knows it won't last. He decides to find a tavern rather than a café, feeling discomfort at the cold rain, just falling, so alien to his Creole skin.

"The game is more trouble than it's worth," he whispers, tightening his coat and re-entering the hurly-burly of the French metropolis.

Chapter Thirty
1859
The Marble Bust of Louis Lequesne

The next day Paul decides to return to London and informs Edge of his decision. There are no more chess games in France, he argues, while in London the Howard Staunton match remains a possibility.

"He will play you eventually," Edge encourages. "His reputation is at stake."

On 4th April Paul's time in Paris is honoured by the chess community in a celebration he cannot escape. Chess players demand his company. He avoids the opera, aristocrats, street players and ladies with admiring letters but he cannot fail to acknowledge those caught by Caïssa's charm. His opponents and supporters expect a champion. Fellow chess player Pierre Saint Amant volunteers to honour Paul's last week, including his victories over Harrwitz and Anderssen, his absence of defeats and his challenge of Pawn and Move that in Edge's words, "no one can bear to accept."

At a farewell banquet in the library of Nicholas Duchamp, a silver laurel wreath is placed on Paul's head. He feels uncomfortable being modelled a king, especially after his recent meeting with the mysterious French emperor. The crown of elegant spikes sits uneasily on his dark features, traps hair on both sides of his head and induces the blood to drain from his forehead. Paul comically but unfortunately resembles Richard III and is clearly uncomfortable in the spotlight.

"The white prince of Death!" cries Rivière.

"If the horse of Death were to ride into the room, you would strike him dead!" Edge says.

"No, I would search for a corner in which to lie down," Paul replies; the audience laughs. He sets the crown on the table and takes a deep breath. Despite the chorus of jollity, he delivers handsome thanks to his Parisian friends from the *Breteuil* and the *Café de La Régence*, plus Anderssen, Nelson Journoud and Jules Rivière. Then a surprise occurs, just as Paul thinks his celebrity is ending. A cunning Norman craftsman, Louis Lequesne, enters the room carrying an easel, plaster casts and a long paintbrush. In his wake trail two boys, his sons, who set to clearing a well-lit corner. At this point Herr Anderssen offers apologies and prepares to leave. Paul cannot help feeling the departure stems from embarrassment, and despite Anderssen's good humour, he senses there is only so much praise a fellow competitor can bear.

"Good luck in Breslau," Paul offers, attempting great warmth in his handshake.

"Don't let them carve you up," Anderssen says, pointing to one of Lequesne's boys sharpening a circular thumb-knife. "I hope to see you again."

"You will," says Paul, smiling uncertainly as he is lowered into a chair along one wall. Anderssen leaves the library, chess papers packed into his schoolteacher's bag.

All is then darkness. The men pass the brandy decanter hand-to-hand and peer into Paul's face, fast disappearing behind plaster bandages cut in big triangular pieces. At his feet, towels surround a container of water. A cream-paste is spread over his eyebrows while a bald cap of saran wrap is hooked over his head and chin.

"Will this hurt?"

Lequesne's rasping voice is far away. "No, no pain. You'll feel a little warm, but try not to fall asleep."

"It feels like a death mask."

Time slows. Paul hears only a muffled babble of voices and some disconcerted laughter. His skin feels hot under the mask but he can't tell if paste or sweat is trickling down his nose. One of the boys wipes his cheeks with a cloth "to help him breathe."

Hearing these words, Paul starts breathing fast and shallow. Cream is applied to his entire face and cap, eyebrows and eyelashes and before he can speak the mask is uncovered. Jokes fill the room and Paul feels a first bout of panic. With fuzzy light behind his eyes, he remembers the playroom of his youth and tries to focus on Basin Street, the fountain…the girl.

He is surprised when the softness of the memory begins to comfort him. He feels sleepy…

"Press air bubbles away, Jermaine!" says Lequesne. "Twist to the edge of the mould. Exactly!" A flurry of instructions follows: "Don't use the bald cap. No, wet the hair! Press the temples down! The paste will stick the plastic to his scalp, if we're lucky."

"Tie the excess behind Paul's head!" Edge jokes. Again the discomforting laughter…

"I don't like this," Paul says. "I can't breathe."

"Patience, dear boy," says Edge.

"It won't be long now," and Lequesne beckons his sons Jermaine and Julius, dressed in plaintive black with white gloves, to his side. "Almost done!"

"You look charming," Saint Amant comments. "A true likeness!"

"Another genius in the room!" a voice says.

There is quiet.

"What's happening?" Paul asks. No one replies.

Suddenly Lequesne says "start moving your face muscles, Paul. The time to escape is now."

"Escape? What do you mean?" He starts to shake in the chair and tries to stand up.

"No!" says Lequesne. "The cast will fall."

"I thought you said take it off!"

"Wait!"

"If you hold the forehead mask…" a mysterious voice adds.

"Yes, do that."

"Pull it down and away from his chin."

Together two men remove the plastic mask. As they peel, Paul feels the glow of the library lights with relief. The boys approach to wash his face and he lets them as the imprisonment drains away. He opens an eye and sees Lequesne holding the bandage to the light.

"Looking for skin damage," the sculptor says, "or I won't be able to make the bust. I intend for marble, Mr Morphy, at the request of your kind friends. If the cast is thin, the marble will tear the effect. You understand?"

Paul opens his other eye. Immediately he receives a shock to discover who is bending over him.

"Hello Paul!" the mysterious voice says and extends his arm. "I received an assignment to Paris as Swedish and Norwegian delegate for Louisiana."

More than ever, Paul feels pinned to his chair. "I find that somewhat hard to believe."

The atmosphere in the room gently sours. The brandy glasses are replenished and everyone takes a sip anyway.

"Gentleman, I am John Sybrandt, Paul's sister Malvina's husband."

The introductions go round in confusion.

"Paul, is everything all right?" Edge asks.

"I am here on Consul business," Sybrandt continues "and I heard of Mr Morphy's celebrations today. As a member of the Morphy family in New Orleans, I hope it's not too pre-emptive of me to pay my respects."

"Pre-emptive?" Rivière inquires.

"Respects?" says Paul.

"I mean *to the living*."

The men realize the joke and laugh. The tension breaks a little.

"I see," says Edge. "We were just saying how the cast resembles a death mask." His words trail away. "The good news is Paul is very much alive."

"I can see that," says Sybrandt. "I hope I'm not interrupting, but perhaps I could have a word with Mr Morphy alone?"

"I'm afraid you would be interrupting," Edge pursues. "This is a private occasion for friends and chess players associated with Mr Morphy."

"I do play chess," Sybrandt replies, looking pertinently at Edge. Paul closes his eyes. "I would not be a member of the Morphy household otherwise. As a family member, am I not also a friend?"

"Monsieur Morphy, the cast is complete," Lequesne interjects.

"Thank you."

"Well, Paul," Rivière adds, "what would you have us do? We still have wine to drink and you need to clean up. But if you have family business to discuss…"

"There is no family business to discuss," Paul says. "Mr Sybrandt has come to bring me home, for sure, whether he is working for the Consul or not. I'm sure his smuggling could wait a day, even if I leave tomorrow."

Sybrandt is taken aback and claims that no such motivation is the cause of his visit.

"I came to see my brother-in-law," he says. "Yes, it's true Paul's family misses him. And no, he doesn't offer great indication of his return date, now it's been over a year…"

"I was in New York," says Paul.

"But that is purely coincidental," Sybrandt insists. He pauses. "I'm greatly pleased by Paul's success in Europe. I just wanted to express that sentiment to Paul directly from his home. That is all, gentlemen."

The eerie silence in the room shifts. The solemn guest John Sybrandt is given a glass of brandy and conversation continues. But the jollity has gone. His sons start to argue, jostling over an old face mask, and Lequesne has to separate them. Edge stands in a corner and tries to engage Sybrandt in a business discussion of the merits of publishing Paul's games. With one eye smiling, the half-welcome intruder stares over his shoulder at the young chess champion.

Finally Paul is on his feet, thanking the men for their visit. He looks tired and hints at his need to be alone. Leaving their glasses on the book cabinet near the door, they all politely exit passing by brother-in-law Sybrandt. Lequesne scurries from the room with brushes underarm and sons trailing like obedient lapdogs. He promises the completed marble bust in a few weeks. Edge reminds Paul to meet later at the *Breteuil*.

"Don't forget to wear your crown," Journoud says, looking back into the room where Sybrandt is patiently gazing from the window.

"Certainly not," Paul says and quietly closes the library door.

Chapter Thirty-One
1859
The Queen's Gambit

T hey return to London by the end of April. With one stroke they escape the Parisian court, growing demands for blindfold games and the envious coterie of the *Café*, not to mention John Sybrandt's intention of returning Paul to New Orleans for the sake of his family.

"He claims my mother is ill," Paul tells Edge, "so I must go home, but I've no reason to believe him. I've already heard from Helena how *maman* ails and recovers. Malvina wants to trap me in New Orleans to legitimate her claim on the family property."

"Your father's estate…"

Paul nods. "So long as I'm back in the city, they can sign over the papers for the lion's share. Done and dusted."

"Because they're married?"

"Yes. Marriage is everything."

Edge sees no reason to disbelieve Paul and sympathizes. The Morphy estate belongs to Edward, he tells Paul, and the remainder should pass to him. "The laws of patriarchy. But the women still run Louisiana families behind the scenes."

"And is England any different?" Paul says. "Of course, I see Helena's and Malvina's claim. But John Sybrandt has no good feeling. He will cut Helena completely out of the will and discredit Edward's character in court, if necessary. Plus, they'll disinherit me on the basis of possessing no viable occupation in the city."

"But you'll be attorney-at-law."

"In six months. Sybrandt will act before then."

Edge smiles his uncertainty at the family complications. "I'm sure it'll work out. You'll be back on Southern soil in two months, as soon as Staunton gives us satisfaction!"

"Quite so," Paul says, trying to be positive.

However, Paul and Edge themselves soon fall out. A day later in the *St. Thomas* lobby, Edge announces work is progressing on his secretive biography *The Triumphs and Exploits in Europe of Paul Charles Morphy*. The title strikes Paul's ear as sentimental but he resists objecting to the enterprise. Frequently raised to god-like beauty and possessing prescience and power in all newspapers, Paul is weary of hearing his praises sung. In print he senses a mythical skin enclosing his body, one he cannot comfortably inhabit, writing his real life out of existence. But the feeling is momentary because all of London beckons with magical possibility and the consoling Lethe of the chessboard. On the English Channel ferryboat from Calais to Dover, he listens to Edge reading sections of the tentative manuscript. The chess player hopes he will warm to his manager's rhetoric. For a while they tread common ground in thinking how to tell Paul's story.

That evening they arrive in London, stepping out under the dreary lanterns. Once inside their room at the *St. Thomas*, Edge sheds his raincoat and immediately reads his latest entry from the biographical work-in-progress:

> "...journeying en passant from London to Paris, this boy of twenty-one, five feet four inches of slim figure and face like a young girl in her teens, positively appalled the chess warriors of the old world: Narcissus defying the Titans...."

"It's just not true, Fred. I know it's the style of the day. I'm a Greek god, a midget and a young girl? Can't you describe me the way I am?"

"So I should make *no* reference to your stature, or appearance, or achievements?"

Paul sighs. "I just don't see the relevance of comparing me to a warrior, or a girl who can defeat older men. Can you draw attention to my heritage, my background or my clothes, without reducing or expanding me beyond all measure?"

"Credibility," Edge muses in reply. "Is that what you want? But your accomplishments *are* incredible. They cry out for a certain kind of writing."

"Fred, I'm asking you not to publish the manuscript. It's embarrassing. I mean, it makes me sound vain and prophetic."

"You think I'm basking in your glory? You want it all for yourself. Is that it?"

"No, you mistake me."

Edge gathers his materials. "Well, it's my prerogative as your manager to paint the world a picture of the great Paul Morphy. Look, you imagine chess pieces being alive. I must picture *words* to capture the essence of our journey. What's the difference?"

"But that's your mistake, Fred. I don't need to explain myself to the universe. Because I play...I don't play chess for..."

"Why *do* you play?" Edge pursues, and stares at Paul.

"I know that I play and that's enough, right? And since you talk of imagination, I don't picture living pieces but more a field of forces around the board. Some are in harmony, others confused. Put that in your book!"

Edge has already left, slamming the door. "Don't forget your seven o'clock match," he calls, "but I won't be there. I have a book to write."

"There he goes...with his exploits," Paul whispers in his wake. "*Exploits* is the right word. That book is officially unofficial!" For a second, Paul relishes his privacy, then shivers at the idea and paces the hotel suite. He sets up the chessboard on the bed and disbands it. In the closet, he arranges the shoes for amusement before retreating to a bath with a cup of *Earl Grey* and lies there feeling a growing sense of isolation from his family. He remembers the recent laughter of the few acquaintances he's made in Paris as potentially mocking, even his chess opponents. He tips tea in the bath and watches the colour drain.

How long will I play chess, he thinks? Will I resort to higher stakes matches? Will I ever see Clara? Suddenly the bathwater is cold. Time has passed.

He clambers out and pours the rest of his tea in the sink. Paul resolves to follow Edge's advice if only to distract his mind. He dresses, boards a moving hansom cab and is soon winding his way through the flea markets of Cornhill. Over the fruit and flower stalls, memories of New Orleans fireflies wash from his eyesight into the foggy London damp. The sky grows dark mid-afternoon.

A Coliseum-style building is suddenly there, part magisterial government, part private club, claiming global dominance. A Union Jack flies high over the building. Paul circles the entire lower floor, wary of the doormen at every corner of the labyrinthine interior, before he discovers a black queen carved ominously over a wooden door. Before he can knock, Augustus Mongredien, the President of the London Chess Club flings open the door, red cheeks boiling over with tobacco. He's been expecting Paul and clears away some beaurocratic papers. Except for a bearded man playing a small boy across a typewriter, no other club members are present.

"Everyone leaves at five," Augustus explains, rolling his flesh as he sits.

They play.

Augustus makes his last move in the seventh game. He loses, folds his king quietly to the table and looks at the boy. Only three hours have passed. Seven games to Paul, nothing for Augustus Mongredien. The President smiles and laughs, undeterred in patronage if a little piqued in pride.

"Good, good, my boy! Good to know you still have it." He looks up and sees, oddly, that Paul is crying.

"There are no more worlds to conquer?"

"I'm sorry…" Before this friendly red-cheeked man, a similar age to his grandfather, Paul has finally given in to feeling far from New Orleans. Augustus takes his shoulder and they sit for a while.

"Chess used to be my forte," the older man says. "But now they made me President because no one else wants the job. I look on it as a kind of ridiculous privilege. Wait here a moment." He returns with two sherry glasses and hands Paul a handkerchief.

"You don't know what President of a chess club is like."

"Actually I do," says Paul, brushing his cheeks. "I'm President of the New Orleans Chess Club. So far I've done nothing and I feel burdened by my duties."

Augustus laughs and proposes a toast. "To ennui, apathy and all the glories of pointless company…no offence intended."

"None taken," cheers Paul and they clink glasses. Off the cuff he adds, "do you know the saloons of the *Marcel Pestel* restaurant in Paris?"

"I'm afraid I don't, old chap. Why do you ask?"

"Well, it's somewhat embarrassing, but I believe in a few weeks a marble bust of my head will appear in the window. Don't ask me the purpose of this endorsement. To frighten the clientele or to motivate thieves, I'm sure."

"To bring people to London, the true chamber of horrors!"

"Quite so," Paul replies, unconsciously imitating the plum-throated Augustus. "Well, could you honour me with a favour should you ever pass the *Pestel?*"

"Surely, I will."

"Just wipe the smile off his face. Or if I'm no longer around, check that he's unhappy."

Augustus frowns at the odd request.

"I will Paul, I will," and they toast before Augustus trips through a pile of books in search of a second bottle.

A package has arrived when Paul returns to the *St. Thomas*. The butler grins and hands over a heavy object marked with the royal seal. Inside is a present from Queen Victoria, a remarkable sheepskin chessboard. A handwritten note reads:

> *Dear Paul,*
> *Well done on defeating Europe at chess to add to your American victories. I am, in no few words, a delicately devoted fan. Accept this chessboard as a gesture of goodwill. I enjoy the game but Albert is currently sick, and we cannot play otherwise I would undoubtedly invite you to the Palace. Please recommend me to your stay in London where my name is known! Enjoy London! With all good devotions for your future games!*

No gold lettering, no scroll work, no ornamentation. But in the lower right-hand corner Paul notices the signature *Victoria R* in brown ink, with a wafer seal.

"She likes to play?" the butler asks.

"In the evenings with beloved Albert," Paul replies. "He's sick."

"Is she any good?"

Paul chooses not to answer but then changes his mind. "She plays wonderfully well," he says, raising the butler's eyebrows. "With the white pieces."

They return to Liverpool that weekend, and leave on April 30th on the *Persia* bound for New York City. Standing on the deck of the steamer as it pulls sluggishly from the docks into the Irish Sea, Paul leans over the railing. "I wonder if I'll ever see Europe again."

"Of course you will," Edge says. "Just a matter of time. They'll *have* to come to you."

"I'm not sure if I want them to," Paul says. "Chess isn't everything, you know. Just a game for adult children. A pastime to kill idle hours."

"Maybe. You cannot mean that?"

"I do," Paul replies, staring wordlessly at the sea. "Why can't I be serious? What good has chess ever done for me, or the world?" He points over the edge with a peculiar, new laugh. "Those grey rolling waves have more genuine meaning than any move on a chessboard. It's only wood. Just pieces of wood."

Edge frowns but decides to look the other way.

Part Three
The Floating City

"Nothing except a battle lost can be half so melancholy as a battle won."

The Duke of Wellington

Waterloo, 1815

Chapter Thirty-Two
1859
The Wings of Caïssa

The departure owes itself to Howard Staunton's final decision to evade playing the new champion. The day Paul leaves, Staunton uses his chess column in the *London Illustrated News* to cut the American down to size, calling him a "cowboy pretender" and "jostler who is not graced in etiquette." Apparently Paul plays a new cut-and-thrust game, dishonouring the ancestry of the *royal* game and its mastery in Europe.

Paul and Edge part ways. Already uncertain of his former manager's whereabouts, Paul holds to his dignity that he was right to challenge Edge's biography. He takes up the Staunton business in a direct letter to Lord Lyttleton, President of the British Chess Association. A series of letters ensues, none satisfactory, but all reflecting Paul's desire not to throw mud or engage in journalistic wrangling. Staunton's right-hand man, Lord Lyttleton, tries hard to mediate between patriotic support of his countryman, Staunton, and the clearly wounded feelings of the new champion.

Lyttleton writes about the omissions in his chess column, serving up private letters for public dissection…

> ...no mention is made of the fact that you play the same game by the same rules, proving yourself by travelling to Europe. You present yourself always as the politest guest of your English and French hosts.

Yet somehow, the letter that Paul receives is further edited for Staunton's column in the *London Illustrated News*. Paul receives the edited version on the day he leaves, realizing how he's compromised by a foreign press. Upset, he retreats to his cabin deep in the *Persia*.

"English pride is at stake," he says to himself, "and clearly there is no trifling with that!" Paul corners himself at the little writing table under the port-hole and writes his worries to Clara. He describes knights committing doughty deeds for their fair maidens, drawing pictures of mosaics on which Caïssa walks in beauty like the night. He makes long digressions into the alternative evil history of how chess was invented by the mythical queen Semiramis, founder of Babylon. Throughout the letter he forgets to ask her the most basic questions. *Clara, we are victims at the shrine of Caïssa. You are my muse!*

As the ship rolls on, Paul scrawls his feelings onto paper, growing into an ever more furious state of discontentment. He sips the claret Edge has ordered for the voyage, soon adding Madeira port in little cupfuls to the wine. Clara is everything to the Creole, she is his *coeur!* He imagines her wearing red ruby slippers and dangling one foot in a fountain. She touches his leg and he pulls away into moonlight. Then she smiles the sly smile he remembers so well from his visit to Minnie Ha-Ha's palace on Basin Street. He does not remember falling asleep.

"Come find me, Paul, I'm waiting," her voice whispers in his dream. "Come to New Orleans. Do not wait!"

"Clara!"

"I may not be here, Paul, when you return. I am waiting. Come to New Orleans!"

In the morning, ink is strewn like blood across Paul's hands. He sits up and takes a few moments, then remembers he is aboard a ship divided between two worlds and two selves, suspended on the ocean. Without reading his letter to Clara he takes the candle flame, ignites the edge and watches the grey loops of flame devour it. Then he retreats to bed. Ceiling shadows roll with the waves. He concentrates on closing his mind, eyes open, and awaits his arrival back into the New World.

Chapter Thirty-Three
1859
The King of New York

On May 18th Paul arrives in Upper New York Bay. He remains on the boat while Edge disembarks, before continuing up the East River alone on a small steam ship to mid-town Manhattan. Edge calls goodbye from the downtown shoreline. "I do intend to publish, Mr Morphy!"

"Publish and perish," Paul calls back and attempts a smile. "I won't be happy!"

The black-coated outline of Fred Edge fades from view. Paul is left to survey the building construction of the east side of the island, cranes duelling with swinging steel girders while the ship approaches land. Stepping ashore, he feels a mixture of elation and sadness. He is making the first steps home. However, he senses his European Grand Tour has been diminished by not playing Howard Staunton.

"There is no going back, that's for sure."

Quietly he retreats to the *St. Nicholas Hotel*. At last he is happy not to be accosted in the street, unlike the last three days of the Atlantic voyage when his identity was matched to newspapers reports, and Victorian autograph hunters stalked him from the shadows. On May 25th at Columbia University, Paul explains how he spent forty-eight hours in his cabin without solid refreshments, a self-enclosed imprisonment he is surprised to discover dissipates with the New York sunshine. The crowd enjoys his speech.

Paul is presented with a silver and gold chessboard by Colonel Charles Mead, who inquires about the difficulty of his voyage resulting from lack of funds? Paul objects to the question and Colonel Mead, sensing joviality, pushes the point. He calls chess "a profession," to which Paul takes great exception. The Colonel is deemed offensive and Paul, as a new celebrity, is judged forgivably eccentric. The session breaks down, and like the *faux pas* of discussing Secession in public, the Creole desires never to discuss money in relation to chess gambling again. Colonel Mead is embarrassed and has to leave the room.

That evening outside the *St. Nicholas*, a carriage draws up and a lady steps out. She asks for a game. Paul feels he cannot refuse a lady despite her abrupt appearance. A table is brought to a window in the dining room and chessmen are placed. The lady is offered the first move. Half a dozen games follow and she proves a self-confident but inconsistent player. Paul draws one game intentionally but despite his efforts to the contrary he wins the next. The lady complements Paul on his speech at Columbia. She is dark-haired Italian and he looks away for fear of staring. At her next checkmate she seems satisfied and leaves while blushing, resting her card with a tenderloin address on the board. Paul knows he has been deceived into believing her a Creole lady. In some ways Clara has been sitting with him. But he knows the impossibility: she does not know he is in America, let alone New York. A trick with clothes and carriages would cost a lot of money.

"You do me a great honour," she says. "I admire your play from the newspapers."

"The honour is all mine," Paul replies without looking up.

"But I must now go."

As though addressing a *femme fatale* Paul asks for her name. She rolls her white-gloved fingers, smiles and strokes Paul's hair as though understanding something no one else could. The next moment she disappears into the morning air, black heels carrying her lightly into the street. Paul is left at the hotel table, the chess pieces scattered uselessly before him. Still the memory of her feet twisting the sidewalk offers a painful and erotic clip to trouble his psyche. Paul stares down at the table. Then, in a single gesture, he scatters chess pieces over the floor and cushions, his head drooping in his folded arms. When he recovers, he is startled by the image of a giant multicoloured chess king staring back at him—a vision frightening and real—eyeing and questioning his whole life. Frightened he collects his coat and umbrella, his city gentleman's hat and hurries home. Can his mind be losing its edge over life's chessboard?

The next day Paul is presented with another chess set by the Prize Council of New York University. He journeys to the large chapel of University Hall to collect his prize, nod repeatedly and make what he deems vacuous statements about America becoming a great sporting nation shoulder-to-shoulder with Europe inside the *sixty-four square madhouse*. The student newspaper of New York University, *The Wise Eyes of the City*, declares the evening "a celebration of great *éclat*." At Paul's closing words, "let us look to a future in which America rivals the European chess masters leading the world in the great artistry of the royal game!" the band breaks fervently into "Hail Columbia!" Later Paul is presented with a little golden cup, marked *facile princepe among chess players and gentlemen alike*.

At the end of the night Paul is introduced to Arthur Napoleon, no relation but a great pianist currently on tour with his light-show performances of Schubert's *Death and the Maiden*. A little in awe, Paul agrees to a chess match in the back stalls and finds Arthur to be surprisingly bad.

"You are no worse than the French emperor," he says. But the joke is not appreciated.

"You, sir, are impertinent," replies Arthur Napoleon with a baton-swing of the arm. "You can play chess like a God, and I am a God-in-Music, but that does not legitimate your impertinence!"

"I was…" Paul begins, but feels more upbraided than usual. He senses the absence of Fred Edge at his elbow to help explain his meaning, the shield afforded by the bravado of his grandfather or the patronage of his uncle Ernest.

"All are a long time ago," he mouths to himself.

"Okay, okay, okay," the conductor replies, claiming he is being distracted.

"Please excuse me," Paul says. "I am tired."

The chess is more verbal blitz than lightning chess. White-haired and face tight like a prune, Arthur continues to try and rattle his opponent with abrasive language. But Paul now decides that even as a gentleman his patience has worn thin and he brings the proceedings to a close with a swift victory. Over the next six moves, he drives Arthur step by step into smothering his own king in a corner. The conductor declares Paul a cheat and abandons the table, his coat-tails knocking over the pieces.

"I've never been so insulted. You sir," he waves his finger, "play like a thug." Paul takes the insult wishing for his brother Edward's anger. But nothing comes.

"Go sir," he merely says. "Go play your music."

But the music has stopped. The evening is over. Before he leaves the theatre, Paul arranges for the delivery of his prizes to the *St. Nicholas*, except for a few stray pieces he pockets. He departs via the back exit emerging on a chilly and garbage-strewn St. Mark's Place. Everywhere is dark. He stares at the rising buildings. Then the city seems to part to reveal trees, a clearing and a grilled gate reminiscent of the Vieux Carré. Brooding, Paul wanders Washington Square Park and sits under the quiet elms at the gleaming white fountain. On all sides, cold-looking people pass by. Night has twice fallen, it seems, and not even an old man or stray dog comes near him. On the grass, a rough-looking boy is selling *The New York Herald*, calling "be on time! Hot as potatoes. Morning edition! Get your *Herald*."

The fountain trickles below Paul. He presses his ears to the stone, slowing his pulsing brain, and tries to picture the courtyard at the back of 89 Royal Street. Above him, the fountain bears a statue of General George Washington, and Paul is reminded of the statue of Andrew Jackson in the old Place d'Armes. Something in the night seems ominous. Water trickles down the fountain bowl as he watches and overflows the rim like blood from a mouth. Carefully he peels leaves from the soles of his shoes and looks at the lights of the city. The lights of Manhattan refuse to blink. Always the same silent people shuffle from work to the shelter of their homes.

Where is Joseph Le Carpentier this evening? Again Paul remembers sitting on piles of books being challenged by his grandfather at chess. The old man would smile malevolently at the pieces, then pick one and force a move. The memory is just a mask, though, for what Clara is doing tonight. Is she alone with her Basin Street comrades? Or hiding from her boss? With someone else? Of course she is not alone....

An hour later, Paul heads to the *St. Nicholas* through Central Park. All the way there he fumbles with the chess pieces in his coat pocket, a king and queen and some pawns. He feels like crying out like a mad lost soul, but fortunately resists. When he gets back to his room, he empties his pockets and discovers two queens and no king. He takes the queens and wraps them in a letter to Clara. From earlier speeches he knows the queens are solid sterling, fourteen carats, and a rich prize for a champion who never played Howard Staunton.

Why did he not take the real bets, the gambles, while he could? Surely he could have won gold or diamonds, given Clara's predicament is greater than his family's? He resists the questions as best he can.

Paul is just relieved to be doing something. Returning the pawns to his pocket, he discovers a white knight in there too. He takes the knight to the window, opens the blind and lets it drop ten stories to the sidewalk. No one calls from below. At that moment he feels a strange heartbreak, the hollow feeling of separating the knight from his chessboard home. Yet he also experiences a new kind of relief, a half formed idea of liberation, a life without chess. He stays awake to write Clara again, constantly flicking candle-ash from his lap.

Eventually Paul retires to bed. He lies down fully clothed and breathes out another leg of his journey in a tour that must come full circle. One day he will surely return to the waiting fountain girl, the clasp of his family and the need to create his own future. That is enough for nightmares. Sleep comes quickly. He doesn't remove his shoes, while behind his eyelids a knight is falling south....

Chapter Thirty-Four
1859
The Dubious Memory of Herr Löwenthal

After visits to Philadelphia and Baltimore, Paul resumes his journey via stagecoach through Atlanta and deeper south. The route is unconventional but he wants to see the Gulf of Mexico along the Alabama-Louisiana coastline.

On the second morning he wakes to a blaze of sunshine. Vast swathes of sand are backed right up to small wooden houses, less suggesting the Caribbean islands promised by the coastline than a whole unseen continent. By the time Paul reaches Baton Rouge he is the last person in the stagecoach apart from the driver, a man close to seventy with a triple-forked red beard. The white blaze of sand, a long day of traversing the unchanging coastline, and the wizened old man create an atmosphere of devilishness that Paul retreats from at the first sign of darkness.

At the heart of Baton Rouge they reach a bar, a crumbling metal shack opposite the county courthouse. After being shown his room, a black coffin with a painted wooden cross over the bed, Paul returns to the bar. No one else is around. With mug after mug of the house ale he plies the lonely spigot until he can no longer stand and, forgetting his room, is directed to a seafarers' lodging house. Waking later, he discovers himself loaded back into the stagecoach with an egg and toast breakfast on his lap and a copy of the *Baton Rouge Watchman*. A note scrawled by the coachman reads *Mr. Morphy, occupy your journey with tales of pirates and rum-runs to Jamaica by restless criminals. Your friendly driver!*

Paul resists turning the newspaper to the game columns having made a decision the night before: he will no longer play chess. But he's unfamiliar with the Baton Rouge publication and the chess section appears just inside the opening pages. A chessboard catches Paul's eye and he recognizes one of his own games. The headline reads *Herr Löwenthal Re-Writes Prodigy's History* and despite his best intentions, his eye cannot resist the article:

Morphy cheats?

We strongly resist the accusation made by Herr Johann Löwenthal, a political refugee from Hungary, in his recent book *Great Games of the Last Thirty Years*. The comments were made in relation to a chess encounter with Mr. Paul Morphy of New Orleans, hinting that Löwenthal drew rather than lost a game over eight years ago when Mr. Morphy was no more than thirteen years old.

The *Baton Rouge Watchman* would suggest Mr. Löwenthal can no more satisfy the heroics of Mr. Morphy over the board, by hoping to create a draw from a loss, than he can turn back the tide of the current Crimea debacle or prevent an American state from exerting her natural free-born rights of self-government! Looking over the proofs to Löwenthal's book, and his other presumptive publication of *Morphy's Games* (his so-called memoir re-living Morphy's life), Herr Löwenthal has taken it upon himself to re-write history!

When is a loss a draw or a draw a win? Maybe in the political centres of Europe! But never in America will winning and losing be thus confused. Whenever there is

---

temptation to split a win two ways—even as plain-speaking creatures we feel this temptation, gentleman—let us remember the honorable origins of the immortal game, precedents Mr. Morphy never forgets. Let's see that a draw is indeed preserved as a draw, a loss a loss, and a win a win!

I hereby admonish Herr Löwenthal's publication of his Petroff's defence game against the teenage Morphy. Such trickery and underhand license! These Old West tactics of the Hungarian play fast and loose with the truth. Let them be exposed for what they are—lies and statistics gentlemen! Support our sacred Mr. Morphy! Never buy this book written by the blasphemous pen of Herr Löwenthal. Surely he is a cheating Grendelesque monster who can only be dangerously corruptive to the honorable sportsmanship and chess glory of our United States! Long may she remain in peaceful unity, unless God Almighty tears her brotherly sides and sisterly states asunder!

Dumbfounded, Paul lays the newspaper aside, revealing a picture of the Morphy-Löwenthal game. He is indeed playing Petroff's defence, there in the back-and-white original, a nonchalant game suspended almost a decade ago. His white knight hovers lonely and daring between bravado and defiance. Paul has seen so few games since Spring Hill College back when Charles Maurian was struck by a brief mania for tabulating their games. And yet the newspaper image is strange and far more lifeless than he expected. The position is cold but the feelings in this glimpse of his childhood have not faded. More than ever, Paul is convinced of the magnificent uselessness of chess. He must finally return home and take up a profession. He must work for the honour of the family name, and less for his own latent ambition, always holding onto his childhood. He must embrace the need to make money, so that the toilsome burden of being known in the world can wear thin and dissipate.

"Chess must leave me," he muses, "to allow happiness to come in." He folds the newspaper away, not without a last fearful glance at the immobile game, the one Löwenthal claims was a draw. Paul knows the game was his painful win because he felt Löwenthal's defeat as much as his father's pride. He can even remember the moves and the winning piece, and suddenly he begins to imagine re-playing the game in his mind—the entire sequence backwards too—until he has the sequence perfectly. Fortunately a jolt brings him to the present and he throws the *Baton Rouge Watchman* to his feet. Then he attempts to eat his breakfast as the stagecoach tumbles down the Alabama sands.

"Clara," he whispers, "I will be worthy of us. We can be together and start a family and I'll support us! *Maman,* too, I will no longer play for stakes or money, or in public, and never again will I countenance publication in connection with my games. I hereby resign as President of the New Orleans Chess Club!"

Immediately he hears a voice, Clara's or Telcide's he cannot tell, calling on the wind:

"Come back home, Paul, the streets of New Orleans are missing you. Do come home..."

He bows his head and empties his mind.

Chapter Thirty-Five
1859
Leaving the New Amsterdam

B y the time Paul arrives in the Crescent City the moon is full and darkness has fallen. The journey has been long. The stagecoach takes him all the way to the Mississippi waterfront to make enquiries at *The House of Rest for Weary Boatmen*. He learns Clara is no longer in the employ of Kate Townsend or *The Twenty-One*, but gleaning from a boy on the street, he learns Clara's new residence. So he wanders back to the stagecoach where the Charon-like driver is waiting, and requests Dan O' Neill's on Gallatin, near the ice house.

Dan's assistant, Mary Rich, answers the door. "As number one queen of the neighbourhood," she preens, "what can I do you for?"

A swarthy beauty, Mary encourages Paul to enter before she'll answer any questions. His desire to see Clara triggers her tongue and she drags Paul from room to room, opining on the wall hangings, trellises and gaudy furniture. Clearly a snob, Mary is keen to outdo her competitors in fake finery and elegant bawdiness. Paul is her audience of the moment.

"Mr O' Neill," she calls, pausing in the parlour under a grand oil painting of a man and woman on horseback, *Mr. and*

Mrs. Hiawatha. He's a descendant of the heroine of that Longfellow's poem. You know, *The Song.* I'm his mistress. So that means I'm descended from old royalty too." Paul braces himself from a compliment but cannot make one. He stares up at the domineering painting.

"And Clara?"

"Upstairs. One more thing, see. *The Amsterdam* is only a year old and Clara is one of our best workers, right? You know what I mean."

Paul smiles weakly as Mary Rich flicks her head and disappears through the darkness of a doorway. Left alone, he climbs the stairs and walks down the corridor. The whole building feels like a remnant of Wild West days, with buffalo heads and ten-gallon Stetsons competing on the ceiling. By candlelight he sees the girls' names chiselled in gold letters on the doors. Each girl is made special by losing her real name. He remembers the granite hitching blocks outside, each with smooth iron rings for the horse's name. He shivers and runs his fingers on the nameplates. Yet the place has a homelier feeling than most Houses of Sin. Paul cannot decide if Clara is better off here or not. He wonders if she's working hard and presumably making money, whether she'll want to see him at all.

At Clara's door is a uniformed black boy in a scarlet jacket, *Amsterdam Dance House* embroidered on his chest in gold.

"I's told to take the gentlemen's carriages," he says.

"I don't have a carriage."

"Well, a bag of apples for your horse?"

"I came here in a carriage," Paul replies a little perplexed. "Most men come here by horse?"

"It's the deal o' the place. Ladies and horses is the theme, sir. *You's* the cowboy and *we* bring o't the ladies."

Behind the boy's head, Paul sees *Clara 'Estella' Young* on the nameplate in scarlet.

"A man is there," the boy continues. "But if you give me your clothes, I's got 'em pressed by morning. Y'ur shoes too."

"No, thank you. But I can wait?"

The boy hunches his shoulders and Paul notices a knife, a heavy five-inch blade, trussed in the top of his trousers. The boy notices and explains "they want us to be protected."

"I see." At the sight of the blade Paul feels his neck pulse and is reminded of his reverie during *Il barbiere di Siviglia*. He steps to the side, remembering he too once carried a knife. "I will be okay in a minute," he reassures the boy. His stomach rolls and he lowers his head to his knees. Staring at his shoes and breathing steadily, he recovers. Clara's door now opens and Dan O'Neill's business partner, Conrad Lehman, exits the room. A burly rough-looking man, he frowns at the doorboy then strides contentedly down the hall.

The boy knocks. Clara replies and Paul opens the door without looking inside, revealing only darkness and a faint smell of musk.

"Clara?"

Suddenly she is before him. Her pale face emerges from the shadows and he can barely recognize her before they embrace. The door closes and envelops them in darkness. She kisses him and lays her head on his shoulder, sobbing. She is wiping tears on his neck. Taken aback, Paul staggers deeper in the room. He shuffles to a chair, speaking all at once and dizzy.

"Paul, is it really you?"

"Really truly," he replies. They release each other long enough for Clara to light the lamp on the table and set a candle beside the bed. They sit together hand-in-hand.

"I wasn't sure you'd want to see me."

"Oh Paul, of course I do. You're my white knight as you always promised you would be! I can't believe you're really here! Oh Paul, I have been so unhappy. Did you see that man leaving? He's a bully worse than Dan O' Neill. They are two pigs! For six months they've been running this place, loaning out the girls and not caring how they're treated."

"What do you mean? We must leave."

"They keep up in fear and panic, you wouldn't believe. And the whole deal was struck with Kate Townsend just because I took one of her scarves. For one evening! And now I am a prisoner and I never see my mother. And…oh Paul, you were right. I have to get out of here. Tell me you've come to help me escape."

"I have, Clara…"

"Please, Paul."

He notices the earnestness behind her eyes. "Nothing is all bad," he whispers. They embrace. Playfully she presses a finger on his lips. He asks her to stop but Clara insists. Then she describes her daily routine before they exchange the possibility of a new life in gentle words, a plan of action: they will leave the *New Amsterdam* after midnight and stay at 89 Royal Street for a bit. Overjoyed at the prospect of change Clara twirls her body in the blue curtain, grinning broadly through the pale moonlight.

"Do you think I can ever be something….other than…?"

"Yes, you will. What do you want?"

"To sing in the opera, I told you. Or run my own business. A clothing store on Canal Street!" Clara trembles where she crouches, her white linen dress circling on the floor. "You don't believe I can!" and she springs up and slaps his shoulder with half-serious indignation.

Paul takes her hand, bolder than ever and escaping his nerves through her predicament. He kisses her forehead and promises they shall leave tonight. Once an escape is decided, Clara realizes that Paul is serious.

"Leaving the house is one thing," he says. "But where will we go? Do we climb out the window?" They discuss waiting until the *Amsterdam* is sufficiently busy with clients to go downstairs for a drink, before leaving via the main entrance.

"Or by the back parlour into the courtyard?" Paul suggests. "If you go riverwards, they'll know you're escaping."

"I have to leave, one way or the other," Clara says. "Conrad Lehman breeds dogs and uses them to threaten us. Last week the piano man had his hand bitten by one and it turned septic and I haven't seen him since. Dan O' Neill is worse. He even has a special mistress to calm him down…"

"I met her downstairs."

"A smiling pack of cards she is. But she's brutal too. Keeps a whip over her bed, n' she's always taking it down. A word in Dan's ear and we'd be out on the street in a gnat's half-life." She pauses and takes Paul's hand. "You know, he used to be with this girl, Molly Mason, until she fled with her lover an' the night's receipts. Then she came back. Dan had her stripped and thrown in the river and she was raped in an alley near here."

"No...please Clara...when was this?"

"We got raided in July and O'Neill got charged for keeping a *house of ill fame.* The 1817 ordinance, you know, bans weapons from ballrooms, n' they found three knives and pistols searching just six people! *The Green Tree* is our rival—did you see it over the road?—run by Johnny Morgan, one-legged Duffy. Morgan set the police on Dan by releasing the story. So Dan had a fire started at *The Tree* the same night. Paul, I just can't take any more! You were right."

"Are you sure it's not the tabloids?"

"Can you doubt me, Paul? I have to get out, please!"

"So the stories are real?"

"Real as you n' me! While you're away playing chess, I'm surviving for my life. Running and ducking to raise a squalid penny in this dump. Every day I wake up I want to forget! That's why the girls drink. Night after night, rum's the only salvation. But I don't want to end up like that."

"Well, that's why I'm here," Paul says. "But you must stop reading those tabloid rags. Life *can* be exciting away from tales of mayhem, Clara, believe me it can!"

She is quiet a moment. Then, from memory, she tells Paul another wide-eyed story from the *Blue Book*. Paul knows the articles are true and is sickened.

"You cannot witness these events, Clara. No one can. You have to stop believing them."

"Take me away and I'll believe in anything," she replies, half pleading, half challenging. "I'll believe in chess if you like!"

"No, not that!"

As they embrace, Paul senses a loving moment that could undermine everything and he pulls away.

"What's wrong?" she asks.

"I just don't want to get too close," he says. "Not yet."

"I'm not about to ravish you," she jokes. "My work is done for the evening."

"Clara, please." They sit side by side. "We can leave in an hour," he says, "to make it seem real."

Cautiously, they talk of when they first met, Clara more clearly remembering their first encounter now.

"I was sure I'd see you again."

"I know."

Softly she kisses his lips, and a little surprised, Paul overcomes his fear of the future and the *Amsterdam Dance House*. He takes her in his arms and she lays him on the bed. The moment is brief because the danger is clear to Paul's consciousness, and he cannot bring himself to completely relax. But Clara is determined and for several minutes nothing is heard but their breathing. Afterwards Paul is very red.

"Not for love or money?" Clara jokes. Paul giggles and lays his head in her lap.

"Napoleon would be proud," he says telling her about London and Paris, of the lights and hotels and dark rooms where serious gentlemen gather for their amusements. "Always the same collection of sour-faced men in fumes of smoke and drink, telling tall tales! Stanley, Löwenthal, Harrwitz, Edge…" He mentions the anomaly of his gift from Queen Victoria.

"And what of chess? I heard you are now champion of Europe and America. The best player!"

"I've stopped playing, Clara. The game is over for me. I didn't play the Englishman I crossed the Atlantic to challenge, but there is nothing I can do. I proffered the contest and he eluded me."

"So he didn't beat you either?"

"I didn't get the honour of a game. But I won't speak ill of him."

"But why stop?"

Paul regards her carefully, looking for sincerity, and convinces himself of her innocence of the wider world. "I have reason to disbelieve you," he says. "Look where you live." Realizing he has spoken aloud, he stops his open mouth.

But she does care. "I know, I'm only a house-girl or simple whore as you would say."

"I'd never say that, Clara."

"But *some* would. And I *do* share your interests beyond this Basin world, Paul. You know I do."

So he tells her, "I know. I'm sorry. But chess is corrupted by money and gamblers. The game is an ancient pinnacle of manners. And all is fair in the most vicious of games. Let's not pollute that with our concerns."

"Paul, what are you saying?"

"I'm saying…chess is not just delightful and scientific, but the most moral of amusements. She remains…"

"…she?"

"My muse is a she, Clara. The goddess of chess is Caïssa, as the poet says. To play her game right, monetary reward is never the goal…and her battles are fought for no prize but honour."

"You make a good case, boy, if a little melodramatic!"

"It is my weakness," he replies. "Chess is eminently and emphatically the philosopher's game. That is why I will no longer play."

"Not with your family?"

"The Morphys are no longer concerned with chess," Paul replies. "Only with money. Especially my sister Malvina. Her husband John Sybrandt came all the way to Europe to scrape inheritance out of me on the premise my family misses me."

"Do they miss you?" she says, and Paul is forced to look her in the face.

"Some of them."

Suddenly Clara remembers, and rummaging under the bed she pulls out a wrap of yellow paper. "Look. They made this already!"

"*Detroit Kitchen & Rothschild superior yara tobacco,*" Paul reads and turns over the packet. He sees his own face staring back slightly mournfully, with a glint of determination he's never noticed. "They made me into a product."

"And tobacco too!" Clara laughs. "Wait a moment!" She kneels again and pulls out a large straw hat like the one Paul wore disembarking at Liverpool's docks.

"The Morphy Hat," he cries. "*A new and novel style by Read Brothers & Co. Good Jobbers of 340 Broadway.* I can't believe it. They made me into a hat!"

"Wear it," she says. Instead, Paul taps it on Clara's head and gives her a kiss.

"Wear it when you meet my family," he replies.

A knock touches the door and the whisper of the boy convinces them of the only exit. Clara begins to pack her trunk, but Paul convinces her she must leave it behind.

"My sisters have plenty of clothes. Wardrobes full."

"Even so."

Clara takes a sheepskin bag and stuffs it with dresses and plastic jewellery. Meanwhile Paul strips the bed and rolls the sheets one by one, tying them in knots.

"We're going through the window like a romantic novel," he says. "Tie this end. Now here, make a loop!"

Minutes later the sheets are tied and Clara is balanced in the window. She drops the bag a level so it clips the balcony and tumbles in the bushes.

"It's two stories," she says.

"One step at a time," Paul replies. "You can do it."

He helps Clara descend the balcony. Instantly the bed sheets unravel through his fingers and drag the bed noisily to the window. Another knock sounds and the doorboy's voice inquires about the time.

"Please, we'll be there," the chess player replies. "Two minutes."

Ready to descend Paul senses something. Behind the pillow he glimpses the *Mascot* newspaper, the stark and distasteful publication he was encouraging Clara to reject. One foot on the window, he reaches for the paper and spies a well-worn page. The *Mascot* falls open on the image of a gentleman decorated with the initials *PM*. The words *fiancé* and *saviour* adorn the page. Stunned, Paul accidentally releases the bed sheets. Clara cries out and Paul grapples as best he can. Then the door is wrapped and the voice of Conrad Lehman can be heard.

"Estella Young, now open this door. You know what'll happen if you don't!" Conrad pounds on the door. "Estella! It will be a long night for you!"

The door rattles and the hinges begin to dance. Paul can only stare at the *PM* initials in the *Mascot*. In the newspaper's image a gentleman stands under a light, dressed in black, and stares up at a window. A pleading look is in his eyes. Paul recognizes his Basin Street doppelganger and shivers, *PM*'s lascivious lean on the wall indicating the libertine and paying customer. Money pokes through *PM*'s fingers and a black-and-white speech bubble hangs from his neck with the words *Come with me tonight and we will live like kings!* Does he want to save the girl because of the money? Does she really care?

The door hinges squeal and burst. Suddenly half the wooden wall and masonry chips collapse on the floor. The door flings open to reveal a barrel-chested Conrad Lehman. He is swaying and sneering. At the end of his arm, an Irish wolfhound rears its hind legs, barely restrained and ready to bulldoze.

"Go!" Conrad cries. Instantly the beast's teeth dive for the scent. Paul scrambles to get to the window. The dog is on him salivating and biting. Struggling without thinking, Paul pins his thumbs in the pits of the dog's armpits. Drool spits all over him and reacting from terror, he instinctively jams the newspaper in the animal's maw. Then he sees the boy throw his flashing knife and ducks. He kicks at the boy, turns his back to Conrad and jumps across the room. Whether Clara or Caïssa see him as a dubious chess player, lover or saviour, he leaps onto the window frame. There he stands swaying alive in the New Orleans night air. He leaps and becomes only a Storyville nobody fleeing a brothel by a hole in the wall. He fully clears the first floor. The wolfhound clambers on the window sill, paws at the moon and sneers at the two frightened youngsters in the garden.

"Go round the front," Conrad cries. "Tell Dan, and alert Gallatin! We'll get this Creole bastard!"

Paul crashes in a mulberry bush, receiving a swipe of thorns to the face. Clara helps him to his feet. Three-legged they hobble for the alley and head north. They are down Hospital Street and between Dumaine and Barracks, zigzagging over to Rampart Street—and away. Paul cushions the bruises on his face, limping a little. They are together, though, and hand in hand.

Clara doesn't look back, dragging her bag of worldly belongings behind her.

Chapter Thirty-Six
1859
The Quarter Sleeps Tonight

Propped up by pillows, Paul reads the letter from Fred Edge and tears it gently into pieces.

I have been a lover, a brother, a mother to you. I have made you an idol, a god....

The house is quiet and Paul is alone. Sleeping all day his mind turns to Clara, already sequestered away to Charles Maurian's house over Esplanade on the east side of the Vieux Carré. He pulls aside the bedcovers and crosses to the little chess table. The pieces stand in a frozen game played against himself and discontinued weeks ago. He takes a white tablecloth and drapes the game. Standing at the open window, he remembers the time in London he stood naked reciting the Civil Code of Louisiana. Already Clara is gone, deciding for safety not to stay at the Morphys' house. She left with only Charles Maurian's address and a kiss for Paul. Meanwhile he wonders if Titi or Helena or even his mother will notice that Clara has slept in his room.

"Three days," Paul whispers in the dark. "Three days." He folds the pieces of Edge's letter and lets them fall to the floor. Outside, juniper trees sway in the breeze. He notices the servants' quarters but cannot see inside. Somehow he cannot prevent his mind wandering back to chess. He tries to block out the image of invisible pieces under the white tablecloth, tempting his mind to position them. Rook takes pawn, sidesteps queen and the bishop retreats to grace a flanking victory. A poisoned pawn remains. The knight takes the proffered pawn, and as soon as Paul realizes, the game is lost and won. "The tragedy of failure and the tragedy of success."

He closes his eyes in concentration and breathes in the night air. He takes his bathrobe, a silken gift from Ernest inscribed *Welcome Home*, and drifts onto the balcony. From an open window he can hear Ernest and Alex in some lively discussion along with the roll of dice. He listens for the sound of Joseph Le Carpentier's peaceful snoring. But there is nothing. "My mind is a crowded room," Paul whispers, "and John Sybrandt is crowding it. But he shall never receive my trophies. I will see him in court first, even if I have to defend myself. A lawyer defending a chess player!" He smiles. "Who would challenge me?"

He decides to leave the house, washes his face and changes his clothes. At the foot of the stairs, memories return of chess played in the *salle de compagnie* and Telcide's musical *soirées*. His childhood home is all too familiar. He remembers his fight with Edward in the kitchen, long ago in the dim and dusky hall. Moonlight from the skylight recreates the scene and Paul shivers. Two boys are struggling on the black-and-white kitchen floor, ghosts of the present. Paul hurries to the front door.

Outside a gentle rain is sweeping the street. The police watch is out. A man in a mackintosh is half way up a lamp-post, igniting the gas flame with a paper quill. After he descends the policeman hands round the quill so other policemen can light their cigars. The tobacco glows through the rain, flickering like molten torches. Paul is reminded of a girl he saw at Kate Townsend's, the night he went looking for Clara. He never knew her name but he remembers how—after she climbed and lit the brothel's red lantern—the *madame* lit *her* cigar.

Something about the rain troubles Paul as he continues down the dark *cañon* of the street. After ten minutes he reaches the richly carved entrance of the French Opera House, Phoebus looming overhead from his burning chariot. A walkway of hanging flowers leads to a mahogany-railed staircase, and he is delighted to discover *The Marriage of Figaro* is being performed. Quietly he slips to the back and watches unseen.

At the interval he promenades the bar for *politesse* with a lady of his mother's acquaintance, but feels uncomfortable. He is reminded of Clara the whole evening. At the final curtain, the movable floor that doubles for *Mardi Gras* balls accidentally begins to rotate, sweeping the cast from the stage to the laughter and applause of the house. In the orchestra pit, a sudden brouhaha develops between the trombonist and the violinist and a clatter of symbols is the cue for the audience to leave while the scene is still relatively calm.

Soon enough, Paul walks the living streets of New Orleans. More than ever he feels the charm and wonder of the city by night. He weaves north on Coliseum to Dryades and enters Congo Square to the echo of midnight drums. Men, women and children sit cross-legged in twos and threes beating open-palm rhythms on the flat earth. Marvelling at the change from the Vieux Carré to Tremé, only a few blocks north, Paul takes a seat. From all sides, wary and welcoming faces are alive.

"Truly this is the Paris of the South," he says to his neighbour, an old slave who smiles intently and offers him a root to chew. Paul accepts and returns the smile. The man has an eye-scar, sores on his knees and looks happy to be sitting among his fellows. But Paul realizes he is not entirely welcome in Congo Square, the only place in the whole country where African drums can be legally played. The huge leather-skins beat in his wake and the colours flare from costumes of dancers imitating lions and tigers and vultures of the plain. Puzzled and amused, faces follow Paul as he scurries across Franklin to Circus Place and materializes under the looming spike of the St. Louis Cathedral. Impulsively he decides on a short cut.

He opens the gate of St. Louis Cemetery No. 1 and the iron portcullis closes behind him suggestive of the wakeful dead. As he floats through the cemetery, graves bob and weave with his every step. Swallowed in the tombs's various faces are names and dates overgrown by Louisiana frog-moss. Everywhere maple and clematis trees hang incestuously over headstones. Wild grasses float like soft Caribbean waves, waist-high in the air, and dandelion seeds brush Paul's face. He stands in the centre of the cemetery. There, he feels enfolded like the Ancient Mariner by the death-alive atmosphere. The tombs lean like treasure troves sunken in quicksand. He crouches and peers into black grates, always open, ready for tipping in the next family member.

Obscured in a corner Paul discovers the family tomb labelled *Morphy*. The grave's pale-white stone is scattered with seedpods. Nearby a pot of basil is growing, still alive from Alonzo's funeral. Its leaves are dry and dead-looking and rest on the family stone with a mournful air.

Paul sits. Time drifts. He eventually takes a bottle of absinthe *frappé* from his coat and sips.

"One to soothe the palate," he says and the wind whistles, "plus one to awaken the mind."

He listens while the night-sounds are lulled. No crickets or toads or fireflies stir. He rests one knee on the tomb, gently touching the hollow iron cross above his father's head. The clouds roll by. He can think of nothing to say, nothing, and his head slumps over the tomb.

Waking, Paul finds an absurd game of human chess is playing itself out between his family members. Edward and Ernest are busy fighting a duel in armour, bishop versus knight. A moment later they vanish and Paul rubs his eyes furiously. Suddenly a woman with a strange head, flat like a rook, brushes by carrying a pawn-shaped child under her arm. Paul watches them dissolve between the trees. The dangling child, upside down, glares at Paul and sticks out his tongue. He whispers "all is lost, all is lost."

The grotesque child makes Paul's eyes reel and he fears disturbing some element in the graveyard beyond his understanding. The sight of the fleeing woman sends him running over a gravestone, and he falls backwards into a freshly dug grave. For a moment he cannot scream or feel anything, before realizing the macabre horror of his predicament. His back has sunk five feet into the hole and his head lies at the lowest point. Fresh-moulded earth begins peeling from the coffin's sides onto his hands and face. He screams, finds himself scrambling from the hole and stumbling under the gently swaying trees. Crashing through some muddy weeds he forces himself over the cemetery gate. Landing in the living city again, he realizes the absinthe bottle has gone. So with no desire to return home and disturb the sleeping Clara, he looks for the nearest gin-bar. But the night is no longer young and the bars are closed. Only the red-lighted part of town beckons, but he no longer sees the attraction.

Instead the river calls, offering comfort and a vista of promise. So Paul ends up on the banks of the Mississippi, arranging rocks on the beach like chess pieces. The shore washes over his feet. He flicks a pebble or two. In desperation he tries to recite the Civil Code of Louisiana, but cannot. He walks narrowly along the grey stones, waiting for a glimmer of sunrise, but nothing seems to happen. He has lost all sense of time. Part of Paul yearns to open his mind to an imaginary game of chess. But his wish to abandon chess to study the law dominates his mind, a little tipsy now from the absinthe. So he announces to the beach his desire to become a lawyer and no chess poseur, performer or celebrity, but genuinely follow in his father's footsteps and proudly honour his family's name.

He wanders on. Reaching the Fulton end of the Quarter bordering the Warehouse District, Paul witnesses the first rays of warmth. The sight of the burnished tip of the sun spreading golden light over a sad swath of the Mississippi makes his heart swell. The promise is made in that moment. Perhaps he *can* leave behind his past and embrace a different kind of future. He meanders to New Levée and Tante Zizine for a *café au lait*.

"I know it," he says. "I can practice the law. I can be someone despite the Fred Edges and Howard Stauntons of the world."

"Yes, you can Paul."

"Believe in me."

"Yes, I do Paul."

"I can be successful without being Paul Morphy chess player." There is no reply from the city but he remains moved by the epiphany of promise.

Over the street Paul stops in a *charcuterie* for little cakes to bring back for Telcide and Helena as part of a proper welcome home. Again it starts to rain and he skips in and out of doorways trying to shield his clothes. When he reaches 89 Royal Street he is soaking and retreats to the bath. He thinks of Edge's letter and whether he was cruel to his manager. But if their adventures are now published in an unofficial biography against his personal wishes, how concerned can Edge be for his feelings? He closes the book on their friendship.

Paul rests his feet on the taps and ponders his future. From the angle of the bath, he can see rain clouds part and a blue sky swell in crystal perfection. Suddenly colours multiply. A rainbow forms in the sky, a premonition perhaps, a hopeful portent of the days ahead.

Later he sits in the grape arbour at the back of Charles Maurian's house on Rampart Street. All is dark in the house. Neither Charles, nor Clara, is awake. Between row of vineyards, curled on the earth with no blanket except a wondering sense of forever looking for home, Paul falls asleep. In a dream he sees his grandfather smoking a cheroot pipe in the prime of his life and striding down Chartres Street. Joseph Le Carpentier bears a whip in one hand, his moustache dripping with merry sweat. But all is illusion. An hour later Paul wakes to the wind blowing strongly in the cypress trees. He walks to Charles's house and raises his hand, tempted to knock, but doesn't. Clara will find him when she is ready. He touches the door with his fingernails.

Paul heads back home. Crossing Esplanade he glances at his grandfather's house, a few doors down from the Morphy home. Paul senses the ghost of the old man. Through the window, he senses the dark picture-portraits of the Le Carpentier generations, no doubt waiting to be sold off unless Telcide finds a space for them in the attic. In the half-light, a rocking chair lies idle, encircled by all those slave-trading faces of buried ancestors.

Paul shivers at the smallness of this world, compared to the vast oceans and what he has seen in Paris and London. He makes his way home to the house of mourning, the coffin and the inescapable sense of a family crumbling into financial worry. Inside, he takes to his bed and looks with brief feeling at the chess table now covered with a white tablecloth.

Chapter Thirty-Seven
1859
The Operatic Tale of Gilbert Rosière

When he gets home Paul discovers his grandfather has died. Knowing only of his illness from Telcide's letter, he feels the shock in his bones. Without having a chance to say goodbye, Paul is devastated. By mid-afternoon Ernest knocks on his door and quietly enters.

"He was always a good drinker. He drank just because he felt so ill. Life just became a vicious merry-go-round."

Paul lies there, wordless.

"In the end, he was in terrible confinement. The world diminished to a point."

"What were his last words?"

"It's not important."

Paul sits up. "No, tell me. Did he say something?"

"Well, he said lots of things. We're not to bury him. He wants to be cremated at sea." Ernest and Paul look across the room past the chess table and into the afternoon air. "And a few words to your mother. There was a terrible moment when he cried out 'Pray for me!' but that soon passed!"

"Oh!"

"He spoke about Jean Lafitte and how he was misunderstood. Something about Lafitte being more the friend to the city than Andrew Jackson! If he had his time again, he said, he wouldn't be an auctioneer. He seemed ashamed by that and repented owning slaves. Then he went quiet."

"I didn't know he was ill," Paul says. "He taught me chess as much as anyone."

"You taught yourself, Paul, in my estimation. But I'm sure you're right...You remember that time you showed your father how the pieces move? Joseph lost a lot of energy after you were gone..."

"Are you saying...?"

"No, of course not. You're not to blame, Paul."

"I know." They don't look at each other. "Did he say anything else?"

"I didn't want to tell you, but I don't suppose it can hurt now. He did say Paul...something like...you should sort out your problems *by the duel*. He didn't think Edward should. But the duel he said was mightily suited to you. Here, I wrote it down." Ernest rummages in his pocket and reads from a scrap of paper. "*Seek out the live-oaks, near the eternal fountains, dripping with Spanish moss. The perfect isolated spot for a duel, my boy.* He told me to say go past the General Beauregard statue at the entrance to City Park."

"I know where they fight duels," Paul replies. "I don't want to go there."

"But have you ever been? These were your grandfather's last words."

"I thought he said 'pray for me!'"

"Listen, Paul. He says 'cross over Bayou St. John and meet under the oaks for a *duello*, if you need to!'"

"Why are you telling me this? It's like an ominous prophecy."

"Then he said 'Presto'!"

"Presto? I don't believe this," Paul says. "The oaks! Coffee and pistols for two?"

"Paul!"

"But *presto!*"

"We all loved him," Ernest says.

"More than what, I don't know," Paul says. "I've lost everyone who cares."

"That's not true. Your *maman* and Helena and me, we all…for God's sake, Paul. Your grandfather just died."

The conversation goes no further and Paul slips under the covers while Ernest calms down. The older man executes a couple of tugs on his beard and leaves. Dark light moves across the bedroom's ceiling. Paul soon drifts in and out of sleep. But he knows he must go out. Not escaping the house of Alonzo's mourning, a full year ago, would be exchanging one death for the pale shadow of another. Eventually he does decide to fulfil his promise to his grandfather, and without understanding the old man's desire, he nevertheless goes to the Fencing Academy on Exchange Alley. He made a promise to meet the *maîtres d'armes* before embarking on his Grand Tour of Europe. Having learned the words of his grandfather on his death-bed, Paul feels obliged to remove his private grief from the house.

So without great desire to pursue any fencing, he meets Gilbert Rosière in the sleazy *Wanton Buck Café* on the corner of Exchange and Timur Streets. There he discovers Edward has arrived first, but remembering his brother's support at Dr Rizzo's Academy, Paul joins all three at a round table. As though wandering in from an Arthurian fable, Marcel Dauphin and Gilbert Rosière are there, attired somewhat ridiculously in body armour. Tapping them on the shoulders, assigning roles, these two King Arthurs make Edward into Sir Lancelot and Paul into the young pretender Gawain.

"Use the rapier," Marcel Dauphin says.

"*Sans doute*," from Rosière.

"I would go straight for the broadsword," says Edward. "You have to draw it eventually. And it's the most reliable. Crack him down before he cracks you," with an eye to Paul. "Works every time, eh?"

"I disagree—use the rapier," Dauphin says. "The trick is to keep combat close. The broadsword is too…"

"Broad?"

"In the *salles d'escrime*," Dauphin continues, "the broadsword is good because the attack can be so loose. But in a soggy field…"

"I didn't know the ground was soggy," Edward says and folds his arms in disgust, eliciting a smile from Rosière. "Otherwise I'd have said…"

"The rapier?" says Paul.

"Perhaps the English longbow. A tidy weapon," Dauphin offers.

"No, no, wrong all of you," Rosière declares. "The correct implement is the spear. Yes the spear is not part of our weaponry. But in a soggy field the broadsword is heavy and a long range weapon will suffice. A simple wooden spear! My *point* gentleman, if you'll forgive the pun, is to match your weapon to your man. Make the right choice, go well armed, and your chances of victory will triple!"

Paul chooses this juncture to make his request.

"Is it possible you still give lessons? Now the city is more dangerous?"

"Why is it more dangerous?" Edward asks.

"There could be a war," Paul says simply. "That's what *grandpapi*…"

"Well, with luck!"

Rosière agrees to lessons by "seeing what I can do," then leans closer to his chosen audience. After hushing them he whispers to the already-converted: "*Maîtres d'armes* lead fast lives! We are spoiled by waiters in cafés and loved by the locals. We're the suave gentleman of the city. Never does a *maîtres d'armes* cross the street no matter who's approaching, politician, soldier or pirate. Only for a lady do we break our stride! Some dress extravagantly and let their handkerchiefs flow from their sleeves, others adopt an elegant style and delicate manner at odds with their quickness to take offence. I prefer the former as you see! But *you*, sirs, are my adoring young bloods, you magnificent duellers, and you're worthy of a brief tale."

Some café-goers look round expecting a story of illicit goings-on or a racy adulterous affair.

"Well, it was a few months ago—Rosière remembers all! We were sipping coffee and liqueurs all day gentleman. Night fell faster than usual. Then as happens, I found myself walking home on the wrong side of town. I was through the Warehouse District and down on Gallatin Street...."

"Incidentally," Edward cuts in, "if you're going to listen to this story, Paul, you shoulder probably drop the Code of Napoleon...for the Code of Honour."

"The boy knows both Codes," Dauphin says.

"Gentlemen," Rosière says, "let me continue. So I cross over the street for a drink and I'm entirely by chance, you understand, at *The Twenty-One*, Kate Townsend's place now run by her cousin Milly Milburn. Before Milly's reign of sheer debauchery, you know, Kate was a wonderful hostess. Remember those days? Well, I'm not quite in the entrance minding my business when this fat man starts to grab hold of me. I'm dragged into the street! He starts twirling me around, dancing and calling me his bride. Now as you know," and Rosière leans in conspiratorially, "I *am* a fan of the opera. *Norma* is one of my favourites. But this guy flits back and forth from *Norma* to *Il barbiere di Siviglia*, crying 'Figaro, Figaro, Figaro!' Well by this time you can imagine the colour of my blade. Blasphemy! I'm fuming! The disgusting paramour dares to treat me as his wench, running his fingers down my tights, and the whole obscene scene, if you'll pardon my pun, is attracting quite the crowd of jeering idiots. Lousy bawds are hanging from the empty windows and the Wild Oak Boys are falling from trees just to glimpse my humiliation. He's spinning me round, the crazy rascal, and singing Figaro in my ear!"

The knights stare over their drinks, some gripped, others politely smiling.

"What did you do? What did you do?" Dauphin interjects, feigning glee.

"Well, what could I do?" Rosière says. "I whipped the man there and then. Gentleman! Herein lines my *point!* A warrior never backs down and never folds. He pushes through the battle to the end. For sure! Edward, don't *you* always fight when challenged? Your reputation is at stake. Better a lion for a day than a sheep for a thousand years! We must face our challengers or leave the city!"

"You don't need a diploma in broadsword or rapier to know that," Edward says, looking at his brother.

"Right!" screams Rosière. "So I met the gentleman in question down by the oaks, my bloods. As is proper! Then we shared a glass of port reserve by the old Salle St. Philippe. Ah those happy days! Unfortunately my opponent turned out to be an Italian professor of counterpoint. So when it came for the duel I was a little too brave with fortified wine, if you'll forgive my pun. So he ran me right through the shoulder and then pulled out the blade. When I awoke he was completely gone, along with his *second.* My own *second* was nowhere. He fled too! You wouldn't believe it! I spent three days in the ice house in bandages. So, you could say I bled all over the wild oaks, but that would be an exaggeration." He laughs with a frown. "But when they sealed the wound they said it looked like an alligator had taken a bite. I told them it was a crocodile and I made love to the beast! That was enough to throw me out on the street. Put it this way I never want to hear Figaro sing *The Barber of Seville* again!"

Rosière leans back on two legs satisfied with his tale and beckons the waiter. Dauphin whistles his compliment.

Puzzled, Edward peers at the table top, "so what's the moral?"

"The moral, dear Edward," adds Rosière, barely discomforted by the sober conclusion to his tale, "is *learn thy enemy's ways.* This business is not always uplifting. That's it. Know thy enemy." He turns to Paul. "So my advice to you, young man, is to return to London and whip that Howard Staunton with your opera glove until he comes out fighting. He dodged you and insulted you and it remains a blemish on your career! Challenge him! You know him for the deceitful cad he is! Go back with the express wish of duelling with him at dawn with pistols, if necessary." He climbs to his feet. "Defend the honour of New Orleans and your good family name, my boy, until you have satisfaction. Proud satisfaction is what we live for!"

Paul is stunned.

"I…appreciate the offer," he says. "And sometimes I do feel like I was whipped from Europe by just one man who wouldn't play me. But I can't return…."

"Why not?" Edward takes the opportunity.

"For the family," says Paul, "and…."

"And what?"

"It's not that simple."

"Find the man," Dauphin adds, whip his face, and force him to a duel. The devil has seduced you over the board and you must have recompense on the field!"

"There is no recompense," Paul replies. "I won't fight to defend my family name. Chess has rules of engagement."

"Then you must play," says Rosière.

"But you don't understand," and Paul stands up. "I can no longer fight for New Orleans, or chess or family honour or my life…" and he starts to sway, "or…"

"You need to calm down," says Edward. "Paul!"

"I can't. The game is over. *Tout est fait. Le jeu est fait. C'est tout*….For me it's the end." He pulls away from the table, knocking over his chair. "Chess is everything. But I will not play anymore. Don't you see? The game does no good. It is useless. Pointless! Pieces move on a board and we pretend that's honour. It's just bits of wood on a board. Don't you see that?"

"But the money?"

"I'm an amateur," Paul says. "*Maman*…"

"Forget *maman*," Edward says. "We need the money."

"Yes, and *you* talk of fighting duels. Life or death, for honour! And I believe you would fight them for money too!"

Edward does not reply.

"My God, Edward," Paul cries. "You will be dead too." He staggers from their knightly round table back through the café. "Play all the duels you want. I will not fight and I will not play!"

That night Paul lets himself into the kitchen of Charles Maurian's house and quietly climbs the stairs. He opens the door a crack on the sleeping Clara. Her hand is cast across a pillow, palm open. Her tangled hair reaches in knots to the floor. She looks clear-headed, caught between dreams and nightmares, but less like a princess than a beautiful Ophelia suspended underwater amid the drowning flowers. He approaches the bed and checks on her breathing.

"We'll find a way to be together."

Kneeling at her side, Paul says a prayer to Caïssa herself, feeling strangely comfortable and exhilarated by addressing the deity. He remembers the ceiling at the *Café de La Régence*. Softly, he takes the testimonial watch, the emblem of his New York Chess Congress victory, and lays it next to Clara's sleeping face, then slides it under the pillow.

"Made of gold and silver," he murmurs. "It will pay for your passage to any city. Go to the North or the islands or even Europe. You are free, you can go anywhere." Clara moans in her sleep, dreaming away her worry, and smiles as though she hears Paul's words.

Quietly he slips from the room.

Chapter Thirty-Eight
1860
Will Deacon the Game Parader

"So you're in a permanent state of lovelorn sorrow? I mean, did you sleep down here last night?"

"I did."

"And your family?"

Paul says nothing. Half sunk in the sofa, he is wearing a pair of pink-and-white striped *culottes* à la Flaubert. Charles Maurian looks at them and smiles.

"Where did you find those?"

"In your wardrobe."

"But they're my sister's."

Paul lifts his feet and admires the silk slippers. "They're very comfortable."

Charles nods at his friend, sensing a change. "You don't seem yourself, Paul?"

"How can I? I'm in love."

"You are?"

Paul frowns. "You know Christopher Marlowe was the son of a shoemaker. And he wrote some great plays."

"And you've played great chess games. But, so I'm told, not any more?"

"That's right."

Charles walks to the window and pours more tea, his dressing gown rolling along the carpet. He is taller than Paul, and somewhat his guardian today, but also the Creole that Spring Hill College made him. He is a private broker, an advocate for new American immigrants establishing a city district beyond Tulane Street. His heartfelt worry for his friend has ruffled his shady world.

"Why do you like chess?" Paul asks.

"The same reason as you, right, it simulates the intellect. Chess alters the structure of the brain and refines it. The joy of predicting the future and testing the mind…."

"What about passion? Chess is just a game, albeit a symbol of art or war or science. And it doesn't bring people together in social harmony. I can attest to chess-inspired duels in three cities. New Orleans is the only city where people care. The rest is ambition and disloyalty."

"Nationalistic fervour?"

"It's a parasite, Charles. A louse that crawls inside your brain…."

"And eats it away, right? A killer game. I suppose the Indians invented chess to curse the Persians, right? Didn't the Islamists bring it to Europe for the same reason?"

"Call me a cynic, Charles, but I just don't like it. The game's vicious. I won't play it any more."

"No one is forcing you. And I thought it wasn't a game?"

Paul shuffles his feet, conscious of Charles's tactic of devil's advocate.

"Look at this," and he hands Charles a newspaper clipping. The headline reads *Deacon Makes His Move*. "This new man on the scene, William Deacon, plays the big names. Then he tricks them so they lose their reputations and livelihoods. It's all in the article. Deacon offers a friendly game and takes moves back pieces *ad lib*. Anderssen, Harrwitz and William Steinitz have all been caught!"

"How can he?"

"Well, he sets up the game in a jovial manner so the champion is at ease. They demonstrate positions, and if Deacon has the nod of play, he writes up his victory for the *London Times* the next day."

"That fast?"

"It's nothing to worry about, Paul. You already know his trick. He's been discovered."

"Yes, but Charles, there could be more of them. Don't you see? These people want to bring down chess players."

"Listen, he's a con man. They exist in every walk of life."

"But this is *chess*. So much is at stake!"

"Paul, what is at stake? You said it yourself. Chess is nothing."

Here Paul goes quiet. "So you agree with me?"

"No. I mean yes. Paul, you have to see…"

"You agree. The game is useless! And I have devoted my life and study to a board game that means nothing."

"No, Paul. You have studied the law and travelled and…"

"I play a mongrel game of rapid attacks in the hope I win before my opponent gets going…but not William Steinitz…he's a master of defence…."

"You are rambling and confusing me, Paul. Remember you wanted to be a lawyer? I mean, you're going to the bar soon right? The *attorneys'* bar of course."

Paul smiles but remains jittery. "Yes, my future years will be devoted to graver and more serious studies….But the whole country is about to break into pieces. Look at this!" and he takes out a slip of paper for Charles. "This is the last letter from my loving grandfather, Joseph Le Carpentier. He is scared out of his wits by this man Lincoln, a bloodthirsty Republican if ever there was one!"

"Well, thirsty for blood because he wants to maintain the Republic," says Charles.

"No, those are my grandfather's words. The poor man died angry. I think Lincoln's electoral win may have brought on his death."

"Paul…"

"There's a perverse joke being circulated—that war is coming—but when we're drafted, we won't be laughing!"

Charles frowns and reads: "*The election of Abraham Lincoln, January 1860, is the final trigger for serious consideration among Southern leaders at state and local level. Make your choices, gentleman, or choices will be made for you. Secession is now a crisis and too many will wrongfully seek the way of the Crittenden Compromise!* Paul, I can't read any more…"

"Look down, too, Joseph has written something."

"Okay, let me see…here it is. *Look my boy. Did I not tell you? Something to behold, my boy, something to behold. Things fall apart and we're going down! Blood in the streets and mighty red rivers! I can't stomach a war Paul. I'm getting old too old for the silly adventure. But you'll have to swap the chess for the sword…*"

"He's amusing you."

"Even so," Paul says and takes his seat. "I'm scared of these reports."

"Well, I'm not," Charles says and pours more tea. For a while the old friends don't speak. Then Charles stands and presses Paul's shoulder. "Everything will be all right, you'll see. There's no war on the way. These journalists are as bad as the politicians, just stirring up fear. One crisis after another or the papers won't sell. But I guarantee this city will stand! They can *try* and take New Orleans! But nothing shy of Mother Nature can take these streets! Our home!"

"You're a patriot after all!"

"I'm just from New Orleans," Charles says. "You used to be too." They stare moodily in the fire when suddenly from upstairs, Clara appears in the doorway. Charles offers her a seat, noticing her stripy red-and-white stockings. She curls up quietly on the sofa.

"Good evening gentlemen," the refugee says and nods a mock greeting. Paul smiles, and Clara takes his hand and squeezes.

"Long faces in here, I'm afraid," says Charles.

Clara grins and holds a cup out for tea. "I thank you kindly sir." Then she turns to face Paul. "So when do I get to meet your family? It wouldn't be right, would it, if I didn't?"

Paul says nothing.

"His mind is on edge," Charles says, generating a chuckle from Clara.

"I'd rather be here than on Basin Street," Clara says.

"And I'd rather be here than on Royal," Paul replies.

They drink the tea and Charles retires early for the night. Left alone, they listen to the rain on the balcony, a strange duet hidden away on the backstreets of Esplanade.

Chapter Thirty-Nine
1860
The Genius of the People

Howard Staunton's *Complete Illustrated Shakespeare* is published in February 1860, a double volume twinned with his *Chess Praxis*. The Shakespeare contains images of female stage roles from Desdemona to Cleopatra, the chess book over a hundred annotated games. None is a Morphy-Staunton match. Ignoring the Shakespeare, Paul throws down the local paper *l'Abeille*.

"I can't believe his games are now reaching the printing presses."

Clara picks up *l'Abeille*. "You know Howard Staunton is reputedly the bastard son of Frederick Howard, fifth earl of Carlisle."

"I didn't know that, but it doesn't surprise me."

They're sitting under the giant oaks Joseph Le Carpentier recommended for problem-solving. After promising his grandfather, Paul still practices his fencing skills. But he's reneged on his decision to abandon chess altogether. So the games compete for his attention. Every now and then he demonstrates a few chess moves, re-enacting them inelegantly with the blade. The afternoon is pleasant and warm: for once his fears are assuaged.

"So if I live with Charles for a few more weeks, I could begin thinking about running the store."

"The store?"

"The clothes store. Like the one we saw one on Canal Street. I could be a glove-seller. Sell mittens to the girls on Gallatin or the Swamp."

"Clara, I thought you'd be an opera singer first?" He places a knight, blocking her pawn.

"That depends on Telcide, Paul. When will I meet her? She is the only one who can start me on the stage. Unless you know someone else at the opera, of course?"

"No, not yet. You're right to pursue these employments, I think. A job is needed."

"And what is your job?"

"Please be a little patient."

The conversation is closed for the moment. Clara sidesteps Paul's knight with an attack of her queen knowing full well the risk of exposing her powerful piece. Luckily, raindrops appear on the back of her hand just as she moves. Paul will not have to face another tricky deception about the family gathering. They hurry the game. Clara smiles, almost tempting him to take her queen, and Paul blushes.

"Chess is not everything," he says.

"No, there is also the opera and clothes," Clara replies and Paul is relieved by her answer.

"I agree."

They hold hands on the way home and receive stares from several Creoles, despite Clara's conservative dress. After centuries of being finely attuned to polite appearance, there is something else about Clara the inhabitants of the French Quarter don't like. She is too dark for their liking. For now Paul is oblivious to the extent of their prejudice and surprised by the acute perception of their eyes. They look, and in looking, some secret of Clara's has been found out. The wrong side of the tracks is one thing. The wrong colour for society is another.

Once again Paul returns Clara to Charles Maurian's house. They kiss just inside the doorway and exchange more promises. The door closes and Paul hears Charles's voice. Here, he thinks, Clara will spend her days in safe, almost dreamlike confinement. The stipend Paul is receiving from Alonzo's estate will pass into Charles's household accounts and take care of her. Admiring the cedars on Rampart Street, sturdy in the air-blue sky, he feels content walking back to Royal Street.

Paul begins a daily routine. With no fixed employment and having resigned as President of the New Orleans Chess Club, he doesn't wish to be reclusive inside the Vieux Carré. Each morning he takes a promenade on Canal Street and visits the ostentatious lobby of the *St. Louis Hotel*. Here he reads English novels lent him by Dr Meek and leather-bound French poetry gifted from Eugene Rousseau. Often he admires the St. Louis Cathedral on the way home. Paul tells people he is still writing a book, a wholly truthful memoir of his chess travels, plus the games themselves, partly to set the record straight with Fred Edge. But swearing off serious chess again to focus on his career, he never writes the memoir. Still, he indulges the occasional chess game with Charles as a favour for his friend's generosity. Weekdays and weekends he attends the opera to see Mozart, Rossini and Meyerbeer. On one occasion he takes Clara to a performance but she is recognized as a Basin girl at the door and refused entry.

Despite trying to regulate his life, Paul cannot escape one appointment. While in Paris he made a monetary commitment, via Edge, granting an interview to Mr Forest J. D. Woodbury of the *Hartford Times*. Months go by before Woodbury smells a likely story. The interview happens in the *salle de compagnie* of 89 Royal Street on a Sunday afternoon. They sit where Alonzo and Ernest played, where Paul made his first chess intervention as a small boy. Woodbury lays his glasses on his writing pad and peers meaningfully at his subject. Then he fires direct questions.

"Genius, it's a word. What does it really mean? If I win, I'm a genius. If I don't, I'm not. Comments?"

"I don't think I said that."

"But can you give us an insight? Did you discover your powers by noticing that others didn't possess them?"

"Well, in a way..."

"Is chess an outlet for hostile impulses, like all sport?

"No, I don't believe so."

Woodbury cocks his head sideways, a bird fishing for a worm.

"How do you respond to people who say you have an anti-intellectual streak?"

"I don't respond at all."

"Some would say Harrwitz plays with brooding murkiness. Steinitz plays with ensnaring defensiveness. But you, sir, play with a crystalline style completely lacking book knowledge."

"Thank you."

"So you play instinctively, like speaking a mother tongue?"

Paul's neck tenses. He tries to glean the kind of article Woodbury might write. Perhaps disclosing chess opinions, he thinks, might limit any interest in his private life. He speaks more freely. Hence he is brought back to the game he wishes to escape, forcing himself out of obligation to comply with Woodbury's line of thinking.

"People like nothing more," the journalist says, "than to know their champions are better than the rest. They want to *feel* that magic sets them apart. You know the kind of thing?"

"*Primus inter pares*," Paul offers.

"First among equals. Go on."

"Well, that's how I see myself, I suppose. I try to attack, it's true, and I like to play fast. What's important, perhaps..."

"Fore sure, Mr Morphy."

"What is good...on the board..."

"Yes..."

"...is not making the best move relatively or for the occasion but the *absolute* best move. That's about as clear as I can put it."

"Right," Woodbury sighs half satisfied. "So?"

"So...other people don't like it," Paul continues. "They envy a gift and...fear it...people see only ambition."

"I see."

"I'm alone," Paul says, "grasping at straws."

"What makes you tired, Mr Morphy?"

"I'm sorry?"

"Or cry. Do you?"

Paul steels himself. "I don't know, Mr Woodbury."

"The end of a chess game?"

"No, not chess."

"Love?"

He watches Woodbury's eyes droop. "I'm the same as everyone else."

"You are?"

"And these questions aren't appropriate," Paul adds, puzzled by how much Woodbury is scribbling. "In chess," he elaborates, "there is only what is true which should be absorbed, and what is false which should be rejected."

"Quite so." Again the pen.

"Is that everything?"

"Let me see. You play with risk and daring. You are a gentleman champion, courteous and never weep at past battles. You know that clear, precise decisions are the key to victory and a happy future. Essentially you're a duellist or a politician!"

"Yes, I think that's everything, Mr Woodbury." Paul rises. "Thank you for coming." More abruptly he guides the reporter to the door and shakes his hand on the threshold. Standing there, a sound from upstairs disturbs their goodbye, a woman's surprise at dropping some object.

"A mistress?" Woodbury smirks and pushes his glasses up his face. "I won't put that in the article, you needn't worry."

"Thank you. No, I mean I'll say one thing," Paul answers, struck now by the foolishness of their talk. "I've travelled to Europe and back and I mean what I say. I've learned one piece of truth..."

"Shoot, Mr Morphy. I have a good memory!"

"Okay." Paul knits his brow, making the journalist step backwards. "When I started winning in Europe, *that's* when I knew all was lost. That goes for every match, every serious game. Do you see, Mr Woodbury? When I started, I learned how to lose. There's no such thing as winning. Winning is losing too. That's it."

"Winning is losing. Got it."

"Thank you, Mr Woodbury."

"The pleasure is all mine. May I come back?"

"By all means. But not this week, Mr Woodbury. I'm very busy, you see. Thank you."

Chapter Forty
1860
The Magnolia Tree

That night Clara leaves Charles Maurian's for an evening walk. She intends to visit Paul in the Royal Street courtyard by surprising him with a stone to his bedroom window. But she keeps walking, questioning what has drawn her away from Charles and Paul, the two men keeping her a secret from the world. She knows her presence in the French Quarter is illegal. But the river offers freedom. She heads down Barracks Street to the shoreline to gather her thoughts.

A strange light is cast over the Mississippi. As Clara approaches, the fog rolls in. The light hangs mysteriously, a will-o'-the-wisp clinging to the fishing boats like a silken thread, couching them in dream-like mist. Something about the bobbing boats and the huge hidden water is comforting. She lies on the beach. Then she picks up a rock and tests its weight on her feet. Without warning the fog rolls over Clara, so thick she can feel its chill on her skin. Something inside her stirs and she tastes its hollowness in her mouth.

"Save me," she whispers. "Take me somewhere." She is superstitious enough to ask the fog whether to stay or go? If she returns to the brothels, she knows that Paul won't find her. But who is to say other men, down by the Swamp or South Basin, wouldn't help her out of trouble? Minnie Ha-Ha would undoubtedly take her back. Even if Kate Townsend doesn't run *The Twenty-One* anymore, Minnie Ha-Ha *always* needs help. Perhaps, Clara thinks, she could even be a *madame* herself?

"Better the devil you know," she says to the breeze. "These Creoles are all slave-traders. So much for my blood! I'm blacker than blue, just like everyone else in this city. They want too much…" and she begins to cry. Fortunately, anger comes. She twists the rock in her hand and tosses it in the water. "Tell me what to do! I'm getting lost. If it's a game like dancing…one two three and turn. But the end of the game is near, I can feel it!" Clara calls out, voiceless in the wind, and pulls her fringe down over her face.

The lighters roll over the water. She lies down and wakes up colder. The mist has gone and reveals the huge expanse of Big Muddy, dark and grinning and no longer a comfort. Men must inhabit these barges, Clara thinks, men who value a good woman. The boats wink back in agreement. Clara is reminded of all the bad treatment she's suffered over the years at men's hands. Even the *madames* were invulnerable to kindly feeling. *Not* going back would mean losing La Cubana—no small blessing—but also mean the end of the milliner's store or becoming an opera singer! But what is the alternative?

Clara turns to face the Vieux Carré and the path that leads from St. Louis Cathedral into one possible future. She pictures 89 Royal Street, its yellow façade and circular windows glowing with family warmth. Little does she know of the Morphys' problems. Instead, she imagines a beautiful invitation card asking her to dinner every Sunday. But the image fades to dark shutters and the doors of the Vieux Carré that keep a trickster and her illicit past well out.

"There's only one way," she says and pictures the single magnolia tree in the courtyard. She closes her eyes and sees its large white flowers, inhales its sweet musky perfume. She makes her decision as the sun is rising, wraps her coat tighter, and walks back to the city.

Chapter Forty-One
1860
Morphy Musical Soirée

The table is cleared of roast pheasant just as the ice cream arrives. Titi brings one tray and removes the half eaten *entrée*, returning with the cherry sauce as the diners move into the music room. A knock is heard at the door and Alex Le Carpentier declares he will investigate. He already has "high expectations a young prodigal chess player is returning." Ernest takes Telcide and Malvina—husband John Sybrandt away on business—arm in arm to 'walk the room.' Meanwhile the front door is opened by Alex trussed up in one of his dandified white suits. He bows magnanimously and peers into the hall with a quip. On the threshold stand Clara and Paul, holding hands. They resemble young people running away from home, knocking at a halfway house for supper, albeit wearing evening clothes. Clara looks less worried that Paul.

Alex Le Carpentier shows them in, but clearly sees what can only be a misfortunate choice for the Creole family. Hanging up the coats, Alex takes Paul aside.

"I can tell she is…"

"Please…"

Alex, ever the cavalier uncle, lays his hand on Paul's shoulder and pats in mock disapproval. "A man after my own heart," he laughs. "It's a case of who finds out first, but I'd never think to bring 'em home!"

"She is not," Paul says and starts to shake. "I don't know what you mean. Clara is..."

"I can see with my own eyes, Paul."

Paul stares at his uncle and for once brushes him away. He is more determined to introduce Clara to his family, regardless of anyone's support or disdain. But Alex takes his wrist and holds tight.

"Paul, I don't just mean she's not from the Quarter, if you see my meaning. What I mean is..."

"Yes, please spit it out."

"I mean...she's not our kind."

"Well," Paul says. "I don't see your meaning. We're all from Spain and living in Louisiana, so what's a touch of sun?"

"Okay, so we're not the whitest Creoles in the Quarter," Alex says and runs out of steam. "But there's a difference...good luck to you!"

Paul stares, before returning to Clara waiting in the hall. The sound of viola and piano harmonizing beckons: Clara takes a shallow breath. Holding hands, the odd couple enters the music room. Ernest welcomes them and flourishes his hand to display the room, the people and a collection of musical instruments. All the faces show bright expectation. Clara curtsies.

Paul steps forward.

"This is Clarabelle Young," he says. "She's from Baton Rouge and also spent time on the islands." The room smiles back. Helena smiles from behind the cello. At the piano, Telcide turns the ruffled pages of her unfinished operetta, *Louise de Lorraine*. In her surprise she disturbs the pages which flutter like feathers to the floor. Ernest retrieves them. Telcide and Clara regard each other over his shoulders, the light-skinned Creole matriarch and the dark-skinned *débutante*.

"You are very welcome," Telcide says. "I hope your journey was not too discomforting."

"No, I assure you. Paul was kind enough to walk me here."

"I see."

Telcide looks her guest direct in the face and smiles, imitating sweetness. She senses Clara is a working girl. Her mind is so preoccupied with the thought, somewhat incredibly and partly due to low light, she fails to notice the darker hue of Clara's features. Rather than unsuitable heritage, she sees only the girl from the wrong side of town beyond the Protestant Cemetery of Camp Street, and born of invisible slums. Telcide does not see Clara's mixed race, only her lack of European breeding. Rather she sees Clara's hidden poverty as progenitor of her unfitness for society. The usual Creole question of Clara's racial background is therefore relegated and her appearance is admirable in the eyes of the other family members, somewhat conscious of their own Mediterranean skin colour. Even in polite society, physical appearance matters more than race; and Clara looks delicate in an air-blue dress with a white cotton hem and neckline. A quiet ring of pearls loaned from Helena drapes her neck.

The spectacle works in silence since to clarify the reality of Clara's racial forbears would end the evening.

"Paul has told me so much about you," Clara trills and stands back. "You are lovely."

"I adore your dress," Telcide says in her politest accent and tugs the hem of her own green frock. The greatest hurdle has been overcome. Telcide rises from the piano and they embrace.

Clara senses her moment, and a newly discovered confidence projects her into the middle of the room. "I'm very happy here," she says, facing them all. Paul blushes slightly, and at his elbow Alex affects a grin.

But near the door, the maid Titi Benevolence reacts differently, staring with peculiar knowledge at the strange arrival. Silently she recognizes a *quadroon* or light-skinned black girl. At the same moment, Clara's twirling accidentally knocks a bowl of cherry sauce balanced in Titi's hands slips from her fingers. The bowl falls with a clatter to the floor. Without delay Clara is on her knees, instinctively ladling the sauce in the pot with a wooden spoon. Paul touches Clara's shoulder and she realizes her mistake and stands.

"*Pas de problème*," Titi reassures her. The room springs into action to hide any embarrassment and the piano strikes up a twirl of notes. As though the cherry bowl never fell, Alex supports Ernest on the viola and the *salle de musique* is transformed into a jamboree of musical dissonance.

"Thank you," Clara says, addressing Titi and betraying her Basin Street accent. In reponse Titi levels her eyes with a sad smile and speaks in her native Cajun dialect.

"Make a lil' harda. Or *allez-y*. You will go-go."

"I see."

"A lil' caution no, okay?"

Clara nods, pretends to understand and watches as Titi clears the floor. Meanwhile Alex adopts the role of guide and encourages Clara to take his arm. Imitating a prince and lady of Napoleon's court they promenade the carpet twice. Telcide then seats herself with Malvina in the alcove window before the keyboard of a so-called mother-and-daughter virginal. Compared to a piano, the virginal has a range of only four octaves: the single string is shared, the truncated octave being a clue to Malvina's limited talent and Telcide's singing range.

Meanwhile Clara discerns who sits where and why, having spent much time among instruments learning the subtle language that connects player to choice of instrument. Paul realizes that no one has experienced more social-musical evenings, albeit in a different context, than Clara. Wondering what she makes of his family, he straightens his own elegant white suit, folding its long lapels of emerald green over a chair. Solo among the Morphys he chooses to sit out Telcide's *entourage de musique*. Helena is not allowed to use the virginal, though, as younger daughter. She is relegated to the clavichord, a smaller quieter version resembling a pair of white wings. Meanwhile Paul and Clara, less on show, remain spectators beside the *armoire* in matching satin chairs.

Clara leans to Helena. "It's very pretty," she says. "An instrument shaped like an angel."

Helena goes red, saying "Queen Elizabeth of England once played it."

"The Virgin Queen," Clara replies and gently taps Helena's knee.

"You are in good company," jokes Alex, taking his position on the viola, freshly tuned by Ernest to the piano. Catching eyes, the whole family begins a countdown again. The room goes quiet, expectation builds and the atmosphere is tense: Ernest finally whips back the piano lid and the cacophony strikes up.

They play for almost an hour until the greater part of *Louise de Lorraine* has been exhausted. During the slow movements Telcide sings, modulating her *mezzo-soprano* voice to fit the tempo while judging the degree to which the instruments fail to harmonize. Now and then, her voice flies to heaven or drops to purgatory due to an incorrect string plucked by Malvina—glee in her eyes and red in her cheeks. So too flat notes inspired by Ernest's rotund fingers are drowned in silent laughter. Gradually the opera draws to a close, the players sighing with communal exhaustion.

Clara claps politely—remembering the piano man at LuLu White's—and Paul joins her in applause. Helena registers a final note on the clavichord to acknowledge her reluctance to join the operetta experiment. Telcide declares the composition shaky and the acoustics of the room ungraceful. A family again, one by one the Morphys pack away their instruments, while Titi returns with fresh cherry sauce and ice cream. As the guest, Clara is happily served first.

"Do you know on Royal Street," she begins, "there's a haunted house where an old woman beat her slaves?"

"No, I'm afraid I didn't," Malvina answers.

"Oh yes," Clara, amusing herself. "A Ms Julia Thomas. She was later overpowered by a mob…."

"Is that true?" Helena says. "How dreadful."

"Terrible," echoes Telcide.

"Yes…A boy's bones and naked servant woman, both tied to a pipe, were found in her bathroom. The mob then got mad and knocked in the windows with pikes on fire…"

"What happened to her?" Paul asks.

"Well, Ms Thomas barely escaped the city alive!"

"Disgusting," says Ernest, "what the mob can do," and changes the subject. "I've been reading, Paul, about the future of your royal game. Herr Kolisch and Herr Anderssen played a game with time controls last month. There was an article in the *Baton Rouge News*."

"Oh," Paul replies, seated now between Clara and Ernest. "Two pretty good tales…"

"It's true," Ernest continues. "The future of chess is clocks. It's a pity Louis Paulsen didn't have that restriction in New York. From what I hear, those games were exceptionally long."

Paul waits for the cry of Joseph Le Carpentier with "inter-min-able!" but no sound occurs.

"Well, the hourglass of old Saturn," says Ernest, "consists of two giant *clepsydras* sandglasses, each giving just two hours! I wonder how they'll play with the sword of Damocles suspended over their heads!"

"I should think faster," Paul replies.

Clara laughs.

"Time is position," says Ernest.

"I'll second that," says Alex. "They'll definitely play better. You know I was never a believer in slow moves…"

Sequestered in a corner, Edward's voice interrupts with a surly tone. "I'll tell you something, since *Papa* is gone no one speaks their mind." He steps into the light. "Any student who needs frivolous chess to please his mind has a carnal, empty mind. If God himself, plus all his books and friends can't suffice Paul's intellectual yearnings, then he has a chess *disease*."

"Edward!" gasps Helena, "I can't believe you. Paul is…blessed."

"Cursed more like. And what has it done for him?"

"I quite agree," Paul says, "and that's why I no longer play the game. Chess is a con man's profession."

"So be it," Edward says enigmatically.

"Well," Paul says. "I have made my journey to Europe and now I need to start a career. And chess is *not* my profession. I won't be a paid gambler or entertainer." Here he glances at Telcide and she smiles approvingly, while Ernest merely frowns. "So," Paul says and stands, "I have an announcement. I'm now partners with E. T. Fellowes to become Attorneys and Counselors at Law. You may remember my old Jefferson Academy friend, Ewan Fellowes. He lives on Orleans Street, No. 199."

"Wonderful," Telcide declares, and stops herself from an overflow of emotion. "That *is* good news, Paul."

Edward and Malvina seem nonchalant but in effect they're happy with the possibility of new income to the family purse.

"Fellowes & Morphy," Paul says and looks around the room.

"Just be careful," Edward adds, "you don't start playing chess on your slow days."

"It's true," Malvina echoes.

"If you lack a meaningful interest," Edward pursues, "how about poetry? *Life turns inward on its root becoming its own poison.* How about *that* for a chess metaphor?"

Paul turns to Clara. "My brother is a genius. Welcome to the family."

"Thank you!"

"You're getting married?" asks Ernest.

"No, I mean, we've been practicing for a week," Paul begins.

"Practicing?" says Telcide.

"Chess?" says Alex.

"No, no," and worn down by questions Paul throws up his hands. "The law! We've been *practicing* for a week now. We have a first client...."

"Let me guess," Edward continues to joke. "Dr Rizzo wants you to absolve him for an opera-night murder *not* carried out under the wild oaks? Let's see. The duel never happens but his reputation *based on* its existence…"

"…means he wants you to *finesse* his chess game," says Malvina.

"Yes!" Edward takes up. "You only play chess with Rizzo during your meetings. From the bench—he's in the dock—you'll demonstrate his right to kill *en passant!*" He smirks and wipes his face. Telcide looks on, bemused.

But Clara does not miss anything. "Paul will make a fine lawyer," she says. Everyone then goes quiet, not wishing to undermine the guest and waits. "I have faith in his abilities."

Eventually Edward delivers the *coup de grâce:*

"So when they come to you for legal advice, Paul, you should be careful. They might not see the attorney, only the magician or entertainer or *chessist.* Am I right? If you *can't* make legal problems vanish like the man in Maelzel's chess automaton, people will become suspicious. They won't understand why you don't use your chess powers, your vast intellect and foresight to win the case? Just a friendly warning from one swordsman to the next! Clients won't allow your victory as a mere lawyer. You'll have to win as a chess-playing wizard!"

"Edward!"

"People won't see me as a chess player," Paul says.

"Oh don't be too sure," Edward continues before he's interrupted by a stern voice. The only possible patriarch in the room, Ernest, pipes up to find some dominant order amid the half bitter conversation.

"Don't say anything you'll regret," Ernest says. "We're still one family. More so now…"

"What are you talking about?" Edward counters. "You're not…What do you mean 'more so'?" He goes pale and looks numb. "What do you mean 'one family'?"

"I don't know," Telcide says.

Ernest rises from the piano and stands behind Telcide. "There's something you all should know," and he coughs into his fist. "Your mother and I…I mean Telcide and…arranged everything last week. The nuns of the St. Ursuline convent are performing a quiet ceremony. And your mother...I mean Telcide...has offered me her hand in marriage."

The silence is broken by Helena who runs crying from the room.

Malvina covers her mouth. "So father's estate?" she begins and stops herself.

"Yes, Alonzo's estate," Telcide says, "is my estate, is my husband's. Even so, the money will be administered as per *our* will. I want you all to know—pardon me Clara—we're waiting until the estate is legally divided. You are *all* benefactors!"

"So nothing has really changed?" Alex offers.

"Not financially no..." Telcide says.

The news hovers. Alex offers his congratulations, followed by Paul and Edward who both kiss Telcide's cheek. They shake hands with their uncle Ernest. The event is not wholly unexpected, even so but Paul cannot look his uncle in the eye. He notices Malvina sitting in a corner biting her nails.

"The family is getting smaller," Alex says, without rejoinder. "I mean...we need an injection of old blood."

"I think it's wonderful," says Clara and, standing, she twirls her dress in celebration.

Meanwhile, a smile crosses Telcide's face. "I'm weary," she says and decides to lie down. Ernest exits by another door to smoke his pipe on the balcony. Alex leaves too, asserting business in the city and no one questions his premise for departure. The party is over, although three siblings and Clara remain. Together they watch Ernest, the great supporter of their family, through the porch window taking the air in his new role as Claudius to Telcide's Gertrude. Alonzo's money will pass brother to brother it seems like a deal struck in childhood.

"We'll never know what happened," says Helena.

"So I guess this makes you Prince Hamlet, the most melancholy amongst us," Edward says. "*The funeral meats did furnish forth the marriage bed.*"

"That would be my line," Paul replies.

"*A little more than kin and less than kind*," Malvina adds. Through the glass, they see Ernest resting his head on the yew tree, arms dangling over the wooden balcony.

"Look how he breaths in the winter air," Edward says.

"It's calming," Paul says. "It can't be easy."

Paul now leaves with Clara joining him and they say their goodbyes. But once in the hall, the door trellis open, they overhear Edward and Malvina. They stop and eavesdrop.

"Paul won't eat anything unless it's prepared by Helena or *maman*," says Malvina.

"So I've heard. And at Paul's office the rumour is—and who doubts it—he carries a portable chessboard and sits there all day ignoring the opportunities. Instead of practicing the law, you know, he practices moves over and over on a tiny wooden board." They continue to whisper.

Clara whispers "*do* you have a portable chessboard?"

"No, I don't," he laughs. "It's nonsense. And everything strikes me more like *Macbeth* than *Hamlet* with all these suspicions! No one believes I can become a lawyer." Clara smiles and takes his arm.

"I believe you, Monsieur Morphy. Thousands wouldn't but tonight, I do." Paul blushes and grips Clara round the waist.

With three-legged steps, they ascend the spiral staircase. Then in honour of their achievement at the family gathering Paul carries Clara, wavering a little, over the threshold. Everything will be reborn in this room, he hopes, calmer and happier. In the cool night air they open a bottle of Möet. The champagne bubbles speed to freedom and their glasses clink. Clara pulls the white sheet back from the chess table and reveals not a single piece and giggles. They toast the welcome Mademoiselle Young has received, at last, on the strangest of evenings at the hands of the Morphy family.

That night, the stalking bishop is absent from Paul's sleep. He dreams instead of Clara. She is riding a sylvan white stallion across a green field and waves the flag of Louisiana behind her. The image is ridiculous but Paul finds it erotic and subduing of his political worries; a dream, it seems, can make sense of any nightmare.

Breathing soundly, he calls out to her. She laughs and throws back her head. The horse gallops past his face and Clara's hair flies free in the breeze. The sunshine sparkles insanely. On the horizon the majestic lady and her steed disappear, while Paul slumbers on in pursuit of the comfort and happiness lying just over the next hill.

Chapter Forty-Two
1860
Quarters of the Crescent

Mainly to escape the house, Paul and Clara spend the morning walking, Clara revelling in her disguise as a Creole lady. Before they leave she lays the *New Orleans Picuyne* in Paul's lap which he opens, without thinking, to a recent chess article entitled *Pawn and Move to the World*. Instantly he recognizes the plagiarism of a dictation he gave to Fred Edge in Paris, following his bout against Charles H. Stanley. By ten o' clock he decides to pay the newspaper a visit to request retraction of the article, published under the staff writer's name.

The weather is inclement, the temperature a steady five above freezing. Wrapped in winter coats, Paul and Clara emerge with a merry glow into the basking false sunshine of the street. Fortified by the success of the evening, a sea change has occurred in Paul. He glances continually at Clara's face and the corners of her green dress escaping her neck and sleeves. From this morning Paul starts to dress charmingly but increasingly fastidiously in elegant suits. He believes Clara's influence on his mind and habits is responsible.

By coincidence at the corner of Bourbon and St. Peter, the newsstand *Louisiana Enquirer* captures Paul's attention. They pause in the street while he reads. *If Mr. Morphy visits the Brown Stone Clothing Hall of Rockhill and Wilson, he will receive a shining canary yellow elegant suit. And should Mr. Morphy's preference be darker, a more sombre suit of black can be arranged, or a double-breasted import from Pennsylvania with crystal stud buttons and silver pockets.*

Clara holds up the newspaper but Paul persuades her to return it. He already has three suits from the local stores of the Vieux Carré.

"It is my duty as a gentleman," he says, "to look smart but not overdressed."

"As a gentleman lawyer," Clara says.

"As a defender of the people."

"And they are advertising to you direct now!"

Arm-in-arm, they stroll down the street like any other couple, a banker and milliner, or office manager and opera singer. Despite Clara's feelings of giddy fraudulence, no one notices of course. They enter the market and for a moment Paul stops, remembering being here with his grandfather the day of Jean Lafitte's funeral. Clara gently takes his hand. The past is there but now it is only the past, unchangeable and separate.

"Ms. Young, what would I do without you?" Today of all days, Paul feels like a child without knowing why. A strong sense of nostalgia and elation fills his heart. They stroll among the market flowers, buying posies and fixing them in each other's clothes. Soon they emerge from the darkness of Bourbon between the façades of old French houses. Everywhere bamboo and cypresses point to Jackson Square. Clara breaks into a skip and Paul follows, amused. Down the riverbank, marigolds and daisies droop from the ears of flower vendors, petals bobbing on the curves of their caps.

At the herb market, Indian squaws stand in the shade selling remedies that Titi finds invaluable for her cooking, plus Voodoo after-hours specialties. Servants straddle doorways in twos and threes. One idly smokes, while the others scrub staircases with reddenin', a brick dust of magic and mayhem employed in curses. Above their heads, multicoloured parrots glare from their prison-cages at high windows.

Hand in hand, the odd couple traverse flagstones and cobbles. They emerge from the French Quarter and peer down the huge rolling wake of Mother Mississippi. The next beachhead brings them onto St. Joseph and Foucher, where ironwork balconies reveal small doors cut within the panelling of larger ones. Gambling is the story of the day. Here, beaten animals are exchanged for fake jewellery and vice versa. More openly, down the alleys old men with crushed faces play dice with young women wrapped in shawls. Festoons of vines cling to mouldering walls. Eventually, through a labyrinth of interwoven bricks, no one residence distinguishable from another, the tiny latticed alleys open Canal Street onto St. Charles.

Here they reach the offices of the *New Orleans Picuyne*, a brass knocker marking the shabby pine door. Paul taps and waits. A flunkey swings open the portal grimaces then disappears, his misshapen head bobbing in dust. Paul peers into the dark and again his memory stirs, this time reminding him of *The Twenty-One* and its descending Dante-inspired corridors.

"Follow me," calls the floating flunkey's head.

Gripping his hand, Clara draws Paul over the threshold. Slowly their eyes adjust, revealing the top of a ghostlike statue surrounded by tangled vines. The face is familiar. Suddenly Paul recoils in horror, sensing his own arrogant grin. Expecting the face of some journalistic founder, writer or patron he comes face to face with a bust of himself, a replica of Louis Lequesne's plaster cast.

"I never saw the finished product," he says. "God, it's obscene."

"Oh, Paul," Clara says and strokes the exaggerated quiff of the bust's hairline, "it's not."

"How did they get a copy? It looks like homage to *The Picture of Dorian Gray!* Look, the plaster is melting."

"I think you look older."

Apprehensive, they hear voices so head deeper. The newspaper's beating heart calls them. Eventually they emerge within the bowels of *New Orleans Picuyne*'s headquarters, surrounded by its clatter of machines and steel trellised offices. After a short delay they learn someone is prepared to speak to them. Offering little satisfaction, he tells them told the article was written by freelance journalist Michel Duphone, without collaboration with either Paul Morphy or Fred Edge.

They request the man's boss, who now marches towards them.

"These rooms are private."

"I can vouch for Paul Morphy," are Paul's first words. "But I can't believe that article belongs to anyone but me. They are my words—just private conversation—but never intended for publication."

"I wish I could do more," says Mr Blackbone, editor-in-chief of *The Picuyne*. "I'm very busy. I have stories to finish on the precarious wildlife of Lake Pontchartrain and Caribbean storms. You have to leave."

He turns around, and doesn't even heed their protests.

"Well, thank you anyway," says Clara.

The flunkey shows them into the light, a couple of moles emeging from a hole.

"I never said those things!" Paul says outside. "Here, listen," and he unfolds the paper. "*The way it began, Paul Morphy could remember nothing further back than chess pieces, including his mother's face. He would play five hours in the daytime, then read chess adventure stories by candlelight at night. Young Morphy's life was passionate but less than ordinary...and the answers lie in the past....*"

"Forget it, Paul."

"But I certainly never called Harrwitz a *Parisian thief*. Or Staunton the *most unreliable man in chess*. Apparently Staunton is now endorsing his name on chess sets! The Staunton chess collection! And we never even played a game!"

"They should send the article to the *Blue Book*."

"But it's hardly racy enough. Just don't believe those stories about me, Clara. Chess isn't my life! My suspicions fall on my lost friendship with Fred Edge."

"He took you for a ride."

"I wouldn't be surprised if that man sells his left arm for another tale of Morphy's European holiday! The papers are keen to run the lies and he's happy to sell."

"It's over, Paul, you know."

"So long as there's no libel…"

"Well that's up to you."

To distract Paul from disappointment, Clara leads him beyond the Warehouse District to the American Quarter. The bamboo and palm-trees grow thin on the horizon and disappear, except for tiny specks in the direction of Lake Pontchartrain. She takes Paul by the hand, coaxing him over Canal Street past the Italian Opera House. They pause to review the billboard performances of the winter season: *William Tell*, *Les Huguenots* and *Robert Le Diable*. Only the last opera is familiar to Paul while Clara has heard of the first.

"I know William Tell shooting the apple."

"Soon they'll open the opera doors for you as a singer," Paul jokes and Clara laughs half-heartedly.

"Or you'll challenge them to a duel?"

"Exactly."

Suddenly a child in rags holding a domino on a piece of string is tugging Paul's leg. A small bell is attached to the domino and announces the boy's presence with a musical flutter. Paul hands down a silver coin as the child returns to the opera steps and the domino tinkers behind him. Only now does he realize the boy is mute. Clara buys bread from a café stall and takes it to the boy. Between the warehouses, wisteria vines lean low as though crying. *Old man's beards*, lonely plants, dangle like cobwebs from their fingers. The mute boy is thankful for the bread and waves at Clara, who waves guiltily back, pained by sins she did not commit. Their journey continues upriver.

Together they pass beyond Carondelet Street, over the plaited osiers spilled by the longshoremen and kaintucks in their drop-offs. They pass the yucca packed everywhere along the coast in squat wine jars, reaching the whipping-post of the calaboose. No slaves are being whipped today. A fish market emerges nearby, each salty haddock hooked in the mouth with bits of green palmetto leaf. They sit on some stone steps decaying in the sand. Meanwhile a rooster, feet tied together with a blue rag, dances proudly round the whipping-post.

"One thing I've learned," says Clara, "is that fine districts border poor ones. Left here, and we'll hit South Basin and the Swamp."

"Yes, I see," says Paul. "The street between isn't called Hospital for no reason. Countries are the same, you know. Clara, when I was in Europe I was treated as an American. But I'm not American, I'm Creole, and it's not the same even though we're all American by law."

"You should know the law, Paul."

"I can recite the entire civil Code of Louisiana, the *Code Napoleon.*"

"Are you trying to tell me something?"

"I mean…if the war comes, I won't believe in any national division, Clara. I'm more a Creole than a Unionist and I've even been to New York City. But I'm not Creole enough it seems to fight for my own country. Don't you see? From the Union's point of view I might as well be European."

"Paul, I don't…"

"I'm sorry. I'm American over there and I'm European here. I just don't fit anywhere."

"Well, look at *me* Paul. I'm not even welcome in my own city. My own history is…"

"…is holding you back but not anymore Clara. You have a mixed heritage. And that could be good, who knows. But everything will change if a war *has* to be fought. You'll see. The Republicans have Lincoln but he can be defeated politically before any conflict. Maybe I see a better future through my own eyes because I can't condone a war."

"It might be the only way. *Secession* is the word, Paul."

"Yes, the big word. I don't believe in it."

"They'll hang you for a traitor."

"So be it, Ms Young."

On a whim he kisses her, trapped between the warehouse buildings and the beach pebbles. Somehow the conversation, the distance from Morphys or Le Carpentiers, brings them close. They lean together in the wind. The kiss lingers, and unconsciously they push back against the whipping-post, scaring away the rooster. A question is asked of Clara and a decision is made. She pulls Paul tighter and he feels her clothes slip loose. The moment is tender. Their breathing is rushed and flesh tightened. For a few seconds the dust no longer sticks to their skin. The residue of a cathartic moment removes their fear and something beautiful and intangible remains. It is over. No one has seen although the market is not far away. Paul's lip is bleeding and he dabs it with a handkerchief.

"Clara, I must go to Havana where I can play chess freely as the game was intended, and practice law too."

"I thought you weren't going to play anymore."

"I know. But I just want to practice the law freely. Here they won't let me *change*. I am the perpetual chess player."

"So you'd take me with you?"

"Of course."

"And you'd be a practicing Caribbean lawyer?" She smiles. "The Cubans play chess sitting in the sun on the beach. There's no money there. Is that what you really want?"

Paul takes Clara's hand as though reading her palm. "Don't you remember my friend La Cubana? We'll be free in Cuba, free to go anywhere. No more family expectations. No more rules on practicing law…"

"No money…"

"Edward is right. Everyone views me here as a chess player. I don't have a single client because they just want to see a knight checkmate or a pawn storm, then have me sign a plea bargain postcard and make the prosecution disappear. But in Cuba, Clara, in Cuba!"

"No one knows us. And La Cubana is from the Dominican Republic..."

"Exactly, no one will know me. Chess will be dead. And no one knows you from the Basin, you see. I could even have the occasional recreational game...and life would be..."

"Paul, you have to stop playing. Like you said!" And before she can get too exasperated, Clara stops his speech with her finger, pressing her legs against his thigh. "No more talk of going away...or the red lights...or chess. Look, we're here!"

"The promised land," Paul replies sardonically. They enter the Garden District of the American Quarter—like Adam and Eve not knowing the flaming sword is at their backs. From this time forth they are Americans in spirit. Wide-eyed, they survey the landscaped streets paved not with the gold of a mythical London, but with clipped lawns, gaslights and drains. All the trappings of new money are on display in plantation houses. On every corner trim gardens roll up to great white columns, while each buttressed tower frames a well-lit drawing room. Unlike the Creoles of the Vieux Carré, these northern European Americans do not cherish the privacy of shuttered windows, private patios or quiet fountains. Bringing wealth from the industrial North, the future of the Big Easy wishes to show its prosperity, one garden at a time. Unlike the French-Spanish gardens, hiding their secret lives of slave plantations, here the great open spaces are conscience-free pleasure gardens. The scent of grass seems fresher, the flowers brighter and the mansions less tainted by history.

The next street even reveals the unusual sight of a white man in working clothes. A second is plying a hose, another carting weeds and branches in a wheelbarrow. Meanwhile the ground is continually watered to escape the East of Eden on the other side of the Warehouse District, the Vieux Carré, that purgatory of mixed European heritage and the Middle Passage from Africa. But here all can be forgotten. This brave world is new.

"A land of Lethe," says Paul. "New Orleans reborn only American!"

The mirage is real. Yet the vision before their eyes of colonnaded houses and beautiful gardens is just as improbable as those islands of forgetfulness, Cuba and Manhattan, one born in vicious sunshine, the other in cramped darkness. Here the blue sky is fretted with clouds of white English, Irish and Scandinavian. For fear of further temptation, Paul and Clara's eyes are filled with the riches of their new American rulers. They will join the great race. But for now, quietly wandering down to the river, they head back to the French Quarter.

"The Vieux Carré is crowded by comparison," Paul says. He whispers *"darkness visible"* to himself over and over until Clara asks him to stop.

"You see things I cannot," she says. "People are happier than you think."

"Only at night," Paul replies.

To break the ominous mood, he picks Clara a carnation and a *boutonniere* for his own coat. Later she buys a bag of rice cakes *calas tout chaud* for the Morphy table. He insists on giving her the money. They walk and eat, feeling jovial by bringing the flowers and hot cakes. Clara tells Paul he must see a professional barber *tout de suite*. Paul touches the roughness of his chin and declares no such intention unless Clara is willing. She laughs again and rediscovers the city streets. The twilight softens into night. Downriver they pass 61 Toulouse Street where Alonzo was Supreme Court Justice.

"My father's old law practice," Paul declares.

"Looks very respectable," Clara says.

"It is," Paul says. "Too powerful sometimes, power I never want."

"But your family still desires it. I can see it in your mother's face."

"Don't forget I have an older brother."

"Edward hardly counts."

Standing under the plaque, Paul reads: "*Alonzo Morphy, Head Judge*. You know," and he remembers a boyhood moment inside Alonzo's book-lined office, "I was once left alone here with only a pack of cards, which failed to amuse me. I could hear my father's voice getting louder and his steps in the hall. I tried to match his coughing with the steps, like a game to myself, until...the door opened..."

"And..."

"Nothing, you know. I just remember the feeling of waiting, rolling the cards in my fingers with those big books looking down on me. I must have only been about seven. I remember thinking my father was a powerful magician and all the secrets to his card tricks were in the books. I was kind of sad too when I opened one of them, a legal journal, because I couldn't understand the secrets of the cards."

"Their magic was lost on you."

"Right."

"You could've had a worse childhood."

Paul looks at Clara. "Yes, I know."

As she speaks, a ringing is heard. Paul recognizes a noise from Telcide's musical gatherings only to discover the sound resembles the *marchand de gaufres*—the shaving cake man—approaching. He is tapping a silver rod, seeking clientele.

"What a coincidence," Clara smiles. Hiding in the alleyway, Paul waits for him to pass.

Clara steps out.

"Can you shave my husband?" she asks. The man pauses from pushing his cart of portable barber's tools, and rolls a finger along his whiskers.

"Of course, *madamoiselle*. So long as you can present the gentleman?"

Paul steps from the shadows and is turned gingerly into a chair. But his reluctance is overtaken by the barber's energy. The *marchand de gaufres* lathers up Paul's face and attaches a neck-bib with a whip of the hand. The customer starts to go pale.

No one is in the street and even Clara seems worried by the sudden turn of events. The barber skips into position and begins to shave. He makes small-talk about the possibility of a *War Between the States*, which Clara does her best to ignore while staring at Paul clamped in his seat. Any second she expects the whole contraption to come to life and the *marchand de gaufres* to wheel Paul riverwards, laughing maniacally, on a handcart to hell. Instead Paul simply glares up with a foamy face at his father's prestigious lawyer's sign.

The barber brings out the blade, touches it to Paul's neck. Suddenly all he can think about is the edge of the Panama hat that induced his father's death. He sits very still and begins to whine. His eyelids do not save him from the soft whipping sound of the blade in the air, the smell of foam congealing on his face. Under his eyelids the blade flashes in the sunshine.

"Do you know Mr McManus?" Paul asks, trembling, when he senses a pause. "He attacked my father Judge Alonzo Morphy with his hat and tried to provoke him to a duel."

"I'm sorry Mr Morphy?"

"What!" Paul cries, confused. "Are you apologizing? Under the oaks! Under the duelling oaks!" He begins to struggle in the chair.

"Please…."

"Are you subpoenaed, sir?" Paul cries. "By my enemies? Tell me now!"

Clara takes Paul's hand as the barber stumbles away from his client's strange paroxysm. Paul stands and staggers from the chair, nervous energy in his eyes, the world spiralling out of conscience.

"You are commissioned to cut my throat!"

"No! No, Mr Morphy. This is too much. Let's adjourn to shave another day."

"A place more convenient to murder me," Paul rejoins. He runs up the street, seems to remember something catastrophic, and runs back down. Clara backs away from him as he drops to his knees, the bib still adorning his neck. "I cannot shout blue murder," he moans. "I know it is not *you*. Others are trying to ruin my family. I have my suspicions! My own flesh and blood and...they are inside the nest, like vipers, sucking away. I...I..."

"Paul?"

"I fear barbers. But I need to keep up appearances. I need to be professionally shaved!"

He collapses on the cobblestones.

Later, after waking and not remembering his fit, Paul is taken home by Clara in a weakened state. He takes a bath and lies down, but when he wakes Clara is asleep.

"My mind," he whispers and sits next to her. He strokes a curl of Clara's hair behind her ear. For minutes he stares and does nothing, then leaves the room.

In the *salle de compagnie* he removes the ornate silver-and-gold testimonial chessboard from the display. He carries the board into the kitchen, together with pieces, and positions everything under the hooded fireplace. Cross-legged he meditates and takes comfort in this collection of carved figures, their shapes and positions. Something deep inside him withdraws now, without his knowing, to the safety of this world...to black-and-white imagination...to these sixty-four squares. The poised tiny armies of Goths and Romans slide invisibly up and down the board in Paul's mind, without going anywhere.

He stares at the grid. A victory occurs, then a draw, a defeat, another victory. He swaps the advantage, swaps it back. He is learning by will-power and instinct alone how to play the game anew. He is challenging both sides, playing both armies against each other without stopping, just faster and faster in a fusion of countless possibilities.

"Endless..." he says. "Rootless...wonderful places, right? Here is magic. Here is darkness visible...visible darkness. Play the game and win, and win, and win..." He coughs, re-sets the board in his mind. "Aren't there more *possible* chess moves in a single game than atoms in the universe? Aren't there more *probable* moves than seconds since the beginning of time? The *possible* number of chess moves can never be played. But the *impossible* number…can…in a way…"

He moves a rook, considers, moves it on and chuckles. "Time flows backwards and the end of the game, and the story, will be the beginning. The king is dead, the king is dead…Long live the king! Long live the queen!"

Another victory and another defeat! There he sits, trying to perfect the perfect game. Pitting his mind against itself, Paul knows a tipping point has been reached. He knows not what—compels him to play, to experiment, to learn—a memory of Alonzo being impressed, the delight of Joseph Le Carpentier, a wish Telcide had…had…protected him. Occasionally the house creaks. He tries to calm down, to relax. But the chessboard is merciless. The kitchen clock ticks through the night….In between times, he seeks himself, ever elusive, ephemeral, and fast disappearing into spiralling mathematical patterns, jewels, pentagrams, pawn lines and bishop flanks…wondering if he can recover the reality of the board again, the kitchen, or Clara sleeping upstairs. Can he convince her of their future together?

Thankfully, around four in the morning sleep comes like death, sudden, with little pain.

Chapter Forty-Three
1860
Tales of the Red-Light District

P aul sits in his office at 199 Orleans Street waiting for clients. No one wishes to trust a strange young man, a chess genius with limited experience of the law. Paul Morphy from the newspapers is a gentleman hobbyist or miracle-worker; but the efficient and reliable lawyer he desires to become is not for the people of New Orleans.

But he waits. Generally by the afternoon he grows tired and opens his doors. One by one they come, requesting demonstration of his *blinding feats* and *mental exploits* in Europe. Each bears a copy of Fred Edge's biography under a sly arm, or cheekily hidden umbrella, ready to thrust under his chin. Paul does his best. Can he sign an autograph? Make a libel case evaporate? Can he transform blame? Turn the malevolence of accusers, or creditors, or jealous family members into financial restitution? How does the castling trick work? Does he practice at home?

Three weeks into business as Fellowes & Morphy, Attorneys and Counselors at Law, the practice is on the brink of failure. His partner Ewan claims to be out recruiting new clients, but Paul guesses he has abandoned hope and can be found in the middle of the day on Bourbon Street with a bottle. Nevertheless he waits, signing, until dusk arrives and the people finally leave.

Then he cannot resist playing. For an hour, he challenges his own self on a miniature chessboard in the drawer of his desk. No need for pieces. The squares are sufficient.

The next day is the same, except by nightfall a knock disturbs his zealous concentration. Troisville Sykes of *The Twenty-One* enters. He sits and hands Paul a copy of the *Mascot*.

"Read."

Paul closes the drawer. He smiles nervously and without a word, reads:

> Kate Townsend, daughter of a dock labourer, born 1839 in a dance-house on Paradise Street, has been openly murdered by her ne'er-do-well Creole lover, Troisville Sykes. The police reports suggest a gleeful stabbing with a bowie knife. More than $90,000 is the disputed purse. The case awaits trail, and must be settled soon, given the new concubinage laws are bound to cause confusion. Ladies and gentleman, a *cause célèbre* is upon us!
>
> We are not a publication to make accusations, but clearly Kate's time in the Basin was ticking away! No angel herself, she would keep Troisville in line with a beating and the occasional lock-up in a dark cupboard, giving him no spending money, cutting his nose once, and constantly threatening to open his belly. But we loved Kate! Accused last summer for forging her name to five cheques in the Warehouse District, an unsolved crime, the case was dropped.
>
> Last month, the city heat no doubt caused Kate's anger to boil over. Her protégé Molly Johnson, a St. Louis

girl with the real name Mary Buckley, took up with Kate's latest fancy man—a young sport named McClean. We have it from a good source Molly and McClean met on Canal Street early last November and got drunk in *Pizzini's Café*. Later that night, Kate and McClean quarrelled and McClean threatened her with a champagne bottle, whereupon Kate cried: "I've got to cut somebody. I'll go home and open Sykes's belly."

But Kate slept off her hangover until Saturday November 3rd when at 9:30am the housekeeper Mary Philomere, an otherwise reliable house servant, heard screams and saw Sykes fleeing Kate's room with cuts to his chest.

"Well, Mary," Sykes was heard to say, "she's gone!"

Paul looks up at Sykes, a giant of a man, and says:

"Well, sir. I'm wondering if the case has not already been tried, in a sense, by public jury?"

"So am I!" is the gruff reply. "But that rag don't mean nothin' in the courthouse. You know that!" Sykes taps his head, an apple with the top cut off, and places his fingers over his mouth. "So I won't tell, if you don't."

"Tell what?"

"That would be tellin'. I won't tell...you know...that I done it."

"Mr Sykes, that's unethical. You can't tell me that."

"Just read the rest," Sykes replies. "We'll haggle terms later." He takes out a long pipe, drooping one end from his lower lip like a pirate, and begins fuming the tobacco in the pipe's cup.

A few hours later Ms. Kate, keeper of the bagnio at 40 Basin Street after losing licence at *The Twenty-One*, is declared killed on police posters by Troisville Sykes, her lover. *The Mascot* reports from the killing scene. Go to the second parlour of 40 Basin's left entrance, ladies and

> gentlemen, and elegantly splayed over the bed, feet resting to the floor, lies our fresh corpse. Kate's body is pierced by four large-sized stab wounds *sans doute* inflicted by a sheath-knife.

"I've read!" Paul says.

"This too," Troisville says, handing over tabloid favourite *The Crescent Hour*...

> Carved to death / Terrible fate of Kate Townsend / at the hands of Troisville Sykes / with the instrumentality of a / bowie knife / her breasts and shoulders literally covered with stabs.
>
> Kate was laid out in a six-hundred-dollar white silk dress trimmed with lace at fifty dollars a yard. Friday will take her to Metarie Cemetery with a procession of twenty carriages. City men, politicians excepted, are welcome after four.
>
> Troisville Sykes is the son of good lower class family of a merchant sailor of Magazine Street...

"I'm sorry," Paul interrupts. "You must be wanted by the police. I cannot take the case while a warrant is open. "I can't...it's..."

"Unethical?" Sykes breathes through his pipe. "What about how she treated me? Ain't that unethical? I don't want sympathy or hate, mister. I want a fair trial. I ain't denying the killing...but there was reasons..."

"Well, now...it's a risk before we even consider a defence," says Paul. "We must move carefully. There is gambling in the situation...and..."

"What are you saying?" Sykes says, removing his pipe.

"I...I'm unsure. It looks like you're guilty," Paul says. "I think we'd lose the case."

Sykes stands, gently lifts his end of the table. "Listen Mr Morphy. I ain't here a-beggin'. I'm just askin' polite now. Can you help me?"

"I…must…think," Paul says. He opens the desk drawer and tiny chess pieces spill out on his lap.

"Yes or no?"

"I don't know that the devil is my expertise."

"Well," says Sykes, dropping a fist on the desk with a clatter, "that's not what I've bin 'earing."

"What do you mean?"

"Only, that you take up with *those girls*. How 'bout that for a fine reputation, mister," Sykes grins. "How long have you been practicing a double trade again?"

Paul freezes, pawns strewn over him dropping to the floor.

"Listen," says Sykes, securing his hat and preparing to leave. "This ain't the first case from the Swamp or Storyville, as they's calling us. There's Fanny Sweet, a devout little Voodoo girl. She pins her faith on that—you know—casket of charms and amulets, right. She carries a brace of pistols and sleeps with 'em under her pillow. But no, that don't save her!"

"Mr Sykes, I'm afraid…"

"I know you are. I would be too. Fanny Sweet is five ten in stockings, eyes thick as pie glasses. Boys from the oaks tried to save her. But Ruth Jeezy gets jealous and puts a fork in her ear, see? And she bleeds to death in the street, n' no one touches her 'til morning. Some girls is too ugly—Ruth no 'ception—even for tha' Big Easy. But they gets it somehow, life or death, 'cos they's greedy as they's vicious."

Paul stares, aghast, sensing he is witnessing a different crime's justification.

He doesn't have to wait:

"Kate Townsend was the same. And the girls that work for her," Troisville tips his hat, "watch out for them, Mr Morphy, if you know what I mean! They's no different! That LuLu White. She drives a bauble wagon she got from New Jersey. She ain't poor. A carriage in plum satin and jewels all got from this rich carpetbagger, one of yours, a Mr William Henchard. The whole thing smells o' money. And where there's money, everything stinks..."

"I know. The blade of the law cuts, Mr Sykes," Paul says, trying, "but I can't take the case. Now if you'll excuse me..."

"LuLu...she lives in a mansion, Mr Morphy, with Mr Henchard's nephew...can you believe *that*? The nephew's a tightwad n' drives a shabby buggy on a little mule. But they's always survivin'...'avin' a good time...drinking wine two bucks a glass, credentials in order, formally presented, goin' upstairs for fifteen dollar....Hand it over, my derringer for your gimlet knife...just a sup at a real gimlet..."

Paul rises.

"Mr Sykes, I can't..."

"Well, well, well. Your choice."

"It is, please."

"Your loss."

Despite his fear Paul shows the giant Troisville to the door and encourages his departure. Descending the stairs Sykes continues to mount his defence, telling more dark tales of the city's underbelly. But Paul can bear no more, bolting the double-lock. Then he listens at the keyhole and from downstairs comes mingled voices, and the words *silly exploits* and *chess fool* and *no winnin' lawyer*. Paul presses his ear.

"Did he take you on, Mr Sykes?"

"I believe he did, good people," Sykes replies, ruffling the head of the premises' water-boy. "Morphy is now closed for the day, everyone, but I believe he did. He took my case!"

Upstairs Paul collects the chess pieces, and sits with his head in his hands. "I cannot bear...this is ridiculous...will no one give me a reasonable client?" He breathes onto his hands.

Eventually he places the chessboard on his desk, free of pieces, and fixes it to his eye-line. The room narrows to a point. The light grows dim. A few lines of attack and defence open up, winning and losing, always, forever, eternal harmony in nothing, equilibrium, and oblivion. Paul imagines other worlds in silent, motionless, amoral struggle, and his soul is softened. Hours pass.

One by one the knocks begin—throughout the morning—and finally cease.

His partner Mr Fellowes does not return to the office.

Chapter Forty-Four
1861
Pelicans of the Civil War

The winter sours. The offices of Fellowes & Morphy, Attorneys and Counselors at Law, are closed. Mr Abraham Lincoln, President of the Union, declares: "A house divided against itself cannot stand."

To distract from the widening social fissures of New Orleans, none more pointed than between Creole and American, slave-owner and emancipation-advocate, flyers are posted in the Bayou and the plantations to bolster state solidarity against the possible aggression of the North. Paul attempts to re-start his law practice with his uncle Ernest, released from his job at the Customs House and replaced by politicians. But Ernest is getting old and their offices are soon confiscated for use as grain storage for the approaching hostilities. The Morphy family finds itself increasingly trapped within the walls of 89 Royal Street. Curfews hit the city. Night movement is restricted so armed operations can commence, and friend and foe, solider and citizen will not be confused. The city has to make a stand and does not know, as yet, where its political allegiance lies.

Events move fast. The message to the Deep South becomes clear. Louisiana will join the race to Confederacy on 26th January 1861, the sixth state in defiance of Lincoln. Receiving no support from Great Britain—already having abolished slavery—the Southern states are alone in making their stand for economic survival. Paul is anxious and torn in his loyalties to the Union and the state of Louisiana. He tries to explain his feelings to his brother, that "one represents his home, the other his soul," but receives no sympathy.

"You've travelled too much," Edward replies.

By December, 1860 North Carolina leads a parade of eleven states in secession from the Union. A new kind of nervous optimism arrives: political decisions made in Baton Rouge bring relief and a sense of purpose to New Orleans. With Edward, Alex and John Sybrandt heading to the military festivities in the state capital, the Morphy family is shrinking.

For weeks prior to aligning with the Confederacy, however, a strange new atmosphere pervades the region. Louisiana declares her independence from the Union, yet feels a strain of individuality: she does not immediately join her southern allies. As her own self-declared free republic, she exists in a limbo of double independence, neither country nor nation but her own slipshod political and military entity, as dirty and unruly as she's ever been. Separate from the turmoil gripping every other state, this loose status creates abandon in her citizens, a disturbing sense of superiority and moral fervour.

Pelican flags, the emblem of Louisiana, are flung in the breeze from hotels, theatres, and public buildings. With nightfall brilliant illuminations—thousands of candles and gaslights—dangle from window ledges. The quarters are crowded. People whistle the catchy new song *Dixie* by day and blow it on horns by night. A brass band is discovered on every corner, praising the wonder of a free Louisiana no longer governed by unseen Northern hands!

"Hurrah for Louisiana!" is heard on every side, "Louisiana is free under her own flag! God bless the great Republic!"

At the Pickwick and Pelican Clubs, the Louisiana coat of arms is draped in shades of blazoned red and inscribed "Union, Confidence and Justice." Every afternoon the Orleans Cadets and Baton Rouge Guards parade in formation. A gold-embossed pelican—the mascot of revolution—is adopted at City Hall. Petty crime is noticeably absent at first, then street thefts and robberies surge. Most citizens decide to stay. Every night, a mock *Mardi Gras* sustains the double sense of celebration and hilarity.

After a few weeks, the atmosphere of Louisiana controlling the Mississippi descends into a strange dream that New Orleans will control its own destiny. The state is now vying for its own nationhood, a never-before realized dream, so why not the city? Talk spreads in the dance houses and drinking dens of the downtown Vieux Carré all the way to the rulers of the American Quarter. One day New Orleans will self-govern. One day New Orleans will be free!

By April the ports are seized. The federal mint and the Custom House are infiltrated by unknown soldiers who barricade all stored goods from the inside. The tipping point has been reached. How and why? The answer occurs all too soon. The Mississippi is blockaded by a federal warship. Trade stops. For a while the newspaper men scramble for the story. People abandon their homes. Looting begins in the poorer corner of the city. The news travels like fire.

In May, Union troops land on Ship Island and prepare to take control of the lower Mississippi. Forts St. Philip and Jackson are bombarded by Captain David Farragut on 18th April. Two warships sail past the new Confederate batteries at Chalmette—the exact spot where the British were defeated fifty years earlier by Jackson's *dirtiest troops who ever defended freedom*—and sink anchor. New Orleans is taken by surprise. Union troops are sent ashore in the night, and without bloodshed they lower the flag and take formal possession. From that single act of flag-exchange, despoiling Louisiana's independence and swapping the pelican for the Star-Spangled Banner, the ebullience of the city's population is exposed as a lullaby of self-deception.

No description can convey the sense of stark partition amid the families of the city itself. The time has come to pick sides. The poor cannot flee, making them a target; the rich are torn by the heritage of having some family with connections to the North. Husbands and wives are separated; brothers declare allegiance for different sides. Family grudges simmering unrecognized for years are re-opened. Mothers and daughters say goodbye. Some follow their husbands north while others miserably come together only to see their men join the militia. The reality of the occupation is imminent, daily, and prayers abound just to one day return to this time and place.

The Morphy family is already split. Edward Morphy is called to the Louisiana Tigers, now a renegade defensive force, half of whose members are incarcerated in the Warehouse District in hastily converted Union-run holding prisons. Edward is not known to have been captured and takes pot shots at federal soldiers, notching his rifle most days, from the Canal Street post office. Meanwhile Ernest and Telcide remain home, hoping to be overlooked by the mob of Union sympathizers stalking the streets at night. Union troops too parade the old town on their way to rip up the gin-joints and honour the whorehouses of Basin Street. There they treat the bartenders to New York tobacco and the girls to a Dixie penny whistle and a touch of Northern hospitality. With fascinated fear, Malvina and Helena watch the troops at night from upstairs windows. By the end of June, John Sybrandt declares his intent to join his relatives in the North and make the long journey upriver to Chicago. Leaving only a note on the kitchen table Malvina joins him, and is gone. Despite losing her daughter,

Telcide refuses to be comforted by Ernest and begins to sleep in Helena's room. *Louise de Lorraine* is abandoned: Telcide reads by night and sleeps by day, drifting into a fantasy world of aristocratic French poems and old English fairy-tales. Alex Le Carpentier is nowhere to be found, presumed fled on a steamship to one of Telcide's elderly relatives, her spinster sister Maya or Aunt Poivre, both of Boston, Massachusetts.

Finding the atmosphere at home oppressive in a way he never imagined, Paul finds he cannot stay. He prefers Charles Maurian's house. There he can properly mourn the absence of Clara too. Did she flee to avoid returning to Basin Street, for fear of being abandoned by the Creoles and being considered a slave? Now she is gone—a week ago without explanation—Paul's visits home become infrequent. Only the kindness of Charles Maurian, whose calm under fire and emphasis on keeping up a good suit, keeps Paul caring.

One night, though, fearing Clara has returned to The Swamp or to Hattie Hamilton's or Minnie Ha-Ha's, and remembering the night he collapsed on Basin Street, his visit from Troisville Sykes and all the possible dangers Clara will be facing, Paul does not come home. Charles returns late from his forced occupation, as riverside clerk for Union munitions, and finds a note. The piece of paper is propped in the fruit bowl:

Charles, I have to go.

I will be okay. Clara's old friend La Cubana came to see me—to reassure me. Clara is in the city, she says, but won't say where. Says the girls are all in danger. But La Cubana was scared and wanted our meeting to look like chance.

Nothing else matters now, Charles. It seems I will chase her over the face of the earth. I cannot live without her! I must find her... Your ever loving friend, Paul.

A pawn from Paul's testimonial chessboard is beside the note, a two-inch figurine of solid gold. Charles picks up the piece and rolls it over his fingers, cold to the touch, and smiles.

"Thank you, Paul," he says.

But another pawn is there too, a wooden one, slippy to the touch. Charles realizes the piece has been sliced in half, revealing a congealed red colour inside. He looks back at Paul's note, senses what has happened. Blood leaks from inside the dissected pawn along the table and onto the floor. *Nothing else matters now Charles!* The dark red notepaper stares up from the table, signed with a blood-lined chess knight as the pen.

Charles drops the pawn—Paul has written the note in his own blood.

Chapter Forty-Five
1861
Night of the Rising Sun

Paul is gone. He wanders the streets of New Orleans, avoiding the lights of houses occupied by soldiers. He flits among the shadows, a pale human ghost. Everywhere he asks for Clara and corner by corner the direction leads closer to the Basin. By midnight he reaches a yellow two-storey at Porter and Bienville, named *The House of The Prodigal Son*. He knocks.

No one comes to the door, but the door swings open. Paul enters the lobby where velvet drapes loop from statue to statue, all headless, and follows the music down the hall. Past gaudy paintings of suns and rocky shipwrecks, a half saloon door creaks under his fingernails revealing—circling the girls in twos and threes—the blue uniformed soldiers of the Union army. Quickly he closes the door. A girl touches his elbow.

"Are you lost honey?"

"Clara Young," he stammers.

"Second floor," the girl smiles, a silver tray with blue drinks in the crook of her arm.

Upstairs Paul finds the door after his second tour, a single plate with 'Young' inscribed in gold plate, and knocks.

"Come on."

Paul waits, and cannot bring himself to turn the handle until Violet Young opens the door. Quickly she retreats in a shroud of shadows, complaining of the light, and Paul has to steal himself into the room. He waits for the darkness to adjust his eyes. Then he peers at Clara's mother—a crib girl herself—as she clambers back into bed and rolls the duvet under her neck. The room is nothing more than a hovel, a bed and washstand, with cracked walls and cobwebs hanging from the ceiling. A candle burns on the mantelpiece. Taking a step, he realizes from Violet's red eyes and face pockmarks that she is not only ageing but dying of the clap. He sees her daughter in her eyes.

"I'm looking for Clara," he says.

Violet says nothing. She moves a wooden box from the bed, places it on her lap and begins to whisper. Paul realizes she has been practicing Voodoo, the belief he discovered at Spring Hill, denounced as a false religion of New Orleans brought to America by the Middle Passage. Symbolized by a snake, Voodoo is banned from the French Quarter; down on Basin Street the etiquette and laws of the Creoles do not apply.

"Voodoo is a language," Violet says and opens the box to reveal the imprisoned serpent. "I take *gris-gris* to cure ailments." With her fingernails she carefully breaks open three tiny red bags containing powdered brick, yellow ochre and cayenne pepper. These ingredients she drops in the box with the serpent and seals the lid to anger the snake.

"Please," Paul says, "I need your help." But before he can persuade Violet, he realizes they are not alone. Half under the bed, and now appearing, is a girl practicing Voodoo. Surrounding her is a piece of charcoal horsehair, herbs and broken bits of horn.

"They create conversation with the spirit world," she says. "Lucky charms for the soul."

"Clara, oh…" and Paul stumbles to the wall and cannot believe his eyes; Clara appears to be in a trance.

"The Nation of Arada lives!" Violet is crying, waving her arms. "We call on the god Voodoo!" She casts the box and it bursts, tossing the dazed snake on the floor. Paul leaps away, taking Clara by the elbow.

"Come with me. We must leave."

"Noooo, I must stay…"

He shakes her. "You have to, Clara, you must!"

The snake flickers at their feet. As though drugged by the powerful odour of Violet's magician-experiment, Clara collapses on Paul's shoulder and he staggers across the crib-room. He lays her in a chair and carefully avoiding the snake, which has pinned itself to the wall, he returns to the bed. He kneels with Violet.

"We're not coming back," he says.

"You must go to a bull n' bear fight," Violet says, eyes wide and bloodshot. "One with a bull-dog and alligator—that is the way to heal yourselves."

"We will," says Paul, and he takes Clara's hand. "We will see the Voodoo dancers of Congo Square, okay?"

"That is good."

Paul gives Violet something he brought for Clara, a black lace *voilette*, a veil she instantly wears and jokes she is a *funeral-bride*. Then he gently lays the wooden box near her arm, and tells her he will look after Clara.

"Are you Dan O'Neill?"

"No, I'm…a friend of the family."

"I opened Pandora's box," Violet says, surprising him.

"Yes, you did," Paul says. "But you can close it…when we leave. Close the box, okay?"

Violet says nothing and closes her eyes. Paul touches her already cold forehead and traverses the darkened room. He listens for the snake and skirts the wall. Dipping his forearms under her legs, Paul now bears Clara half toppling into the hallway. He goes the wrong way over a balcony and *The House of the Prodigal Son* is awake. Bodies are everywhere. Girls and soldiers and the regular johns intermingle with musicians and bouncers and rough-looking *madames*. Clearly, escaping with a house-girl is less than polite.

Paul moves to the staircase and lays Clara down. He considers leaving her and then coming back, but there she lies dressed in a green evening dress and heavily rouged. The image of the working girl is so foreign to Paul, tears edge into his eyes and fall onto Clara, his chosen girl who did not wish to be chosen. He does nothing to wipe them.

"We are like pieces of opposite colours," he whispers. "I cannot express it properly." Leaning down, he lays his head on Clara's breast and leaves it there amidst the noise of the brothel. "No, we are only pawns. Just pawns in a bigger game." Unsupported, her head falls and hits the wooden floor as Paul is wrenched at the shoulder to his feet. Clara herself is lifted by two girls who drill her down the floorboards and back to her mother.

"Please!" Paul cries out. "I cannot leave her. Not…" His words are stifled. A hand like a meat-hook takes the back of his neck and squeezes the breath away.

"Get gone, *idiot savant*," the bouncer shouts, laughing. The stairs approach rapidly and Paul has to negotiate them four at once as he crashes into the lobby. Velvet curtains cover him, sending images of butchers' knives—and blood—rushing to his brain. Then the kicking starts, three to his ribs, a stomp to the chest and the rest everywhere else. A dog barks, seemingly far away, but a burly man now appears with the dog chained, its teeth snarling in Paul's ear.

"No, wait," someone is saying. "This is the chess player."

Chain rattling, dog salivating, men laughing, Paul feels the blackout coming.

"What do you mean?"

"I know him—the genius. Let him go."

"*No one* is let go," says the man with the dog.

"You heard him."

Paul is yanked to his feet.

"Let the dog on him. He'll live…he doesn't play chess with his legs, right?"

"Right," says the first voice which sounds familiar. "He plays with his head."

Drunk with the violence and swaying, a strange recognition now cuts through Paul's confusion. Here is his uncle Alex about to save him. No longer a drinker and client down on Basin Street, Alex is a working man, a doorman.

"Paul's famous, and if they trace him back to us, we'll be in court. His family's in the law…"

"New Orleans doesn't have courts."

"It has military courts."

"Listen, I say we let the dog have some fun!" cries the dog-man and there is a hearty cheer.

But by this point Alex has cupped Paul's head and is carrying him to the door. No one stops him and the lull in violence affects the atmosphere. The men complain but there will be another unruly customer before long. So they let Alex do his work—the last move—which they don't bother to witness. To reduce suspicion and not lose his job, Alex must first throw the genius chess player out. Anyone could be watching. So he takes a swig of whisky from the door-girl, smiles and hawks his charge to the entrance. Paul finds himself in a tragicomedy more tragic than comic. A sensation of light-headedness, the air on his cheek, makes him curious before impact with the street. Mud slides over his cheek and cuts open his mouth. He lies painfully. That is all he remembers—for minutes—until Alex finds another moment to come outside and help him stand.

"I cannot stay out," Alex says. "I'm sorry, Paul. Please don't come down here. It's not like it used to be."

"You…hurt me," Paul says.

"I think I saved your life," Alex replies. "Can you make it home?"

Paul does not reply and drifts into a shadow. The hour is late for a night-carriage, especially here, even if he had the money. No hospital is nearby: all he has to do is make it home. Clara clearly is back under the bordello's thumb. Cautiously, he leaves via South Basin but on the last block he stops in a barrelhouse to clean up. He soothes the pain with beer at the spigot, dipping his mug in self-disgust.

Meandering back to Royal, he passes the dog-fighting and rat-killing at *Hanly's Dog Pit* on Girod Street. The den is a mirage of handheld lanterns giving a last glimpse of a rough, lost world. There is Derrick Hanly's dog Cabbage and Dan O'Neill of *The Amsterdam* with his bull-mastiff Twitches. Dog and man lean over the pit and bark illegal gambling. Paul moves closer to the noisy circle of spectators reminding him in a confused way of *Le Café de La Régence*. Below the pit-dogs dance, teeth back and eye for eye, until both are seriously injured.

"...fighting like that makes the whole world blind," Paul says to his neighbour, and then moves on his way; but the man pulls him back.

"You know who I am?" he barks. "I'm Charley 'Largerbeer' Lockerby of the Wild Oak Boys. Who is you? You just can't speak to me in that educatin' way an' not expect nothin' back..."

"What do you mean?" Paul says.

"I mean...clever boy...I is short but I is powerful and I shot a shopkeeper named Keppler this week. He's dead now in the Charity Hospital. Got my meaning? You gamble if you stay *here*, boy, not just make quips."

"I'm not a gambler," Paul says. "Never was, and..."

"Never will be..."

"Right."

"Well get the hell out of here!" Lockerby scowls at Paul then strokes the scar on his chin. "Hang on, I know you..."

"I'm a Storyville *demimonde*."

"You're that chess player...well, chess player, get back to your own people!" He raises his fist.

"Good advice."

"Get gone."

Paul drifts through the busy streets until he is back in the Warehouse District. Unintentionally he finds himself in the alley where he kissed Clara, the day they went for a walk, months ago.

The memory is painfully sweet and in his bruised and drunken state, Paul changes his path and heads for the Mississippi. The doormen who abused him—his uncle Alex included—he now realizes will never be arrested. "I'm supposed to be a lawyer..."

Doubling back to avoid the occasional patrolling Union solider, he remembers the case of Hattie Hamilton from *The Herald*. She shot her paramour and police broke in the building in seconds, rushing to the gunshot. They found Hattie holding the smoking gun. "…but she is released without questioning. Why is no one ever judged?"

In the distance the bell of St. Louis Cathedral sounds. The breeze revives Paul a little. He drops on the muddy beach with the river silently rolling by. The Mississippi flows ever on. Looking at the moon, Paul speaks: "*My* love is from Cynthia to Saturn changed." He touches his face, feels more encrusted blood. A cypress palm for a pillow, he lies on the beach in the shingle-mud. A few stars glint, only a few, and when they do it seems like an act of courage. But Paul can no longer appreciate them. He closes his eyes and dwells on the bizarre meeting with Clara and Violet, the snake and Alex, and can make no sense of anything: the world of New Orleans creates itself a new nightmare every night, always hopes to wake to the promise of salvation in the morning.

Paul's jacket feels bulky and remembering something, he half smiles, half laughs, lying there alone. From his pocket he removes the miniature chess set rescued from the failed Morphy & Morphy Attorneys. Laying the board on his chest, he sets up the pieces without looking. The pieces are only the bodily containers of improbable chess powers. He no longer needs them, but still desires a physical connection to the living game. Before he completes the opening—for both sides—he slips into a disturbingly conscious sleep.

He dreams of the endless depths of chess, the sheer purgatory of its infinity. With a frightening sense of his persecution and imprisonment, he lies beside the Mississippi without controlling his dream. Sand and mud in his shoes, he reclines on a giant chessboard trapped by a pawn army, and tied down with ropes. The sword of Damocles swings over his head, falling lower and lower with his every struggle and cry. He tries to justify the tactics but even the perceptive moves—crossing to the French Quarter, putting Clara in Charles Maurian's house, not playing

Howard Staunton—all seem wrong and helpless. The sands of time run low…his opponent wears a mask of terror…white skeletons and the black girls of *Mardi Gras* dance fiercely before his eyes….Then, without so much as a hush, the god-like blade becomes the black widowing Guillotine of the Revolution and loosens…falls…sings like steel…with rank and files screaming for blood…*la fin*…check…mate!

Paul rears awake crying out across the sands of time in his consciousness:

"Darkness! Darkness visible!"

No one hears. The black bishop returns and the cowl is drawn back to reveal a changing face, one moment Telcide, the next Alex Le Carpentier. Paul is on his feet striking at invisible enemies, falling on the pebbles and swinging an imaginary broadsword. The malleable face of his persecutor is Ernest, now Alonzo, now John Sybrandt…"Leave me!" The face is Daniel Harrwitz sneering then Violet Young cramped in bed with her Voodoo snake and her pockmarked face. Howard Staunton raises self-engraved chessmen over his head, the standard issue pieces for the future of the whole world!

"Darkness visible!"

Paul cries and wakes in a sweat, feeling all the pain of his heart beating for the loss of Clara. He staggers down the beach, railing at himself for the decision to leave Clara and fire Fred Edge and return to New Orleans. "I could have made a career in Europe! But I couldn't take the money! Why? Because I am a gentleman?" He wades into the water and washes away the imaginary blood. "Yes! I am nothing. I'm no gentleman!" He takes the pocket chess set and spins it carelessly into the Mississippi. To his disbelief, the chessboard lands on a pieced of driftwood and floats on. The pieces themselves scatter in the water but the board remains flat, and Paul shouts out: "It was meant for the water! It was meant for the water!" Down the Mississippi floats the miniature chessboard, pointing out Paul's future, though he does not know it, to the Gulf of Mexico.

Eventually Paul makes it home and hides in his room. He washes himself at the washstand. That night he dreams of a huge furnace and his old Spring Hill adversary, Father Beaudequin, who wanted to beat him at the royal game and for the rest of his schooldays remained jealous. Beaudequin is stirring a giant pot, a cauldron with chessboards bouncing around and endlessly boiling. Paul shivers in the night. Intoxicated by the fumes, he senses his mind separating, the parts splitting. Beaudequin cackles at his shoulder as he peers in the chess-pot. The sight is horrific. Amid the flailing kings and horses are the decomposed bodies of schoolboys' faces and St. Ursuline nuns. John Sybrandt is there too, twisting his knuckles. Clara is there too, wrapped in a black robe and leaping burning chessboards, softly mouthing her Voodoo rhymes.

Chapter Forty-Six
1862
Island of Lethe

L ate in October Paul boards the Spanish man-of-war Blasco de Garay, bound for the Caribbean islands. The ship enters the harbour between the grim batteries of La Punta and El Morro and sails under a midday sun into the bay of Havana. Already prepared, Paul is wearing a cool white linen suit. As he descends the gangplank a new world, free of the swamps and the claustrophobia and the soldiers lining Bourbon Street, welcomes him with the promise of forgetting everything.

Far from the Mississippi mud of New Orleans or the rolling grey waves of Liverpool, in Cuba luscious fruits line the boat dock. Pomegranates and mangoes are stacked on the wooden welcoming jetty, and now and then topple on the beach in merry plenitude. Someone hands Paul a coconut concoction wrapped in a green bamboo tube, followed by a cocktail of rum with sugar and lime juice. Moments later the evacuees, refugees and ex-patriots—Paul awkwardly included—crouch at the edge of the forest, ankle to ankle, drinking planter's punches and smoking strong black cigars. They watch ripples lap the white sand.

Bound for the only lodging, *Hotel America*, the international band shares breakfast of green pepper omelettes, pompano fried in olive oil and *guanábana* sherbet. Questions are asked about their backgrounds and journeys, and Spanish and English mingle happily under the cooking sun. By eleven o'clock, Cuba's twin newspapers *La Gaceta de la Habana* and *El Mauirian* are available, delivered in trucks to the port. The front page covers Paul's arrival with the inevitable challenge: *The chess master is willing to play a partie with anyone who feels brave today.*

Finishing his breakfast, Paul politely declines: "I am only the North American champion," he says. "Europe doesn't have a tournament, and the Caribbean and South Americas remain undecided. So what is the benefit of playing me?"

"One game with you," a fisherman jokes, "would create the Cuban champion!"

For several days Paul fends off challengers. The local dignitaries begin a cart-and-mule service to *Hotel America* on the proposition that—with new Americans arriving—the tips are good. A hundred locals hear the promise and scale the hotel walls. The atmosphere becomes untenable. Many villagers must return home having walked miles to see the wonder of 'the chess magician.' The solution for Paul becomes a tour of Havana's hotels, accepting invitations simply to escape his current staff's desire for autographs. He soon learns that his signature alone exported to America sells for a month's pay.

But escape is at hand. An invitation from one Don Eduardo Fesser begs Paul to grace *L'Hermitage*, his mock-Victorian *morada* fitted with wrought iron balconies in the style of the one-time Spanish rulers of the French Quarter. Paul sits on the balcony overlooking Havana Bay, conscious that a chessboard will eventually be produced. He soaks in the overpowering scent of the night-blooming *damas de noche* from the garden, breathing deeply the mingling scents of tobacco, sugar and coffee. Over the whole house men wander in their cool linen suits, beacons of gentlemanly Caribbean dignity, with girls no older than their sisters. Drinks are presented with *canapés* skewered to their pineapple lips.

Toasts ring out over the valley. The guests are presented one at a time: a Chicago baseball player; a cousin of the inventor of the telegraph; a Norwegian Olympic backstroke swimmer; and the chess champion of North America *if not the world*. Laughter mingles with conversation about Greek mythology, the future of Cuba and tales of the conquistadors who raided the Aztec gold. Paul feels captivated by the elegance and aristocratic welcome of the Cuban dignitaries, the powerful men of the island and their delicate *coquettes*. The men bow robustly and push back their dark hair; the women sport beautiful air-thin dresses, mock-peacock feathers, and wear eyes flashing with purple mascara. Wives or mistresses, they flit around the men like fireflies courting their mates by the light of the moon.

Paul feels like a child, found after being lost so long no reprimand takes place. Even as a nervous observer he is exhilarated by the glamour, celebration and self-importance. He knows too—like in New Orleans—poverty lies only a street away. But something about the mingled Spanish and Cuban setting connects him to his European heritage. In this swirl of sweet island drinks, he feels closer to home.

Then at midnight two young boys, buttoned up in silver and black, deliver the chessboard.

"Now for a little game," says Don Eduardo. "What shall we stake?"

"Only honour," suggests Paul.

"I couldn't agree more."

The drinks are cleared and the game arranged. Cut from a single slab of ivory, the board illuminates two sets of chessmen, one ruby-red and the other emerald. The red king bears the thunderbolts of Zeus while the emerald queen reaches to the oceans for the trident of Neptune. Paul is reminded of his testimonial chessboard. But he no longer feels the burden of performance inspired by the royal game, and seats himself with an uncharacteristic flick of his coattails. He plays the game deliberately, not thinking about the moves for fear of slipping back into a turbulent feeling of ambition, perfectionism and self-torment. Ultimately the feeling of losing amid the throbbing heat and spectators affects him less than he expects.

Don Eduardo is pleased with his surprising victory, to be published in Cuban newspapers the next morning. But the evening's play does not end there. With the reversal of the pieces and more coconut rum intoxication, Paul cannot help his mind from racing. He wins the next three games, and the crowd applauds with pleasure, nor is Paul's opponent sour. Don Eduardo remains pleased with his refugee-guest from New Orleans.

"How do you like your stay in Havana, Mr Morphy?" he inquires.

"Wonderfully well."

"Would you like another game?"

"I thank you," Paul says, "but I may have finished for the evening."

"One more."

The game goes to Don Eduardo. Soon after Paul retires to his room, only to discover his veranda overlooks the party. Again he admires the elegant guests, company he would grace in the French Quarter if he held a successful profession. Getting ready for bed, Paul notices a card under the door and recognizes the handwriting. Wishing to let sleeping dogs lie, he nevertheless reads from curiosity how Fred Edge is back in Paris, recovered from their falling out. With dizzy admiration Edge describes the *salons* of noble Faubourg and the Chausée d'Antin. Women are playing chess now, not only in theatres and behind the scenes at the opera but in private clubs where men are *interdit*. But depicting this heady atmosphere is Edge's smoke and mirrors, a distraction from his true intent. It seems a new arrival in the chess world, Herr Ignatz Kolisch *The Incomparable*, wishes for a game. Without hesitation Paul lays his *midori sour* on the bedside table and pens a rapid note thanking Fred for his missive. However, he concludes by stating Herr Kolisch has not beaten Adolf Anderssen or Louis Paulsen. The comment is not intended as a boast—Paul does not care for pyramids or hierarchies among players—but the implication is that beating someone's victor is not equal to beating the original loser.

Unfortunately for Edge, the note is indication of Paul's new slide into arrogance and the sly security of the reclusive champion. Paul is becoming Howard Staunton, no longer desiring to play the game that made his name.

"The difference," Paul says, anticipating this judgment, "is that Staunton still desires to play chess. I do not."

To cement his words, Paul dashes off another letter to D. W. Fiske clarifying his renunciation of the game. In a recent telegram Fiske has already indicated *the sad events that are transpiring in our distracted America.* He hopes that Paul might consider a few exhibition games in New York on behalf of New Orleans Chess Club: at a pressured time the games might generate *a spirit of togetherness.* Paul laughs when he reads the lines, amazed at the idea chess games could have any effect on the national crisis. He writes back to Fiske:

...I agree, my dear Fiske, upon the issue of the war depends all our lives. In these circumstances, though, I feel it is insulting to engage in the goalless strife of the chessboard. I am more strongly confirmed in the belief that the time devoted to chess is literally frittered away! It is, to be sure, a most exhilarating sport, but only a sport.... Those who have been passionately addicted to the pastime should ask themselves whether sober reason does not advise its utter dereliction. Cuba is another matter. I am being grandly hosted, and resting up. Chess is, well, a hobby and no more. I'm finished with the nightmare of the board. Sometimes I cannot even sleep for fear of a wrong move, an unintentional slight to my opponent or the fear of victory. As a Creole, I have liberty to say in returning to Paris I would no longer patronize the *Café de La Régence*: it is a low—and to borrow a Gallicism—ill-frequented establishment. I no longer gain pleasure from checkmate, and if that alone doesn't communicate my need to forfeit chess play, I sincerely do not know what will.

As you know, I have been called an agent provocateur during recent Union-Confederate skirmishes by those who do not understand me. I'd be grateful if such stories have to be spread, they contain a kernel of truth, don't you think? Please can you inform my detractors, or at least those newspaper editors you know about town? I plan to return to New Orleans soon, to practice law and give up chess for good. I will remain impartial in the current conflict to preserve the Republic of Louisiana and the United States of America. I will do nothing to diminish the Confederate cause, although I make no shame of my disproval of raising arms against our sacred and constitutional Union. As you know, I was turned down for military service because of my health or I would be *aide-de-camp* to Pierre Beauregard, an old family friend. Now I only wish to cleanse body and soul from chess conflict and the more deadly field of strife. The chess pieces can be repositioned after every fatal game. But will I one morning read of my brother Edward shuffling off this mortal coil? Well, I only hope you can join me in this desire—the end of chess—and spread words that need be spread accordingly. Caution those who denounce my family name.

With loving peace,
Paul Morphy

Sensing the dramatic tone of the letter, Paul writes quickly and tips the dregs of his *midori* to his lips. With more drinks any memory of Royal Street, his family and Clara's circumstances drains away.

For his remaining week in Havana, Paul walks the dusty streets, pushing away the past. The sun beats hot and flat. The houses lean with orange walls and dark shutters, their top halves unpainted for a reduction in taxes. All day old men play dominoes on their doorsteps, while through a crack in the light their wives can be seen peeling sweet potatoes in the back kitchens. Small girls and boys are everywhere; for hours Paul sits on street corners encircled by children with deep questioning black eyes and demonstrates how to roll a coin in a circle, how to spin one coin on top of another. The tricks are magical and the children giggle with awful glee and run away. One boy remains, always quietly watching, saying nothing.

One afternoon Paul says: "What is your name?"

"José," the boy replies. "José Marveilles Julius."

"Well, José Julius," Paul says, "how would you like to learn to play chess?"

"Are there swords?"

"There can be."

"Is it dangerous?"

"Always," Paul replies. The boy runs away, dust swirling at his heels.

But Paul waits for him, wondering what he said to frighten or over-excite him, but José does not return. Later, rainfall cleanses the street, the bins and gutters. Roof-water loops from one house to the next, splaying walls in rivulets, but Paul does not move. He takes a stick and draws a chessboard in the mud. Despite his better judgment he waits for the boy with silent curiosity, conscious he is seeking an image of his own past. Why is he trying to make friends, he wonders, like an out-of-town Pied Piper? The rain dissolves the chessboard squares into diamonds. He decides he must return to the adults.

The next few days, Paul decides to go swimming and is instantly calmed. He lounges in a tide pool close to the bay floating up to his neck, and picks barnacles from the rocks. Sometimes white bubbles of surf go up his nose. Resembling a child learning to swim, he waves to the strangers on the beach.

Floating out there Paul feels safe, at home and possessed of no greater fear than a crab surprising him or the possibility of slipping on seaweed. Though he tries with a pole, and a baited hook, fish elude his eye-dexterity if not his patience. But the pleasure of failure is its own reward. Lacking aplomb, he enjoys sinking a rapier-like stick into shallows and is rewarded time and again with nothing.

Most of the time he is alone except when a lady or local from *Hotel America* asks for his autograph or wishes to learn his chess secrets. Always polite, Paul discovers his status as amateur fisherman-in-training soon tires their curiosity. More often than not they retreat with disdain, while he senses a new liberation in no longer acting the gentleman. He gains no pleasure from displeasing those who seek him out. Yet in Havana Bay with the ocean rolling, any slight to Paul's feelings is minor compared to the tight world of the Vieux Carré with its etiquette of Creole manners and carefully constructed claustrophobia.

One morning he tries climbing the large rocks strewn along the hump of the beach, protruding like meteors among the shaggy-alien sand dunes. Despite witnessing the ease of Cuban teenagers' tide pool leaping, rock-climbing proves too arduous for Paul. He settles for laying out shells, then paddling in the shallows for starfish to fix at the heart of his beach display. At last when he finds one, to his horror Paul realizes he has laid out two rows of eight shells all pointing the same way, the linked pawns of a chessboard. Trying to face castles in the air, Paul feels he is once again slipping into a chess fever masquerading as healing and amusement. The projection of his mind, a grid of sixteen squares, stares back from the sand.

He shivers, and feels he is losing.

"I don't understand...I want to slow down....Please can someone..." But telling himself pictures are better than games does no good. Caught in a world of vidual habits, he continues to create shapes in the sand. He even draws in the pieces, a bishop here, a rook there, and stands back trembling. The game is already begun. He is rooted. Eventually the tide rolls over the game, dissolving all, and Paul forces his body to go swimming.

That night Don Eduardo Fesser begs for another game of chess and Paul has to excuse himself to his hotel room. Here the sound of tinkling glasses, champagne corks popping and imagined covetous hands gracing zips of dresses find their way into Paul's dreams. He tries to forget why he came to Cuba—to escape himself—but now knows he must go home to the Big Easy.

"Checkmate," the black bishop whispers in his dream, cornering him in a net. "Congratulations, Mr Morphy, you are no longer the champion of the world. Chess fame and fortune is blunt. You cannot hope to be remembered if you do not defend your title."

Chapter Forty-Seven
1862
Le Jeu Est Fait

Despite the continuing war and the streets occupied by Union soldiers, by the end of the summer Paul keeps his decision and returns to New Orleans. The party in Havana is over. The Foreign Minister is impeached and the political situation is edgy. The rebels wait in the hills for the chance of a military coup. All foreigners are advised to cut short their holidays, but while the timing is disastrous for Don Eduardo—as a rebel sympathizer his house is likely to be confiscated—for Paul the extended mirage of Cuba is Dante's descending spiral. He has received a letter from Malvina, signed by Telcide and Helena, saying he must return to divide up Alonzo's estate. The family is splitting. Along with those who still care, Paul must be there to witness the death rattle.

The doors of 89 Royal welcome the idler home, refreshed but anxious. For twenty-four hours nothing is unusual: a surprise incident then occurs. Over Sunday dinner coordinated by Telcide and her children plus John Sybrandt, another guest is announced and Léona Queyrouze enters the room. Without further ado,

Telcide explains how Léona has been abandoned yet is happy to come to some arrangement in the Morphy household, should Paul be willing to turn his chess skills to mutual financial advantage. The meal turns surreal when Telcide, somewhat deliriously, proposes future marriage to Léona on Paul's behalf but the bribe-to-be refuses, hinting she expects Paul to deliver the proposal.

"*Maman*," Paul says, "I cannot believe…this is happening. I've been home less than a day."

"We cannot cope any more, Paul," she says. "Do you *not* understand?"

Paul turns to Léona, seated in a white gauze dress, looking pale. "Clearly, times are fraught and…"

Léona looks deeply embarrassed.

"The match is a good one," Malvina says, openly smiling at Léona. "And…"

"I will not play chess, not even for a thousand dollars a game. And I have no intention of marrying yet," Paul says. "The pursuit of excellence in chess is not appropriate…"

"Appropriate?" says John Sybrandt. "How is the situation not appropriate? The money is desperately needed…"

"And you are quite welcome to raise it," Paul replies, "outside the walls of this house."

A quiet descends. Léona stands and politely excuses herself and Telcide watches her depart with genuine melancholy. Malvina and John Sybrandt leave the table too. They begin colluding in the kitchen, their whispers intentionally half audible.

"Listen, *maman*," Paul says. "Malvina and John…they are…I can't say it any other way…plotting the end of the family, so any money you still have from *papa*…"

"Paul! Not now…"

"The truth is…is…"

Helena lays her hands on the table. "Please," she says. "We *have* to be a family…and Uncle Ernest…"

"…is not for discussion," Telcide replies. "We need the money, Paul, now…"

"I will not play chess for money," Paul says. "I won't be a professional. I might as well be a carpet-bagger and build a whore-house!"—going a little red—"or…you said it yourself, *maman*…the name of a chess player is no better than the mud of the Mississippi! We would be falling a social class…"

The conversation suspends. Titi enters with a cream flan, lays it on the table, and leaves. No one volunteers to play waitress so the flan merely remains, silently commenting, wobbling on the tablecloth. Someone smiles. The absurdity of the scene becomes apparent and one by one the family members discover a lost humour. Their amusement dies away, though, as the conversation in the kitchen is over and the scheming couple returns. Malvina and Sybrandt have Titi remove the flan before they focus their sights on the chess player.

They brand Paul "lazy." In light of John Sybrandt's job as a clothing distributor working closely with the Confederate cause, Malvina feels Paul's contributions to the Morphy name and the state of Louisiana, aside from enhancing his reputation on a "self-promotional world tour," have been limited.

"As a career, the law is too partisan," Paul says in his defence. "The people are…unreliable."

"That's the point of the law, Paul," his senior sister insists. "You can play with wooden pieces but not with people's lives; no one will take you seriously."

"That is just it, Malvina, I don't wish to *play* with people's lives."

"Well, you have to take something seriously. Or…"

Paul looks at her closely.

"Yes?"

"Or…you don't deserve your share."

"That's not your decision," Paul replies, glancing at Telcide, who says nothing.

"Seriously, litigation is like gambling. And you refuse to take a risk, Paul. But you must! You need gainful employment if we're to live under one roof and maintain a certain respectable way…and the privileges of the neighbourhood."

"You're not suggesting…" he begins and then stops. "I take risks all the time."

"Make-believe moves on a board, Paul."

"The risks are real!"

"In a game of fantasy! Come back to the family and stop playing obsessive games in your head. Look at you, all stiff collars and no blood in your face. You're completely ill with silly games!"

Paul stands and Telcide stretches her out hand, but he excuses himself from the table.

"I suppose you're all in agreement?"

No reply.

"So I salute you king and queen," Paul says, addressing Malvina and John. He bows low. "I hereby resign as a member of the Morphy clan. There is no more family, just squabbling hens and a few greedy cockerels."

"Paul!"

"…I don't mean to put it that way…but…I can't think what more to say."

"Life is just learning to lose the things you love," Sybrandt says, smiling.

Fixed to the spot for a moment, Paul watches as Telcide cries, her hand supported by Helena. No one speaks, asks Paul to stay, or encourages him to survive on chess alone. The idea of Paul Morphy, solo Attorney At Law, is not even mentioned.

Paul leaves 89 Royal Street as though backwards through the past: he traces his steps through Telcide's music room *soirées*. He walks through the kitchen where he once fought with Edward, out to the balcony where Alonzo and Ernest would play their evening game of chess smoking Havana cigars. What did it all mean, only to reach this point?

The courtyard is little unchanged, nestled in overgrown vines, the magnolia tree leaning on the greying fence, the moon peering down. Alone in the centre of the past sits the fountain, symbol of his youth, a stone block, its water frozen like the one across Canal Street where once he met a young girl, now also gone…

Paul turns on his heel and is gone too, still searching and wondering who—if anyone—is playing the next move.

Paul rents his own rooms close to Charles Maurian beyond Esplanade in Faubourg Marigny. He spends his days in the empty office of Morphy & Morphy, no longer frequented by Ernest. He opens Ernest's *Decline and Fall of the Roman Empire* and sometimes *Don Quixote* while shuffling papers around the room, but never reads more than a few pages. Pretending to practice the law, he makes the occasional speech, files incomplete cases and waits for clients who never appear. One afternoon a telegram arrives from his lost partner, Ewan Fellowes. The message ends with the words "please keep the furniture." He then realizes the letter is months old.

Even on weekends Paul returns to the now defunct office. He sits behind the large Maplewood desk, salvaged from Alonzo's former practice, and opens drawers. Late one Sunday, he discovers the knife he used to carry around Basin Street over a year ago. He remembers how Alex would wave its double-blade to cut open envelopes, shivering at each cut. He also recalls how after about a month of curiosity about Morphy & Morphy—mostly inspired by Alonzo's name—the lawsuits brought by new clients ceased altogether.

As uncle and nephew attorneys, they fought a single case in open court, but Ernest was too ill as barrister, Paul too shy as solicitor. A farce ensued in which Ernest wrote defence speeches from bed, while Paul read them out in court as though Ernest, somewhat disguised beard and all. The case was awarded to Kate Townsend. Even with his new partner, Fellowes, Paul's law business was a non-starter. Troisville Sykes, who eventually persuaded Morphy & Fellowes to represent him, was incarcerated *for the foreseeable future to life*. That time is gone....

Now truly unemployed, Paul returns to his lodging at 912 Governor Nicholls Street. A small room with cracked floors, its only redeeming feature is a view of the woody bayou bordering the Vieux Carré. Paul crouches at his writing desk under the attic window, peering at the misty landscape. Here the land rises to swamp—the city being lower than sea level—and hundreds of dour elms fork in the wind. Today is stormy and the trees yearn riverwards to the Gulf. On the horizon their treetops tower over the canebrakes.

Here shifting wetlands are born and die with the season. Here wild bayou begins, endless streams, feeding the rivers and lakes, bogged down for miles into the swamplands of southeast Louisiana. Here is a place of magic and mayhem, of old wars and future battles, of duelling under the oak trees, of missing people and unsolved murders, buried bodies and vigilante reprisals. Here float, ten feet down, the watery death-graves of escaped prisoners. In a land half liquid, half solid, ghosts of the soldiers of Ship Island are tortured. Tied to their execution oaks by day, they wander free by night.

The mist rolls over the forest, thick and vanishing, clouding Paul's mind one moment then clearing his imagination the next. He peers from the attic window, sensing on his skin the glory and despair of New Orleans, his home. Trapped within a confusing history, his journey incomplete, he wishes only to be here.

"Basin Street is my home too."

A dram of ol' *Raleigh Rye* whisky, left in the house by the previous inhabitant, sits on the writing table Charles has lent him. The liquor is bitter with a hint of the brothels, and provokes a memory of the barrelhouse where he first tapped the spigot with his uncle Alex, now nowhere to be found. Edward and Fred Edge enter his thoughts too, but he pushes them away, no longer wishing to return to the false glories of his travels, as he sees them.

"The name *Raleigh Rye* has nothing to do with whisky," he tells himself. "Yes, I know that. Bourbon Street has nothing to do with whisky. But I'm still going to drink it…."

Fist on the table, he pours a third drink, tips the bottle to his face and hay-coloured juice trickles down his chin. After a good burp he wipes the liquid from his hair. Outside a young magnolia tree, the child of Royal Street, trembles in the wind until the whisky is all gone. Paul lays his head on the table. Just as suddenly he wakes, remembering the mail he rescued from the Morphy home.

Taking his German knife, and twirling its blade in imitation of Alex, he opens a letter from Alexander D. Petroff, the 'Northern Philidor' and Russian chess master. Quietly he dips the feather in the ink and writes a reply, steadying his hand on the wood. Feeling like Howard Staunton running away from his challengers, Paul escapes having to break a lance with the Nestor of Russian chess on the basis that a meeting is unlikely, even if he could endure the trip to Moscow. He politely declines the chess invitation with the words "retirement," "attorney" and "amateur." Despite the drink, Paul's reply reads well and not without classical allusion in desiring to *lay aside his armour for the next generation of chess players*. Similarly, in opening the next request, he turns down fifteen hundred francs for two weeks at the Vienna chess club.

"Despite my family's financial losses and your kind offer," Paul mouths as he writes:

Estemmed Sirs,

I am now embarking on editing a manuscript of my own games. So my time is sadly pressing. I keep no record of my chess bouts except in my head. I hope to offer some insight into my time at the chessboard, you see, without making money from the royal game. In view of this enterprise, I must decline your offer to play in Vienna at your esteemed chess club.

Kind regards, your humble servant, PCM.

In the next letter Paul is astonished to see a request for a match from Howard Staunton, recently dated, but several months after the possibility of an encounter in Europe. The memory of the grandest opponent he crossed the Atlantic to play, even the sight of Staunton's name, deeply pains Paul. The consciousness that he was evaded, rebuffed—just so Staunton could avoid defeat—remains fresh. The main excuse in the letter is the same as before: *The Illustrated Works of Shakespeare*. Defeat, defeat…he thinks…what is defeat?

"Defeat is the rest of life. Long years await defeat. Why bring them closer?"

Dipping his pen with annoyance, his emotional weakness offset by alcohol, Paul finds the strength to write a personal reply:

Mr. Howard Staunton,

If you will….Allow me to repeat what I've declared in all chess circles in which I've enjoyed the honor of participation. I have never wanted to make any skill I might possess a tool for making a profit. I only wish your invitation were timelier to my career in the chess world. Let me take this opportunity to inform you of my official withdrawal from the field of Caïssa! I am now a busy practicing attorney-at-law and I envisage very little of my future time can be devoted to a pastime that has brought me so much happiness. Once again, I send my heartfelt thanks for your invitation, but I must decline, and wish you all the very best in your future games, exploits and publications.

Kindly, your servant, Paul Charles Morphy

He seals the letter with his family coat of arms, an underused relic of his childhood, and doubles the reply to Lord Lyttleton and the bulldogs Mr Avery and Mr Wills *addresses unknown*. No one, he hopes, will be under any illusion as to his public position with regard to chess.

"I am no longer on the board, so to speak," Paul says to himself and grins, the whisky now taking steady effect.

The next two letters are non-chess related, one an invitation to a costume ball on 27th March given by Colonel and Madame Norton. Paul considers such frivolity a touch inappropriate during wartime and tears the card up. The second is a newspaper article from Spring Hill College requesting Old Boys to join the militia resistance of *the great state of Louisiana in its current duress as an occupied colony of the Northern aggressors.* Paul learns how Abraham Lincoln— in a plan formerly ridiculed by the Northern press—advises the North how a blockade of the South could split the Confederacy along the Mississippi. *Can we just stand by and let this happen? What were you educated for if not to protect your land, your people, your state?* Already Lincoln's heinous tactic appears to be subduing any chance of a Southern rebellion. The committee of Spring Hill intones: *We are an enslaved people! Let all alumni honor the good fight of Spring Hill pelicans who fought the Revolutionary War. Educate yourselves in the art of resistance, and we shall prevail. Boys, do not let us down!*

Once again Paul tears the letter in two; momentarily he ponders the condition of New Orleans under long-term Northern occupation, but he knows it is not right to challenge the Union despite the secession of the South. He cannot fully explain why. Certainly slavery has little concern for him, always being close to the servants of the house. A gentleman of his time, he does not see the issue as one of master and slave so much as the rightful control of America being by the United States of its name, in Congress and the Constitution, and that nothing should break that bond asunder; it is wrong to rebel under such circumstances no matter how deep the love of Louisiana, New Orleans or the Vieux Carré. Paul sets none of these words on paper: he simply scatters the torn request alongside the ones by Lord Lyttleton and Colonel Norton and they drift to the floor like snow.

The next day Paul returns to 89 Royal Street. Despite his rejection letters to Europe, he realizes he needs the comfort of the chessboard if only to set up positions. He has no intention of playing with anyone professional. Charles Maurian requests the occasional friendly game and for his kindness Paul feels he has to play, especially now Charles has moulded his game into a significant challenge once Knight and Move have been offered. Climbing the stairs in the early morning, Paul ruminates over choosing the testimonial set with its ornate gold and silver figurines, or the simple wooden board. When he discovers Telcide has removed the testimonial set from the glass cabinet, the decision is made and Paul enters his old bedroom. The room is suspended in half-darkness. Everything feels eerily familiar, and yet distant, as though he is saying goodbye to his past. Leaving home inspires a peculiar feeling in Paul. Once again he is a trespasser and traitor to his family values, a living ghost wandering the walls without intending to stay.

He is distracted en route to the table by the closet door ajar. Inside are an old brown coat and a pale cream suit he cannot abandon; he throws them over his arm and shoulder. There, low down in the closet, two pairs of pointed shoes—tanned leather—smile in green and streaky red-and-black. Paul finds it impossible to resist their charm. Taking his old leather school satchel, he finally reaches the table only to discover the chess pieces are stuck. Tipping the wooden base achieves nothing. Then the king's crown—a simple wooden cross – snaps in his hand.

Paul is left surveying the broken king.

"It cannot be," he says and begins to dwell on the idea Malvina has glued the pieces to the board; the pieces are central to their squares. The whole enterprise seems calculated and vicious. Paul mulls over the thought anxiously then drops what remains of the king. "Clearly Sybrandt is at work," he shouts out. "That's it! Malvina is provoking Sybrandt to some dark deed. And we'll all suffer for it!" No response comes from the room. Paul sways, hair falling in his eyes. Then he balances the bag of shoes and tears the queen from the board. "Malvina is Lady Macbeth! She wishes to kill us all. Steal the family money! Well, she won't have my share." Proudly he tosses the king's tiny crown on the bed only to notice another revelation.

The *Hartford Times* is laid out meaningfully amid the sheets announcing the headline *General Winfield Scott has retired from active service, November 1861.* The newspaper is two years old, its appearance coincidental, but Paul does not know the news. He stares at the headline remembering his first boyhood challenger, the loud Winfield Scott. He reads:

> *Old Fuss and Feathers* and *Grand Old Man of the War*, as he was affectionately known, yesterday retired from active service. Golf and ornithology—his twin passions—will occupy his retiring years. We wish him every success...

The article is a glowing review of Scott's career of leading the American army mostly in Canada and Mexico. Momentarily Paul is happy to have outlasted the military tactician, bully and poor chess player. Then he remembers: he too is retired, and the games will not be remembered, only the wars.

Strangely though, next to Scott's eulogy is a minor article: clearly the correct article intended for Paul's notice by the person who left out the newspaper. Forest J. D. Woodbury's brief column, a profile of Paul, includes a picture of the chess player at twenty-one, dark-green pit-like eyes and a slightly fleshy face. Paul peers closer, the bag of elegant shoes suspended from his arm, and reads how Woodbury calls him *The Edgar Allen Poe of Chess*. "Very tragic," he says, sounding out the writer's name. "Edgar...Allen...Poe. But there is nothing tragic about my lifestyle." He is flattered by the article nonetheless, remembering his reading of Poe while recuperating from fits of illness in Paris. Even then he knew Poe wrote on chess.

"One day I will see Maelzel's chess-playing automaton," he says. "I'll guess its guilty secret. Some say there's a man inside. Who could ever build a machine to play chess? I don't think so! Clearly there is some other magic at work."

So saying Paul closes the newspaper and for the last time, constantly looking back, he leaves the family home. Like a man trapped inside the chess-playing automaton, he must prove—to others and himself—there is still a way out of the box.

Chapter Forty-Eight
1865
Brothers-In-Arms

One morning a knock at 912 Governor Nicholls Street brings Paul downstairs. He peels back the door and reveals Edward, his brother lost to the wars, standing there solemnly, wondering how he'll be received. Paul smiles and they embrace. As they enter Paul's two-storey house, now more decorated with furniture acquired from the settlement of the Morphy estate, Edward glances at his brother and Paul does the same.

"You haven't changed," Edward says, noticeably calmer, older than his years.

"Neither have you," Paul replies, his face more worn. They hug and before Paul can suggest tea or a meal, Edward proposes a visit to the grape arbour behind Rampart Street.

"I plan to spend the rest of my life," the veteran says, "in my favourite rocking chair. Now that the war is over." He looks at Paul. "It's been too long."

"I know."

"Damned war. Two years."

"Yes, two years," Paul repeats but does not seem to register the time. "The family has missed you."

Edward laughs, revealing a flash of his old self. "I shouldn't wonder, but thanks for the sentiment."

"So you want to see the vineyard?"

"Sure."

A block away, the brothers perch on the garden flagstones behind Edward's new home, an abandoned house set aside for returning Confederate soldiers. Edward shares the upstairs with two other men. He prefers not to talk about the war and Paul is careful not to dwell on asking. The garden is bare of flowers; the weather is cooling at the end of winter. All round, bare trees line the patio circling a fountain green with stone-moss. From an upstairs window comes the *staccato* of a waltz played on a violin by one of Edward's fellow renters.

"I plan on being a gardener down the warehouses," Edward says. "Maybe along St. Charles, who knows, there's some rich houses down there." He does not ask Paul what *he* is doing. A second later, he lifts his arm in momentary spur of excitement. "Look around you. All this greenery and it's so...I saw trees up North when..." but the sentence ends. "What's that line from that poet? *Honeysuckle vines, peach and figs...golden fruit...beds for mint and basil.*"

"I never thought..."

"I know," says Edward, knotting his brow. "I do read sometimes you know. So how are *you?*"

"How is anyone?" Paul says.

"You still play?"

"Now and then, with Charles." He smiles weakly. "Not seriously. Not anymore."

They stare at the fountain. Edward tosses a pear seed in the pool. The atmosphere is strange, expectant. A photograph would reveal a ridiculous sight: Edward sporting full military regalia in a grey coat with gold tassels, Paul in a white chiffon shirt and black waistcoat resembling a cocktail waiter. Their cold breath illuminates the air.

Suddenly Paul asks, "Have you ever been in love, Edward?"

Edward frowns. "Sure. Once or twice. Takes a fine woman to pin me down."

"I was in love," Paul says.

"There was one girl. Suzy-Jane. I met her in Maryland on the way home. A fine girl, but...well...she was already married..." He reminisces then claps his boot on the ground, not hearing Paul. "How 'bout you? Why did you never marry that Léona girl?"

"Too young," Paul offers, for an answer. He waits for Edward's next question but nothing arrives. "Do you think of her?"

"Sometimes...And you?"

"Me?"

"Léona?"

"Sure—all the time."

"Are you serious?"

They go back inside. In the living room, to satisfy something lost and somehow lay the past to rest, Edward dares take out a chessboard. Paul says nothing. He must play or Edward will be offended, but perhaps for once the gambit is good. The game is their first since childhood, idly begun. Ten minutes of play go by before Paul offers knight advantage. Edward accepts the gesture without inquiry. Little seems to have changed in their respective chess tactics.

"Tell me more," Edward says, not looking up. "I know about the other girl."

Both players feign interest for a move or two, but now the necessary expansion of the lines brings threats and opportunities, inspiring temptation. The brothers resemble a single entity. They huddle over the board, fingers lightly moving as if without care. But the human need for an ending, the last wound—setting the trap no matter the player or the position—becomes all too clear.

"The other girl?"

"I know, Paul. Go on."

"She...lived down by the river, closer to the Warehouse District. There's very little to tell."

"Her name?"

"I..."

Spying a winning position Paul is tempted to let his brother win. He knows Edward will miss the move if less subtly offered, so he rotates his bishop into plain view.

Edward frowns, hesitates.

"I could take it, but it might be a trap." He makes the move anyway, gingerly claiming bishop in one hand, pawn in the other, and looks into Paul's face.

"But now there's no going back," Paul says.

"Too right, young brother. *Touché*." Moments later the game goes to Edward, marvellously relieved, and proud of his achievement. He straightens his waistcoat and grins at Paul.

"You sure you didn't let me win?"

They return to the flagstones and settle into two wicker chairs on the courtyard.

"Yes...I mean of course not," Paul says.

"So the girl's name?"

Paul senses his brother's lighter mood. "Look, she was a prostitute," he says. "She...was special. We could have been married, but...it's a secret..."

Totally surprised, Edward leans forward, not untouched by Paul's confession and grateful for the excitement. "Of course, of course. Tell me. What is it?"

Paul looks at the mossy fountain. "She was a girl when I met her...I was...I don't know...only chess meant anything....Just Sundays at the chessboard, the moves of the king and queen. But I felt drawn to her...I can't explain it. That's all. I would go to sleep at night thinking of Clara and chess, chess and Clara, and wake with the same feeling. Waiting for my next game...waiting until I could see her again..."

"Two worlds."

"Yes. Nothing else, the city, family, could...I don't know."

Edward is tempted to talk about the war, but resists. He looks over at Paul and says:

"I'm sorry."

The words surprise Paul and he finds he has to turn to Edward. Somewhere in the grey uniform, the pale face and pride on Edward's sleeve, he sees the civil war battlefield of Antietam he has survived.

"Thank you," Paul says, at which Edward puts his head back and pretends he is not moved. "I…wish…"

"No," Edward replies. "No, you don't. We're here. All of us. *Maman…*"

"Don't," Paul says.

"No, Paul. *Maman* and Helena, you and me. That is our family now. I no longer trust Ernest and John Sybrandt and Alex Le Carpentier. They're the other side. Somehow it happened while I was away, and well, it's all about money…"

"That's not what I mean," says Paul. "Don't say these things. I can't see how…"

"Paul, you have to take sides. Think of it as just another game of chess. There might be a court case, but in the end *we'll* be the victors."

"Edward, please…no more games!" Paul cries. "I can't bear it."

They don't speak for a while. The moon appears over the yard, seems to offer another chance. Paul retakes his seat, and they watch her slow, grinning ascent.

"Clara was her name?"

"Yes, Clarabelle," Paul says. "We were going to be married."

Edward murmurs, lays his hand on his brother's shoulder: "She is there, Paul, I'm sure. If you want to find her, you can."

"Okay, thank you."

"No—not thank you. You're always saying 'thank you'."

"I know, Edward."

"You can find her, your *bella* Clara. The one that got away…"

"*Clarabelle.*"

"Yes," Edward says. "Exactly. Do what you need to do."

Down along the brick wall enclosing the garden, light shimmers in the walnut tree. Caught between the chessboard and lifelong feelings of love and resentment the brothers decide not to play anymore. Edward tells jokes to Paul instead, knowing that the apology relieves past crimes as far as possible. Their chess games are done. For the next hour or so until the light fades, and cold edges under their clothes, they study the newspapers. They sit on the porch, reading snippets out loud but avoiding the war news.

"The Baton Rouge Sailing Club," Edward says, "is attempting to sail Cape Horn. No one seems to be betting on them."

Paul smiles and searches for an accompanying piece. Much to Edward's amusement, he reads:

> Lost on Solidelle Street, old man Thomas Frère-Jones, seventy-five, eventually discovered in drainpipe," "Foul play not suspected. Wife of thirty-five years, Mrs. Gracie Frère-Jones of Athens, Alabama, spoke Tuesday of her husband's hobby of climbing into disused industrial pipes. Even so, Mrs. Frère-Jones 'never expected a tragic outcome.' For details of…

"Fetish," says Edward. "They always call it a hobby when it's a fetish."

Paul says nothing.

"Here's one," Edward continues:

> The original layout of the city's sixteen squares along the river, as established by engineer Pierre De La Tour as a network of drainage ditches—the whole bounded by a canal—is no longer deemed worthy to withstand the mightier storms…

"Okay, it's too small…can you read?" He hands the paper to Paul:

> Since architect Benjamin Latrobe described New Orleans in 1819 as *mud, mud, mud* and the construction of *levées* under Governor Etienne de Perrier, nothing has been done to improve drainage in the city since Francisco Luis Hector,

> Baron de Carondelet, served as the Governor of Louisiana and in 1795 constructed the Old Basin Canal from Bayou St. John under the Vieux Carré…

"After that bit…"

"I can see…okay," Paul says, and continues:

> The New Orleans *levées* are being raised to cover the new hurricane standards. The Orleans Drainage Company received the contract Wednesday from George T. Dunbar, the Engineer of the State of Louisiana, to improve drainage and *levée* protection for the city; higher standards must prevail to combat future outbreaks of yellow fever and malaria from poor drainage, and to free the city from the water purges that occur during the season of Caribbean storms. The *levées* are inadequate, we know them to be inadequate, and we must protect the city at all costs because protection from destruction is *no* cost at all…

"Poetry," Edward says. "Plus there may be jobs in the managing of construction. That's what I hope to pursue, Paul. I don't intend Ernest to have me logging shady shipments in the Customs House forever. There's already talk in Baton Rouge, you know, of state investigation into the seed barrels that roam the city. Someone's got a suspicious amount of Caribbean moonshine between his wooden teeth. Probably Ernest has a finger in that cherry pie too! But, *believe you me*, I won't be no piratical rum-runner…"

"Edward, what are you saying? Ernest is…"

"Just like *grandpapi*, you'll see. A lovable rogue, maybe, but a bad man. Ha! I plan to be one of the first men, Paul, to be completely straight in this family! The drainage company…you should consider it…"

Paul frowns and twirls a copy of the paper to Edward, where it falls open at the chess column.

"Listen to this," Edward instantly reads, leaping to his feet:

> Mr. Morphy plays serenely with a delicate nervous touch as if the chessboard were a musical instrument. His moves are the musical notes, and his fingers elegant endeavours to bring peace to the confusion of the table, and joy to the lives of the pieces.

"That's nice," says Paul.

"Henry Wadsworth Longfellow," Edward says and opens the double page spread. "So who's Longfellow? Look, another announcement.

> Herr Adolf Anderssen last Tuesday received an honorary degree from the University of Breslau. He was credited with service to the mathematics department and for *international endeavours on the field of chess*. No one stands higher than Mr. Anderssen, except of course, our own Paul Morphy.

"Edward, I'm not sure I want to hear them."

"Didn't you play him? The *field* of chess? Here, another quotation. *Morphy is the fastest player of our generation, a genius, a prodigy and a tragedy for rest of us!* That's Anderssen again."

"Heard it before! Please, Edward. I hate...the game!"

Edward steadies the newspaper:

"Okay, I'll stop."

"Please...I don't like chess. Anymore...it's..."

"That's all you had to say. Anderssen is a nice man. A good German it seems."

"He is," Paul says. "But chess is not everything. That's what I was trying to say. I refuse to play chess because it serves no purpose. I want to help New Orleans. But not with chess—not now! How will that help Louisiana?"

"The war is over, Paul. You missed it."

"Well...I *want* to work at the Custom House, or with the drainage company."

"Paul, they both dirty jobs."

"Well, I mean, I want to be an attorney-at-law!" Paul is on his feet, desperate-looking, hands pressing his forehead.

"Paul..."

"Don't you understand? I want to...to be of service. I want to...help people!"

"You...do?"

"God," Paul whispers, and falls to his knees. "I think I might have done the wrong thing with my life. Wasted it..."

"No, you haven't."

"I don't have a life..." Paul collapses in the wicker chair. Then he starts to shake, uncontrollably, and within seconds, passes out.

Edward is left in shock. "Christ!" he cries, and begins to fret, then starts to farcically bound around the room. "My own brother, I've killed him! I only wanted to persuade him to get a job...oh..."

The moon rises over New Orleans and keeps grinning down on the lost city while the *levées* hold.

The house is quiet.

Hours later, Paul wakes in the dark. He is half undressed and sweating from the heat. Furtively, uncertain where he is, he takes off the rest of his clothes. Then he meanders to the kitchen, and drinks tomato juice direct from the window ledge where the jug is cooling.

Suddenly Edward's cat Geronimo—a scrawny tabby—wakes from beside the empty bottles and scares him. Paul squeezes tight on the jug and does not drop it; the cat flicks its tail in disgust. He sees her slink off into the night of Rampart Street, glancing over her shoulder with yellow eyes. Moving to the door, Paul sits on the black and white tiles, feet on the cold step, and drinks the tomato juice. An unseen sunset is only moments away.

Paul realizes the empty bottles are Edward's moonshine. So much for the straight and narrow, he thinks; then noticing a newspaper he picks it out of the bin and reads:

> They were of two worlds, one of Tobacco Road's gaming houses and illegal cotton brokerage, the other of subscription balls and fencing academies. But the lore of ill-starred romance could not stop them...

Paul's eyebrows go up. He looks for the title, only to discover more troubling coincidence. What is real, he thinks? What can I trust? Surprises everywhere! Nothing I do brings any help, he thinks. Every person, reference, line or instinct seems to beckon the past into the present. The article ends overleaf. Paul discovers the article is in fact a short story called *Another Southern Girl* by 'Regina' L. Queyrouze. Underneath is the lady's signature: the single word *Léona!*

"She is following me!" Adjacent, Anderssen's words are repeated as though by fantastical torture:

> It is impossible to keep one's excellence in a little glass casket, like a jewel, to take out whenever one wants.

Lying down, Paul stares at the words but they offer no new meaning. "Impossible...a jewel...what jewel? A little glass casket...keep one's excellence...excellent what?"

His mind buzzing, the jar slips from his fingers and breaks over the kitchen floor.

"Spilled milk—no such thing? Like blood? Tomato juice...from heavenly skies...from heaven?" He lays aside the newspaper and lays down face forward. He touches his head on the cold tiles. Raising his head, again he touches the tiles and receives a strange, cooling comfort.

Lying there alone, Paul recalls the night in Clara's when they first sat on the bed together.

"Like the budgie in your room," he whispers. "The budgie the cat never saw...but I saw...like the budgie in your room...the budgie in your room..."

Chapter Forty-Nine
1872
Woodbury's Teeth

In 1868 Louisiana is readmitted to the Union. Nevertheless New Orleans remains an occupied city holding the ruby of the river port. Union soldiers remain. The citizens become accustomed to life under siege, always waiting but no longer holding their breath for the end of Northern control.

Meanwhile the chess world shrinks. Paul declines entry in Paris's International Chess Congress of July 1867. In December 1871 the Second American Chess Congress takes place, and once again Paul declines. He is adamant in his decision and only plays chess on Sunday afternoons with Charles Maurian. Now in his early thirties, he eerily resembles his boyhood self. He wears his hair almost to his shoulders and reminiscent of the Parisian pantaloons of his childish years, he takes to more garish and feminine outfits. No one comments but the flamboyancy of Paul's clothing does not go unnoticed.

He also begins reading about his family background, but less about the Morphys than Le Carpentiers and especially his *grandpapi*. For days he sits indoors researching the romantic figure of Joseph Le Carpentier, discovering the true black sheep of the family. He learns Joseph was not a rich man, and travelled all over the United States and Mexico. But he learns more about Joseph's beloved wife Modeste Blanche who inherited 89 Royal Street along with her brother, Julius Louis Blanche, both now deceased. Slowly Paul realizes that the Morphy pot of money comes more from *this* source than the earnings of his father as Supreme Court Judge. Being public service any income from Alonzo is restricted, while much payment occurred covertly as perks of the trade, namely in food products, wine and clothing. The big money, it seems, comes from father-in-law Le Carpentier and the lucrative merchandise of slaves.

After digging in the Library of Public Recordings on Pastiche Street, Paul discovers two transactions, one in which Joseph sells a black man named Ayr for 1750 francs in March 1806; the notary's name is Captain Marc Lafitte. In April 1820 he buys a forty-seven year old woman named Maranthe for 1090 pesos, again trading with the pirate. Joseph Le Carpentier is even authorized a *Certificate of Debenture* by the U.S. government, acknowledging his slaves and making him respectable. In a special Bill passed by Congress, sales are thenceforth subsidized. Business is maintained as usual and money flows like liquid gold.

Here is proof of the blood money that has long supported his family, Morphys and Le Carpentiers. Here is the hidden shame accepted as right and just rule, the leisure of afternoons at the chess table, the pleasure of a good education, lessons in piano and swordplay, fine dining and society, not to mention his gentleman's Grand Tour of Paris and London. Yet the guilty feeling remains impersonal: any connection with past slaves is swallowed by the wrongs of history, not unknown, but already faded. Titi is part of the family and Joseph Le Carpentier is dead. The North is winning the Civil War, if only recently, and life in the segregated South will go on. For now Dixie will fly. Reconstruction is a myth of coming years. So finding human sales with precise dates and monies, Paul expects to feel numb.

But he does not. Instead the past consciously frees him from unconscious guilt, the benefit he has taken from Titi's direct help since birth. As grandson to Joseph Le Carpentier, he is a piece on a chessboard being forced is to move; he is responsible for the next move yet understands any position he makes is a forced hand of history, a cog in a vast, infinitely free, yet necessarily deterministic machine. The game of life is a rigged game, with the appearance of progress but trapped within itself. Once the game has begun, no play can be taken back; no piece can be cleaned of feeling once touched.

So Paul turns to the only outlet he knows to help comprehend his family, slavery and the past. No matter how far he moves, the game of chess—a tangible reality, a symbol of self-control—is always there. Will he always be enslaved by the sixty-four squares?

At this time Paul receives a letter from Forest J. D. Woodbury of the *Hartford Times* explaining the new craze of postal chess using rubber stamps and played by telegram, as an easy way for *anyone* to get back in the game. Paul refuses the inquiry. But Woodbury's ridiculous chess games, played over weeks between a woodpusher and a world champion, are only the prelude to a visit. When he knocks on Paul's door to find the chess player returning from an afternoon walk, the journalist wins the opening gambit: the need for politeness induces Paul to welcome Woodbury into his home.

After preliminaries and a polite rejection of tea, the two men face each other in the living room. Eleven years have passed since their first meeting. The downstairs room is so small Woodbury's elbow touches the kitchen door. A pencil drawing of the whole family hangs on the wall, plus a single portrait of Joseph and Alonzo, forearms on shoulders, saying nothing. On the table sits a watercolour painted by Charles Maurian of Clara Young in a splendid crimson dress.

"You received my requests?"

"Yes," says Paul. "I have a little while, but not too long."

"Of course, please continue."

Paul sinks in an armchair, fingers to temples, eyes darting but never directly at his interviewer. Woodbury is curiously feline, upright and alert. There is something of the ferret about him. He sits with elbows on knees, pencil in one hand and tobacco between his teeth.

"Tell me about Europe."

"It was all long ago. Can you remind me?" Paul says, attempting humour. "This is for the *Hartford Times*?"

"Yes, Mr Morphy. Weren't you travelling with a companion? A Frederick Edge?"

"Not a companion, he was my manager...no, secretary. A...good man...we parted ways."

"Over the book?" He looks up. "You said in the mail."

"Yes, you know—over the biography. A fabrication."

Woodbury grins. "I see. Would you say you had a relationship with Mr Edge? That went sour?"

"Mr Woodbury...we agreed..."

"Never mind. I was wondering, Mr Morphy, if you could enlighten us on your family history, as background of course. Our readers enjoy...how can I say...the local colour of any great person."

"What do you mean? I am not a *great person*, Mr Woodbury, and I wish to be left alone. I have no responsibility..."

"No, of course not, but our readers...as a *public figure*..."

"Your readers? I am not a public...man."

"They like to feel in touch with the source of talent or genius, if I can be so blunt."

Paul begins to sweat and shifts in his seat. His eyes close. But all he can see is Woodbury chewing on a pencil and his yellow teeth staring from the pit of his mouth. Somehow Paul cannot look away. He starts to panic, freezes.

"Are you okay, Mr Morphy?"

"Why are you here?" Paul says. "I know you're a journalist. But tell me...*why* are you here? Did Daniel Harrwitz send you?" He leaps to his feet.

"Harrwitz? A chess player, correct?"

"Malvina...she sent you? No!"

"Paul…"

"She is plotting something…"

Woodbury chews so hard the pencil snaps in his mouth. "Please, Mr Morphy."

Paul is dancing foot to foot as though imaginary flames have caught his feet. He looks pained as though chastised by Telcide for interrupting a musical *soirée*. "The spirit of the professional," he cries, "is no longer the true spirit! Only the amateur enjoys what the professional lacks in spontaneity and carelessness. Professionals *damage* amateurs, you see, by contamination. The professional endorses the amateur to *suffer* from *inferiority complications*."

"I'm afraid I don't follow, Mr Morphy."

"No, you cannot. Only the white heat of chess play can bring grace to the game. Money is dirt on the shoe. Hence the gentleman amateur really damages the royal game. Don't you *see*, Mr Woodbury?"

"Please calm down," Woodbury says, staring at Paul's hopping around the room in a melancholy madness. "I will ask some different questions."

"I'm a private man. Can I go now? I'm a private man."

"But you were quoting something, Mr Morphy? You were quoting an article I read…"

"Myself! I was quoting myself in Paris."

"*…the professional is the curse of the modern game.* Do you really believe that?"

"When I was younger, yes, I did," says Paul and calms down a little. "Quote me if you like. Do you want to see the house?" Woodbury is stumped by the question but notices a kind of pleading in Paul's eyes, and agrees.

"So long as you don't murder me," he says, and laughs.

"No chance."

A flight of stairs leads to Paul's dwelling-rooms. He opens the door to reveal a quiet room. Woodbury puts his head inside, Paul still holding the handle of the door.

"Looks comfortable."

"I know," Paul says. "I had it specially made to look like my bedroom at home."

"I see."

Woodbury looks again. A single bed under a window nestles in the corner, a washstand nearby. Over the bed hangs a wooden crucifix of the St. Ursuline nuns. Woodbury gestures to the cross. Paul admits he no longer goes to church, "but I used to enjoy the Catholic ceremonies at St. Louis Cathedral very much, mainly for the family gatherings, and the smell of incense." He is about to close the door when Woodbury notices the chess table. "You can't move the pieces," Paul says. "My sister Malvina stuck them down to try and stop me playing."

"Did it work?"

"I suppose so. I keep the table, though."

Woodbury is about to leave when over at the window he spies another sketch, one of a large ballroom with bodies twisting and leaning together in candlelight, with a woman twirling in a silk blue kimono in the middle of the crowd.

"Clarabelle," Paul says. "A gift from her *madame*."

Woodbury says nothing but notices the row of elegant shoes underneath the sketch, all in a neat line. He smiles. "And those are her shoes too?"

"No, those are mine," Paul says without further comment, and softly closes the door.

Downstairs Woodbury makes his excuses and shakes hands with his interviewee, revealing his teeth. Paul now realizes he was imagining the wolfish canines; the journalist's teeth are strikingly white and carefully aligned.

"*Toute est illusion d'espace...*"

"I'm sorry?"

"Oh...nothing, sir, nothing..." At the door Woodbury turns back. "Oh I forgot to mention. Did you know Howard Staunton died?"

"No, I did not," and Paul returns to his chair before the door is closed. "Thank you for telling me. He was..." But he doesn't finish the sentence.

Woodbury's article appears in the *Hartford Times* three days later with an editorial biography which Paul, increasingly upset, forces himself to read. The column concludes:

> Once the brightest star on the stage of world chess, Mr. Paul Morphy has faded, sadly, to no more than a soft lantern...

He gently turns the page.

> Paul Morphy is poor and morbidly sensitive to misjudgement. He lives in the quasi-French society of Old Orleans for which he maintains the fine delicacy and nostalgic values associated with his debonair days. The impression one receives is that manners, gentlemanly conduct and finesse of Creole breeding are far dearer to Mr. Morphy than either wealth or renown. Mr. Morphy is melancholy-faced, full of dignity, his brow overhanging with self-consciousness...

He flicks the page.

> ...as to the question of his former New Orleans fame, the champion insists he is an amateur and averse to notoriety. Let us hope that, as a bastion of antebellum glory, Mr. Morphy returns to his former splendour soon. Mr. William Steinitz would dearly love to play him. Far more than New York trails and London tribulations, we the people would love to see that match too! Fame and fortune can only fleetingly live and Mr. Morphy has a duty to the city of New Orleans and the great state of Louisiana. Do not let us down Mr. Morphy. Make the right move!

Paul takes the newspaper upstairs. He lays the words gently over the covered chess table, above his shoes, and below the picture of Clara and the cross of the St. Ursuline nuns.

Tentatively he enters his own mind. He looks for a way back to the boy Morphy before the champion. There he lies sliding into the past. Move on move he topples himself until the pieces grow few, space opens up and the board grows bigger and bigger.

"Am I going mad, at last?"

Later, before sleep he reads the Woodbury article again, taking in the promise, the sadness, the challenge to play rising star William Steinitz. He has no interest. He wishes he were not cursed by that moment of first contact, aged only four in the Chartres Street playroom, so long ago.

Chapter Fifty
1874
A Thousand Shoes

Two years go by. Then one spring, Paul reopens his law office and defends a few small cases, some successfully. This time his partner is his former co-editor of *Chess Monthly*, the more reliable D. W. Fiske. But the practice folds unexpectedly, however, because Fiske is struck by yellow fever, succumbs and dies. People avoid the office. The remaining clients are suddenly only interested in Paul's autograph or a blindfold performance. The operation of keeping the office running, for the third time, becomes wearying and pointless. Paul again faces the failure of his legal career—chess, it seems, is Paul Morphy and the law is a world apart. Then one morning a rugged-looking man enters the office.

"If you defeat me at chess," he says, "I'll pay you $250."

"I will play you for nothing." Paul confirms his amateur status, explaining how he no longer bringing his miniature chessboard to work. But he remains somewhat affronted by the brusque offer. He leads the man to the *Elysian Fields Coffeehouse*. They play a quick bout, Paul abusing the game and intentionally constructing his own loss. "Next time I will give you the queen!" he cries. "I will never play chess for money."

"You just did," the man replies.

"But you won," Paul says.

"Yes, and now you owe me the money. You can only refuse to take the money if you won."

"But I'm still an amateur…"

"Just pay me the money."

Later Paul pretends to pay bills in his office and await clients. He knows this month is his last. So he retrieves old newspapers full of Alonzo's legal cases from a cabinet. One by one he ignores the law cases, and instead cuts out the chess problems. In a four-by-four grid he arranges multiples on the table and solves them with disaffected relief. As he searches for more patterns, challenges, shapes, the hours go by: chessboards blizzard tiny chequered paper all over his office. Then half way through a bundle, he discovers a photograph of the Prague champion, William Steinitz. He tries to turn the page but the photograph holds his attention, a grainy image of Steinitz behind a chess table and smiling mischievously, his comic fingers dancing over the board. The headline reads *Chess Has A Merry New Master*. Sensing the implication of chess as dull and serious before now, Paul cannot bring himself to read. Nevertheless his eye falls to the last line where Steinitz claims: *I could give Pawn and Move to God himself!* No comment is made by the editor. Paul reads the line again, remembering his own *Pawn and Move to the World* challenge made in Paris years ago.

"Perhaps Mr Steinitz should offer me Pawn and Move? No one ever replied to me!" Paul folds the newspaper in two, looking at himself in the mirror behind his office door. "I've never even heard of Steinitz. Who is he? Challenging God! The man is clearly mad. He has already moved into the cosmos!"

Despite new chess rivals and opponents seen and unseen, Paul practices law for two more months. One option emerges. He encourages people to be represented in the Criminal Court of New Orleans, still ominously guarded by Union soldiers but now permitting Southern defence attorneys.

The trials play like a repeat of the Civil War and no less vicious. Southern ingratitude and rebellion are punished by Northern military courts while tales of legal battles—and ensuing defeat of Southern lawyers—are continually sold to Northern newspapers. In one week-long trial, Paul defends a single case of an old man accosted and made to strip in the street by drunken Northern legislators; the politicians are asked to leave the city and lightly fined because their politics are sympathetic to the South. At last, Morphy the old man's lawyer accepts defeat. Paul's legal practice ends. The office is closed.

For days Paul meanders the streets between his room on St. Nicholls, the ghostly family home—where only Telcide and Helena remain—and Charles Maurian's house. He does not visit Basin Street. At night, sometimes half the morning, old dreams and delusions crowd his mind. Having no occupation and no pension from the family estate, now controlled by Malvina and John Sybrandt, Paul grows increasingly suspicious. He is certain he has enemies; attempts are being made to poison him. Eventually he confides in his mother and Telcide promises to keep his fears a secret, telling only Helena. But the difficulties of hiding Paul's mental ticks become more challenging.

As though to compensate for this manic worry, Paul himself becomes more obsessed with his upper-class heritage. More and more he dresses for the formal evening in the day-time; twice a day he washes his clothes and wears fine suits, primed and heat-dried, with debonair flowers in the lapels. He begins to tell people of his past adventures touring Europe. Stopping strangers walking to work, he describes Alonzo as *juris-consult* at the Louisiana Bar, member of Legislature, Supreme Court Judge and grandson of consul to Spain in New Orleans. The people brush by, sometimes calling names, mostly unnerved by the odd gentleman with his intense gaze and dandyish clothes. By night he develops an eccentric habit of arranging women's shoes in semi-circles in his room. When asked about this choice of shoes by Charles, he puns: "I like to look into their soles," and no more is said on the matter. But Charles advises Paul to keep his passion a secret and to hide the shoes as much as possible. "The display is what matters," Paul says, "not the shoes," and looks almost tearful.

One Sunday, Paul dares to bring some shoes to Charles's house and ties and unties the laces while they sit reading the newspapers. When Charles enters the kitchen, he finds a bag filled with more shoes, and Paul feels immediately guilty as Charles holds them up in the air.

"Clara had ruby red slippers," Paul says.

"That time is long gone," his friend replies. "The shoes remind you of Clara?"

"A little."

"She is probably down by the river and you can always see her. No one is stopping you."

Paul looks up. "What can I offer her now?" he says. "What could I ever offer her? Tell me. Answer me that, Charles."

"Your energy. All good things come of energy."

"I suppose," Paul says, smiling weakly.

Later, Paul continues learning of Steinitz's exploits, this time in the *New Orleans Bee*. Mr Steinitz, it seems, has *a defensive style of play luring his opponent into attack, encouraging him to overreach and then grinding him down.*

"It all sounds so ugly," Paul says.

"The way he tempts?"

"No, nothing," Paul says, learning how Steinitz *wears a black silk top hat which, when he wins, he slams on the table and cries 'Damn! I'm a chess player!'* "I mean, the way he dresses is...unrefined. All cloth rags and silk ties."

"Very uncouth," Charles says quietly. "You shouldn't read the chess columns, you know. It only gives you nightmares."

"Who are you? My mother?"

"I'm nothing like your mother." They laugh for once but continue to read in silence.

For the rest of that week, Paul tries to put chess away for good but reminders constantly crop up. A tablecloth from his childhood with red and blue diamonds is donated to him by Helena. Despite the skewed shapes and monotone colours, only a glance at the tablecloth is sufficient to make his mind race. Paul imagines chess armies in the red and blue waves, men crawling over one another like ants bearing weapons. He hides the tablecloth at the back of a cupboard and locks it. The next afternoon, though, he sees a boy and old man playing chess on Carondelet Street and is reminded of his grandfather. The old man is much thinner than Joseph, but Paul finds himself running and tripping on the banquette to escape the scene.

One bizarre incident follows another. Alex Le Carpentier recalls Paul asking him for money, a simple loan, but Paul not taking it when offered. According to Alex they agree Paul will call for the money, a few hundred dollars, the next day, but Paul does not. Meeting Paul accidentally in a café, Alex asks for an explanation. Paul says he "just wished to know the money was there—a security against poverty." By the time Malvina, Helena and Telcide hear the tale, Paul is deemed forgetful or vindictive or both, while the whole episode walks a narrow line between fiction and a ring of truth. Then Paul begins to remove objects from his room that resemble chess pieces, anything from photographs of landscapes to toy soldiers from his childhood. Only the delicately-painted shoes he collects prove a distraction not leading him back to chess. The shoes calm Paul in a way he cannot understand except through a dream-like connection to Clara, or the Clara he prefers to keep in his mind. He does not try the shoes on for fear of breaking the illusion of their visual spell, their suspended beauty: he fears opening a doorway back to chess's *sixty-four square madhouse*.

Slowly Paul learns. By the following Sunday he even folds the newspaper the wrong way in order to eclipse the chess problem inside the back page. If he glimpses the position for a second, he begins solving its possibilities; then he cannot turn his mind off chess for the whole afternoon. As though feeding a laudanum addiction by dissolving opium into alcohol, he must locate real chessboards to dissolve his growing anxiety.

Usually he plays a slow game with Charles and that provides some respite, but only as a last straw. This Sunday is no exception. By the evening, though, reading something he does not like in the *New Orleans Bee*, Paul takes it upon himself to pen a reply.

Dear Esteemed Editors of *The Bee*:

I just read that Mr. Meyiner, Editor of *The Louisiana Biographies*, will tomorrow begin the publication of the first part of *Governors of the State*, and I quote "following those biographies the reader will find equally entertaining biographies of Paul Morphy, the most celebrated chess player of the world, and that of Jean Lafitte."

If you'll permit me: my father Judge Alonzo Morphy of the Supreme Court on his death left a fortune. The inventory of the succession made in November, 1856 is available at the office of Theodore Guyol, Esq., Notary Public and amounts to $154,590 and the share to heirs is ample enough to decently defray all expenses. Since that time, gentlemen, I have followed no calling for the last ten years and given no cause for a personal biography. I have received a diploma as a lawyer. There is nothing more to say on my life story. I am quite retired.

I am ignorant of the spirit in which *The Louisiana Biographies* are conceived, but I am Louisianan by birth and in my heart. I am the son of a father who acquired the reputation of juris-consult at the Louisiana bar and who was a member of the Legislature, Attorney General and Judge of the Supreme Court, and I am grandson of a grandfather who had the honor of representing Spain in New Orleans during the first quarter of this century. I cannot approve of a work that would bring to light the quite legal auctioning services, recent or old, rendered to Louisiana, or in any way questioning my family history. I therefore have the honor, Messrs. Editors, of presenting you with my most distinguished sentiments. I wish to hear no more of biographies, fictitious or otherwise, and I encourage you to inform me of the formal, courteous abandonment of the project. I thank you.

> With all due respect,
> Paul Charles Morphy
> Attorney-At-Law
> > 912 Governor St. Nicholls Street
> > New Orleans, Louisiana
> > United States of America

Charles edits the end of the letter before Paul mails it the same evening. That night they play word games over a bottle of brandy. Around midnight Paul falls asleep in his chair and his friend covers him with a blanket before silencing the grandfather clock and retiring to bed.

"I don't know," Charles whispers to the walls. "Perhaps Paul is right. Chess has *no social purpose*," and he blows out the candle.

Chapter Fifty-One
1875
The Devil's Asylum

W hen the weather is hot again, Paul escapes the city with the only person now willing to help him, Alex Le Carpentier. They travel to Chalmette where Alex treads the boards of the barrelhouses in the same way he introduced Paul to drinking on the seamy side of town when Paul was only twenty. Chalmette has little to offer, though, and at the end of their stay Alex leads them to a rich friend's house, ostensibly to show off Paul's chess skills but in truth to acquire more wine, shelter and some indelicate last-minute entertainment.

Paul is now thirty-eight and Alex in his fifties, yet both resemble their younger selves when the Morphy and Le Carpentier families were whole, before John Sybrandt and Malvina had acquired a great proportion of the family money and before Telcide's and Helena's recurring bouts of illness. The events of the past few years, largely overshadowed by previous catastrophes, do not fail to register with Paul. More than ever he walks with a mystical air, opting to use a cane but ever the polite, shy and exquisitely dressed gentleman in public. Edward is now head of the family, in terms of maintaining the house at 89 Royal Street, and feels a sense of responsibility towards the remaining female members. Ernest works from the Baton Rouge Customs Office and sends money on occasion. The legal practice is closed for good. The music no longer echoes from Telcide's musical *soirées*, nor do guests come. Amid this communal malaise the decision is made for a break to Chalmette. When they return, Paul must at long last find an occupation and vocation. Chess is a penniless devotion worsening his health. Now and then people even forget he was champion of North America and Europe, preferring to see him as a failed lawyer with immaculate dress.

The day before they leave, Paul does again try to find Clara Young but with no luck. The old palatial brothels are now in new hands. Some of the *madames* including LuLu White and Minnie Ha-Ha are dead and gone to the brothel in the sky. Even Dan O' Neill's *Amsterdam Dance House* is newly occupied, rented under the table to a Scandinavian circus troupe. More than ever Paul and Alex need a distraction and the short carriage ride to Chalmette suits the purpose. They disembark not too far from the Union barracks, the source of Louisiana military rule, near makeshift brothels lining the fort's walls. Here the soldiers and working girls rub shoulders in drinking shacks, while conscripts provide ditch-drainage and food to encourage a Roman-style prostitution village.

After a night in this dark and dangerous backwater, Alex drinking himself into oblivion and Paul trying to remain proper and upright, they repair to the backstreets and Alex's friend William Henry Malpotha's house on the corner of Regal and Benefit Streets. The evening passes without incident; Malpotha cooks a fine turkey. The warmth and the port feel like paradise in contrast to the hell of the previous night, near the barracks, having slept on cold straw surrounded by shouts and screams and the rain coming through the roof. After dinner they move to the gentlemen's smoking room; Malpotha's wife is away with cousins on the Alabama coast. The three men sit and smoke; the only interruption is the soothing chirp of grasshoppers at the window. A servant boy Malpotha has purchased at a local auction—now illegal in New Orleans, but not for forty miles around—brings the drinks.

"How do you like your city today?" Malpotha asks, swishing his hand.

"As ever," Alex replies. "The city likes us."

"A bit restricted, wouldn't you say?" Malpotha pushes, taking a gulp of brandy. "A bit...."

"No worse," Paul says feeling a touch defensive, "than Chalmette. We cannot move about as freely. And the curfew is still in practice…"

"We don't go out in a big-style way," Alex adds.

"No," Malpotha adds, "I expect not." He winks, a portly man with a red face stupefied by years of drink. "I don't either." Then he laughs and staggers to his feet. "Come follow me, let's indulge a little billiards. The table is my muse, my mistress."

"Billiards is a great sport," Alex says and downs his brandy.

The evening is getting late, but nevertheless the men adjourn to the billiard room. Malpotha unfurls a huge damask curtain, serving no other purpose than dramatic introduction, to reveal a gold-baize billiard table, a book-stacked cabinet and a series of paintings adorning the walls. Paul is reminded of the library-billiard room in Paris but this room is larger, the table itself more magnificent and ornate; the books are for show but the paintings, giant multi-colours from all ages and styles, tower from the walls like goliaths. Alex finds the cues in a rotating wooden vase and proceeds to dip them in a bowl of black chalk.

"Clearly you fancy yourself as a player?" Malpotha says. "Or do you just fancy yourself, hey?"

"I've played before," Alex says. "In lesser places…with more distractions."

"I see."

Surprising the other two, Paul clatters the balls around the table. Malpotha stares at his presumption, and Paul smiles back, momentarily released form his private thoughts.

"I feel," Paul says, "like improving my fencing skills."

"Wrong sport! There's a little difference," Alex says.

"An expert fencer too?" Malpotha says, and strikes the baize with the point of his cue. "Blue ball in the corner!" He cushions his stomach over the wood and cannons the target, hard. The balls spin out of control chasing one another in formation like overzealous little dogs before slowing and parting company. Nothing goes in.

Alex frowns but compliments his host: "Just like at Rizzo's."

"I was only there a month ago," Malpotha says.

"So you know the man?" Alex says.

"He believes fencing solves all conflicts," Paul says.

"Just a swish of the sword," Alex replies crouching to the table and fixing his shot. He sinks the ball and the next three. Dizzied by the paintings Paul takes a seat and Malpotha does too, a tactic to feign confidence in his opponent, and Alex misses. Meanwhile the orphan boy returns with the drinks, tops up their glasses and disappears from the haze of the darkened room like a ghost through the bookstand. Paul cannot see the doorway. He only hears the clatter of shots as Alex and Malpotha vie for superiority. Then looking up he is struck by the tremendous oil painting of a horse rearing up on its back legs, a white stallion with no rider, the background completely black. Paul's eyes wander to what the horse with surreal intelligence appears to be watching. The adjoining painting depicts two opponents seated before a darkened chessboard, one pale with fright, the other scowling with deliciously malign intent.

"Moritz August Retzsch," says Malpotha, appearing at Paul's elbow. "Mephistopheles is playing a game of chess with the young man for his soul. Look how the boy cowers…"

Surprised by the realization, Paul drops his brandy on the carpet. Malpotha's back is facing Paul and the host fortunately concentrating on his shot. So while Paul watches, Alex pours a jug of water on the spillage. Paul looks back at the painting and stares… mystified…horrified.

"Yes, his Satanic Majesty is winning!" cries Malpotha. "Look, the Devil has the Vices for pieces, the young man the Virtues. The young man is falling for sure…"

Without hesitation, Paul says: "I can take the young man's game and win. I can…beat…the Devil."

"But the game is done. The boy is struggling. Look at the pieces."

The players laugh and toast Paul's claim. But realizing Paul is serious, not even smiling, they see potential sport in the game. The servant-boy is called and despite the warnings of Charles Maurian and Paul self-proclamations, the chessboard is arranged. The game in the oil painting is reproduced piece for piece. Mephistopheles is clearly waiting—Alex happily takes the role—so Paul's move is next. Meanwhile Malpotha refreshes his own glass; he will drink himself into a steady stupor, hand resting on a belly already bloated with turkey and brandy.

"Bravo," he burps. "Alex, be sure the Devil plays his best!"

"I'm playing for my own soul," Paul replies, smiling faintly. "And *still* it's possible for the boy to win. See!"

He picks up the rook and demonstrates all four ways the Devil is trapped, cornered and suffocated by his own pieces. Alex applauds his nephew and adds:

"Let us play out the moves the old-fashioned way!"

"Yes of course." Paul makes his choice. Then he looks up at the painting.

"Don't do that," Alex says. "*Malchance.*"

Paul waits under the glare of Mephistopheles: the Devil's yellow fingers are poised over his next move, the pale young man trembling, the playfulness of the Lord of Darkness repressed by his certainty that one more soul is about to join him. Keeping to the rules of the game, just this once trying to win fair and square, the Devil hides his surprise in a scowl.

Thus paint and flesh and blood compete for Malpotha's attention. He glances from painting to players, one scene suspended in cosmic art, the other dramatized in changing reality. The matching chessboards flicker under the lights. Alex's sidelong look uncannily captures the leering scrutiny of Mephistopheles. Paul has the blank face of the pale young man. So the game is played in a curiously shaky manner, pieces floating and trembling, until the Devil's position unbelievably weakens. A sigh! Alex Le Carpentier is forgiven in the falling of a wooden king and Paul snatches victory. The pale young man is saved and the boy in the picture will never know his fate!

"You kill me!" cries Alex and cheers! They toast the victory and defeat. The table is abandoned and they agree not to look at the painting. Their host, slouched over the billiard table, is asleep.

The game is eternally concluded. Alex and Paul feel it is time to retire. They wake and leave the shocked Malpotha, a drunken Count Dracula who shakes their hands in his steely white claw, to the remains of his meal, drinks and the scattered items of the billiard room.

"Goodnight chess kings," he calls as they leave.

Outside the sky is dark and the moon is nowhere. In their *Chalmette Lodge*, across Main Street and past the train station, Alex and Paul reach their room and sleep comes fast. Paul has dreams of a fantasy place called Kalmykia, a country devoted to endless chess. The rivers of Kalmykia flow in straight ranks and files, but the roads are blocked by guardians dressed as pawns who leap unbidden from the hillsides. They stab the traveller...a lost outsider from New Orleans...with long pitchforks as he floats down the river; they swing at his eyes with sceptres stolen from queens as he wanders the abandoned streets. Paul wakes in a screaming sweat with the words "Kalmykia, Kalmykia!" on his lips. He wakes Alex who is shocked by Paul's wasted look. A nip of Alex's laudanum does the trick for the rest of the night.

The next morning they seek out Paul's nightmare country by examining a world map. Just as they are about to abandon the guessing game, Paul's finger strays east beyond Prague and Breslau to lands where chess originated. Tracing a circular route, there, between Persia and China, is a small Russian state.

"That's it."

"That's not Kalmykia...or however you say it."

Paul looks up. "That's it. My home. Kalmykia."

"It says Elista."

"Elista is the capital. A place of beauty, but landlocked, don't you see? *Zugzwang!* Not like New Orleans in any way."

"Paul, calm down...you look funny."

"*Zugzwang*," Paul replies, and looks intently at Alex but a thin string of saliva dribbles on his cheek. "Yes, home...my home...zugzwangg-ggg-ggggg!"

Alex stands back and stares. He whispers something under his breath, but Paul remains hunched over the map, circling the tiny province with his fingernail.

"Don't remove my finger," Paul says. "Never! That is my home. Kalmykia...Elista. I'm sure of it!"

"You're imagining it. That's Russia, Paul, where Russians live. You know, Russia!"

Paul starts to gurgle, and then abruptly in two stages, collapses. He twists on the floor, kicks out and rolls on his back. His face is twisted and loses even more colour, the muscles leaping out as though the flesh is trying to flee. Alex cries out, and stumbles, and is helping him. He drags Paul to the kitchen. Suddenly Paul awakes on the chequered tiles face-down and screaming. Alex grows frantic but the chess player is silent and does not move.

"I'm sober now," Alex jokes, the last thing Paul remembers as Alex shakes him. "But where are you Paul? Where now? What does Zugzwang *mean?* Where are you now?"

After a fitful return journey and the breaking of his fever, Paul moves back in with Telcide and Helena. They begin to look after him at home and he ventures out less and less. What they call "Paul's delusions" reach a climax when he suspects a barber being in collusion with one of his father's friends, Mr McManus; while Paul is at home being shaved he attacks the barber, trying to slap him with his bare hands for drawing a knife—the standard barber's razor.

"Under the oaks!" Paul cries. "Under the duelling oaks!"

The barber escapes, while seated at the piano Paul declares how barbers are in a vast conspiracy subpoenaed by his enemies to cut his throat. Usually quiet even on home visits, Paul now shouts blue murder as though in fear of his life. Later that day and from now on, he takes to wearing his father's Panama hat—a symbol of his fear of barbers' blades—as though by some perverse magic he can warn off attacks.

"The sad part, *maman*," Helena says, "is that Paul now fears barbers, but he still wishes to be professionally shaved."

"He likes to look good," is Telcide's reply, but she is aware of Paul's increasing difficulties. Surprised by Helena's conservative tone for her brother, she knows how upset her daughter will be soon. In private, Telcide makes plans to remove Paul from 89 Royal Street for his own good. From the St. Ursuline nuns she hears of an establishment called the *Louisiana Retreat*, a hospital run by the Sisters of St. Vincent DePaul. She does not know, however, that the *Retreat* is an experimental hospital to treat the mentally ill. But over the next few weeks Paul's behaviour becomes disturbingly unpredictable, with more incidents closer together.

In one incident, he walks out on his balcony overlooking the garden and declaims: "*Il plantera la bannière de Castille sur les murs de Madrid au cri de ville gagnée et le petit Roi s'en ira tout penaud!*" For three nights Paul makes the solemn cry, but on the last night the outburst is brief then stops altogether. Helena translates: "He will plant the banner of Castille upon the walls of Madrid, amidst the cries of the conquered city, and the little king will go away looking very sheepish!" In Paul's voice, the words sound like a nursery rhyme spoken by a gentleman. Yet mother and daughter do not overlook specific mention of a king's move or Spanish roots— chess and history—in this strange midnight song. A week later, just as all goes quiet, Paul cries out in his sleep:

"I want to live the rest of my life inside a house built exactly like a rook. Like a bird in a nest! Like a rook in a rook-hole!"

Silence for a while, then:

"The black bishop! Save me Elista!"

Helena crawls into Telcide's room.

"Who is Elista?"

"I don't know! Go to sleep. We will help Paul tomorrow."

That night Telcide decides: by mid-morning they are en route by horse and carriage. First they cross the Bayou St John named Tchoupic or 'muddy' by the Indians and head for Lake Borgne and the Gulf of Mexico. After a night in Venice, Louisiana hoping the Gulf air currents will clear his mind, another of Paul's midnight fits brings them to Venice's only General Practitioner. Without knowing his patient's background, the doctor of Venice recommends *chess as a means of distraction and change of thoughts.*

A small man with round glasses, he grins as he diagnoses:

"The aesthetic beauties of interaction that appear with surprising unexpectedness in the unfolding of a chess game, you know, are harder to explain than the miracles of the human body. For a chess player, I would recommend a *blitz* game to get the system going."

"A game of chess," Helena whispers. "That is…"

"…not possible," Telcide finishes. "Chess has caused all this…destruction!"

"Do you know there are fewer atoms in the universe than moves on a chessboard?" the doctor pursues.

Telcide is polite enough to listen, then says: "Tell me what's happening to my son. That's your advice? He's an atom of time?"

"He *will* awaken simply because chess is infinite…he will find a way, if we leave him alone…"

"Or if we shake chess pieces in his face! I won't believe it!" She grabs Helena by the hand, and walks Paul coolly outside. They resume the trip. By early evening the sun is setting in the poplar trees surrounding the *Louisiana Retreat.* The carriage rolls impatiently down Henry Clay Avenue. Between Coliseum and Chestnut Streets, a nun appears from the side door of a large granite building.

"Welcome," she says, and hands Helena down from the buggy. "I trust your journey was good. I am Sister Clare. Welcome to the Sanatorium Charity Hospital."

Paul immediately realizes he has been misled, believing the destination to be one of rest and recuperation. Standing before a nun in a nursing uniform, he begins to panic.

"I am the patient!" he shouts. "I don't...I won't be..."

No one is touching him but to prove his sanity Paul begins to expound the *Code Napoleon*. Reciting the lines seems a lot like madness. Meanwhile like a mirage alongside the building, a patient is being strapped down by orderlies in black coats and removed into a van.

"This is the right place," Sister Clare says, blocking Paul's view and gesturing for help. Paul suddenly realizes what is happening. Arm in arm, Telcide and Sister Clare walk him forward still reciting the Code. As they reach the entrance Paul starts to struggle. Over his head a sign welcomes: '*The Louisiana Retreat for the Feeble Minded*, 1040 Calhoun Street, New Orleans and 616 Henry Clay Avenue, Baton Rouge. *Welcome!*'

"Just be patient and trusting," says Sister Clare. "Make the right move, Mr Morphy. We can cure you of your demons."

Paul screams and falls to his knees and says his prayers in the street.

"Elista! Elista!" he cries. "Please! Let no merchant traffic in my heart...Clara, where are you? Help me! Save me Clara! Come now..."

"You have persecution mania," Sister Clare continues, "and you must be cured." A burly man now takes Paul, wilting under his arm. Helena is in tears.

Sister Clare puts her hand on the wall to catch her breath. "I think he'll be alright," she says.

"*Maman*," Paul cries. "*Maman*...Titi...Clara!"

Telcide watches her son being dragged down the corridor. "I'm scared!"

"That's enough," she says. "We made...a mistake."

"Mrs Morphy, we do have time."

Telcide turns to the nun. "I know and I'm sorry for your time. But please bring my son back. I've signed nothing. I've made a mistake."

"We made a mistake," Helena echoes, looking up.

Sister Clara is amazed and tries to persuade the women but they are adamant. Feet dragged behind him and semi-unconscious,

Paul is returned to his family. The burly man folds his arms, unhappy with the outcome, either from embarrassment or pride. Sister Clara chooses not to help their departure.

"You will never bring him back, Mrs Morphy!"

"My name is not Mrs Morphy," Telcide calls as she leaves. "I am Thelcide Le Carpentier. I am a French Creole woman and my son will not…be treated….My name is *Le Carpentier.*"

Sister Clare and her orderly have already left. On the threshold of the huge granite hospital, Telcide and Helena support Paul over their arms and bear him into fading light down the drive and under the popular trees. At the road they wait several hours for the first empty carriage.

"Am I ill, *maman?*"

"No, something made you ill."

"Or someone," Helena says.

Paul is silent but troubled. Then he adds from memory: "James Alexander Cockburn, *Idle Passion: Chess and the Dance of Death*, 1774…A sport or activity where expertise has no convenient slot in society…can produce angst and neurosis…James Cockburn, *Idle Passion: Chess and the Dance of Death*, 1774…A sport or activity where absolute expertise has no convenient slot in society…"

He repeats the lines two or three times. Helena covers his lips with her fingers and he is soothed. Under the fig trees lining the road they mop his brow and share a jug of water. They promise to get Paul home. As the light fades, a carriage appears on the red glow of horizon.

Later Telcide destroys all the chessboards in the house. She safeguards the gold and silver testimonial set, wrapping the pieces in handkerchiefs with one eye on the metal market in Jackson Square. The remaining wooden boards, gifts from the New Orleans Chess Club belonging to Paul and Alonzo, she wraps in a scarf and takes outside. In a clearing near the fountain she lights a bonfire and watches the wood burn.

Later that evening opening the mail for the day, Telcide finds a package for Paul bearing the insignia of a chess knight. The postmark is New York, New York. The package is awkward so she fetches the carving knife; a slip of paper falls out declaring an honourary award for *Mr. Paul Charles Morphy* from *The Union Chess Club at Buhler's Restaurant, 8th and Broadway*. From a cover of gauze, Telcide unravels a spiky wreath handsomely cut into a crown of silver laurel leaves. The beautiful blasphemy of the martyr and the messiah's crown is too much for Telcide. She looks up at the bonfire burning outside—all Paul's chess possessions—while holding his latest prize. After the bonfire goes out, as though by cue, Telcide extinguishes her bedroom candle.

"Put out the light," she whispers. Alone in the dark room, she places Paul's silver crown on the table. She determines not to be upset. Then she cries.

By 1874 Louisiana is bankrupt to the tune of $53 million and cannot pay the interest let alone the principle on its loans. The longer the state remains in debt, the longer the Union troops will stay. A group called The White Leagues is established to combat corrupt government, but admonishes Northern control of the city as equally suspect. On 14th September 1874, a pitched battle erupts between the northern governor's Metropolitan Police and the White Leagues led by John McEnery. The riot lasts fifteen minutes and kills twenty-seven men and McEnery is soon disenfranchised of power. President Ulysses S. Grant sends troops and three warships to New Orleans to take back control. McEnery can't fight the US Army and Navy and the fate of New Orleans hangs by the day.

As Paul Morphy lies in his childhood bed, watching the moon cross the sky, shells sail over the eastern districts. The guns boom at night and then go silent. The city remains the same. Military rule is kept in New Orleans. But by 1877 Grant is no longer president, and New Orleans becomes a constitutional question. The honourable retreat for the sake of the Union befalls President Rutherford B. Hayes. The new Supreme Commander orders Union troops from New Orleans on 27th April 1877.

Paul watches this scene from the roof of his house from where he can see the river. As the federal troops retreat, their guns pointed at the town, the mayhem of a providential *Mardi Gras* breaks out across the city. After years of curfew, rationing, harassment and civic control by a recent enemy power, New Orleans cannot contain the *joie de vivre* at its dark heart. The skeletons must dance and the bearded ladies drink, and the politicians and prostitutes reopen their revolving saloon doors. The great unwashed—never happier than tonight—flood the streets of the Big Easy.

In 1879, due to accusations of corruption, New Orleans loses its political centrality and influence; overnight Baton Rouge becomes the state capital.

Chapter Fifty-Two
1884
A Chance Encounter

During the downturn of the city, Paul continues recuperating from his breakdown. As the seasons pass he moves his winter chair from inside the house to the courtyard, where it becomes his summer chair. Night on night he observes the stars from his room or from the balcony where Alonzo and Ernest once played chess. Paul avoids all contact with the game, reading the *New Orleans Picuyne* and avoiding the chess columns. One evening he learns how in the eighteenth century Frederick William, King of Prussia collected the tallest men from across Europe to create an elite troop of royal guards, the Potsdam Giants. Paul stops reading in case the giants and the chess pieces fuse in his mind and deliver more bad dreams. But now and then he dips into Thackeray's *Vanity Fair*, the tale of plucky Becky Sharp, hot off the serialization press. The instalment depicting Becky's heroic escape from Miss Pinkerton's Academy—her prison of a finishing school—stirs old memories of the opera, schooldays and his childhood.

To vary his reading, so Paul claims, he also subscribes to the *Blue Book* of Basin Street. Every Tuesday he picks up a new copy on Canal Street. One time he learns Troisville Sykes will not be prosecuted for the murder of Kate Townsend; instead he will receive 10% of her posthumous earnings due to concubinage law. Next week's *Blue Book*, No. 88, is a double edition. Kitty Johnson's two lovers, Billy Walsh and J. J. Heley, fight an open duel on the banquette before her barrelhouse, *The Morbid Drinker*. Kitty is fined $60 for not referring the men to the Wild Oaks. Every detail of the bloody fight is glamorized with gleeful comedy down to Walsh's death and *The Drinker* preparing a meal for the victorious Heley. The next page is an article charting how the Basin has changed over twenty-five years. The grainy photographs show how the brothels have doubled in height. Billboard advertising—everything from *Jane's Saloon Stockings* to *Classic Raleigh Rye*—has tripled on every street. Still the claptrap houses of old remain, delightfully incongruous amid the palatial palaces and themed wonder-bordellos of today.

Paul tries to stop reading the *Blue Book* extracts but their fascination takes hold. *The Twenty-One*, sold by Kate, is now a mulatto house run by Hattie Strauss *the half-caste*. A hard-hearted whore with a glass-eye, Hattie is rumoured to have provoked the killing of *her* lover, Senator James Beares. Paul runs his finger over the images of *The Twenty-One*, remembering his brief visit with Clara, when his eye catches one paragraph. Hattie is quoted:

> That is how Clarabelle Young came to us, by way of her grandfather who was from St. Louis, Senegal in West Africa. I was first to inspect her health and assign her Violet as mother. Violet's now dead o' the clap. But Clara is here forever. She hides from the money and the lights down Hospital Street in and out of the ice house herself sometimes. But we know she is half-slave, that girl, and every black woman has a place down at *The Twenty-One*. Clara is always welcome back, if she wants to see her time out. Yes, she did well by *The Twenty-One*. And we'll do well by her again!

The article stops.

Paul takes his head in his hands, and stops reading. The mention of Clara is too much to bear. For the first time he knows why Clara cannot bring herself to be among the Creoles or in the French Quarter: "She's just been too long on Basin Street."

But so much time has passed Paul cannot be sure. He knows his family cannot tell Clara is a *quadroon*, quarter African, less welcome in the Quarter than the other side of Rampart Street. Maybe Helena knows. But nothing is definite. In his blood Paul has always known. "Nothing means *less* to me. Why would it? Clara is Clara," and he sits there lost in thought.

The next Sunday, tired of resting before the sun goes down, Paul takes his walk early. He draws aside the mosquito net, purchased by Telcide in panic at new cases of malaria, and steps on the cold floor. On his wooden table—once home of his chessboard—fresh linen is laid out with trousers and a frilled shirt; from the dresser he takes his fine cambric handkerchief and pearl-coloured gloves. After dressing and shaving he waits for his face to dry at the window.

Still adjusting his monocle Paul picks up his walking stick and leaves 89 Royal by the front door. He walks the same route to Jefferson Academy he made with Joseph Le Carpentier over thirty years ago. Glancing in the new tobacco storefronts, he plans to aim for the opera. The West End opera is showing *Madame Anget's Daughter* while *Patience* is ending its run at the Spanish Fort. He decides on the West End to keep closer to home, pausing for a newspaper at his local vendor on the corner of St. Louis and Royal.

Paul tests the air with his finger, decides the prospect is good and tapping his cane jovially against the iron railings he turns onto Canal. Almost immediately he is struck by a flashing sensation from a shop window and twists his body instinctively. As the light clears there behind the glass is a delicate air-blue dress, a lady's ballgown. Paul stares in wonder, admiring the beautiful cut of the dress. His hand presses gently on the pane. In the store there is no movement, no one attending the shop front, no one adjusting the dresses. Paul takes advantage of these absences and allows his mind to drift in harmony with the dress, almost willing a gust of wind to float under the mannequin's skirts and lift them with extroverted majesty in the air. Looking down he sees the silent lady's shoes, a ruby red pair, and the effect is too much. The ghost of Clarabelle is before him; with a gentle gurgle his face touches the window.

"Are you alright?"

In the window Paul sees a small face with a goatee beard reflected. He turns to find a diminutive man holding an umbrella, a bowler hat in his hand dangling free.

"The fresh air, I believe," Paul says.

"Aren't you Paul Morphy?" the man asks.

"Well…"

"Yes, Mr Morphy. Please to meet you. I am Mr Steinitz. William Steinitz of Prague. What a surprise!"

"Yes…"

The man, half a foot smaller than Paul, stares in wonder.

"Let me present you my card."

Paul gives him a wild look for a moment. "You are…the future…" he says.

"The future, Mr Morphy? Here let me write down my address for you. We should play a game—a casual game, of course. I assume you still play?"

"No, Mr Steinitz," Paul says. "You are the champion now…not me. I do not…play…." He goes very white and looks afraid.

"But that's nonsense," Steinitz continues, trying to take Paul's hand. "You know as well as I, there are many champions. We simply have to play each other. Everyone has a different style. Respect is what is important, Mr Morphy. Honour is what matters. Don't you agree?"

"Of course."

"If you'll permit me," Steinitz says, tracing an arc with his bowler hat through the air, "I am the founder, one might say—and proud of it too—of the positional chess school. You were the founder of...well...speed chess...."

"Speed chess?"

"I mean...only in the sense of rapid attack. But play a bout today...."

"...were?"

"I'm sorry?"

"You said 'were'...'were the founder'?"

Steinitz frowns. "Well, presumably, you founded it sometime in the past? Listen, would you like to go for a coffee, Mr Morphy? I know a little place just down Canal off *The Barber's Cut*. We're there now practically."

"The positional school," says Paul.

"Yes, of course. Where have you been, my friend? The idea is many combinational attacks are a success only because of defence imperfection. See?"

"Yes, I see."

"Saving of strength is the basic principle of the defence. Defence is the best kind of offence. Spread to the flanks." He winks. "But I might tell too much, eh? You've got the old flame in you, right?"

"Of course, Mr Steinitz."

"May I have your address?"

"I'm...I'm afraid not...you see, I've retired from chess," Paul confesses, edging away from Steinitz. "I...I just don't think it's good for my health and well-being, you know."

"Oh."

"Yes, it's true. But I would enjoy playing at the New Orleans Chess and Whist Club. We could play a round of *écarté* or bridge or something?"

"Cards!" says Steinitz, sneering slightly. "You want to play cards?"

"I won't gamble, Mr Steinitz, if that's what you mean?"

"If not chess or cards…then…maybe you would join me for a drink?"

"Well…my mother and sister don't like…"

Steinitz stares at Paul, and nods.

"I see."

"I may change…my mind," says Paul. "So please write me your address. I will play chess again, please, one day. Who knows? How can we to know?"

"Yes, you're right." On a piece of paper he writes his address, a street not far from Paul's own. "I'm only here for a month, Mr Morphy. So feel free to look me up before September."

"I will."

Slowly they back away from each other offering pleasantries. Paul then turns on his heel and says:

"Incidentally, Mr Steinitz, do you know the oldest name for New Orleans? You should do, while you're a guest in the city. It's not the Crescent or the Big Easy."

"No, I don't believe I do," Steinitz replies, raising his umbrella against the sun.

"Well," Paul says, "the name comes from the *portage* the Indians used. It means *the portage of the lost*. New Orleans is for the lost. The silkworms and the mulberry trees…"—he looks up at the sky—"and the enormous cypresses that never find a home….they find a home here. Do you see?"

"I…"

"Back when this land was only dreams…and carved, Mr Steinitz, carved out of the wilderness!"

"A land of milk and honey?"

"Yes," Paul calls. "Yes, a land of silk and milk mulberries, and honey."

For a moment they regard one another.

"I heard you had an accident with a barber?"

"I was mad then, and violent. It was bitterness which they mistook for frolic…"

"Well, I hope you get well."

"Once I saw a painting," Paul continues, "of the Devil playing chess against a man. And the Devil was winning."

"I know the painting," Steinitz says. "*The Chess Players.*"

"Yes. Well, I set up the pieces and I took the boy's side and I won. Yes, I could...see clearly into the painting."

"Oh."

"And I beat the Devil at chess," he says innocently.

"I'm sure," Steinitz smiles, "you could give the Devil Pawn and Move, Mr Morphy. But can you really beat the Devil? Next time play God. Give him Pawn and Move. I know *I* could beat *Him.*"

The two men stand there neither knowing who is stranger, the one for playing chess or the other for fearing to play. But a connection occurs between them, a nod and understanding for being drawn to chess and failing to comprehend its incessant compulsions.

Steinitz grins.

"I have to go now," he says. "Your gambit is good."

"One day you have to stop playing," Paul replies. "You do know that?"

They separate and yet this time Steinitz—challenger for the world chess crown over Paul's lingering claim—pauses. Without turning he calls out: "Give the Devil Pawn and Move, Mr Morphy. Offer the advantage. Always give the Devil Pawn and Move!"

"I am getting married," Paul calls back inexplicably. "I am getting married, Mr Steinitz. We can have that drink you promised. I will invite you to the wedding!"

Paul turns to the dress in the shop window, and a young girl is now adjusting the ruby red shoes. With lingering embarrassment he turns away and heads home, pushing ahead with his cane and eye monocle, and no longer feeling like the opera.

Chapter Fifty-Three
1884
Disaster in the Sun

Provoked by the high rainfall of April, the cruellest month, every year Big Muddy turns blood red from the sedimentary mud. Sometimes a storm follows the flood and cleanses the districts of past sins. Often wind and rain arrive in torrents, lashing buildings and people, bringing devastating censure without the promise of re-birth. The French Quarter shields itself on the high ground.

This year is no exception. Down through the bayou the big river roars. Along the coastal port she rolls, spews and hustles, rattling warehouses and blasting Rampart Street into Faubourg Marigny. Down through the Vieux Carré the big river comes. Monseigneur the Duc d'Orléans is nowhere: long dead, he will be spared witnessing the city threatening by sinking once more.

Over the *levées* built in 1723, this river—vast and snaking through the heartland of America—will flood tonight. New Orleans past and present has one foot above sea level, one foot in the mud. Without warning, the storm begins. Lake Pontchartrain cries and swells like a broken heart.

Chapter Fifty-Four
1884
Nor Any Drop To Drink

Meanwhile the heavens open and down come the summer rains. Paul barely makes it back to 89 Royal Street, abandoning his walking stick the torrent is so fierce, and not wishing to shelter in any bar or doorway.

"Every game is a work of art, a work of art, a work of art," he mouths as he hurries. Eventually he makes it home, where Telcide and Helena are sitting in the kitchen sipping tea and remarking on the brewing storm. Saddened by his encounter with William Steinitz, Paul says goodnight and disappears to his room. No more sound is heard upstairs. He retires with the bedcovers to his chin and listens to the endless rain. Sleep intervenes. He wakes to discover no respite in the weather. If anything the rains have become harder.

For three days and nights Telcide, Helena and Paul do not leave the house and no one comes to see them. Mother and daughter spend the time brewing up potato lentil soups and gumbo and encouraging each other to eat. Hour by hour the rains get worse. Looking outside periodically, Paul senses the rain torrents are only a warning. Storm surges are forming unseen, temporarily moving underground, linking up patiently, preparing. After midnight, rising walls of sea water begin gushing up the canals of the Vieux Carré. Outside all is black and neither the Creoles nor their servants know what is about to happen.

§

The *levées* break. The waters rapidly become foul, a mixture of gasoline, sludge, snakes, canal rats, sewage and decaying bodies. Flotsam is carried inland. From Biloxi Bay to Pontchartrain's shores the change in sea level spills the Mississippi over the deltalands. Swollen by rains from the oncoming cloudburst, the unborn storm waits in the Gulf of Mexico to move inland. An abnormal swell of coastline delineates the path of the menace forming in the Western Caribbean, crossing Mexico's Yucatán Peninsula and turning north across the Gulf. Through the night the edge of the storm's eye skims over the Louisiana islands. Storm waters surge. From Pascagoula, Mississippi to Vermilion Bay the slope of the eyewall doubles in size. Rain-light shimmers inside black clouds promising fraught winds. At dawn the weather joins hands, becoming an incestuous union gleefully fermenting its stomach and sharpening its appetite. Trees are stripped and the threat of deadly destruction breathes moment by moment closer to New Orleans. The *levées* are broken.

The next morning Paul opens the front door to witness a flooded street. All down Royal is a low river of floating cypress trees, mud and Spanish moss. Only tough canebrakes and orange trees ride the wet foot of mixed sea, river and rainwater. Paul touches the floating objects. There, before him on the step and drenched to the bone, shivers the outline of a girl. Her dress is torn at the shoulder, hair bedraggled and eyes down, her body shaking uncontrollably.

"Paul!" she cries, looking up. "Help me, please! They're all gone…there's no more…"

He pushes the door, she half stumbles into his arms as he bears her inside the house. Her body is no longer warm.

"Clara!" And then: "*Maman, maman,* where are you?"

Tentatively he carries her into the house: they collapse on the hall floor. Helena appears at the top of the stairs and Telcide from the kitchen.

"It's her," Paul says. "She…came back. I think she's…"

Immediately the women bear Clara to the kitchen and tell Paul not to worry. They begin peeling off her clothing before closing the door. Paul is left alone. He imagines Helena lighting the fire and Telcide drying Clara's face and arms. They will cook up a hot toddy on the stove and wrap her in Titi's old dressing gown.

"How is she?" Paul calls through the door. He knocks but is told to come back in ten minutes; so he retreats to the front of the house. The brooding wind and rain whips into the hall. Before closing the front door he looks into the street again. Water rides the banquette in rivulets coursing over its own flattened body. Suddenly he witnesses a *pirogue*—an Indian canoe hollowed out from a tree trunk. No one is inside. The mysterious *pirogue* turns at the next corner and is gone. No one responds; no one is outside. Somewhere within the storm, a siren wails and a dog barks a pleading answer. He slumps in a chair and waits.

An hour later, Paul is allowed to see Clara. She is asleep beside the kitchen fire. He is left alone with her, but told to call if she wakes. Only minutes later Clara begins coughing. She looks pale and weak so Paul calls for help. Her eyes half open, white and flickering, and dart around the room without recognition.

"She is delusional," Telcide says. "I have nothing to give her. I'm sorry…I…"

Paul catches the edge of her tone. "What do you mean? There must be something we can do." He looks again at Clara. She is draped in Titi's black and white gown, a wedding and burial gown in one. "She looks angelic."

"She needs a doctor," says Helena, and for once she does not cry. Instead she looks Paul earnestly in the face. "But we can't contact one."

"Nonsense," says Paul.

"Don't go in the rain, Paul," Telcide says. "You need to think about your family…"

"I'm always thinking about my family."

"Now that's not true," his mother says.

"I will find Dr Chambers on Bienville. He works from home and is likely to be…there."

They look at Paul and say nothing. Clara looks deathly pale.

"You have no way of getting there."

"There's a way," Paul replies, and sways to his feet. "I must…go…now."

Without further discussion he runs to his room and flings open the closet. Pulling out the women's shoes, at the back he finds an old pair of walking boots. He secures them over a thick pair of socks and stamps about the room. Rain patters at the window, hinting at absolution by tapping out a warning. Paul ignores the threat. He finds two pairs of old britches and fixes a thick leather coat over his head. Then he grips and pulls the belt, takes a deep breath and is downstairs again. On the threshold of the *salle de compagnie* he smiles at his mother and sister, and then plunges out into the street.

"Clara, please come back." For a moment he waits on the one-storey balcony built precisely to avoid excessive rain. "Come back. Don't go!" Then judging the street depth he jumps; instantly the water surges to his waist. Cold enters his body—a flame of ice over his skin. He panics and begins slapping the water. But his toes find the streetbed and he treads water. A stench of spoiled cabbage is everywhere; it whips his nostrils and fogs his face. Royal Street has become a mixture of merciless black mud dragged from Mississippi oil steamers. Like a hundred random icebergs, everything from tea chests to baseball bats—to Panama hats and imaginary chess sets—floats just below the surface.

His chin dips in and out. Slowly, one tentative foot at a time, Paul fans through the flooded streets of New Orleans. Sheltered earlier by the view from 89 Royal, the wider destruction is now apparent. At Bourbon and Bienville, the side of a building is slumped in the water; masonry blows like snow off its roof. Iron railings opposite—torn from their supports—are jammed like knives underwater with no telling where their spikes might be hiding. Two gaslights lean together like a Maypole promising good tidings, then before his eyes, they slip and clatter into the low-gushing stream. Paul decides to take another route. Weaving around St. Peter he is lifted into Jackson Square. Now an *islet*, the entire plaza is sunk by a good ten feet, disappeared from the Earth. A whole half block of the city is gone, taken by the mighty river rushing by no more than fifty feet away. Freed by wounded levées, the Mississippi is exposed in all her conquering glory.

The shock is enough to send Paul underwater where he splashes and emerges coughing and fearful of his life. Already he is swimming frantically. His head fills with memories and an image of Clara breaks into his consciousness. She is racing by on the *Mardi Gras* float all those years ago when he could have thrown him until the heels of her black stallion. Ahead of him bobs the former Place d'Armes and Andrew Jackson's horse. The animal is semi-submerged while the president—face merry as ever—waves his hat in celebration of British defeat as his horse gently drowns. Again Paul feels his feet escape the street and half striding, half swimming, he retreats to Exchange Place. No one is there.

Eventually though, Paul finds Bienville on fractionally higher ground. With intricate pleas and promises of double his normal fee, he persuades Dr Chambers to come to Royal Street. Paul can hardly believe the old man is home. But there he sits on his porch, waiting out the surprising weather with his prize medicines. Paul offers to carry his briefcase. He knows the route now and the storm appears to be dissipating. Dr Chambers carries the rest of his equipment overhead, and keeping north of the French Quarter they wade ankle-deep heading east.

As they circle closer to Rampart some boys jeer at them from a rooftop, and they receive whistles from a man cross-legged on his roof, a banjo across his knees. Looking drunk and grizzled, the banjo man plays them a tune and then encourages the boys to throw a couple of stones, which they do.

"Double the money, you say?" Dr Chambers enquires once stones have flown.

"Yes, of course," Paul says. "Without question."

So they push on, navigating the final three blocks by clinging to the same piece of driftwood. The stench makes them swim the rest of Royal. Emerging from the waters, they drip heavily up to No. 89. Telcide answers their knock; again her son remains in the hall. The doctor examines the patient while Helena waits with Paul.

"Shouldn't you dry off?"

"No, I'm okay. I want to be here when Clara wakes up."

"You still..."

"I do," Paul replies, looking at his sister intently. "I do. She will come round, you'll see. She has to..."

"You don't have to say it like that."

"But I don't have any other way of saying it."

"You've done enough for now, Paul. Get some rest."

"Yes...thank you."

They hug, and Helena goes to bed. Then whisky in one hand and Clara's scarf in the other, Paul retreats to the *salle de compagnie*. He sits at Alonoz's chess table where he learned to play. The pieces are all cleared away, long gone. He puts his head down. There is nothing except his mind and the board in between, only memory of the past. Water sluices down the street only yards away. The family portraits look down wordlessly. Paul is sleeping in moments. The fire dies down.

Another day passes with no restraint in the storm. It seems the wind and rains only get worse. But by evening a breakthrough occurs and Dr Chambers reassures Telcide that Clara will live, and Telcide hands over the week's housekeeping money in payment. Clara is removed to Paul's room and becomes his responsibility. For now the women sit in the music room and prepare the accounts for the house, determining how they will last until the end of the year. Telcide plans to give music lessons to the neighbourhood's children while Helena will knit clothes for the cheaper stores on Canal Street. But all is castles in the air. Neither occupation will bring in a packet of money.

Meanwhile Paul nurses Clara, laid out in his bed. For hours he looks in her face, older now with a brutal scar from her lip to her ear. He promises never to ask her about it—it has damaged her enough, he thinks, however it happened. She will stay the Clara he remembers. Through the woman on the bed, so quiet and peaceful, he sees the careless, carefree Clara he met long ago at the fountain.

"I'm glad you came back. I often wondered…" He touches her forehead. "There are no more moves. No more…time away. The chess is finished."

She continues to sleep. In her waking hours Paul feeds her soup and lets her sleep again. She says little. By the third hour her fever is fading. They do not leave the room for the rest of the day. It is the only time they have together, a few moments away from the brothels of Basin Street and the restrictions of the Morphy household. The rains have washed everything clean and dead: all the vicious life down in the Storyville red-light district and uptown in the once-prestigious Vieux Carré. They hold hands and Paul prays. Clara quiets his lips with her finger. So they sit there, saying and sharing all that is necessary. The storm rattles the casement like *The Eve. Of St. Agnes* as they remember the meetings, the declarations, the escapes—all the lost opera dreams.

After the storm the Americans will run New Orleans. But Paul and Clara know the Creoles and the illegitimate working girls of the city will be no more: the former will slide into history and the latter into obscurity. But for this brief moment, drained of all their energy and after so long, they find the strength to be together. They slip under the sheets and lie *en passant* but for fear of everything Clara simply holds Paul. Their tenderness, born in memory of a life shared separated by letters, is unsayable. They recognize what could have been and what they now most possess—this hour. Soon there is a lull in the eye of the hurricane.

The sky is clear to the north and the stars shine brightly. A very light breeze conjures an eerie whistle. Paul and Clara exist in this moment in the uncertainty and anxious respite before the storm. They kiss and hold each other. Together for the last time the storm is within them, sweetly expressed and then over. Outside and miles away, Lake Pontchartrain floods night water into New Orleans and the last *levées* break once more.

The Mississippi cuts through New Orleans in a mighty torrent sending the houses under eight to ten feet of water. For now, after four days of rain, a lull is palpable. As the eye of the sleeping hurricane drifts over the French Quarter, birds become trapped in the clam air at the hollow centre. They settle on the ledge outside Paul's room, while inside he sleeps with Clara arm to shoulder and hand in hand. Outside a devilish wind flings sand down to Bayou St. John. The beach is whipped into electronic charge, the sand particles growing frenzied until they become magic lights—millions of sparkling fireflies—invisible to the human eye. The pieces dance under a blue Voodoo moon. Somewhere, somebody knows this is not the end and *Mardi Gras* will return and take possession of all.

When they wake the four inhabitants of 89 Royal Street remain in their rooms because they fear their new guest: the stinking river water. The downstairs sloshes back and forth with furniture, musical instruments, portraits, the house itself. The grand piano slides and squeaks across the music room. Paul sees his silver testimonial plate slip under the black water. From the attic he surveys the desolate cityscape, the houses beyond St. Louis Cathedral now shacks, sunken, wayward and teary-eyed in the morning mist. The wind and rain have gone: the waters remain. Everywhere the wet grave of New Orleans is exposed and the hopes of thousands now buried.

Paul returns to bed and buries his face in the sheets. Without reason or warning Clara has gone too. He cannot face what has happened. No note has been left. The imprint of Clara's side of the bed still retains her smell and her shape on the ruffled sheets. He clings openly to her absent body.

"The waters….She would not…leave me now…" He looks around the room for any sign of Clara but nothing remains. Nothing—no testimonial pieces, no gold or silver or wooden boards, no crown of thorns. Reaching out he gingerly opens the closet. Out tumble a collection of women's shoes into a chaotic jumble. Perhaps if he lines them up, he thinks, they can take the edge off growing despair? For now he simply lies in bed not wanting to plan or dream, only to disappear.

"The end must come," Paul whispers, "and everything will just be over, checkmate." He presses Clara's shape on the bed. "Please deliver me from the everlasting move…and bring the end soon…"

But in that very moment, turning back to the bed, Paul realizes he was delirious. Clara has been there all along, all night. Paul is scared—knowing he is hallucinating, but he tries to remain calm. He must keep this a secret. Clearly his nightmares have not receded completely, but he is thankful, despite a chill from the storm, to find her there. "But in this storm, what is a dream and what reality?"

He climbs into bed and goes back to sleep.

Chapter Fifty-Five
After the Storm
1884

After the storm the rains fall for three days. Paul stays by Clara's bed while Helena brings them *sirop d'orgeat* and *petit fours* on a silver tray. As the light improves Paul sees how much Clara has changed; the years have not been kind, but the old Clara is beneath the crowfeet edges of her eyes. As she wakes and yawns, Paul balances apprehensively on the bed. Clara sits up and looks around the room. She sees the shoes Paul has been hoarding but says nothing. She is much older: fifteen years have gone by since he last saw her down on Basin Street when Edward saved his life by pretending to throw him in the street.

"Good morning," says Paul.

"Bonjour," Clara replies and pulls the covers a little higher, whether joking or from embarrassment, Paul cannot tell. She sips her tea, a strong mixture of *camomile* and *l'herbe cabri*.

"*Maman* makes *mamou* tea made with beans or roots," she says. "Or *crapeau*. That's toadgrass, you know."

"Toadgrass?"

"Toadgrass." They stare at each other. Paul says she sounds like the little girl he once knew, but Clara affects not to remember.

"I can hear the rain."

"You were caught in the storm," Paul says. "And you came back…"

Clara squirms a little. "I was on my way somewhere else, and I remembered where you live."

Paul, for once, does not take the bait. "You were on your way somewhere," he says.

"Yes, I was on my way to the opera."

"In a hurricane."

She stares at him. "Yes, Paul. In a hurricane. I'm going to become a singer. I was running away, and then I got caught in the storm."

"And that's your story?" Paul stands and crosses to the window. He sits lightly in a wicker chair and takes up the book he was reading. His one word surprises Clara, absent of concern for her own predicament. "Thackeray," he says. "I've been reading Thackeray." He quotes from the book: *New Orleans, in spring-time— just when the orchards were flushing over with peach-blossoms, and the sweet herbs came to flavour the juleps.*"

He stops. The moment is surreal; Paul peers over his shoulder through the window at the grey slanted rain. "Three days and nights, and now three more days. When will we be delivered into a new spring?"

Clara is uncertain what to say, leans forward, and begins laughing out loud. "I can't understand a word you say!" But something about Paul's weariness she mistakes for nonchalance. "You seem different, Paul."

"Wiser," he says and resumes his book.

"Not just older then?" The room goes quiet, the walls restless. Clara leans back in the walnut bed on the plain white pillows and sips her tea. "You know, that time you came for me, I wasn't ready…to go anywhere."

"And you're ready now?"

"Perhaps I am, Paul, yes."

Paul turns to her. "That was a long time ago, Clara. I've changed now, too. Why don't you rest, and we can talk when you feel better. In the morning."

"In the morning, in the morning," she mouths. "It is the morning."

Clara looks at him and pouts, affecting coyness. Paul blushes slightly and Clara waits for more reaction, but he is calm. Dissatisfied, she lies down again. Suddenly at the window a wild parrot lands on the gallery, cocks a glassy eye and squawks.

"Hello," Paul whispers. "What do you want? Some kind of warning, are you?"

He lets the parrot pick at his fingers, then withdraws his hand when the bite is too sharp. A flash of blue and orange, the brazen bird hobbles up and down pecking the wooden ledge. Now and then the creature shakes water from her wings then cries half in consternation, half disgust. Paul crumbles one of the *petit fours* in his hand and is surprised to find her politely nosing at his palm, apparently no longer wishing to hurt him. The bird stares at him, rolls both her eyes and tips into the dark rain. When Paul turns back to the bed, Clara is asleep.

In the swirl of the final storm, Paul sits brooding. He wonders how the city will survive, washed clean by rains seemingly born of Biblical times. Even now he thinks of the streets wiped clean, the people sheltering in their homes, the shine of black and white cobblestones, the mystery of surfaces caught between emptiness and overlong days.

Chess is not forgotten in Paul's mind. Every move he made was a move for himself, he now realizes, and winning contains its own loss. Was Clara playing the opposite colour in the past? Perhaps two people are destined to be together in the end, so long as they remain in each other's minds. Only the forgetting sours the future, or that is what Paul now thinks. Again the lines of Thackeray enter his head: *New Orleans, in spring-time—just when the orchards were flushing over with peach-blossoms, and the sweet herbs came to flavour the juleps.* Perhaps a new season of re-birth is coming, if he can believe long enough.

The next morning they go for a walk. Paul believes Clara should rest, but the rains have cleared, the sky is azure as though the storm never happened, and Clara insists. As Paul slips out of the house, he glances next door where Telcide is asleep on her cherry four-poster bed. Helena is curled up in her arms, and for once Paul feels like the future might be good, be different. Clara takes his hand descending the stairs and Paul does not let go.

Still, the pain of the lost years lies heavy on him and he finds a way to release her hand at the door and not feel too bad. For once, after so much unhappy struggle, Paul relishes his own composure.

Frenchman Street leads them through the Faubourg Marigny neighbourhood. The Quarter is deserted but people are slowly drawing back their window blinds and opening their doors to the street. On a corner an old woman is brushing down her step, flinging the branches in the street with a twisted broom. There is an eerie sensation of loss, but of rebirth too, a suspension like purgatory that could inherit good or evil. Again Clara takes Paul's hand, uncertain of her surroundings, and without anyone watching—what he desired for so long—they walk through the empty, motionless backstreets of the Vieux Carré. Soon they pass the Ursuline chapel garden opposite his childhood home, the beautiful pink convent with its shiny black balcony covered with ficus. Clara faces it with slight trepidation.

"It's a long time since I've been to church," she laughs, but Paul is looking the other way at 1113 Chartres Street. The house has not changed much, a little weary in the stonework, a slate or two dislodged from the roof. It looks so much smaller, even though he passes it every month or so, but today it looks tiny. Walking to the corner he sees a solo banana tree that has blown down in the garden. The tree rests on the wooden fence, appearing to be breathing its last and melancholy beyond expression, the roots awkwardly and obscenely striking into the air where nothing can support them.

"What is it?" Clara asks.

"Nothing, nothing," Paul says. "I used to live there. It was where I was happiest, I suppose." He points to the attic. "I used to look at from that window at the world, a sort of skylight on the future…"

Clara grins. "Your boyish dreams…"

"Yes, just dreams. Then I found a chessboard in there, and a map, and the strange power of those black and white squares. Like they held the possibilities of new worlds, but always coming back to this room, safely. That's what that room told me…with no one around…when I was alone."

"Paul, you need to forget. Live a dream for today." She squeezes his hand, but he hesitates.

"And what is that dream, Clara? Are you that dream? You rejected me after all our letters. But now you'll stay and be my dream?"

"I can be," Clara replies. "If that's what you want."

Paul is stunned. "You mean that? You want to be here?"

"I came here, didn't I?"

"Yes," he says. "But in a storm. You fled the Basin because the rooming houses were washed away, and the rain came in and…"

"That's not true, Paul. You remember I was living at LuLu White's? She has the best show-palace on the whole row. The roof was built by the Mayor of New Orleans himself. Why would I want to leave there?"

"I don't know…"

"That roof held in the storm, I can tell you that much. And I'll tell you why! It's because Violet—my mother—could take it no more. She was tired with everything and she left in the storm." Clara sits down in the street, and her dress, a green day-gown, billows around her knees as though floating in water. But the water has all gone and Chartres Street is dry in the midday sun, its camber hustling away the last drops of the evaporating deluge. Soon there will be no sense of a hurricane's patronage only the residue of damaged buildings, and trees, and the souls of the citizens. The water will disappear like a magic trick.

"Go on," Paul says.

"So I followed her," Clara stutters, "but she just kept going and I couldn't stop her....She found the tide and let it float her down to the river. The last I saw of her, she was calling to the Mississippi...her hand was in the air, and she clung onto the Levée Street sign for a few minutes, but before she could speak the waters had taken her..."

"Clara, I didn't know..."

"It's all over, Paul. There's nothing there for me now. So I realized that you were the only one who ever cared for me, really."

Paul takes Clara gently and lifts her to her feet. He holds her in his arms, and she leans on his shoulder.

"Thank you, Paul," she whispers. "You can still save me, I know you can."

"Your mother..." he says, but cannot find the words.

"It was her time," Clara says, her voice shaking only slightly, "and I'm convinced she did it, so I could find my dream. So I could escape this trickster life, at last. So I could come and find you in the Quarter..."

"Clara, you mean that?"

She pulls back and kisses him full on the lips. Together they stand there, the storm gone, the reunion complete. Paul and Clara walk side by side, alone with each other, together at last. They enter Tchoupitoulas Street on the downriver side of Canal Street. They follow the curve of the crescent bend of the river, first crossing Napoleon Avenue, and soon they arrive on Elysian Fields, the main thoroughfare of Faubourg Marigny and the grandest boulevard in the city. The route is unusual for Paul as it leads away from his clubs and the St. Louis Cathedral—the brief walk he takes daily—but Clara has never been here before in her life. All the beauty of New Orleans is on display. Grand oak trees, each hung with a sprawl of magnolia, line the street and sway in the breeze, while mysterious cobblestone alleys disappear off the main thoroughfare. No one is around, even at midday, the storm having quietened people. Each house stands out individually, the finest of the Creole domiciles rivalling the new Americans of the Garden District upriver.

"Where shall we go?" Clara says.

"Anywhere, we can go anywhere. In a few hours the city will come to life, you'll see."

At the corner, Paul and Clara emerge from a cabriolet before the Porte-Saint-Martin Theatre. Blackberries and banana plants bow from the theatre along the patios, with chindolea bushes hiding the grander mansions. Family nameplates for Duponts and Béarts glint in the sunset from open doorways, the pretty terrazzo floors winking back at them. They could be forgiven for walking the streets only hours after the abatement of the disaster storms of the last five nights, but as Clara says, "we could not stay inside forever."

Heading upriver, but avoiding the route to the Basin, they follow Toulouse Street across Bourbon and plan an arc across Canal. Here a local carnival *krewe*, a group of acrobats practicing for *Mardi Gras*, appear from Jane's Alley in a place called Brick's Row, and suddenly dance before their eyes—a flash of clapping and colour as surreal as anything that could happen on this day. Several men and women with silk shirts, white hats, black pants and streamers pinned to their arms cartwheel around them, beg for pennies "though not for char-itee" and vanish into Perdido Street. One swarthy man dressed in white, his dark skin only visible at the wrists and ankles, bangs a drum with a handkerchief under the snare, tunk-a, tunk-aa-a. Heat haze trembles between the bodies. *"My Brazilian beauty down on the Amazon / that's where my baby's / gone, gone, gone."*

"I think I want to go back," Clara says. "I don't know these streets. Even the French Quarter is better for me, Paul."

"It's a long way back."

"But we should go. I feel like the Swamp is not far from here, you know, where I grew up."

"Well, it's not," Paul says, but listens to her plea.

On the way back Clara's mood changes and rather than the sweetness of her earlier self, she begins to complain of how humdrum the city has become. "They weary me, those dancers. But that's because I'm low on energy. I could do with some gumbo."

"We'll eat," Paul says, "but nowhere is open yet." He looks at the sky, its curtain shimmering white. "I don't believe the people know the hurriance is truly gone and won't come back. It's been a few days. They are superstitious."

"No more than us," Clara says. "In old years, before embalming, you know, some bodies came to life. The river would turn 'em out."

"I know, Clara, I know why we bury them above ground." He peers at her. "You're not thinking about Violet, about your mother?"

She turns to him, upset. "How can you say that? My poor mother was washed away in this same flood. How can you be so slight with me?" Before he answers, from nowhere—as though watched by dark powers beyond their control—a black cat with a ginger tail strides across their path. Clara screams. "Draw a circle with nine horseshoes," she cries. "And kill a black cat in it!"

"You don't mean…"

"Throw it in a boiling pot!"

Understandably the cat vanishes. Paul is surprised and takes Clara by the elbow: he does not feel he can be responsible for her. He feels much has changed between them and he shakes her. "Stop it, Clara, you must stop it. You've got to be…civilized," he says and regrets it. "That's frightening talk."

"I am afraid, Paul, can't you see?" She stares at him, her pale dress and cravat shaking. "Don't you know what I've been through? While you've been all over the world, I've been here the whole time. I've been trying to stay alive!"

"I know, Clara, I know. And I've been living, but I've not really been alive. I tried to find the meaning of life in a game, just a game. But instead I got caught up with people who tried to take advantage of me, my own brother-in-law, my manager, Mr Howard Staunton, oh it hardly matters who."

"No, it doesn't, Paul, that's all in the past.

"It doesn't?"

"I think I made a mistake," she says, now looking in his face intently. "I should have listened to you long ago when you came to take me away and we escaped through the window."

"No, don't say that, Clara." But a feeling of immense sadness takes hold of him as though he knows she is right but doesn't know whose fault it is. "It's never too late. We have each other now."

"Let's go back," Clara says, and without replying Paul begins to lead her away from Elysian Fields Avenue through Jackson Square and past his old school. Before they reach the door of 89 Royal Street, however, they pass the grandiose old Mint building at the corner of Dauphine and St. Ann streets.

Together they are captivated by the beauty of the building, and the moment offers some respite. They stare up at its proud redbrick façade, an Ionic portico and four monumental columns circled by square pillars.

"I can't believe it survived the occupation..." Paul says, touching the outside wall.

"...and the flood," Clara says, and presses her face on the dirty glass window. Inside is a mahogany staircase and large rectangular windows, beautiful high arches supported by freestanding piers.

"It's a Greek temple! There's a coin vault in the basement," Paul says. "A symbol of a better time. When my grandfather..."

"I don't need to hear about your family," Clara says and stops herself. "I mean, we're alive now, aren't we?"

Paul hesitates, and then agrees, "yes, I suppose so. And my father wanted me to play chess, and look what happened there."

Clara's hands go up against the glass. "You didn't want to play?"

"I did at first, when I was playing generals, and my father's friends. I remember one, Eugene Rousseau..."

"Where are they now?"

"Who knows, probably not New Orleans." Lost in thought Paul steps back to survey the building. He touches the flood watermark over his head, stretching on tiptoes, and deliberates over the strange power of the flood. "Given the water receded, the weather last week seems unimaginable. The Mint was a symbol of Union occupation," he says, knowing Clara's Basin Street magazines, annexed by the North, will not have reported this story. "They once hung a steamboat gambler from this building. I remember his name, William Mumford. People protested so strongly there was almost a military curfew re-imposed on the city." He turns round and is surprised to find Clara listening.

"That wouldn't have affected me much," she says.

"No, well. This Mumford was hardly the most gentlemanly of rebels but more power to him, right. The people wouldn't tolerate what happened."

"What did happen?"

"Well, the Union soldiers, the Marines, came in on General David. G. Farragut's orders. After they captured the city they took the Mint for their own purposes. They reversed the dies and coined their own half dollars, like the Morgan silver dollar. You can still find them in odd shops around here! Anyway, they flew the Union flag on night they captured the Quarter, and the next morning Mumford tore the flag off the roof while they slept—you see, no one expected retaliation—and stuffed it in his pockets. Then he went home. Later he was hung from a flagstaff projected out from the Mint. It cost him his life and the Yankees sang all night long, *Ranzo* and *Boney* and such. *Hangin' Johnny* and *Fare-you-well, My Bonny Young Girls!*"

Paul stops talking and takes his hand off the wall.

"That's dreadful," says Clara.

"I'm not saying I'm against the Union. But times like that have left their mark on people. How can things be the same? A man hung from a flagpole and left to rot, like a gibbet in medieval London…."

"I don't know."

They don't look back at the Mint glowing red in the overhead sun.

Clara presses her hand into Paul's and says, "here, a present. It's just a cracker toy, but it's a key to unlock every door.

So you won't need to worry about leaving New Orleans, finding a new place to live."

"Thank you, Clara, but I don't want to leave."

She says nothing.

"It can open *anything?*" Paul says, playing the game.

"Except," Clara laughs, "the door to a cold, cold heart."

Paul smiles and yet cannot tell if she is joking. Gradually they wind their way down Royal Street just as people begin to emerge into the street, gingerly looking around, amazed at the day and the retreat of the terrible waters. The smell of Lake Pontchartrain is delicate and they hold their noses, just in time to see Paul and Clara disappear down the side-alley of number 89 and enter the Morphy house via the back garden.

Telcide and Helena are not home, gone checking on their neighbours while awaiting the opening of the levée markets. Inside Clara takes to her bed, complaining of a headache, and asks Paul for a jug of water. When he returns he finds her sitting upright in bed. She is wearing a blanket coat and *chapeau blanc* and suddenly she begins talking in a strange half Cajun patois, telling him to light six black candles one by one and to arrange them in the pattern of a moving serpent. "Pray for our mortal souls, Paul," she whispers. "Pray we can be together at last."

The moment is surreal and he cannot tell what's changed. "Clara, we *are* together. And I'm Catholic. I shouldn't be doing this…"

"What, harmless magic? This is just to help us sleep, that's all." Clara looks at the ceiling and begins a low chant. "Queen of Comus, grandest of the Mardi Gras galas, bring luck to us. Be generous and bring us good fortune!" Paul stares at her in disbelief. "You know that John Sybrandt, the one who is causing you trouble?"

"Yes?"

"You must write his name on a slip of paper and drop it in a sugar bowl. Add some red pepper, one sixpenny nail, twenty cents of ammonia and three room keys."

"You're still delirious," Paul replies, looking down at the bed. "Clara, you should sleep more. And forget these charms. It's the fever you caught from the storm—it's still inside you, inside your mind. You need rest."

"No, Paul. It's not me. You just don't believe in anything anymore, not your family, not yourself. Do you believe in me?"

Paul sits on the edge of the bed and pulls the blanket to Clara's neck. She is mumbling recipes cures for unknown ailments. He listens to one that sounds like a curse:

"Carve the heart out of a potato," she says, eyes rolling over white. "Write my name three times on some paper and fold it inside the potato. Close it replacing the cut-out..."

"Hush, now, Clara, tomorrow we will go for another walk. But rest now."

"...or on a hot day, take a cold bath, it soothes the muscles under the skin. Or for a burn—if you burn a finger lighting a cigarette, Paul, stick it behind your ear, quick."

Later he brings her some food, a *papabotte* with chicken-wings. When he returns he finds her sitting upright in bed, a bottle of St. Julien beside her from an unknown source. "Where did you get the wine?" he asks.

Clara is playing cards in bed—Paul realizes they are Tarot cards.

"I'm adding potions to the wine. Don't you know I'm a magician? I'm not really here. I've been a ghost this whole time." She laughs without looking up.

"Clara, you have to stop."

"Trust me, Paul, we're better off if I'm a ghost. A spirit that keeps you company like a friend." She turns over one of the cards, sighs and turns it back. "It's death," she whispers. Mock fright clouds her face, her cheeks grow pale and for a moment Paul feels scared. "Death," Clara says, "the last knight of the realm. *Le beau monsieur sans merci!* The card no one wants to see."

"I agree with that," Paul says, trying to calm her fears. He watches her pick up a pearl comb, no doubt borrowed from Telcide's room. The chicken-wings are untouched beside her, the cards scattered across the duvet and sheets. Suddenly Clara parts her hair to reveal something never seen before, her accentuated widow's peak and the dark sun-blistered skin of her forehead. Paul starts back in surprise. But just as quickly Clara folds the hair forward, her smooth face returns and the damaged skin disappears.

"How about an after-dinner *framboise?*" she says, hinting at something more than a drink. She rolls over grappling with the pillow and is quiet. Just as quickly she rolls back, her blouse buttons undone to the throat and revealing the soft curve of her cleavage. "I am not really here, Paul, do not mistake me for anything. I am dying, I can feel it!" Her mouth falls open and she moans slightly.

"Clara, you will get better. It's just a fever. I've had them myself in recent times. It's some kind of shock, that's all."

"I'm not unwell, Paul, but that's why medicine helps. A good cure against croup—a charm if you like—is to wear a dime in your shoe heel. Add a pinch of salt then hang chinaberries about your neck. Or even better," she adds with a quick grin, "wrap your head completely in leaves from the castor oil plant, the Palma Christi. Then sweat it out."

Paul laughs and says it sounds blasphemous. "I'm not the one who's sick," he dares to say. For a second Clara glares at him. In her dusky eyes Paul sees his own reflection multiplying and shrinking into her giant pupil. He shakes his head in confusion. "These cures contain the world," he mumbles, "the whole mighty world, flat and endless. I'm amazed, Clara! You're not gone from me, not gone from me." He tries to distract her with questions about the future, to remind her about her desire to run a business. "Remember, Clara, that milliner's store on Canal Street?"

"It's too late. I don't have the energy."

"Not yet. But we could set up in the Warehouse District. You can't go back to the Basin, Clara. Look what happened to….Anyway would you rather work in a *petit ménage* in Perdido

Street for fifty dollars a month, or establish your own store? I can help you. Then we get you registered in the Quarter. It might mean changing your name."

Clara laughs despite herself. "There you go, Paul, trying to save me again. The American way. You always want to change me."

"I'm only an American in spirit," Paul says. "By blood I'm…"

"A gentleman."

He takes her hands and smiles. "Exactly! And if I want to make you a lady, maybe I can. We'll have lemon-haired children with dark faces," he jokes. "They'll be Gothic, a brood of real horrors."

"But how could they be happy as octoroons, Paul? How could they be?"

Clara sits up in bed, the cards all tumbling to the floor. "Oh, Paul" she says. "I saw an awful sight, dreadful and beautiful. It was the balconies of houses in the flood. From waist-deep I could see them, the grilles rising from the water. Like cages! I imagined the people trapped inside them. Under the water….Yet they were beautiful too, shining in the evening light despite the rain, and that only made it uglier. Oh, Paul, it was terrible to find such beauty when the homes were drowned…"

Softly Paul lays her head down on the pillow, pulls up the covers. "Sleep," he says. "The waters are gone, remember, we were out there today. Sleep, and in a few days I have a surprise for you."

"You do?" Clara says, sounding like the little girl by the fountain. "What kind of surprise?"

"Well, that would be telling!" and he kisses her on the forehead, acting the gentleman he wishes to be.

Clara touches his face in return. "Such a soft face. You're a good man, Paul."

Without another word Paul takes away the wine and leaves the room. For a moment he listens outside the door, but there is no noise. Downstairs he waits in silence, sitting in the *salle de compagnie* where he first learned chess.

Later that night he goes to the Pickwick Club on Tchoupitoulas Street. He orders warm oysters half-shelled, and steaming pompano *en papillote*. On the way home he passes the St. Louis Cemetery No. 1 and remembers the time he visited the family tomb. Tonight he turns his eyes away and hurries home, saying a prayer outside Our Lady of Guadeloupe Chapel but not looking up at the weeping figure of Mary above the door. He is ashamed of the decisions he is making, the desire he still feels for Clara, the hope that burns in his chest for a happy future. It is not too late to be happy, he believes, so long as the Morphys and the royal game can both be kept at arm's length.

The past cannot sully the future endlessly. The words come to him from nowhere, suggesting the long struggle ahead but the possibility of redemption, a parole from his own skin. "Is that how the world works?" he asks. "The old world must be abandoned in the forging of a new one?" The night does not reply.

It is the story of the continent, and now the story is his. The solid gates of the St. Louis Cemetery close behind him, and like Adam banished to wander with his newly discovered Eve, he can make the loss of Eden bearable, so long as he plays the right move, the best possible move in the best of all possible worlds.

Paul walks eastwards through the night. All around, and with scarce any sound, the high walls of this low city shiver with warmth and desire. Not unfriendly gargoyles grin from rooftops. A labyrinthine mass of oleander and jasmine, tangled like hair between street signs, promise long nights in New Orleans, city of ghosts and dreams. In the forgotten Old South lantana and mimosa feed the bare earth with the food of unseen gods. The ground will heal and the people will sing again.

That night Paul dreams feverishly of the storm. He sees someone caught in a tree-top. But when he gets closer, the shape twists into a black cat with a ginger tail. Waking abruptly, he turns to Clara in the bed. She is sleeping peacefully, her heartbeats slow and death-like, something he has not witnessed before. Her breath is barely noticeable as her chest falls, as the hour of midnight passes into the good spirits of new dawn light.

But Paul lies awake. They say the darkest hour is the one before dawn.

Chapter Fifty-Six
The World's Fair
1884

Clara's fever lasts for two more days then the worst is over. Life at 89 Royal Street settles into a fresh pattern. Telcide and Helena spent their time together whether in the *salle de musique* or in the city's slowly reviving *salons*. Paul and Clara keep to themselves and gradually everyone realizes that Clara is going to stay. After a month or so, even Telcide notices the calming effect on Paul and is especially pleased when Clara begins to dress more in line with the ladies of the Vieux Carré. Nothing can hide Clara's complexion, however, her *sunburned hue* as Telcide calls it, but at the same time Telcide deliberates whether to invite Clara to the rejuvenation of her musical *soirées* or to the parlours of her friends for coffee, conversation and discussion of the revival of the city. She never quite manages it.

Remembering Paul's promise, one morning Clara asks what her surprise is, and Paul asks her to wait another day. When the time comes, they leave the house just after sunrise and begin walking north.

"I know where we're going," Clara says as the route reveals itself upriver in the direction of Audubon Park. On the way they pass the riverfront streets packed with immigrants and the rejuvenated and colourful levée markets. They take North Peter's Street out of the Quarter, then pick up St. Charles through the Garden District and finally onto Magazine Street. At the foot of Canal Street, the girls look out with steady expressions from behind shutters and windows, and Paul is pleased to find Clara gripping his arm tighter.

"Don't look," he says.

"I know," Clara says. "I know."

Today is a Sunday and Paul is wearing a salt-and-pepper linen suit, black and white shoes and a jewelled stickpin in his silk tie. A Panama hat, a sign of celebration and his overcoming the fear of his father's death, signals a new beginning. Despite the distance they've walked, almost five miles, the day is relatively cool. Clara walks beside Paul with a ladylike air, a transparent parasol borrowed from Helena's wardrobe. The hem of Clara's skirt is low, fashionably purple, and a beautiful banana-coloured hat, wide-brimmed, sloping on one side and set with a white sash, keeps her face covered.

Hand in hand, the lovers take Perrier to Laurel, to Annunciation and finally Calhoun to Exposition Boulevard. A blue mist envelops the parkland, then lifts to reveal a transparent tent enclosing huge iron and glass buildings. The World's Fair, the World Cotton Centennial, is before them, an event Clara is newly familiar with from reading the *Times-Picayune* and the *Red Book*. Entering the main gate, Clara sighs and touches her hat with a gesture of pleasure and astonishment.

"Oh, Paul, our first real date, and you brought me here!"

Why is this our first date, Paul wonders? But he believes she is joking. He smiles through his tight-buttoned suit, satisfied because no man can be prouder than he is today. "Of course, this is what the city has been waiting for. You have been ill, and know so little about the preparations. But it's the best thing for the city, to finally end the Reconstruction era, Clara, by bringing money from Washington."

Clara has stopped listening, but she squeezes Paul's hand and does a twirl by the entrance fountain. The statue at its centre is a cherub raised on a stone plinth, water bubbling from its playful mouth. A marker underneath reads, 'Peace, the Genius of History' which Paul puzzles for a second, deciding it means no more than 'be at peace with the past.'

"That could be our son," he says, pointing at the fountain. But Clara has already gone, swirling into the park to see the carnival delights. There she finds the park's continuation of Magazine Street bisecting International Drive, revealing a vista of live oak trees nodding their heads together. Visiting families and the refined *hoi polloi* of Louisiana adorn the walkway, stout gentleman with thin cigars and ladies in splendid hats borrowed from the Creole Race Course. Rotten leaves have been cleared, stone paths swept of branches and the drive planted with chinaberry bushes. Now and then a man passes in a buggy powered by an experimental electric motor, and the crowd leaps back in surprise and alarm. A child screams and a dog rushes forward, drooling and giddy, looking back at its master for the correct emotion. Here, evergreen trees of spring intermingle with the oaks while a calm grey sky looks down peacefully on the serious pleasures of the domed buildings.

Clara claps her hands and twirls her parasol while the crowd surges, tensely expectant, hundreds of the city's finest citizens cramming to the entrance to the World's Fair. Side by side, Paul and Clara pass under a red banner extended between two oaks: *New Orleans, a Desirable Place to Live and Work*. Some people jokily scoff at the claim, others shout 'hear hear' in mock seriousness. The path narrows, the oaks lean closer and lower bringing the bodies tighter, and all darkens. The world goes quiet.

Then in single file the people burst through a clicking wooden turnstile, manned by no one, and enter the Main Building. For a few seconds each person is alone on this day, 16 December 1884, at the centre of the world's beating heart, witness to the latest innovations of the peaking industrial age. At the back of the building a giant swollen sun hovers over the Mississippi, visible through a huge crystal dome.

Once inside, Paul and Clara find each other by sensing their surroundings step by step. Facing them is a long Horticultural Hall stretching endlessly into the distance. Tropical and semi-tropical plants dangle from wooden bridges while overhead, suspended electric lights and give the feel of an Amazonian Central Park.

"Why have you brought me here?" Clara asks.

"You'll see."

They pass through the hothouse phenomenon, witnessing groves of orange, lemon, mesquite, maguey and all the flora of Louisiana. Here they discover another fountain, a replica of the entrance display, only three times larger, again adorned with a cherbum statue of "Peace, the Genius of History". The effect is overwhelming and, feeling dizzy, Clara needs to leave the building, Paul leading her by the elbow.

"Follow me," he says. "The opening ceremony is taking place on the west-side in about half an hour. It will be quite something…" So saying Paul thinks of his grandfather and the day they toured the French Quarter funeral of the pirate Jean Lafitte. He cannot say why the past is invading the present, except his current boyish excitement is strong enough to summon images of his hard-drinking buccaneer of a grandfather, the auctioneer and slave-trader whom Paul loved but in no way wishes to emulate. "Sure, quite a something to behold," Paul adds and leads Clara away between scenes of Creole families picnicking on the Horticultural lawns.

Next they enter the Tent of Industry which is busy demonstrating the advances in steam and electric power New Orleans can expect to benefit from in the new century. An iron doorway, rotating seemingly by magic, ushers them into the half-light of a noisy cavernous building, the roof as high as a railway station. Smoke trails to the ceiling from the countless pistons and wheels all blurring together across a cobbled floor like a military parade ground. A small dapper man accosts them and begins explaining the machines to the crowd, how the Lamm fireless engines are being replaced by experimental electric trams, and how one day a passenger trolleys will roll down Magazine Street or St. Charles Avenue. Paul is curious—but Clara grows bored.

A crowd gathers. A few guffaws escape the gentleman leaning over her, cigar smoke wafting, until she simply digs her elbows backwards. Twisting her shoulders, she wriggles free of these grey industrial men and the machines their gods.

For a second she wanders away, distracted by the noise, only to find an adjacent room with a sealed door. Here Clara discovers a special exhibit of 'Women's work' and 'Negro Exhibit.' Her distaste for their relegation doubles the insult. A small prim woman sits at the table of 'Women's work' mending a broken porcelain jug, a delicate repair operation in itself and requiring no small skill. Clara is about to speak, glancing down at the lady's hand-painted label on the desk displaying her name, Léona Queyrouze, in loopy pretentious handwriting.

"Hello," Clara says.

The lady looks up, a tired expression behind her eyes and in that moment she notices Clara's skin colour and looks down again. "The Negro table is next door," she says and then smiles as though not in the least perturbed. Her fingers resume sticking the jug.

"I am here as a woman," Clara replies, hesitantly, but also finds herself saying "thank you" to her shame, believing that is how a lady behaves. Still, she cannot bring herself to examine the exhibits Léona has scattered across the tables, mostly beads and textiles, a quilt showing the Confederacy colours melding into the Union flag.

Instead, Clara steps over to the dubious 'Negro Exhibit' which consists of wood cuts of African masks and shields and spears of all sizes but very little to represent life around Basin Street or Congo Square, no drums or festival descriptions or Voodoo. Clara smiles at the ignorance on display, even for a room secluded at the back of the industrial hall.

Glancing up, she realizes even the individual in charge of the exhibit is a quadroon gentleman, whose blue eyes and yellow hair misrepresent him in the extreme. Nevertheless Clara smiles at him, he looks so eternally bored sitting on the table next to the objects, and touches her forehead in a quiet salute. He simply grins back at her, and then spoils her attention by quietly licking his lips. She passes back out of the doorway into the white light of an industrial world, uncertain as ever which side of the doorway she belongs or what belongs to her.

Clara returns to Paul but finds him gone, so she strolls past the machines looking for him. Her memory of first meeting the Morphys and their realization of her African blood—their prejudiced guess at her poverty—now causes her to sweat under her hat. She hurries down the wooden slipping on the sawdust until she can see the exit. Above her the boiler room with its forty dynamos of the Edison, Brush and the Louisiana Electric Company are rattling with mayhem. The pistons thrust out towards her, their heavy shoulders of steam-powered glory crying out against the flash of purple and yellow colour dashing for the doorway. But Clara is through the door, breathing hard.

Next she enters a Factories and Mills centrepiece room with cotton, sugar cane and rice showing the process of sugar refining. The horror of her mother's plantation life is all around her, not only in the sweet sickly smell, but its taste in the mouth too recreating all the perfumes of boarding-houses and bordellos of her childhood. Clara runs on again, knowing she must be free from the present as well as the past—she is no longer looking for Paul, just a way out.

At last she comes to the recreation of the New Orleans Cotton Exchange, a room of bartering and trade, where she finds Paul sadly looking at the stone plaques commemorating those who served the Supreme Court of Louisiana.

"I have to get out of here," Clara cries, laying her hand on his arm. "It's too oppressive."

"My father," Paul replies pointing to the plaque, where inscribed in silver is *Alonzo Michael Morphy, Head Judge*.

"Yes," says Clara, "just like the one we saw."

Paul turns to her. "You remember that, when we went looking for that journalist?"

"Of course I do."

Without another word, Clara hurries Paul from the Cotton Exchange to a side window view of parkland. Outside the festivities of opening day are all around, a military parade of the first American soldiers containing northern and southern men harmoniously mixed. Gradually, by watching the soldiers, Clara forgets the Women's and Negro displays and allows Paul to lead the way.

They reach the Main Room, a vast dream of iron and glass with numberless glass portals and triangular towers. A lofty bell tower set to chime every half hour divides the entrance; a statue of angels adorns a plinth bearing the clock. On a distant grass path, a gold-plated flaming sword marks the final oaks of Exposition Boulevard, descending once again to Tchoupitoulas Street where the river can be seen in all her rushing glory.

Here Paul presents their tickets stamped with 'World's Cotton Centennial Fair,' then whispers to Clara, "this is the surprise!"

"Oh, really," she replies.

Smiling, they enter the so-called 'Tent of Privilege' hand in hand. Soon Clara realizes they are here for the actual opening. The room dims. A slow electric glow—another modern innovation—reveals a room semi-circular in shape, and behind the central stage, an auditorium capable of seating five thousand people and six hundred musicians backed by a Medieval-looking organ. Large industrial fans maintain a pleasant cooling temperature as the people file to their seats. Before long, an opening prayer is said by Reverend DeWitt Talmage of Brooklyn, "one of the most noted divines of the day," as expressed by *The Washington Post*.

In this surreal tent constructed of pinewood flooring, situated between Gothic arches reflecting the fields beyond, the politicians and worthies of the city chatter with absent minds. Diamonds drape the backs of the ladies of the hour in the style of the moment, a single row of pearls hanging from their arms. The men wear the newly fashionable top hat, a single white ribbon twirling freely from its hem. Although the top hat will be gone from the milliners' shelves next month, Paul removes his Panama as though already a decade out of date.

All at once the room hushes, and in strides the governor of Louisiana, an old Civil War general called Francis Tillou Nicholls. He is accompanied by the new Mayor of New Orleans, brusque and husky-voiced John T. Monroe. A curious thing then happens. Holding a giant pair of fake scissors, Nicholls and Monroe extend a white ribbon between them, and announce that the President himself, Republican Rutherford B. Hayes, will open the ceremony.

"This is a special time," calls out Mayor Monroe, newly appointed and keen to make an impression. "If you please, ladies and gentlemen," he clears his throat, "this will happen when the engines in the machinery are triggered by an electric key."

"The touch of this key," Governor Nicholls takes up, "is delivered by the President at the White House in Washington. The Presidential hand will directly commence the World's Cotton Centennial!" In response to a flourish by the brass band in the orchestra pit, the audience breaks into applause. Whistles and cheers bounce around the auditorium. "But first," Nicholls adds, "a little culture before the greatest show on earth is official!" The politicians step aside.

A small boy takes to the stage, no more than seven years old. He is wearing the knickerbocker clothing of a girl, the style reminiscent of Paul in his youth. He is instructed to stand by an amplification machine, a system of metal cabinets which ricochet sound before releasing it into open space, tripling the volume of his vocal chords. The oddness of a small boy at the distance from Paul and Clara, half way near the back of the room, is distinctly felt when his voice is enhanced tenfold. "Welcome everybody," he says and politely enunciates a poem by Mary Ashley Townsend, a local *salon* writer; then he introduces music by the Mexican Band and the Currier's Band of Cincinnati. Suddenly the music trails into a last fanfare with the squeaking of a cornet, a patriotic salvo, and the announcement is made that the President of the United States is on the line.

Mayor Monroe and Governor Nicholls step forward awkwardly, still bearing the oversized scissors and white tape. Nicholls begins a speech about the importance of the year 1884, and the significance of the Cotton Centennial owing to the earliest record of cotton being repatriated to England from the United States in 1774, "when a shipment of six bags of cotton, amounting to about one bale, was made from Charleston…"

At that moment he is interrupted seemingly by the modern industrial age itself.

"Electric communication has been achieved," a woman off-stage whispers, but is mistakenly amplified around the vast amphitheatre. "We are in range. The East Room of the White House and the Main Building are in play."

"…taking the octagon room, and redressing the curtains…"

"Mr President?"

"…Hello? This is the President."

"Yes, this is New Orleans. We can hear you, Washington. This is Governor Nicholls of the great state of Louisiana…" The rest of his words are momentarily drowned out when the audience realize their President is with them. A local hero, only three years earlier President Hayes had ordered all Federal troops out of New Orleans, so Reconstruction in the city in a sense is beginning today some fifteen years after the end of the war.

"…and we thank you too, Mr President, for joining us on this historic day. New Orleans has suffered a lot in recent times, what with the dire weather of last year, the unseasonable cold, not to mention Hurricane Georgina. Of course we don't have to remind you how honoured we are to have you in the room with us." A few crackles on the line, and Nicholls is a little unsure how to proceed, so decides to conclude, "and of course, no citizen of this mighty state of Louisiana is more pleased by your recent actions to grant our citizenry their freedoms—free of military presence—than I am."

"Well, I am pleased to hear that, Governor, or you wouldn't be doing your job as well as you are." There is a brief pause. "I heartily congratulate you on the great job you're doing down there,

Nicholls, with the Fair. The World's Fair no less, and I myself have received wonderful gifts from all over the world in honour of the great spectacle. I believe you have a man down there called Samuel Mullen?"

"Yes-sir," Nicholls replies, a little surprised. "He's our floor manager, I mean, chief of installation, down here at the Fair."

"Well, he's a cousin of mine, and I wanted to single him out for sending the Siamese rugs from your great state and all the Mexican pottery…"

"Er…of course, Mr President…we'll do that for you."

"And now, what do you need me to do?"

"Well, in your own time, Mr President, we have a room here filled with the dignitaries and newspapermen of the city and they are very much looking forward to you opening the Fair. In your own time, since I'm informed we only have a few more minutes before the connection goes down…"

"In that case, Mr Nicholls, shall I proceed?"

"Certainly."

"Let me see, 'I hereby declare on behalf of the twenty-six nations invested in this international project, an exchange of goodwill, culture, industry and technological advance between the developed nations of the earth, the New Orleans Cotton Centennial World's Fair now open!'"

The boy on the stage does a little jig, the band blares up, and the Governor and the Mayor—clearly relieved to finally use the scissors—cut the white tape and a torrent of magical balloons, red white and blue, each filled with helium gas, tips heavily from a velvet canopy. The crowds cheer and tap the balloons playfully to the stage, Paul joining in the fun. For once he embraces the game, the challenge of family and chess exploits beyond his consciousness. He sits there amid the commotion fielding away countless bright-coloured balloons.

Gradually the air clears and he can see his neighbours, a bony woman and her burly husband who for a moment resembles Troisville Sykes, the killer who came to his law practice for aid, but fortunately the resemblance is all. Only then does he notice that Clara is away from her seat.

Sitting very still, Paul watches as Clara appears on the stage and shakes the hands of the politicians. There is no sign that she does not already know them. She curtsies to the crowd. Paul instantly wipes his eyes, pressing them softly with his fingers. Perhaps he has mistaken this woman on stage, with her flowing purple dress all the way to the ankles and her brash yellow hat, as Clara's look-alike. The longer he looks the more he is convinced of a surreal dream. Yet as the politicians leave and she is bathed in a single spotlight, she is Clara only, the girl he knows, the one he has kept in his heart despite all the struggles, all the voyages to New York, London and Paris: there she is, in the crescent city, back in the soft afternoon light of his home.

Clara positions the microphone away from her; she won't need its modern amplification. The auditorium goes quiet, so quiet that the song-birds of live oak trees can be heard until a veil is drawn across the turnstile entrance way. A balloon or two rolls around the stage. "This is a song taught me by Charles Boudousquié," Clara begins, "from the grand ol' opera *William Tell*—the one with the shooting of the apple off 'er 'ead!"

"Hear hear!"

"Take it or leave it," she adds, not knowing how to continue, her voice charming, querulous. She is clearly nervous as she peers up into the crowd, a long way from the section where Paul is silently watching. She begins singing.

No longer is Paul's back to the audience, as in Paris at the French Opera House for *Il barbiere di Siviglia*. His full attention is on the stage. For a half second he wonders if a joke is being played. But he realizes that he has not known Clara in many years, and there is no reason to suppose he'd have seen her at the opera, given his penchant for the esteemed Orleans Opera House. If she has been learning, and practicing, clearly it has been under the impresario Charles Boudousquié of the French Opera House, the one he has avoided following his unhappy experiences in Paris.

Here, now, he listens awestruck by her presence down on the stage. Clara again becomes the little girl he once knew, whistling to herself alone by the fountain. The vast music hall is captivated, and no one could know, for the briefest second, what Paul knows. He listens in silence, marvelling at her talents, and for the first time, he knows something new. He feels a strange mix of admiration and emotion in his stomach, not the feeling of love, the little butterfly he once knew, but a new feeling, a stronger surge of respect and passion, a burning. He wants to know this new Clara just as much as the old Clara, and now he is certain why he has loved her all this time. Seemingly everything makes sense now and overcome by his feelings, Paul stands in the middle of Clara's performance and is told to sit down by the spectators behind him. He squeezes his hands together, barely able to contain himself.

The lights go low. Softly, sweetly, Clara sings out the loving-plaintive cry of Susanna, chambermaid and confidante to Rosina in *The Marriage of Figaro*, the sequel—unknown to Clara but known to Paul—to *The Barber of Seville*:

Giunse alfin il momento
che godrò senz'affanno
in braccio all'idol mio.
Timide cure,
uscite dal mio petto,
a turbar non venite il mio diletto!
Oh, come par che all'amoroso foco
l'amenità del loco,
la terra e il ciel risponda,
come la notte i furti miei seconda!

Deh, vieni, non tardar,
oh gioia bella,
vieni ove amore per goder t'appella,
finché non splende in ciel
notturna face,
finché l'aria è ancor bruna

e il mondo tace.
Qui mormora il ruscel,
qui scherza l'aura,
che col dolce sussurro
il cor ristaura,
qui ridono i fioretti
e l'erba è fresca,
ai piaceri d'amor qui tutto adesca.
Vieni, ben mio,
tra queste piante ascose,
ti vo' la fronte incoronar di rose.

Paul wishes his Italian were better, but the feeling is momemtary. All too soon, the performance comes to an end, and Clara is bowing to the sound of the ribald orchestra striking up the start of the World's Fair. High up in the audience, Paul waits to see if Clara will come back to him, nervously pressing his feet together and rolling his fingers. He looks down at the ground. When he hears his name, he looks up.

"Paul Morphy, it can't be!" A woman in a purple dress is staring down at him. "There is a break now," she says and takes his hand. "Won't you please follow me, sir?" Paul laughs as Clara leads him down the aisle of floating balloons to a Japanese tea break. Outside the politicians and the businessmen, their wives and daughters, all mingle under a comically expanded tea pagoda while Heno tea is generously dispensed.

"Siam apparently sent a small display of cotton fabrics," someone says.

"How did they hear of the Fair?"

"It's a success."

"In the South maybe, the Northern newspapers have barely noticed…."

All conversation fades as Paul and Clara exit the pagoda. They spend the afternoon among the national exhibits witnessing the gifts different countries have sent to the Fair. The Bohemian Czechs and Venice vie for the most delicate glassware, Guatemala and British Honduras for the finest rosewood and redwoods, Jamaica strong rum, delicious sugars, fibres and fruits. Most extravagantly, from Russia a wardrobe of handsome furs is displayed with a collection of malachite tables, some *droskys* and a bronze bust of Rutherford Hayes. Overwhelmed, Paul and Clara escape the grand Smithsonian rooms and flee past the Main Room down to the beautiful river gardens. Here, protected from the sinking sun, they notice two old men slouched under a banana tree playing chess.

One man says: "You have no common sense."

"No," the other replies, "it is all genius."

Their grizzled faces, worn by the horrific possibilities of chess like the grip of an opium den, barely see the spectators. Paul does not even turn to look at the board. He considers, nevertheless, how the whole day has transformed his past. No longer is his time with Clara the stifled *zugzwang* of his imagination, the impossible move, the forcing of time to flow backwards like a troubled stream in a storm. Chess is tragic, he knows, because its logic requires a move when any position would be worse than the current one. That is *zugzwang*. But no longer! Here today, briefly reminded of the royal experiment that has occupied so much of his youth and manhood, he has a chance for recovery, for life. Since Clara has provided her own move, no longer running away and teasing him into pits of despair, instead she has countered with *zwischenzug*, a play to interrupt the initially expected consequences. She has taught herself a skill to finally escape the Basin Street life. It is their chance to dance a middlegame, to parry each other pleasurably rather than painfully, to dance to the music of present time before it is too late.

"Tell me, Clara, do I know you at all?" He turns to witness her childish smile under the great yellow hat. "I know we haven't seen each other for a long time…but you never thought to tell me you could sing?"

"I learned a few years ago. One of the Basin Street men helped me. He runs the French Opera, or he's the house manager at least. He said if I got some fancy clothes, he'd make me an introduction."

"So you did…"

"That's right—what more is there to say?"

"I don't know, I just never expected."

"You thought I was helpless? That I couldn't find my own way?"

"No, not that."

"That I didn't have the talent?"

"You've always had the talent, Clara. I just…" Paul smiles and unexpectedly Clara takes his hand. He doesn't ask any more questions. Instead they pursue Mayor Monroe and a small party heading riverwards, everyone curious how the exhibits are carefully fired by water power.

"Almost better than our levées," the Mayor says with a stern face, "except the drainage is funded internationally, and that makes all the difference, you see. The most reliable energy-source is Big Muddy herself. I'm told our power is furnished from the river by means of two compound duplex Worthington pumps, five miles of pipeline, and as Mr Mullen informs me, by fifty-six fire hydrants spread throughout the building." A cool ripple goes through the crowd followed by Paul's extended applause.

"Astonishing!" says Clara for her own amusement. "The river is the saviour of the city—a shining wonder of Mother Earth!"

Paul squeezes her hand for fear of his own embarrassment. "How did you get included in the ceremonies?"

"Why, Paul," she turns to him and frowns slyly. "I got asked. Not everything is about you, you know, despite your world travels."

A little puzzled, Paul smiles as the light fades then jokingly lets go of Clara's hand. When she looks at him, he feigns indifference and it's her turn to smile.

But before the night creeps upon them, they witness the greatest spectacle of all. The central theme of the Fair, they now realize, is light and its advances in technology. Along the slippy side of a former *levée* they clamber over the embankment, some people deciding to turn back, but a small party venturing onwards, Governor Nicholls and Mayor Monroe among them. Paul even notices the small Creole boy who began the stage events; he remains unaccompanied, swinging a toy fish on a rope over his shoulder.

While the sky darkens for loss of light, a clicking is heard in the tress, more a sound of man-made ingenuity than the scraping of the spring cicadas. The trees themselves come alive in a thousand winking lights, a huge electric display of a hundred thousand candlepower.

The new lights blare down on them, frightening at first. Like the first people who travelled in motorcars believed they couldn't breathe, the people crouch in surprise. But slowly adjusting to the incandescence of nature and artificial light fused, they take to their feet again. They are enclosed in a playground, a heaven of whiteness bounded in five directions by tall lights on delicate towers for the grand illumination of the entire grounds. The boy squeals whether from fear or delight, as the politicians lead a crooked path out from the trees. All around, tiny jenny lights buzz at their feet, while the mighty Edson bulbs draw them over the oldest *levées*.

Paul treads on one of the jenny lights and cracks it.

"Who-oops!" laughs Clara and begins singing a line of *The Marriage of Figaro* in her soprano.

"A human error," Paul says, looking back on the consequence, a small crushed light buried in the grass.

Together they take Riverside Drive to a bend in the river. Paul thinks of his childhood, Telcide's voice at her musical *soirées* dominating the room, that time he saw a female face glowing red in a window on Bourbon Street during Lafitte's funeral. Is this where everything led? Is the future this technological innovation, science and industry? Yes, he thinks, don't we need great minds, moral attorneys, and good leadership? Or is Paul Morphy just a sideshow at a fair, a memory of a more refined era, one of life's lost amateurs? The answers lie in the cosmos tonight, he knows, now he is holding Claea tight.

Downstream, the sun is setting in grey-orange splendour along Algiers Point up to white villas overlooking the city, the dark brooding trees, all the lights and sunken beauty of New Orleans. This way, the trees seem to call, this way to your future...

Chapter Fifty-Seven
The Steamboat Race
1884

The Fair ends with a steamboat race. Everyone strides down to the river as the melancholy jenny lights flicker and Paul and Clara continue their extended date. They pass more century-old live oaks, leaning like hanging baskets and engulfed by soft Spanish moss.

"Where are we going?" Clara whispers.

"Into the past," Paul replies.

Descending the last *levée* onto stone steps, the first impression they receive is a draft from upstream. The scent of jasmine sharpens the air with the cloying taste of sugar refineries and the musky sludge smell of the Mississippi. For a few seconds the light disappears, the sun is down, and the moon takes a breath before announcing her presence on the horizon. Then over the dock appears a wooden grandstand, hastily constructed but filled with the beauty and the chivalry of New Orleans. The crowd of a hundred people step gingerly onto the grandstand, testing their weight a foot at a time and laughing at the possibility of being swept into the river.

Mayor Monroe walks to the end of the pier, spins and leans on the railing. With the shining river as his backdrop, he tucks his thumbs in his lapels and looks cheekily at the crowd, whiskers lifting his ears as he speaks.

"Life and death feed each other in an endless cycle," he says and pauses. "Just like those two goliath mirages, look for yourselves, bobbing at their moorings, either side of us. See our huge Mississippi steamers!" Timed to perfection, two steam-boats are magnificently illuminated on the water, all ropes and shining hulls, and the crowd actually coos. "So, my good friends, I am reminded of the first ever boat to power up this great river. Those were the days when the marshes were impenetrable, before we tamed them, when a single bark canoe could be crushed by the tide. But no more! Now the colour of the water has changed and we, the people of New Orleans, we rule this river. We decide!"

"Hear hear," from his supporter Governor Nicholls.

"The Mississippi may only be a third of a league wide at its estuary," the Mayor continues. "A musket shot in width, and the cane-breaks thick as mountains, but men came here, our ancestors, and we planted those trees which bring the river down to the sea. So let us now sing a *Te Deum*, in gratitude at our discovery of the entrance of the river."

The audience realize the speech is over and begin to applaud. The *Te Deum* is sung somewhat awkwardly as the grandstand sways gently on the silent waters. Then everyone faces the spectacle before the crowd, the steamers moored a quarter the way out: the *Robert E. Lee*, a New Orleans boat, and the *Northern Lights* from Chicago. The boats sound their horns boisterously, repeatedly.

"Now I'm not a betting man," Mayor Monroe says, "but I do like a little flutter. And since we're refined sophisticated people, you'll notice this table is manned by my secretary Miss. Evangeline." He gestures to a prim-looking girl of about fifteen in a flower dress, clearly his daughter, perched under a parasol canopy among a table of papers. "Miss. Evangeline will be happy to take the orders. But first let me introduce the players." And he waves his arm over the vast swath of river. "The boat on the left, the slightly larger of the two, is the *Robert E. Lee* captained by John W. Cannon, a fifteen year veteran of the route to St. Louis. The *Lee* is arguably a more powerful engine, tugging a greater load, yet stripped of excess weight in passengers and cargo." Whistles from the crowd! "While on your right is the beautifully streamlined *Northern Lights* captained by Thomas P. Leathers, a man of slightly less experience but filled with youthful zest and vigour. The *Lights* promises less risk of being curtailed by tides or river obstacles such as sandbars and islands and the like, but her engine is smaller. The choice is yours, good people, for the boats leave within the hour!"

Paul and Clara near the edge of the viewing platform and survey the boats, mysteriously suspended, making their final preparations. Paul waves to the captain of the *Robert E. Lee*, who is clearly preoccupied, while Clara has her eye on the other boat. For a few moments she walks away from Paul, stops and leans over the river. The shimmer of moonlight makes her eyes feel heavy while the long day in the dark city, the bright Fair and the Mississippi ready to be lit up by two steamboats roaring into the night, is almost too much experience. But not enough to change her plans...

The game changes when a small fire breaks out on the back of the *Northern Lights*. Little can be done and the shell of a lifeboat burns as her bow is eaten by some inflammable substance. Murmurs go through the crowd but quickly young Captain Leathers is there, angrily cajoling the men responsible. In his hand is a large bowie-knife, one of those murderous weapons more efficient than the Roman *gladius* and the horror of its use ripples through the crowd. But then Leathers ostentatiously salutes the spectators, calling out inaudible words of apology and reassurance.

"Ever a betting man," the Mayor calls back nervously. "A captain with fire in his belly is a good bet," he adds for the benefit of the gamblers.

"To the ol' Mississippi!" the Governor echoes. "Too thick to drink, too thin to plow!"

But Clara's mind is elsewhere. Even now, she feels the uncertainty of things—that they could go on forever—but marred by an indescribable feeling of everything fading. "Nothing lasts, and yet we feel everything," she whispers. In the grey haze of crescent moonlight, the present slips interminably into the past.

Suddenly there is a flash with a glitter of paddlewheels and an arm of water spouts from the *Northern Lights*. With seconds the *Robert E. Lee* counters in spirit and the mutual signal, a second foghorn, sounds the opening of the race. Nearby a keel boat trembles in the bay, a tug to pull the boats, and begins making towing adjustments as the steamboats edge out into the heart of the Mississippi.

Paul and Clara reach the betting table, and for amusement they mark a different boat each, Paul for the hometown *Lee* and Clara for the streamlined Chicago challenger, the *Northern* upstart. All around a violent rattling noise, the scrape of wood on iron, accompanies the churning of frothy yellow waters.

"You know the weather is different in the middle of the river," the Mayor's daughter is saying. "Sure, the river has its own sandbars and shoals, but the winds are faster lower to the water with strong rains, shifting winds, that kind of thing. But an island can slow things down, sure."

"Which is the safer bet?" Clara asks.

"Hard to say," Evangeline says, her father's daughter, eyes latent with crafty promise. "A steamwheeler race, a week long, between steamboats with paddlewheels? The boats are so similar, your guess is good as mine. Both have a shallow draft, flat-bottomed enough to nose up to the riverbank. Both hulls are wood-strong with keelsons and hog chains hooked to the keelsons, sure, up the hog-post and down the hull. They're both designed the same way, basically."

Clara frowns at the technicalities and thanks the girl who is already stamping the next betting card. Without waiting any longer, Clara turns to Paul who is staring up at the steamboats, their paddlewheels and parallel funnels already pouring out wood smoke.

"Come on," she says, "I want to get a closer look."

Likeminded people have already disembarked in smaller boats, their oars hitting the grandstand below. These intrepid spectators, mostly young men impressing their dates, are already rowing close to the steamers, a discouraged activity but there's no formal control. A few boys stand on the *levée* and skim stones at the tug as it swerves near the banks. Amid the activity the Creoles of the city consume cocktails, ignoring the increasing rabble on the river beneath. A general mood of expectancy, sleepiness and impatience falls over the crowd.

Meanwhile Clara takes Paul back to Riverside Drive just behind the last trees of the entrance. From there, she knows the westbank ferry will be disembarking soon for Algiers Point. "I reckon we have about half an hour," she tells Paul, "and we'll get a better view from the jetty anyway."

Paul struggles to keep up with her. "But I don't need to go to that neighbourhood," he says. "How will we get back?"

"When the steamers have gone, of course, and we'll see the race better. Look, there it is!" Already, just around the bend a few hundred metres, the *Thomas Jefferson* ferryboat is ready to disembark on the hour with its usual nightly crew. "No time to lose!" Clara cries out. Paul skips aboard at her heels and, for a moment, she sings a line he heard once, long ago. *"For I know all de cops; I stan' in wid de roughs, Yer kin bet yer sweet life I'm er Nu'leens tuff!"*

Within minutes the *Thomas Jefferson* is downstream from the steamboats and has launched a path into the Mississippi using a wider arc to avoid the fanfare. Paul is feeling nervous without consciously knowing why, but he doesn't have to wait long.

"You know, Paul, I am leaving," Clara says.

He turns to her, silent and desperate-looking. "Clara, you just came back. You can't...don't leave again." Her hand touches his forehead but he brushes it away.

"You were always leaving *me*, Paul, don't you remember? The chess adventures, always another city, another opponent."

"Yes, I remember, but..."

Clara turns her face to the river, upstream to northern cities, to St. Louis and beyond. "I never said I would be here forever."

"You didn't," Paul says, "but New Orleans is your home. Mine too."

"Well, that's because you have one. Wherever you lay your chess pieces!"

"That's unfair, I don't play anymore."

The ferryboat pulls away. Leaving the shore, Paul and Clara see white geese and black snipe flying towards the swamplands. The moon turns a pale red blood and the people around them—bundled-up washerwomen and tired-looking fishermen, uncertain of these finely dressed passengers—edge to the other side of the boat. Suddenly, all down the Gulf Coast the night sky is lit up by the incandescence—the last dying lights of the World's Fair. Seemingly at the same moment the twin decks of the two steamboats, closer now, become a great firework. Their chimneys launch a host of black stars into a white glowing sky.

Within seconds the specks fall on Paul and Clara and the lights flash all the way to the Vieux Carré across the mighty stream.

Old man Mississippi will join his love, the Atchafalaya for whom he sluggishly plows the riverbed. Separated, the old man carries a tragic love for the considerably younger and swifter river, for whose forgiving waters he yearns and digs deep into mud.

"I must say it," Clara says. "You helped me once, but you cannot fulfil my dreams, Paul. It's not something you can do. New Orleans is your home, and always will be. You belong here."

Angry for a moment, Paul grips her hand. "But you belong here too, Clara. My home is always open for you! And my heart!" Behind them, the river glints and almost grins but is silent.

"Not on the chessboard, Paul. I cannot live on a chessboard. And your mind is organized by the game, your habits, the way you life. You are too...you are too polite for me!"

He releases his grip. "But this isn't a chessboard," he whispers.

"I know, Paul. I know that. Not everything is chess."

516   *THE KNIGHT OF NEW ORLEANS*

"Clara, we can do it. Why did I come to see you? Why did we go out after the storm? Not because of my career, for the law or chess or any of that. I came to see *you*."

"To save me from myself? It's not enough, Paul." Again she touches his cheek and lets her fingers lie there. "It's not enough."

"Don't Clara, don't patronize me."

"I love you, Paul. I always will. Take this from me now, I will always remember you." And gently she pins a *lagniappe* in his lapel and twists it around with *élan*. "I'll be out there, and I'll come back. But first you must let me go to come back."

So saying Clara walks slowly backwards from Paul. She raises her finger, and he does not attempt to approach her. Between them a river island appears, a black formless mound drifting in a grey drizzle that the *Thomas Jefferson* carefully navigates past. The glow over the island comes from the moon, placidly watching the scene unfold. For a brief moment they are back at the fountain, a boy and girl playing without the adult world watching and without any future or past, just a game to indulgence and each other to entertain. They manage to exchange a smile, standing still, until suddenly the ferryboat is swerving behind the engine of the *Northern Lights*. The giant red paddlewheel rises over them threateningly. A torrent of water hangs a moment, like a beautiful frozen waterfall, before crashing in the Mississippi, the backwash breaking over the side of the ferry.

"Over a thousand steamboats arrive in New Orleans every year," Paul says. "How will I know when you come back?"

"Don't wait, Paul, not this time. Just don't wait."

He trembles in the wind like a small boy in the heat of Canal Street, his whole family lost to him. "I am trapped."

"Paul, stop thinking about chess. You're not a piece on a chessboard."

"I can still be a knight," Paul replies. "I've done all I can," and he stares uncomprehending.

"Threaten me then," is Clara's reply. "Sacrifice me! Do anything but what you're doing. No move at all is the worst move."

"I just want to save you…"

"Don't you see, Paul, we're opposites and you can't save me. All we can do is end the game!"

Paul crouches and puts his head in his hands. He does not understand.

For a moment the ferryboat dips in the water, swings and cuts a path free to Algiers Point. The *Northern Lights* turns under the power of her own tugboat, and in that moment, with eyes closed, Paul knows Clara is gone. He waits nevertheless. After a lifetime seeing the future in motionless chess pieces, a graphic stillness beats behind Paul's eyes, memories in search of lost time. Then he looks up and sees her, Clara in her flapping purple dress, the yellow hat missing from her head, her dark hair undone in the wind. He says nothing, but open-mouthed he watches as she falls without a care into the cold waters of the brooding Mississippi— she coughs herself immediately to the surface and begins swimming for the mighty hull of the steamship. The siren on the *Thomas Jefferson* sounds. Everywhere passengers clamour across the deck pressing hands to their eyes. Paul feels deafness embrace him. Wordlessly and sightlessly he stares at the ocean of a river, utterly immobile and paralysed.

A moment later he is on the edge of the ferryboat, calling out to Captain Leathers who appears on the deck of the steamship, a pistol and his dagger in his hand. Almost at the same moment, a gun blast from the World's Fair grandstand signals the great steamship race is halted, but neither boat heeds the signal. Leathers runs in opposite directions, his race to attend to, grappling with his First Mate on the way and shouting something about a crazy woman who has thrown herself in the river.

Within minutes, two red-hot steamboats are coursing neck and neck, straining every rivet in the boilers, their locomotive engines gunning from bow to stern. White-hot steam shoots from invisible pipes, pouring black smoke from the chimneys, raining down sparks, parting the river into long channels of hissing spray.

"Make it to Chicago," Paul calls out to the river. "Just come back!"

The lifeboat is launched. The *Robert E. Lee* searchlight turns on the water, but the paddlewheel is clearly sucking Clara nearer and nearer. The devilish red grin of the revolving wheel bears down on her. A boatlight flashes in Clara's eyes and she screams and startles hserself. A solitary beast—an aged alligator—turns and watches in disgust from sleeping on the riverbank, then laughs his way into the water not for the smell of flesh, but for the fun of the struggle and to witness the commotion first-hand. Only a hundred yards away, the creature disappears underwater.

Then a gun-blast goes off, a pipe has burst, and the paddlewheel scoops Clara up and hurls her brazenly over the lifeboat, but not into it, in an awful gesture of macabre comedy. The searchlight eyes her like a roving lighthouse, playing in her hair, and before she can disappear again someone leaps in the Mississippi, dragging her down accidentally as he wrestles her towards the lifeboat.

Meanwhile the *Robert E. Lee* whips its engines into a frenzy. The paddlewheel blurs water in its struggle to get the great hulk moving, and at last, Clara is pulled from the river by the Ship's Cook into the arms of the First Mate, sitting on his haunches in the lifeboat and who immediately places smelling salts under her nose and jerks her back into life.

Moments later, it is clear she is not hurt, nor seems to be too shocked by the whole episode. From the docking *Thomas Jefferson*, Paul is uncertain if the person standing on the deck of the mighty steamship is Clara but he imagines it to be her. Again he says a prayer under his breath. He sits on the wooden jetty exhausted by the episode, bizarrely wondering what the *Red Book* will say about Clara's daredevil exit from the city—the escape no doubt of a soul-abandoned woman, blessed and cursed by a life of her own choosing. Along the riverbank the alligator slouches back onto shore, half entertained by the drama but having seen enough for the night.

Someone is singing behind Paul, but he does not turn to see. *"My Brazilian beauty down on the Amazon...that's where my baby's...gone, gone, gone."*

The steamboats straighten for their journey. A bend in the river draws them into a narrow path and Paul watches them away. He is alone. His fellow passengers scatter, heading to their nightly dens along Algiers Point.

The river is higher than the city. Clara stands on the stern of the *Robert E. Lee* and stares down at the roofs and streets and trolley cars of New Orleans. Mission accomplished, she thinks, glancing over at the ferry. There is no sign of Paul on deck as she turns away.

In the grey light of morning, Clara sees the future for the first time. She is going somewhere for once. Not London, or Paris, or New York. She is going where they make the hats that sell in the stores along Canal Street. She is going west but not too far west: not to California, or the heat of Texas, or the barren rocky slopes of Arizona or New Mexico. She is going north to the cool summers and cold winters, to steady her nerves, and sharpen her mind, and one day, perhaps, to bring back the hats to sell in the stores.

She is going to be a businesswoman. She is going to Chicago, an expanding city, but one not overpopulated and clogged with human grease, little work and even less daylight like Manhattan. Instead she will walk along the shore of Lake Michigan, touch the breeze and see people go about *their* business. Just watch everyone go by, free of the fetid past of Basin Street, free to wander with no games or tricks. Free at last...

After a time, the *Robert E. Lee* passes beyond the Eads Jetty and the vastness of the river opens with the last, uneasy swell of the Gulf behind. Clara makes her way into the unknown heart of the continent, aboard the Mississippi that will eventually become a Minnesota stream. "I will create my new home in the North."

Paul must take the returning *George Washington* ferryboat home. Half way across the river he can see the *Robert E. Lee* from a new angle, but only for a few seconds. He decides not to torture himself yet and turns away, looking back at the city streets lying slumped below the curve of the Mississippi sweeping down into the Gulf.

A flatboat emerges from nowhere to steer the tired *Washington* ashore, strong winds in mid-steam crook the bow as it sways, rocks and slouches downstream. Unseen, a man ties a hawser to a tree stump, and the great gunwale anchor is set down. She won't be moving for a long time now. All the sailors come ashore, the roustabouts, timber cruisers, fish market workers and poker-sharps, ordinary thieves and hustlers all, returning to their beds aboard industrial barks on Levée Street for a few brief hours. Only the humped *levée* remains, black in the moonlight under the artificial glow of the jenny lights.

Paul sits down. She is gone. New Orleans is gone, gone. He is left among the demented music of the trees. He can see them along the river, leaning down sad and expressionless in the wind. All the strangeness and the glory of the world is his once more. More than sickness he feels his insides turning out. Hands gripping the sinking earth, he is physically sick in the mud, and then again; he kneels there shivering as the ferry slides into the dock.

For a few minutes he contemplates throwing himself in the river, then realizes he would have to climb the jetty. Ending the painful game is hard, and—as a thoughtless act—just something he cannot do. "I cannot even drown myself," he whispers. "I am resigned to my fate, wherever it is. Now it must be without Clara."

He looks through a break in the *levée* at the black heart of New Orleans, deathly quiet in the night-time rain. For a while he is motionless. Yet something draws him home, the solitude of Royal Street and Faubourg Marigny, the calm of home perhaps, the remains of his family, his collection of unworn shoes.

Nevertheless he stands and decides, moaning, to head back. He is supported by the ancient great city, the only thing now keeping him alive. Instinctively in Audubon Park beside the World's Fair, the buildings all shimming and abandoned, he looks up and sees a miraculous sight, a blizzard of snow geese, truly a beautiful lonely sight. The snow geese are surrounded by a thousand purple martins, numberless as pawns on a forgotten chessboard, and shielding the smaller birds like chaperons, both species travelling west through steaks of chequered moonlight.

"Too much," Paul whispers to himself. "I resign. It is all too much!"

Chapter Fifty-Eight
The Phantom
1884

L ife in the Quarter resumes its flow. A full year goes by. On certain afternoons, light filters arabesques through the grilles of the balconies. No one would know of the thousands of steamboats docking at the New Orleans port each year, or that races were becoming more common. As Paul knows from his travels, people will eventually grow accustomed to wonders in their midst, such as the Tulieres Gardens or the *Café de La Régence* chess players.

Trying to forget Clara, Paul adopts a fresh routine. Wearing a palm beach suit, he enjoys walking in the Lafayette Cemetery on Prytania Street. The presence of the gravestones is somehow soothing, though he never goes there at night. By late summer offshore breezes bring a warm molasses smell from the sugar refineries into the city. With the Carré's gardens in full bloom, streets below the St. Louis Cathedral begin to choke on the scents of tangy honeysuckle and too-sweet ivy cascading the walls.

Paul knows he could spend his life here, sipping *café au lait* with a beignet before bed-time, so long as he keeps the past at bay. For now it remains a quiet life living with his mother and sister.

One afternoon he is reading the *New Orleans Item* and learns that the Cotton Centennial Director-General, Edward A. Burke, also editor of the *Times-Democrat*, has fled to Brazil with one and a half million dollars of the World's Fair treasury.

> The architect of the Fair's Main Building, landscaping over two hundred and fifty acres of the Audubon Park-to-be, was a genius of space. From St. Charles Avenue to the Mississippi, the Fair could be approached by railway, steamboat or ocean-going ship. The Main Building alone was the largest roofed structure in the United States, costing three hundred and thirty thousand dollars, a sum now deposited in a Rio de Janeiro safety deposit box *sans doute*.
>
> Not since young Paul Morphy's mastery of the chessboard has a talent emerged for utilizing space so well. Burke's grand palace of glass and iron reputedly housed an opera stage divided by classical Greek pillars, overhung by a domed crystal roof...

Paul lays the paper down, but cannot resist the chance of finding more mention of his own name. He reads on:

> Before his unfortunate theft, Mr. Burke developed a Horticultural Hall, an observation tower with electric elevators, prototype street-cars and a spectacular silver cage containing hydra plants and tropical fruits. What these accomplishments fail to mention, though, is that the New Orleans extravaganza, running from 16 December 1884 and recently closing on 4 June was popular for the city, but not a good investment. Ultimately the buildings all went for scrap, the logging sold cheap to Alabama forest companies, totalling financial losses greater than the initial investment.

> Mr. Burke has therefore robs us twice! Let him try and return to the city! We do not welcome back our heroes, not those who line our pockets with dust and then rob us blind!

Paul puts down the newspaper with a sigh. He knows there is no way of forgetting, no wiping the board clean, no taking the pieces back or starting again. The game was in progress and there was only one resolution: the defeat of the player who would call himself the king.

Clara may have been his mistress, his queen, his angel or devil, he can no longer tell. But she played the queen's gambit in the end by jumping in the Mississippi. If he was supposed to jump after her, save her or even feign saving her, the move was rejected: neither of them believed in the white knight, the clichéd hero, only in escaping the pointless stalemate. In his heart Paul knows Clara did not want him to jump. If he had, Clara would still have surfaced, but would he? The thought is ironic and absurd to him now, though it would have been desperate at the time.

But the memory cycle is something Paul cannot stop. At night, he suffers phantoms of the eye and descends into fierce chemistry of dreams of the past. In the darkness he seems to deliberate with phantoms long gone, his uncle Alex dragging him down to Basin Street, or struggle in alleyways with Gilbert Rosière and Camille Rizzo. He begins drinking again, both the green-eyed goblin absinthe in the evening, and then sipping the Swamp favourite, *Raleigh Rye* whisky, in full daylight out on St Ann Street. Now and then, proud and sorrowful, he sinks half a bottle of gin and passes out. In a random act of discovery he becomes obsessed with Thomas de Quincey's *Confessions of an Opium-Eater*. Though he has never tasted the drug, not illegal for Creoles in the city, he believes: 'whenever two thoughts stand related to each other by a law of antagonism, and exist, as it were, by mutual repulsion, they are apt to suggest each other.'

"Like two pieces left randomly on a chessboard," Paul whispers. Now, like Thomas de Quincey himself, every night Paul descends into chasms and sunless pits, less disturbing than the sensation, repeated nightly, of the vast expansion of time or the feeling to have woken and be living again as an old man. Sometimes the room seems to expand and shrink without measure, fuelling a kind of latent terror, fear that cannot break into consciousness until morning.

Delighted and horrified both, he is once again a toddler crawling on the floor of the Chartres Street playroom. The orange map of the world covers his head, the chessboard slips from his feet and he falls heavily. His finger is bleeding and the chessmen await his soul…

Absently, wandering the streets once more, Paul goes to the dead-letter office on Burgundy to see if Clara has written. A grizzled-looking boy of no more than sixteen, scratching nose and sideburns, goes to check but returns empty-handed. Paul seems unwell.

"You want a cure for hiccoughs, Mister. Look directly at the point of a knife blade. Cures any sneezing too!"

"Thank you."

"Get well, Mister Morphy."

Paul starts. "You know who I am?"

"Mister Morphy," the boy says with a cutting look, "everyone knows who you are."

That night the alligator Paul saw on the riverbank returns inside his dreams. A dark figure in a torn black cloak, half knight half chess piece, is sitting on the alligator's back, riding the beast uncomfortably and lashing its head with a stick. Waking in a sweat Paul sits up in the moonlight, loathing and fascinated by the sight, and decides to give up the *Raleigh Rye*. The next day, Sunday, he visits Our Lady of Guadalupe Chapel to see the St. Jude shrine behind the altar, and he prays kneeling before the relic of St. Jude.

The next night, rather than exorcize reptile spirits from his room, Paul dreams of Clara as a ghost trapped inside a shawl of black crepe. When he wakes he feels her presence within the walls. All other dreams promptly vanish, and the following night he dreams only of this women in black, blended with a woman he dreamed of in his childhood, a desperate smile he once witnessed looking up to a Basin Street balcony, repeated now in a tormenting dream, a recurring nightmare. For his own comfort, Paul plays a game of chess against his own mind, first with the English opening, second with the Two Knights Defence.

"For I am two people, and I must let one of them go, else I'll go mad. I must let myself go from Clara, from the past, from chess!"

He thinks of all the men he's played, Steinitz, Staunton, Harrwitz, Löwenthal, Winfield Scott, the Duke of Brunswick at the Café, Louis Paulsen in New York. The faces of these men, some gone, some alive and still puzzling over chessboards in Europe, all blur together. Suddenly a noise distracts him and he stops playing, folds away the chess table in a panic, and takes to his bed. After imagining another chess game, the presence in the room is stronger. He knows Helena and Telcide are knitting quietly in the next room, but suddenly he hears a voice, laughing from a single direction, a high-pitched cackle. He immediately goes next door only to find his sister and mother gone. A note lies on the table explaining a visit to the doctor, claiming they did not wish to disturb him.

Again Paul hears the laughter, only this time coming from his own room. Shivering with fright, he takes a wine bottle from Helena's room and backs into the hallway. Again the sound—a shrill voice mumbling a plea, only he cannot detect the direction. Cautiously, he pushes open his bedroom door revealing the strange scene of someone sitting by a chair at the window, the figure of a woman dressed head to toe in black mourning.

"Clara?" he whispers, and the figure utters a pained sound. She raises her hands, letting the sleeves fall down, and he notices the whiteness of one of her arms and the blackness of the other. He can see only one of her cheeks, a pallid colour reflecting a strange and serpentine sort of beauty, until she turns the other cheek to reveal darkness. Lifting her head she grins with an empty yellow mouth. Paul shivers, frightened, and grips the bottle tighter as he stares through the woman's veil at two black opal eyes. "Clara," he repeats. "Is that you?"

At that moment, the door swings shut and a gale blows through the window. Paul swirls and pulls at his bedroom door, but it's jammed and he pulls so hard, not daring to turn, that he falls to his knees. Somehow he can hear a Chicago chorus-line, a strange dancehall melody for New Orleans in the middle of a hot summer afternoon. Somewhere he hears the popping of champagne corks. A perfume of Havana tobacco drifts in from the open shutters, and mistily hangs on the shrubbery along the veranda. He turns in time to see the ghostly presence dissolve, its mouth stretching wider and wider. *You lose*, it says without feeling. All Paul has proven over the chessboard vanishes in a moment of terror and supernatural belief. Instead of leaving the room, though, he grabs a bottle of rum from behind the door, and hurls it at the chair, desperate for some kind of reaction, the most uncharacteristic moment of his life.

But whoever was there, her white throat shimmering in the heat for a lingering few seconds, is now gone. What remains is broken glass slung from Paul's hand, and a dark stain of rum juice down the wall. Awkwardly he wipes blood from his fingers. A clock nonchalantly ticks near his wooden chessboard, the pieces long passed into his imagination. His bed is untouched. The wind moves the lace window hangings. The drowsy odor of a Basin Street woman lingers like incense.

Paul remembers what he has read of ghosts. "*A broken fan lies on the lonely rocking chair,*" he whispers. "*A bouquet of camellias dying on the mantelpiece.*" Whoever she was, she seemed to be more than a *doppelgänger* or the image of Clara bestowed on his inner eye. Paul knows she has been following him since he was small, and is no more Clara than Caïssa herself, the ungrateful chess god who devours men and thirsts for another gift of the impossible game.

The room is calm at last. Paul senses she was a solo visitation, and reassures himself about the limited powers of ghosts. A spirit would not appear in multiple rooms, surely, and her feet would be silent, nor could she float through the house opening and closing doors noiselessly like a phantom, answering questions before they were asked. In other words, Clara is not haunting him....Surely a survival move, and a viable story for sanity's sake. The last home he wants to revisit is the *Louisiana Retreat for the Feeble Minded*.

Wherever she is Clara can sleep now, and at last, so can Paul in her absence.

A week later, Paul has managed to stop drinking altogether. His cut hand is beginning to heal, and feeling claustrophobic in the house he decides to visit the fishermen he remembers from the afternoon on the *Thomas Jefferson* ferry crossing. So he makes his way down to the Mississippi.

Crossing Levée Street and leaving behind the flower markets, he embraces the breeze rolling in from Big Muddy, the air tugging at his Panama hat. Once on the shore he strides the dark sands of the beachhead, parting the sand-dunes and warily glancing down the blunt drop in the embankment. Along the drained riverbank, he watches the oysters being hauled from the small docking boats, the shell-fish with insides fleshy and savoury, caught by the local *écaille* for their tender hearts.

Here are the oystermen with their backs to him, working as his Uncle Ernest once worked before taking over the management of the New Orleans Customs House, patrolling the docks, separating the fish, making dubious deals of an unknown nature: men who spend days and nights scraping shell-fish from their natal beds and dragging nets ashore. Paul thinks of those creatures as himself, soft within but an exterior of endless resistance.

He watches one oysterman pry open a solo prize with a knife, lifts out the puffy centre, leans back and drops it in his gullet. Shivering at the intimacy Paul walks away, soon passing a clutter of red fish-boxes on the shore. The shell-fish are entombed in busy piles, wooden signs pinned in the mud rejoicing *fryd, rost & in the shel* and *de bonne huitres toutes frais et poisson de la mer—un véritable collection!*

Now he sees that Clara was like that too, a hard shell whose cracking led to more layers and a deeper enigma within, the inverse of himself. But he sees her shell was open for business and love—and ambition—from the beginning too. She had to leave her birth city in order to seal it closed, to protect herself. But could he ever really understand her motives?

Paul loops back along Peter Street up from the river. Soon he stands before the central courthouse and the Morphy plaque. He remembers his father's dedication to New Orleans and the proud legal history of his family—all its Creole history in France and Spain—that must soon end or else be channelled through him. He knows he is not up to the task: he cannot be the savior of the Morphys. He just stares at the building, a red-brick box itself, well weathered and needing paint but having survived prior to the Civil War. The clock strikes the hour and Paul moves slowly down the street. He goes home.

Back in his room at 89 Royal Street, Paul takes up the *Times-Picayune* and reads how

> ...both boats left New Orleans Thursday, 30 June 1884 at 4:55 PM before the *Robert E. Lee* docked at St. Louis at 11.25 AM on Thursday 4 July, 6 hours and 36 minutes ahead of the *Northern Lights!* Clearly, Captain Cannon won because Captain Leathers did not use barges floating alongside the *Robert E. Lee*, which the *Northern Lights* realized was a good idea after getting stuck on a mudflat for 6 hours—without which occurrence the race would have been very close.

Paul folds the newspaper and dangles it from the window, eventually letting it fall. The pages scatter over the garden and drift into the fountain. Looking from his window at the sunset, Paul remembers how he once saw Edward crying by the fountain and did not comfort him, did not go to him. Would it have been so hard? He remembers how Edward stuck up for him at Spring Hill Acdemy, also how he bloodied his lip with a fencing sword.

He looks up over at the trees and the dark swamplands beyond. "Pine forests were here a long time ago....No people, only trees," he says. "Surely trees do not fight, not like people?" He laughs a little at the thought.

Softly, a stray bird lands on the window-ledge, no longer the parrot Paul is expecting. The bird raises its foot and Paul is seemingly saluted not by a hummingbird but a mockingbird, the cruellest of night-time joys. He remains there a few hours when he wakes to find the bird gone. In the intervening dream he's been lulled by a nightingale.

"They are not the same," he whispers to himself, thinking back on his life. But he is no longer able to tell one memory from another. "They are different, such opposites. I cannot measure what I have lost...Lost by not knowing how to live!" He senses no absurdity in his plea.

Paul is about to put his head in his hands, but forces himself back to his bed, and collapses.

Chapter Fifty-Nine
1884
Perpetual Check

Paul does not see Clara again. Almost three months go by. Life in the French Quarter establishes a steady routine. The Morphys accept what remains for them. Helena is not going to marry, and neither is Paul, nor will he pursue a career. Telcide resists trying to influence her children in the ways of marriage and career and accepts no one is going to come along and rejuvenate her with a third marriage proposal. The storm of four years ago marks history, the end of history.

Life adopts a steady routine. An uneasy acceptance, the malaise of contentedness, settles over 89 Royal Street. Telcide plays the piano at friends' *soirées* and sleeps in the day. Helena turns her knitting into a small enterprise with two other spinsters of Bourbon Street. They run a dress shop on Canal Street near stores where the Basin Street girls acquire their dresses. Paul does not bother Telcide or Helena in their environments. Titi is finally freed by federal statutes no longer resisted by Louisiana, and leaves for Chicago.

Ernest Morphy is never heard from again except for a white carnation he sends to Telcide every year. Telcide has the flower pressed in a book on the mantelpiece beside a portrait of the two brothers shaking hands down by the Customs House in the noonday sun; Alonzo is wearing his Panama hat.

The family soon hears no more from Malvina and John Sybrandt. Once the storm waters recede they see a divine wind blowing their fortunes to New York where they purchase a Bronx townhouse with the greater share of the inheritance money. Edward joins the American Reserve Navy and is briefly stationed in Hawaii. One summer he is reprimanded for inciting a superior officer to a duel; Edward wins and in revenge the duel is made public. He is decommissioned and sends home giddy and incoherent postcards from around the United States. The only family correspondence from beyond the city, Paul pins them on the kitchen wall. Meanwhile Charles Maurian lives on Rampart Street and plays chess regularly at the New Orleans Chess Club. Even now he invites Paul for friendly bouts, but does not seem to understand what Paul has overcome, gained and lost. The chess players of New York or Europe no longer write to Paul.

Once he receives a note from Fred Edge, thanking him for the favourable description Paul created of his former secretary-manger in a whimsical travelogue piece, *A Knight's Adventure*. Considering them a charming favour, Edge quotes Paul's lines back to him:

> *Edge is a decent, supportive man who guided me through the labyrinthine chess worlds of New York, London and Paris. He helped me down corridors I could not have gone down alone. The journey was self-destructive but we took it together bravely and we would do so again. I commend my old friend and wish him well.*

Paul writes the article for *The Alumni Journal of Spring Hill*, a favour undertaken for his old school knowing the article will not receive wide publication.

New Orleans is changing fast. Many laws are challenged and Paul is no longer legally qualified as a lawyer. He has no career. Months have passed without any chess, not even idle games, thoughts or dreams. But Paul is content. He maintains his daily walk and opera visits around the Vieux Carré.

One afternoon he begins a long stroll beyond Canal Street where he seldom now goes. He enjoys walking where his grandfather did. But moving deeper into the American District he misses the familiar sounds and smells of the French Quarter. There are no nuns walking two by two, no bright-turbaned quadroons. No roistering sailors line these streets, nor vendors of *calas tout chaud* and *estomac mulâtre*. The carriages look different, safer and privately sealed; the horses trot faster and appear healthier. No booths of *bière douce* or fruit stalls curb the streets. No scents of strong coffee or rich food drift from unseen kitchens and mingle with the fragrance of flowers. The American District is its own tailored quiet of self-conscious isolation. The half-glimpsed courtyards reveal magnificent paths to giant white houses; the French Market is a covered store at the street corner; Jackson Square is a lane for parking the delivery carts. But for the children of the Louisiana Purchase, a vibrant and vociferous life is missing in these strange orderly streets. The colours are subdued, the voices controlled, the boulevards trim. By the river no one is patrolling the banquette, singing and selling or lying in the afternoon sun.

Paul passes on, not sufficiently confident to stop and feeling like an illegal alien. House by house he grows more and more weary. The ominous porches and colonnades offer the image of welcoming patronage, but despite the sequestered order Paul senses he does not belong here. The false propriety is beautifully overwhelming in a way he never expected. So he weaves back through the Warehouse District, adjusting his collar as the day grows hot. Passing Button's Coffeehouse he doesn't stop for a *sirop* or cooling lemonade. The sun is so sheer in the sky that no shadow projects off his shoes.

However, he insists on playing the confirmed fop, pacing a little fast and saluting an imaginary acquaintance or two. Light-headed, he reaches the *St. Andrew's Hotel* down a narrow corridor splitting Anne Street. He traverses the courtyard, skirts the barroom and pauses in the rotunda to admire the famous ceiling mural by Canova. *The Parting of Venus and Adonis* smiles down, four hands extended, mournful and tragic; the goddess and the youth parting ways forever. Paul settles in the reading room—occupied by a few early risers—with the newspapers. The time drifts and he begins to slumber when he hears voices, then his own name…

"Some say he was violent for a while, you know. His family tried to lock him up…he fancied his brother-in-law was stealing his inheritance…"

"No, trying to poison him…that's what I heard…his family *did* lock him up…and his brother *was* trying to poison him…."

"Well I heard he wouldn't eat anything his nurse didn't cook."

"He didn't have a nurse…his mother did everything…."

"Who in Rome feared poisoning? Caligula?"

"Right."

"They all did."

"Morphy was never afraid of his family…except when they trapped him in his room…that's how he learned to play chess…."

"I thought his father chained him under the stairs."

They laugh.

"I heard his mother taught him…"

"Left him under the stairs, more like, with a bishop and some confession paper…"

Paul rises from his chair and can smell the cigars; he pauses at the backs of the speakers' armchairs, seeing only an elbow or arm, the shiny top of a bald head. They do him the courtesy of restraint. Then he leaves the room without looking back only to hear voices, the rumours.

Outside the heat blast of the city is back, the sense of suffocation after the cool air of the *St. Andrew's*. Heading home to change his clothes, Paul paces a little fast and to avoid the humidity he enters the shadow of the St. Louis Cathedral. The large oak door opens slowly. From his favourite seat behind a pillar he listens to the silence.

Over the altar St. Louis of France—half painted and half chiselled in stone—proclaims the Seventh Crusade. Like Joseph Le Carpentier, Paul admires the combination of knighthood and kingly promise in St. Louis's proud gesture. Gazing up he feels close to his *grandpapi* and the strong presence of the old pirate-lover. As the bishop appears and the Credo begins, Paul retreats to the door and takes a coin from his *portemonnaie*. He hesitates and then drops the offering in the small pewter cup. For the last time he leaves the cathedral.

In Jackson Square the waters are long retreated. The statue's arm is higher: the president-general towers over the *islet* daring any invader—foreign or domestic—to challenge New Orleans. But Paul does not look up. Weary now, he skirts the Pontalba buildings on his way to the French Market. He is back across Canal and calmed by the Vieux Carré. A peculiar thing now happens. Passing recognizable courtyards, streets and fountains, Paul tips back his neck and exclaims to the sky:

"Yes…this I love. And this I love. All of this…I love." The streets reply inside his mind with a private music of their own. He spends another hour in the sun.

A chessboard has been set up back in Paul's room, one he prepared earlier. There are no pieces except a doll with red shoes. For a while he quietly moves her from square to square. On the doll's back is the label bearing her name—written by hand, *Ms. Young*—and the words *forever young*. He sits her on the mantelpiece where she looks blankly out at the trees while a crescent moon rises along the horizon.

Everything is so hot. Despite the temperature Paul clambers into his bath as per his routine. On this occasion he feels particularly overheated and isolated. So he tries hard to be comforted by the shoes that surround the bath, always close enough to be touched by a stray hand from the tub, always near enough to quiet his nerves. There he lies. With one foot he runs the water cold, hoping to drown out the memories of the hotel gossips, to prepare himself for his late afternoon sleep. Cold water, he tells himself, will deliver safe and pleasant dreams. At three o' clock the bath is full and he is surrounded by water to his neck and lingering. His fingers are crinkled.

Paul's mind is drifting. He remembers a childhood fear— the Cannibal Monsters—that Telcide used to tell him lived at the mouth of the river between driftwood and sand-bars, eating both. He remembers his chess game against General Winfield Scott and how upset the old soldier, leading the American Army to Mexico, felt losing to a boy....He remembers Louis Paulsen playing so slowly and Daniel Harrwitz playing so maniacally...the bizarre game of croquet with Napoleon III...the unexpected gift from Queen Victoria.

He wanders in reverie, feeling hot in the cold water. Above his head hang tree-lined walkways and blue nights, a land of palm trees and sweltering summer afternoons. Where did chess come from? Where did it come from, he thinks, to torment me so? Quietly he sails through the world's one ocean. A cabin boy looks out from a ship. The boy spies two mermaids on a rock playing chess. When the game is finished the boy is already an old man. Paul shifts in the bath, perturbed, and wakes with a jolt. The water feels hot, so he runs more cold...more cold....His eyes feel strange like they are burning up with a fever. At seven o'clock, Telcide taps on the door but hears no response. She enters Paul's room, calling his name, and is filled with dread and knowledge. She sees a red doll on the window sill.

"Helena," she calls, but Helena is downstairs in the music room.

Telcide enters the bathroom and finds Paul clinging to the side of the bath. She sits beside him. His eyes move to the ceiling with an expression of calm surprise, of some struggle but mostly resignation. Telcide takes hold of his hand and stumbles backwards, knocking her head on the sink. Quietly she begins to cry.

"Your suit…" she says.

Paul has taken his bath fully clothed in his white shirt, black suit and black pantaloons, the young gentleman's costume he wore as a child. A magnolia blossom droops from his lapel seeking the bathwater; something there and then dies inside Telcide. She can hear Helena playing the piano downstairs. Once more she dares to look, and there in Paul's arm overhanging the bath is a piece of paper. Gently she peels it from his fingers and holds it to the light. Scrawled decades ago, it bears the only chess problem Paul ever constructed—the knight's trick he wrote as a boy, only a few pencil lines, a daring move trapping the king. The lines bring together the perfect act of self-destructive genius: three moves that win the game through self-sacrifice.

Dr Meux visits the house within the hour. Paul is pronounced dead on the evening of 10th July 1884. The cause is deemed congestion of the brain, an inexplicable haemorrhage, a clot, an accident.

Strangely, the secret is kept from Helena, now early middle-aged herself, because Telcide does not know how to tell her. Instead Charles Maurian comes to the house and, on Telcide's behalf, tries to tell Helena. He sits with her in the *salle de compagnie* and says:

"In India, a princess—with no other family—designates her brother as her heir…okay?"

"Mr Maurian," she says.

"Well…one day…a nobleman brings a carpenter to the palace and instructs him to make a board of sixty-four squares, in back and white tanned leather, and carve thirty-two small figurines…"

"A chessboard."

"Yes… well, when the job is complete the carpenter says: 'This is war without bloodshed'…The two men play, and when the game is complete, one side checkmates the other…"

"What do you mean?"

"The message is then understood….The game is done, and life has taken away…our….Paul is…" Helena bows her head and begins to sob.

Charles waits, slightly confused and worried his story has caused more harm than comfort.

Shaking, Helena looks up.

"You have said it," she says. "Say no more."

Chapter Sixty
1884
Notes from Underground

S herr Spens, a notable journalist, writes the following poem about Paul Morphy in the *Glasgow Weekly Herald* of 9th July 1884:

> *Tis wrongly said the greatest art's concealed*
> *Behind art, for he never strove to hide*
> *His forte to see beyond the opposing side!*
> *Most dreaded was he when he seemed to throw*
> *Piece after piece away, for then all knew*
> *Swiftly approached the inevitable mate.*

The New Orleans Item, Friday morning July 11th, remarks how

The Golden Age of the royal game began with Philidor, the French composer who died in 1795, and ended with Anderssen and Morphy…Paul Charles Morphy who never did but scratch the surface of his marvellous ability. Beyond a doubt Morphy was the most extraordinary chess player who ever yet lived; his brilliancy was unequalled. Nor can we guess what Philidor or Morphy might one day have accomplished by alchemizing their remarkable faculties to more useful everyday pursuits. The many-sidedness of genius is too well known, though, to permit the assumption that Morphy, whose legal education was superior, would not have distinguished himself at the bar had he so wished. But it is the misfortunate of genius to almost always lack perseverance….

The Daily Picayune on Saturday morning, July 12th 1884, reports that

Paul Morphy, born in a beautiful country built on cake-brakes and wood, now rest (RIP) in ashes inside a large white family tomb in St. Louis Cemetary No. 1. The burial site is above-ground to prevent feted memories being stolen, as much as bones to the surface (in case of dire flood). Let the deceased now rest under the single stone marker, our son Paul Morphy at peace with his father and grandfather. At the family's request, please send flowers to 89 Royal Street, c/o Helena.

In April 1885 in *International Chess Magazine* William Steinitz announces how

...the fearful misfortune which ultimately befell the pride and sorrow of chess, as Sheriff Spens justly calls Morphy, can only evoke the warmest sympathy in the coldest human heart.

Chapter Sixty-One
1884
Redemption

On Sunday Father Mignot officiates as Paul's face is exposed at the house. Numerous flowers are laid in his hair. Before the pallbearers lift the casket, a small woman arrives from outside the Quarter. She is dressed in red rags. She asks Charles which side is Paul's heart on? He tells her "both sides" and carefully she places a white carnation in the centre of his chest. She kisses his forehead, Telcide and Helena turning away. They cannot see her face but they don't feel the need to question her presence.

On Tuesday the coffin is carried to the cemetery. The pallbearers are Edward Morphy, Charles Maurian and professionals Léonce Percy and Edgar Hincks. Containing only ashes bound in a jar, the coffin is light. Paul will begin his long rest—his eternal endgame—tipped into a vault of lacquered white stone behind a black iron cross. Everyone is struck by the mechanics of the tomb, the absurdity of its letterbox slot. As the procession departs Telcide and Helena cling to each other.

"What will we do without Paul?" Telcide asks her daughter.

"*Il n'y a pas de point.*"

Telcide hands her the chess problem taken from Paul's hand.

"Keep this among your treasures."

They walk in silence as the brass band plays behind—more quiet than raucous—a miniature episode of Jean Lafitte's last hours only without the crowds, singing or praising followers. The band is temporary and disperses. All that remains is family sadness and local pity. Some of the curious join the procession but leave half way down Bourbon for a drink. Two journalists hover on the corner of Esplanade, pencils in hand. No children, no dogs, no horse and carriages change their course for this uneventful, missable parade.

At the gravestone Helena reads Sir Walter Raleigh's *The Nymph's Reply to the Shepherd*, calling the poet a 'discoverer of new worlds' to reference her brother.

She reads:

> *The flowers do fade, and wanton fields*
> *To wayward winter reckoning yields;*
> *A honey tongue, a heart of gall,*
> *Is fancy's spring, but sorrow's fall.*

Helena glances at her mother. Sensing the pause, Charles Maurian steps forward and reads two lines adapted from Samuel Johnson's *The Vanity of Human Wishes:*

> *Around his tomb let Art and Genius weep,*
> *But hear his death, ye blockheads, hear and sleep.*

He steps back.

After the rites, and the prayers, and the casting of the earth, Father Mignot says:

"Even in his years of eccentricity he was still a knight of courtesy and a man of heart. This is the funeral of a good man before a great chess player…"

"…as Paul would have wanted," says Charles.

Meanwhile Edward is walking between the tombs. At the heart of the cemetery he finds Voodoo queen Marie Laveau's grave, her plot well attended with flowers and graffiti.

Father Mignot's words echo over the headstones:

Now there is at Jerusalem by the sheep market a pool of five porches which in the Hebrew tongue is called Bethesda meaning House of Mercy. Therein lay a great multitude of weakened folk, of sick, of blind, of lame, of withered: waiting for the moving of the water.

He pauses to lay a hand on the casket.

And an angel went down at certain seasons into the pool and the water was troubled. And whoever after the troubling of the water stepped into the pool was made whole of whatever disease he lay under.
John Chapter 5: Verse 2.

Looking up in surprise Telcide sees a woman in red rags. She is standing far behind the other mourners. Their stares cross and flicker of recognition occurs, but that is all. They wait. Under a pale sky the coffin jar is tipped and the ashes are freed. Already Paul lies with his forefathers. The ceremony is over. The mourners start to disperse. There is no brass band in the Southern style, only pallbearers disappearing and the family heading home.

But there Clara stands silently, neither troubled nor included. When everyone has gone she steps forward in sunshine to the tomb and crouches before the carved word *Morphy*. She whistles low and waits. A small child materializes beside the grave. Clara twirls her into view—revealing a sturdy head, clear-sighted eyes. Wasps of black hair break over the child's forehead. No more than five years old, she stands patiently at her mother's side.

"This is your father, Bea."

"*I* know."

The girl is busy watching a grasshopper that has landed on the headstone.

"He is Paul. Say hello…we knew each other a long time."

"I don't like it…here."

"Say hello."

Bethesda looks pleadingly.

"Can we go?"

"Yes, of course. Say hello first."

"Hello!"

"Bea, say hello properly. Say hello, *father*."

"Hello *father*."

"Good."

Now Clara stands and without looking back leaves the tomb. She takes Bethesda to the north end of the cemetery where they sit on a wall and look into dusty Rampart Street.

"There," Clara says, pointing downriver to South Basin Street. "It stretches al the way home. Can you see?"

"The black-white man talked about heaven," Bethesda says, swinging her legs. "What does heaven look like?"

"It looks like paradise," Clara says smiling. "And like a river."

"Like that river?" the girl says, pointing.

"Yes—exactly like that one."

Bethesda is quiet and soon they exit the St. Louis Cemetery. For the rest of the day they wander the French Quarter. They stop for fruit from a stall, and sit on the banquette as the sun fades. Later they make their way upriver along the banks of the Mississippi. Bethesda grows tired.

"Can we go home *maman*?"

"Not yet."

On Burgundy they head for *The House of Good Drinking*. Long ago in the same spot, Paul Morphy bore witness to the funeral parade of Jean Lafitte, the renegade pirate celebrated in death by the merry lonely souls of New Orleans; equivalent solace would only be found by Paul moving wooden pieces about a board. But Clara and Bethesda do not know that history.

The original source of Paul's inspiration was Lafitte: the beginning of Paul and Clara's struggles, separations and triumphs. All originated on that fateful day. *He* felt the need to excel, to travel, to find meaning beyond the closed Creole society of the Vieux Carré; *she* felt the need to remain, to not be saved, the power not to be shaped or invented like a piece on a board. In the end, too, it was the boy who could not leave and the girl who got out.

For now, Clara and Bethesda lean on the wall near the crook where Paul sheltered. They stare at the dusty street, a mother and daughter waiting for nothing and something, much as Violet and Clara once worked the Swamp down by Girod Street. The tidewaters of Ol' Man River, Clara thinks, will one day roll again, broken and sad through the fountains of the city…down to the Gulf of Mexico. Meanwhile, always the two New Orleans, brother and sister, father and son, mother and child, hero and anti-hero, polite and less polite, will co-exist inside *The House of Good Drinking*.

They enter, and Clara takes a cloth from her bag and spreads it on the table. She drinks a cup of *Raleigh Rye* and tips the bar-girl for Bethesda's orange juice with its nip of vodka.

"Now, look at this tablecloth," Clara says. "You see the black and white squares?"

"Yes. They's dirty, Bella."

"Well, Bea, can you tell which are black and which are white?"

"Yeh, I do." The girl looks up innocently and grins.

Clara then proceeds to teach her the rules—in a fully business-like way—not of chess but of a similar and older challenge: the classical puzzle of the *Knight's Tour*.

"This is the knight." Clara takes hold of the salt cellar and walks the feet in a circle, two squares up and one across, then one across and two squares down. "See how it moves. But the trick is to never touch the same square twice…"

Bethesda follows the rotating diagonal with her eyes, struck by its beauty but not seeing the pattern. Witnessing the curiosity in her daughter's eyes, Clara frowns at her half understanding.

"See, the knight must tread on every square," she says. "But only once…you see? Never the same square twice."

"Look!" says Bethesda, and she grabs and clips the knight round the table in her own new pattern.

"But that's backwards," Clara says.

"Both ways," is the reply. "Watch the horsy go. It's more fun this way!"

"Yes, Bea," Clara says, watching and not really grasping the arc, but happy too. "That's the fun." She stares at the girl as though for the first time. Bethesda's skin is more dark than pale, having inherited a lighter strain of Michael Morphy and a darker hue from Clara's grandfather. She is pretty. Around her neck dangles the fool's gold necklace-locket bought for Clara years ago. The locket sparkles in the dim light as Bethesda sips her orange juice.

Giggling while drinking, the little girl keeps the salt cellar moving. Then something happens, without warning, clicking magically into place. The lesson is over. Bethesda is mesmerized by the speed and strangeness of the looping circuit. The knight moves faster and faster...one-two...two-one...one-two...until the circle is complete.

"Look!" she cries. "It's back in the same place. Look, Bella, look!"

"Yes, I can see. I can see."

Bethesda holds the knight firmly in her fingers and determinedly makes the moves. As the minutes pass, her face lines with puzzled intensity. She has inherited her father's desire for risk without feeling the risk; Paul's melancholy and caution are there. The origins of Bethesda's strength and weakness remain elusive however.

Given the diversity of her parentage, and the potential for revival in New Orleans, her future will remain unknown. For now, Bethesda tires of executing the *Knight's Tour* and Clara encourages her to drink to make her sleepy. They have only two hours before Clara is working Violet's former crib on Girod—her daughter's only inheritance. Bethesda must wake up to her mother's profession day and night. As they leave *The House of Good Drinking*, though, Bethesda takes the salt cellar with her—to practice.

Dusk comes early today. Provoked by the funeral, Clara decides to take Bethesda to the fountain where she met Paul. As they enter the courtyard from Burgundy, two children are playing marbles there. The image is too much even for Clara, and she sits in the street and cries, and wipes her eyes on the hem of her dress. Bethesda lies on the cobblestones, nothing between her head and the ground, already asleep. The minutes throb. Soon Clara must go to work. Darkness is visible.

The music begins palpably at eight when a clatter of doors brings the first clientele to *The House of Rest for Weary Boatmen*. Despite herself, Clara drags her daughter back to the crib-hole. That night, she tells Bethesda stories of the French Quarter's beautiful people, the games of cards, the opera, and the sword-fights. She reassures Bethesda that nowhere do they have prettier and more elegant dresses than *The House of Rest for Weary Boatmen*.

"You see, the dresses of the opera are no finer. We have the finest clothes, Bea. We have the elegant stockings and shawls. We always will because...we need them. We always will..."

"Yes..." says Bethesda, taking out the borrowed salt cellar, her imaginary knight.

"You know, Bea Caïssa, that piece is part of a magical game called chess. Your father played chess too."

"I know."

"You do?"

"Yes, the funeral men said. But not chess as good as me, Bella."

"Yes, Little Bea. Not as good as you. Can you make the whole *Knight's Tour* yet?"

"I think so."

"Where's the beautiful watch I gave you? That was your father's too. What's your father's name?"

"Paul, mama."

"Yes."

Bethesda retrieves the testimonial watch from her apron. She holds up the dial, grinning, and it sparkles with chess pieces.

"Yes, my love," says Clara. "You will sing in the opera and you will be a chess player one day, Little Bea. An actress too! The Creole men will love you too, my love. They will love you so...so much."

"I hope so. Will they forever?"

"Yes, but first let us get through tonight. You will see, Bea. You know I will always be here to see you grow and play…"

Postscript
1884
A World Apart

In the courtyards of New Orleans the heart of the old French Quarter has stopped beating. The narrow cobbled streets are hushed. A world of faded elegance and soft candlelight has passed away...Nearly a hundred years have passed since a great fire burned the original French town of Nouvelle Orléans to the ground in 1788. In its wake rose a stately Spanish city. Wood was turned into brick, plaster into oleanders, banana trees and wrought iron trellises. Everywhere, courtyards and houses were built flush to banquettes with fan-shaped windows. Now the city is French and Spanish and all-American. Freed slaves, Cajuns and Creoles from the Old European empires mix liberally and uneasily with the whites and blacks of the New World.

New Orleans lives in the remnants of its history amid the splendour of a forgotten world. If the city were a room—one of the many rooms we have visited—the ceiling would be adorned with painted cupids, cherubs and from the centre a silver statue of Venus would gleam with the smile of Clarabelle Young. The rug would be patterned with flower garlands, the window draperies of rose-coloured brocade rising and falling in the hot summer breeze. A great golden bench would stand on a raised dais, a table of royalty where the families Morphy and Le Carpentier would argue and joke while Paul Morphy stares into the mist of Jackson Square.

Even today along Royal Street in the heart of the French Quarter you can hear Paul's footsteps or the sound of him wading through the flooded streets of New Orleans. He calls aloud names over and over, sometimes those from America, sometimes Europe, sometimes those of his lost family but mostly Clarabelle...Clarabelle...Clara...and never knowing his beautiful dark-haired daughter lives.

Paul Morphy is forgotten now. For three months after his death, The Manhattan Chess Club drapes a portrait of Paul in its central banquet room: he is twenty-one again wearing a black tuxedo with a white carnation. Telcide writes them a letter offering thanks *for the glory of the son and the everlasting grief of the mother.*

Paul's bedroom at 89 Royal Street remains unchanged. Telcide keeps a plain wooden chessboard open there for good, never intending to use it, the pieces ready for a game never to begin. The house falls quiet. No one comes and no one goes. A veritable Miss Havisham, Telcide locks her door and only takes meals from Helena. Little can stir her grief. Six months after Paul's death, on January 11th Telcide induces her own in a self-constructed romantic bower surrounded by flowers. Her opera *Louise de Lorraine* remains unfinished. Confusingly the coroner declares the death one of natural causes provoked by misadventure. Empty laudanum bottles are later discovered under the bed and destroyed without Helena's knowledge.

For weeks Helena finds her world empty. Not even a surprise marriage proposal from Charles Maurian can convince her of a new optimistic path in life. Without Telcide, or the increasingly rare visitations of Ernest or Edward, Helena shrivels up willingly.

Only a year and a half later she is gone, choosing the vast Mississippi as her final home, again declared misadventure. For those left behind, Helena remains an enigma who lived for her mother and family. She leaves no notes, no clothes, no trace she ever existed.

In December 1885 William Steinitz of New York and J. H. Zuckertort decide to play a match for Chess Champion of the World. Neither claims to currently hold the title of world champion—in latent honour of Paul's legacy. But at the conclusion of the match Steinitz officially recognizes himself as *the world's first chess champion*. Paul is cut from history.

By Steinitz's declaration, his predecessor's memory is relegated to *the last unofficial world champion*. For future tournaments, Paul Morphy is nothing and nobody, a footnote beneath the finer lines of history.

On January 23rd 1890 the New Orleans Chess, Checkers and Whist Club burns to the ground. The letters Clara sends to Paul in Europe were housed there after Paul's death. Now they are gone. Only Paul's letters to Clara survive, bequeathed to Bethesda as a warning note not to remain in Storyville. On the backs of the letters Clara writes additional advice to Bethesda, mostly to leave New Orleans for good and pursue happiness in the 'Victorious North.'

But Chicago cannot cure the girl from New Orleans of her past, her habits and increasing addictions. She feels no guilt, but she never forgets the chess player from the 'Embittered South.' Clara dies at the age of fifty-four of alcohol poisoning. She is buried with her mother Violet down by the Swamp. History is no less favourable to her story...

No one knows what happens to her daughter, although it is believed Bethesda remains in the city of New Orleans. Decades later during the age of Can-Can, a dance hall queen of Storyville is known by the double stage names Cherie Young and Bethesda Violet. But no proof is traceable to Little Bea Young as the original birth-line. The names circulate in the new red-light district as stage name pseudonyms, real or unreal, and in some way fulfil Clara's own desire to have her name in lights on the stage. Clara herself would have been amused, if not entirely surprised.

Eventually these names too—with all the long-ago women born astride the grave on the wrong side of Canal Street—dissolve into a deeper history.

Edward Morphy and Charles Maurian see each other one more time. They pass by chance in the street, much as Paul ran into William Steinitz once. Edward is looking for Malvina, still chasing his share of Alonzo's money, but Charles cannot help.

"Paul was right...," Edward says, "and we doubted him. That John Sybrandt took everything."

"It's possible."

"And they eloped to leave the rest of us rotting—now it's just you and me, Charles, we're all that's left."

The conversation tails into a drink. They decide on the river. Side by side they sit in the sun watching the muddy tide lap the dock. *Kaintuck* sailors are unloading grog barrels one by one from a moored whaling ship, navigating a single plank to the shore.

"You know," says Charles. "I was reading James Lowell the other day, one of the Fireside Poets, you know?"

"Not really, but go on."

"Well, Lowell called Paul's chess exploits *a new clause to the Declaration of American Independence.* How about that?"

"I don't really remember my brother," Edward says, and tosses a twig in the ocean. "Not any more."

Charles is quiet.

"But I still play chess."

"You do?"

"After Paul died, I found I could play. Like when I was a boy."

"You're still a boy, Edward," Charles says and risks a laugh. Together they drink glasses of navy rum from a stray barrel. "You know," he continues, "I used to ask Paul now and then 'where does chess *come from?*' He would give some odd answers. I don't think he really knew. But chess has changed over centuries…take the queen. She's more powerful today than long ago…"

"Like all women," Edward says.

"Or the *Knight's Tour*…that trick's older than chess itself.…But where does chess *itself* come from? That's the question no one can answer. Because no one invented it—it invented itself—and people refined it over time. They speeded it up. What we have is what remains…bequeathed from the past, see…"

"Like evolution."

"Yes," Charles laughs. "Just like evolution."

"I vote for Persia."

"What about India?"

"Maybe both. Or Siberia."

"Too cold there for anything else!"

They watch the *Kaintuck* drop his barrel—the lip cracks—and the sweet rum juice seeps down the harbour.

"Most likely chess comes from China," Charles says, "and moved west…"

"And will keep going…back to China."

"I went to school with Paul," Charles says. "You know what Paul would say? He'd say, 'Nothing has changed—it's all a myth.…Chess came from the real sunken city of Atlantis…and the lost city of El Dorado. Chess is a gift of two civilizations that crossed sometime in the past…an offering of peace during war time…you know…disappearing and reappearing constantly.' You believe that?"

"Not really. But chess was never my game."

Charles's eyes are wide and earnest. He grins and lays his hands on the earth. "And then it came to us…from places forgotten…and places sunken…that is the truth…and it will return to Atlantis…it will return to El Dorado…and one day we'll all come back…to New Orleans…That's what Paul said."

"A prophet," Edward says.

"A prophet," Charles echoes. He raises his hand to the sun. "Good night, brother."

"Sweet prince, good night…"

Edward and Charles stand up and toss the empty bottles in the river. The sun has long gone down. They watch the *Kaintuck* as he bends and lick dregs of the broken barrel from the deck. He gets a taste—you can see it in his eyes—before the empty barrel falls between the wooden slats and is lost to the river below.

Acknowledgements

I owe the following authors many thanks for their knowledge of New Orleans, Paul Morphy, chess and Louisiana history: David Lawson (*Paul Morphy, The Pride and Sorrow of Chess*), Lyle Saxon and E. H. Suydam (*Fabulous New Orleans*) and Al Rose (*Storyville, New Orleans*).

My thanks to everyone at Parkgate Press, Parkgate Originals and Dionysus Books for all their hard work, patience and commitment to publishing a novel about a chess player. Grateful appreciation to Katharine Willers, Jennifer Fullerty and Charlie Greenhill, three readers I couldn't write without.

Special thanks to Clare Tanner of Bookhabit, who set me on the road to publication, authors Geoff Cush and J. C. Hallman for their buzz and kind words, three-time Virginia State chess champion Macon Shibut (coming to a tournament near you), and Tom Standage Digital Editor of *The Economist*. I am indebted to you all for your encouragement and support of *The Knight of New Orleans*.

Also by Parkgate Press (F Street Books)

www.parkgatepress.com
www.fstreetbooks.com

Katharine E. Willers

WHAT TOOK ME OUT TO THE BALL GAME

The Determinants of Attendance of
Major League Baseball Games from 1989–1999
and the Implications of the 1994 Labor Strike

Matt Fullerty, Ph.D.

THE PROFESSORROMANE

The British and American Academic Novel 1945–2012
Lost in the Academy
The Comic Campus, The Tragic Self

Also by Parkgate Press (Dionysus Books)

www.parkgatepress.com
www.dionysusbooks.com

Tom Robertson

NAPOLEON Vs. THE TURK

A play based on the chess match of Napoleon Bonaparte and 'The Turk,' the famous 18th century chess automaton. Who will triumph, the master tactician or the technology? First performed at the Toronto Fringe Festival.

Engin Inel Holmstrom

LOVESWEPT

A Cross-Cultural Romance of 1950s Turkey. Neri falls in love and marries young, but which of three men will win her heart?

About the Author

www.mattfullerty.com

Matt Fullerty has been playing chess and writing fiction since his schooldays. After a visit to New Orleans and Paul Morphy's tomb in 2005, he was struck by the story of the only American chess world champion before Bobby Fischer and Morphy's remarkable youth. Matt is currently Lecturer in English at George Washington University in Washington, DC, and recently taught Creative Writing (fiction) and the University of London, Royal Holloway.

Matt is the author of novels *The Murderess and the Hangman* and the forthcoming *American Con Artist.* Originally from Warrington and a graduate of Oxford University and the University of East Anglia, he has published reviews, articles and interviews for *The Daily Mail, The St. Ann's Review*, BBC Radio London and the Discovery Channel's *Deadly Women* TV series. In 2011 he attended the *Vermont Studio Center* on an Artist's Grant.

Matt is married with a chessboard and divides his time between Arlington, Virginia and Cambridge, England.

This title is also available in hardback from Parkgate Originals and as an eBook from Parkgate Digital.